ROBERT SHAPIRO
WALT BECKER
MISCONCEPTION

"A breathtaking thriller. The courtroom scenes are stunningly real but what makes *Misconception* a page-turner is the way it takes us inside the hurricane of media hysteria."

Joel Siegel, film critic, "Good Morning America"

"They got it right: The Arrest—The Trial—The Media—The Spin! It's the next best thing to sitting at counsel table at 'the Big Case.' Compelling!"

Mickey Sherman, Esq., Sherman & Richichi

Also by Robert L. Shapiro
THE SEARCH FOR JUSTICE: A DEFENSE ATTORNEY'S
BRIEF ON THE O. J. SIMPSON CASE

Also by Walt Becker
LINK

ROBERT SHAPIRO
WALT BECKER

MISCONCEPTION

AVON BOOKS
An Imprint of HarperCollins*Publishers*

AVON BOOKS
An Imprint of HarperCollins*Publishers*
10 East 53rd Street
New York, New York 10022-5299

Copyright © 2001 by Robert Shapiro and Walt William Becker
ISBN: 0-380-73323-4
www.avonbooks.com

First Avon Books paperback printing: June 2002
First William Morrow hardcover printing: June 2001

Avon Trademark Reg. U.S. Pat. Off. and in Other Countries, Marca Registrada, Hecho en U.S.A.
HarperCollins ® is a registered trademark of HarperCollins Publishers Inc.

Printed in the U.S.A.

10 9 8 7 6 5 4 3 2 1

To three special women—Mary, Francoise, and Linell—and all the others in the world who perform the most difficult job on earth—being a mother

MISCONCEPTION

PART ONE

PROLOGUE | SAMARITAN

No one ever found out who shot the man.

The motive wasn't robbery. The shooter didn't stick around to take his wallet, the Mercedes he'd just stepped out of, keys in hand, or the gold Rolex around his wrist. Just popped him in the chest once, and watched as he ran away, blood streaming from the wound until the man's white shirt was matted to his flesh.

The victim ran with superhuman strength, across the parking lot of the convenience store where he'd stopped to buy cigarettes, out to the highway, up the embankment, and across the road. A few cars' headlights picked up his fleeing, crazed form, bright and manic in the hot, moonless Louisiana night. But he was across in a few seconds, and no one stopped.

The man found himself in another parking lot, this one almost empty, surrounded by the darkened windows of an electronics store, a bakery, a drive-through bank.

His breathing was wrong. An awful pain was building in his chest, as if each breath were a ratchet pulling some internal vise tighter and tighter, a fist closing on his lungs, his heart, his life. But he didn't stop running. Before him were the lights of a restaurant that was still open. The wounded man used the last of his waning strength to make for its doors.

He burst into the sudden brightness and sound, bloody and wheezing, a bizarre invasion of the carefully crafted elegance of the restaurant. Patrons and staff looked on in confusion as he stumbled a last few steps, then fell to the floor. His arms flailed once, rolling him onto his back and revealing the crimson mat across his chest.

There was complete silence for a second as the dumbstruck crowd looked down at the motionless, bleeding man. A waiter stood paralyzed a few feet away, his palms open to the sky in the universal gesture: *What is this?*

Then the wounded man took a harsh breath. The sound was liquid, like a column of air passing across some wet and loose membrane. It transfixed the onlookers for a second more, as if all shared some memory of this sound.

It was a death rattle.

A woman screamed, and the room burst from its frozen state into a blur of action. The nearby waiter knelt and held the man's head. A rush of shouted suggestions and clamorous movement filled the room. There was a low murmur of beeps as several patrons pulled out cell phones and began to make calls for an ambulance.

One man stood, calm amid the chaos. With a serene authority, he walked from his table to the shooting victim's side, firmly pushing away the waiter, who was inanely repeating, "It's okay. It's okay."

Dr. Daniel Wyatt looked down into the man's glassy eyes, then bent an ear close to hear his breathing. He ripped open the shirt, which was heavy and wet in his hands, and saw the entry wound. A small bubble appeared there, swelling in rhythm with the man's breath.

It was not okay.

The man was suffering from what doctors referred to as "tension pneumothorax." Some fragment of the invading bullet had perforated one lung, ripping aside flaps of loose tissue and creating a small but deadly aperture, a one-way valve. Air could pass out of the man's lung through this valve, but not back in. With each breath the man took, a small amount of air passed into the chest cavity outside the lung. In his careening, panicked run across the highway, his chest cavity had been filled with air, pressurized like an inflatable raft by the involuntary and persistent pumping of the lung. The pressure was growing, pressing against the wounded lung and beginning to collapse it. With every breath, more air reached the chest cavity and less entered the lung.

The man was, in effect, breathing himself to death.

The process was reaching its last stages. Suffocation was not the main danger; the other lung would probably function for another twenty minutes, possibly more. But the pressure was building on the other organs inside the chest. It was as if the man's heart were held by a boa constrictor that gradually and relentlessly tightened its grip. The end could come at any moment.

Dr. Daniel Wyatt stood up and walked to the waiters' station. His hands sifted through the silverware, selecting a small, serrated steak knife from the pile. He lifted a pitcher of ice water, which was hardly as sterile as boiling water, but it would do, and plunged the knife into it. He walked back to the struggling body, moving now with such confidence that no one sought to question him. They just watched with growing horror and fascination.

Wyatt wrapped the handle of the now icy steak knife in a cloth napkin, to give himself a better grip. He tipped the pitcher of water over the wound, washing away the thick layer of coagulated blood. The man's breathing quickened with the sudden shock of cold water, and the dying sound that rattled from his mouth grew more pronounced.

Dr. Wyatt fitted the tip of the knife between the tenth and eleventh rib on the wounded side, drawing blood. That was good. The knife was sharp. It had to be for this to work.

Wyatt held the knife steady with his left hand and raised his right in a fist. When the crowd saw what he intended to do, there was a solemn gasp.

One of the onlookers was Cynthia Feld, a reporter for KLIF News, the local Lafayette, Louisiana, television station. She had been the first of the restaurant's patrons to reach 911, seconds after the man had stumbled in. Her cell phone was still in her hand. As Wyatt raised his fist, she pressed the code for her line producer's number.

Like a stonemason wielding hammer and chisel, Wyatt brought his right fist down, driving the knife a precise few centimeters into the man's chest. It passed between the ribs and into the inflated cavity. Wyatt turned the knife slightly, and used his right hand to press up against the tenth rib. He bent to listen, and heard the unmistakable hiss of aspiration from the new wound. The trapped air was escaping, releasing the deadly pressure. It went on for a few seconds, a bubbling sound that increased in pitch and intensity as Wyatt leaned his weight against his patient's chest.

Then the man jolted under the doctor, drawing a ragged and sudden breath, almost sitting up as his body demanded more air from the newly freed lung. His eyes cleared as oxygen reached his brain, and he stared up at his savior in confusion. One hand reached out and brushed Wyatt's face, leaving a streak of blood across one cheek.

The nearby waiter pulled the protesting arm gently away and pushed the man back down to the floor. "It's okay," he said again, nodding his head and looking at the doctor with a strange mixture of respect and fear.

Wyatt let the wound close around the knife, but he left it inserted in the chest. The man's breathing would immediately begin to build the chest pressure again. He might need to aspirate again before the EMTs got here. They would certainly be carrying a needle and stopcock, a one-way mechanical valve that could be inserted into the chest, where it would continuously release the air escaping from the perforated lung.

Until then, he could only wait and listen to his patient's breathing, weighing the risk of reopening the wound against the dangers of tension pneumothorax.

Seven minutes later, the EMTs burst through the door.

When Dr. Daniel Wyatt left the restaurant, a television news van was waiting outside. Cynthia Feld stood before the camera, immaculate in the bright lights.

"And just coming out now is Dr. Daniel Wyatt, the man of the hour, whose quick thinking saved the life of local businessman Roger Eastermeadow, a father of three children and pillar of the community."

The camera zoomed over her shoulder, finding Dr. Wyatt, whose face was still marked by a streak of blood. He walked carefully, dazed by the lights and the emergency's sudden conclusion. His wife, Ellen, stood at his side, supporting one arm with an iron grip. She had given the reporter her husband's name.

The grainy footage taken that night was kind to Daniel Wyatt. In the harsh shadows of the television lights, his strong features seemed cut in stone. His graying hair looked distinguished even in disarray. And the single stroke of blood down his cheek gave him the appearance of a wounded warrior.

The story was played relentlessly by the local station for twenty-four hours, and was picked up by the national network for the next evening's news. Roger Eastermeadow, the man whose life Wyatt had saved, owned a car dealership just outside Lafayette, and the lot's giant sign, which could be seen from the highway, read THANK YOU DR. WYATT! for a month. The Associated Press ran a seventy-five-word story that was picked up as filler in almost every paper in the country. A Lafayette stringer for *Time* magazine interviewed Wyatt two days after the event, and the doctor mentioned his work with a nonprofit women's health organization. The stringer expanded the story, writing a one-page history of the organization.

In existence almost ten years, the Lafayette Women's Advocacy Group suddenly found itself on the national map. Its director, Claire Davis, launched a new fund-raising campaign, enclosing the *Time* article, along with a freeze-frame snapshot of a bloody Daniel Wyatt for good measure. The media found Daniel Wyatt and his partner useful. Davis and Wyatt suddenly found themselves in the strange world of CNN regulars, as pundits, experts, talking heads. A southern white male, courtly, handsome and pro-choice, Daniel Wyatt was always needed to balance some panel or other on the politics of women's health. Sharp-tongued, brilliant, and a veteran of Louisiana trench-warfare politics, Claire Davis could always be depended on for a brutal sound bite.

But Dr. Wyatt continued his private practice, and was invariably introduced as "a country doctor." In a way, his life did not change much after the incident. His fame was of a limited kind, and it had always seemed that everyone in Lafayette knew his name. His patients were the same men and women. The Women's Advocacy Group still struggled for cash. His kids grew older and less interested in watching their father's occasional and "boring" appearances on television.

Then, two years after Daniel Wyatt saved Roger Eastermeadow's life, a call came from the White House.

Nothing was ever the same again.

1 | FIRST PAGE

Dinner was over, and one by one the guests rose to make their speeches.

Terri Porter recounted the time her teenage son fell from the towering oak tree on Tarragon Street. Walter Rory spoke of his wife's long battle with cancer while Alexandra Rory herself cried quietly and held the guest of honor's hand. Rebecca Schroeder told of her first child, who had been delivered on a roadside by a man then unknown to her; a passing stranger, an unexpected angel. And Henry Sinjin, of course, revisited for the thousandth time the car accident that had resulted in the wide scar on his ample abdomen. But this night no one minded hearing the tale (or seeing the scar) once again.

Tonight was special.

The stories were of accidents and sickness, but the gathering at which they were recounted was a celebration. All the endings were happy, all the toasts were to good advice, to speedy recoveries, to bones well mended. And to Dr. Daniel Wyatt.

Seated next to his beaming wife, he listened with that combination of embarrassment and unwavering attention that comes with being the object of public praise.

"I've known Daniel longer than most any of you," Ernest Magley was saying, his rich Louisiana accent resonating as it always did after three glasses of wine. "As the man who was his roommate for two years in med school, you may assume that I came prepared to offer some special insights tonight."

Laughter filled the small, private room. Dr. Magley leaned back against the faux wood paneling and took a leisurely sip from the ruby-filled glass in his hand, letting silence return.

"But I am afraid that I must disappoint you," Dr. Magley finally admitted. "For Daniel Wyatt was the second-most boring drudge at Harvard Med."

Another artful pause.

"I was the first."

"Oh, I doubt that," Claire Davis called through the laughter. "At least the last part. But you stick to that story if you're called upon by the Senate."

"Already planning for the confirmation hearings?" Magley chided.

Claire shrugged her shoulders, and those who knew her well enough realized that she'd been planning something like a Senate confirmation hearing for years.

"Should the esteemed senators ask my humble opinion, I'm sure I'll be ready with the proper words to describe Dr. Daniel Wyatt," Magley continued, straightening his shoulders and putting his glass on the table. "For many of us, he's been a counselor. For all who live in Lafayette, a leader in the community. To those lucky enough to know him well, a good friend. But if asked to choose one word to describe Daniel, I would say simply, he is a healer."

Applause filled the tiny room. Dr. Magley looked pleased with himself.

"No way am I putting that pompous ass in front of the committee," Claire Davis whispered into Dr. Wyatt's ear.

Daniel Wyatt nodded his head, but he was remembering a night fourteen years before, when he had delivered Ernest Magley's first child. Sixteen hours of labor, ending in a footling breech. It had been a very risky delivery, and when it was all over, Ernest had cried harder than the baby.

"And now we must hear from the new attorney general . . . um, I mean, counsel general to the surgeon general nominee," Magley finally ended. "I give you Claire Davis, esquire."

Claire rose, and put one hand on Wyatt's shoulder as she spoke. Wyatt sneaked a quick glance at his wife, Ellen, but she was smiling broadly up at Claire. With any other woman, especially one as attractive as Claire, the intimacy revealed by the touch would have made her furious. Wyatt had learned early in their marriage to avoid beautiful women at parties; Ellen found even a moment of public conversation between Daniel and an unknown woman humiliating. It wasn't jealousy in the usual sense. She trusted him. But when *other people* saw in Wyatt a hint of something that even remotely smacked of infidelity, Ellen's mind began to spin. She had grown up in Opelousas, a small town to the north of Lafayette, and she had a lifelong fear of gossip.

But with Claire it was different. In the years that she and Daniel Wyatt had worked together, spending long evenings developing the Lafayette Women's Advocacy Group, Ellen had come to accept her. Claire was a consummate professional, a strong-willed lawyer, and a fearsome politician. Despite her beauty and the powerful sexuality she exuded, Claire was, in the eyes of a genteel southern woman like Ellen, less a woman than an honorary man.

A waiter passed through the doors that led to the public part of the restaurant, and the sounds of the crowd of diners briefly overwhelmed the room. Claire, never one to allow her voice to be drowned out, paused until it was quiet again.

"When Daniel and I began our work creating the Women's Advocacy Group—or WAG, as some wags have dubbed it"—Claire paused again, allowing a moment for the room's warm laughter at the decade-old joke—"we certainly weren't thinking of Washington."

Wyatt smiled to himself, wondering how many in the room were credulous enough to swallow that one.

"But now that we're headed to the office of surgeon general, I'm sure Daniel will be remembered for more than just telling Americans not to smoke."

"Uh-oh," Ernest Magley interjected, stabbing his cigarette

into his mashed potatoes. No one dared laugh at his antics while Claire held the floor.

"We began with one simple goal," she continued, effortlessly ignoring Magley. "To help the women of this city and state take control of their bodies, their futures, and their lives."

The applause was loud and long, then Claire continued to tell the story of her partnership with Daniel Wyatt. Watching her words grip the crowd, Wyatt realized how much she had changed since she had first come to him with the idea for an advocacy group. It seemed absurd back then. A pro-choice family-planning and domestic violence organization based here in the most conservative and Catholic state in the union. To make matters worse, Claire was a Yankee-educated lawyer, inexperienced and sure to be seen as an outsider in small-town Lafayette. But even then, before her skills as an orator and trench-warfare politician had been honed, Claire wouldn't take no for an answer.

"You, Daniel," she'd said, "*you* will make it work. A respected small-city doctor with small-town values, who deeply cares for women."

And it *had* worked. Here, a thousand battles later, they'd been recognized in the best possible way. Dr. Daniel Wyatt had been nominated by a fellow southerner as the next surgeon general of the United States.

"There is, of course, one last hurdle to jump," Claire was finishing. "The wise *men* of the Senate must confirm the president's choice. But I'm sure that regardless of our politics, we're all very pro *that* choice."

More laughter and applause. Then Wyatt felt Claire's grip tighten on his shoulder. "Please welcome my colleague and very dear friend, the future surgeon general, Dr. Daniel Wyatt."

Wyatt stood. He looked out over the smiling faces and was overwhelmed for a moment by the love and respect he saw in their eyes. A shy man, Wyatt usually left the public speaking to Claire. But for once his usual fear of crowds was mysteriously absent. So, this was how success felt, he was thinking. The feeling of an audience waiting eagerly to hear your words. He saw why Claire pursued politics with such energy.

Dr. Wyatt took the index card with his notes from his breast pocket and glanced at it. He and Claire had gone over the points carefully the night before. But then he shook his head and crumpled the card in his fist. These were his friends. They deserved to hear him speak from the heart. He didn't need notes to speak here.

This was home.

But before he even opened his mouth, his pager beeped.

The row of numbers on a pager can say it all. Those whose professions demand constant availability—stock traders, police detectives, doctors, soccer moms, drug dealers—learn to glance at those short sequences of numerals with trepidation. Some adopt a weary fatalism. Too many emergencies begin with the sharp cry of a pager, a coded string of signs that spell disaster in numbers rather than letters.

Dr. Wyatt knew by heart the numbers of perhaps two dozen of his patients. Heart problems, a kidney recipient, the panicky calls of an asthmatic kid's parents.

As he unclipped the beeper, there was laughter in the room. He smiled and shrugged his shoulders. A doctor's duty. His moment of triumph had come off as an expertly timed gag.

Wyatt squinted as he stretched his arm out in front of him, holding the pager at that ever-greater distance that age had begun to require. For a moment, he didn't recognize the number. It wasn't one of the usual suspects, but it was somehow familiar.

Then Wyatt remembered, and the realization of who had paged him rushed in suddenly. He had been confused by the extra three digits at the end of the number, which came into focus only now.

. . . 9-1-1.

A small, sharp sound escaped Wyatt's lips, like the grunt of his male patients when he tested their cremasteric reflex the old-fashioned way, a firm grip on their testicles as they attempted a dry cough. He tried to swallow the sound, to erase the dry feeling in his mouth, but it went down as unblunted as a sliver of ice.

He returned the pager to his belt, felt his wife's questioning eyes upon him, a smile fading on her lips.

Wyatt nodded at her reassuringly. That part was easy. He was used to smiling in emergencies, at children with broken arms who were bug-eyed with pain, at women with lumps in their breasts who waited for test results. He gave a quick "Excuse me" to the audience and pointed toward the pay phones. He hoped his stern look said, *I have to deal with this right away*.

Ellen nodded back at him and rose to apologize for her husband. She must have made some joke about the duties of a doctor, for more laughter followed Wyatt as he hurried toward the pay phones.

Later, during each of the countless times he replayed that night in his head, some trick of memory made it seem to Wyatt that he'd already known, even before lifting the receiver, every word that would be spoken.

"Sarah?"

"Daniel."

"Are you all right?"

"Daniel." Her voice failing, almost inaudible against the background noise of the restaurant.

"Listen, Sarah. You shouldn't be paging me. Unless you're . . ." He heard her breathing, heavy like sobs. "You're not sick, are you?"

"No. I mean, I vomited."

A strange feeling of relief came over Wyatt. Sarah was calling as a patient. The familiar routine of procedures, the safety of assuming the roles of doctor and patient settled into his mind and pushed out the panic of the moment before.

"Tell me what you've ingested," he said. "Any alcohol? Drugs?"

"No, Daniel," she replied. A sob rose to thicken her voice again. "That was two days ago that I first got sick. And I was already late."

Already late. Wyatt squeezed his eyes shut. He was not hearing this. Instead, he listened to the high-pitched roaring sound in his ears.

Sarah sobbed once more, and then said it. But by then, the scream in Wyatt's mind had faded a little and he already knew what he was going to hear.

"I'm pregnant, Daniel."

2 | DOMESTIC CALL

The two deputies crouched on either side of the garage, pinned in the headlights of their hastily parked police cruiser. One of the small windows in the garage door was shattered. The shards of glass were on the outside, Sheriff Mark Hicks noticed, so the window had been broken from within. It crunched underneath his cowboy boots as he strode up the driveway, almost powder. It would take a shotgun to blast it that fine.

"Watch out, Sheriff!" one of the boys called to him. "He's in here!"

"I can see that, Ray," Hicks said flatly.

Hicks stooped a little as he approached the garage, keeping an eye on the shattered window and a hand on the pistol in his holster. Hicks had never fired the pistol in his nineteen years of service. He hoped tonight would not cause him to end his streak of good luck. He knew Jack Williams and his daughter. The Williamses had lived in Lafayette back in his grandfather's day. That made them good people. Hicks knew that Jack Williams respected the Law. Maybe today he just needed reminding.

"You in there, Jack?" he called.

"That you, Mark?" the man answered from inside the garage. His voice was hoarse and strained, but somehow it didn't sound like the voice of a murderer. Hicks guessed that no one was dead yet.

"Yes, Jack. It's me." Hicks took in both deputies with a glance, Tom Jenkins and Ray Dallop. They were shit-scared, backs to the stone-covered columns on either side of the door, guns out and ready to shoot. They made Hicks more nervous than Jack Williams did. "Who else you got in there?"

"This son of a bitch Wayne Roderick!" Jack yelled, fury breaking his voice.

"That's no way to talk about family, Jack," Hicks responded, a careful measure of chiding in his voice. In his view, civility and decent speech were both servants of the Law.

"This bastard ain't no son of mine!" Jack yelled. "And I'm fixing to put him down."

"Fixing to?" Hicks called. "Well, that means he's still in one piece. Hey there, Wayne."

"Sheriff! He's crazy!" came Wayne Roderick's voice, high-pitched with fear.

"Shut up, you sack of shit!" Jack cried, the reasonable tone of a moment ago utterly gone.

"Wayne," Hicks said calmly. "You better just keep your mouth shut, like old Jack says."

"Better say your damn prayers!" Jack Williams muttered. But that measure of control was back his voice. Like all good people in a crisis, Williams wanted to be reasoned with. Hicks knew he had better stay on Jack's side in this conversation.

"Now hold on, Jack," Hicks cautioned. "Law's here now. You done your part. Maybe you should hand over that boy to me and my men."

"Did you see what he done to my little girl?" Williams called.

"No, I haven't," Hicks said thoughtfully. "Maybe I'll just go do that. She inside the house?"

Tom Jenkins nodded.

"You all just stay right here, then," Sheriff Hicks ordered. "I don't want nothing happening while I'm gone, hear?"

Assured of the power of his words, Hicks didn't wait for an answer.

Hicks had seen Lynn Roderick beaten up before, but this time Wayne had really worked her over. Hicks shook his head and sat heavily on the reclining chair across from Lynn and Deputy Mary Jackson. The first-aid kit from one of the cruisers outside was open on the couch, but Mary was mostly just holding Lynn. A cut above her right eye was bandaged, but the rest was bruises. Lynn looked like a prize-fighter, her face puffy and turning from a bloodless gray to bruised purple.

"Hey there, Sheriff," she said. Her lips were cracked, and the words came out with a slight lisp.

"Hey, Lynn. That boy Wayne has really done it this time, hasn't he?"

"I hope that son of a bitch dies in hell!" she cried. "Look what he done to me!"

"Yep," Hicks agreed, shaking his head. "It's past time to lock him up. You know I wanted to last time."

"I know," Lynn said a little sheepishly.

"And now your daddy's fixing to put Wayne down with a shotgun, Lynn. Unless we can talk him out of it—"

"I hope Daddy blows him to hell!" Lynn screamed, her face contorting. Mary glanced at Mark and shrugged her shoulders, then tut-tutted as she saw that Lynn's eye bandage had popped from her sudden movement.

"Now you just settle down, Lynn," Mary ordered. "Look what you done."

Blood began flowing again from the cut, spilling into Lynn's eye.

Hicks sighed. The sad thing was, Wayne had done himself pretty well for a Roderick. His daddy had been an alcoholic who'd made money fixing cars and passing bad checks, and who had a noted lack of respect for the Law. But Wayne had done well in school, and got a good job wiring homes for the cable company. When he'd married Lynn Williams, her mother and daddy hadn't liked it, but they couldn't complain. But since Wayne had been laid off last year, he'd taken on the sour disposition of his father. He'd started drinking, methodically destroying himself. Not long after, Sheriff

Hicks's daughter, who worked for the parish as an EMT, had first told Mark about the beatings.

"Now, Lynn." Hicks leaned forward imploringly. "You don't want your daddy in jail. Why don't you come out and talk some sense into him?"

Lynn's face twisted; it was almost unrecognizable as swelling began to set in. "I hope he kills that son of a bitch!" she hissed.

Sheriff Hicks stood. "Well, okay then."

Hicks checked the kitchen, where another deputy covered the house's entrance to the garage. He motioned for the man to stay quiet. He didn't want Jack Williams to get the feeling he was surrounded. Hicks walked back out through the front door.

An ambulance was just arriving. Millie Hicks jumped from the driver's side with a shouted "Hey!" to her father. The sheriff waved her over to the other side of the lawn. He didn't want his daughter in the line of fire if this all went to hell. Millie nodded and led her partner to the Roderick house's side-porch door.

Hicks returned to the garage, where the deputies still crouched nervously.

"Just talked to your daughter, Jack."

There was only angry silence.

"She said you should come out of there. She says you done your part by capturing Wayne. Now let me and my boys handle this."

"Son of a bitch ain't fit to live!" Williams shouted.

"Well now, he's fit enough to rot in jail, I figure. And Lynn's gonna need her daddy now."

"I reckon you might be right," Jack Williams said reluctantly.

"Just let the law do its job," Hicks said.

"Law hadn't done my little girl any good lately!" Williams shouted.

"Only so much we can do, Jack."

"You should have *told me*, Mark," Williams accused. "You should have."

Hicks considered this. He'd thought about telling Jack, but he had expected something like this to happen once the man found out. With Lynn unwilling to press charges, there hadn't been much he could do. Sheriff Hicks hated men like Wayne Roderick for one simple reason: the crimes they committed were turned inward, so to speak, against self and family. Such men not only abused their wives, they forced them to lie about it, to reject the Law's help. These private crimes were the one gray area in Mark Hicks's world of black and white. It shamed Hicks to think it, but he was almost glad this family matter had spilled into the public world, where he could do something about it.

"You're right, Jack. I'll take that blame," Hicks called, emotion in his voice for the first time. "Wish I would've done more."

There was a sound from inside the garage. Suddenly the door began to slide upward. The two deputies jumped, and Sheriff Hicks glared at them.

Jack Williams blinked uncertainly in the cruiser's headlights. In one hand he was holding the shotgun by its barrel. Hicks reached toward it slowly, but Williams didn't hand it over.

"Man's not fit to live," Williams said, looking back toward Wayne Roderick.

Roderick was crouched in one corner, hugging his knees, his eyes still closed. There was a brown bruise on his cheek that looked like a blow from the butt of a shotgun, but otherwise he looked okay.

Hicks took another step into the garage, casually lifting the shotgun from Williams's grasp. The two deputies rose from their crouches a little shakily. It looked like Ray Dallop's legs had gone to sleep.

Wayne Roderick opened his eyes, staring at Hicks as if he might shoot him.

Then Sheriff Hicks caught the smell.

"Phew, boys. Looks like this fellow's had an accident!"

The deputies laughed, and Williams joined them. Even Wayne Roderick, the stain spreading on the seat of his jeans, smiled hesitantly, in a pathetic display of relief.

Hicks removed his hand from the butt of his gun, where it had been clenched during the entire encounter. His streak remained unbroken.

He smiled. Hell, he hadn't even drawn the weapon.

That was the power of the Law.

3 | SHOOTING GALLERY

The nine-millimeter jerked in FBI Agent Eduardo Costilla's hand, beating out its sharp tattoo. Three shots almost silenced by the bulky earphones, a pause, three more muffled explosions, another pause . . . five sets of triplets until the weapon was empty. Costilla ejected the magazine with a practiced flex of his right index finger and swept a fresh clip into the nine. Though he didn't fire again, Costilla never let a weapon stay emptied. It was an old superstition: bad luck to let an ejected clip stop bouncing on the cement floor of the firing range before he had reloaded. Bad luck to let a freshly fired weapon stay empty for more than a second.

One day, he was sure, the superstition would make a difference. Like playing the same sequence of lottery numbers for years, you didn't give up a habit like that. One day your numbers will come up. You will need those bullets.

He reached for the rocker switch that brought his target to him. With a click and the grinding of gears, the memberless torso swept forward, the concentric circles of the superimposed target rippling in the wind.

Costilla swore when he saw the results. High and to the right again, fifteen precisely grouped holes just above the target's left eye. It must be these damn earphones. Up here at the CSIS firing range, they issued ancient, bulky hearing protection. Eduardo Costilla felt like an arctic explorer in them, or one of those guys with two flashlights who brings the airplane into the gate. They were clumsy as hell. But Canadian Security Intelligence Services regulations required that they be worn while shooting. At the FBI Academy, Costilla's shooting instructors had always complained that he tilted his head too far, almost resting an ear on his right shoulder. With these earphones on, he felt as if he was trying to shoulder-cradle his cell phone while firing.

Costilla pondered the target again, and for a moment his mind flashed back to the images he'd studied on his laptop all night. The target motif was popular on the websites he was monitoring: the crosshairs of a rifle sight, the lozenge shapes of scoring regions, diagrams punctuated by bullet-hole graphics that looked real enough to have been punched in your screen. The names of the websites still rolled around in Costilla's mind. The most famous, now shut down by a lawsuit, had been called *christiangallery.com*. How many art students had pointed their browsers there, expecting to find Michelangelos and da Vincis? Cherubs and seraphim? Sorry, no angels here. The site was called gallery as in "shooting gallery." There wasn't much art there, unless you appreciated the aesthetics of guns, dead fetuses, and abortion doctors whose photographs were so grim they could only have come from their driver's licenses.

Costilla shook his aching right hand. The cramp hadn't come from shooting. It was from clenching a damn computer mouse. He had spent hours scrolling through the rants of the sites' regulars, searching for a telltale hint that would lead him to his killer.

But he'd found only anger. And lists and lists of doctors, carefully coded with the letters "RGB."

The radical fundamentalists at the Christian Gallery had started the RGB convention, as Agent Costilla and his team called it. Red, gray, and black. If a doctor's name was in red, he'd been killed by an antiabortion activist. Gray meant that the doctor had been wounded, perhaps injured when a round was stopped by the regulation bulletproof vest. Get you next time. Most of the doctors' names were in black, though. Targeted, but not yet made to feel "God's" wrath. And the websites didn't stop at names. There were phone numbers—most probably changed once they hit the sites—license plates, and the addresses of clinics, hospitals, private practices, and doctors' homes.

Costilla shuddered. Even the names and schools of some of the doctors' kids were posted. The sins of the fathers visited upon the children.

"Santa Maria," Costilla whispered, touching the small gold cross at his neck. For three years he had tried to understand these people, and sometimes he saw the twisted logic in their interpretation of faith. Costilla himself was here at a shooting range, practicing to skillfully break the Sixth Commandment should the need arise. History had shown that there were times to kill. But whenever Costilla spent time on the shooting gallery websites, he saw only gleefully self-righteous hatred. The cartoon blood dripping from the screen titles, the gun porn lovingly scanned from small-arms catalogs, and the portraits that matched Costilla's last four victim files, their names in red, with captions that seemed to taunt him to turn the perpetrators into martyrs.

Fine. He might just do that.

Agent Costilla stretched his fingers and listened. The firing range was deserted now, almost ten o'clock. Fuck regulations. He pulled the earphones from his head and let them drop with a heavy thud to the concrete floor. He clipped a fresh target to the wire and watched it travel to the other end of the range.

To hell with his hearing. It was time to hit something.

4 | LOCAL HERO

"Look!" Ellen cried. She was peering up, one pointed finger pressed against the top of the windshield.

Dr. Daniel Wyatt panicked for a moment, his shoulders hunched to follow Ellen's gaze upward. His hands clenched the steering wheel of the Saab.

Ellen looked at him and gave a surprised laugh.

"Relax," she said. "Nothing's falling out of the sky. Didn't you see that banner?"

Wyatt swallowed and nodded. The banner. He and Claire had passed under it earlier that day. Suspended above Main Street, between the Vermillion Cinema and a gas station, fringed with the fluttering little flags of car dealership grand openings. It read:

LAFAYETTE CONGRATULATES DR. DANIEL WYATT
U.S. SURGEON GENERAL

Civic pride. The small-town doctor goes to Washington. Wyatt wondered what the banner would say if Sarah Corbett started to talk.

"Yeah. Claire and I saw it earlier."

"Well, I'm sorry if it's old news," Ellen sniped. "But *I* hadn't seen it yet. And I think it's very exciting."

"It's very nice of . . ." he started, then found himself at a loss. "Of whoever puts up banners," he finished lamely.

"Well, you don't seem very happy for a local hero," Ellen complained.

Dr. Wyatt took one hand from the wheel and rested it softly on his wife's knee. He tried to soften his voice, to make the sounds of a confiding spouse.

"I'm just nervous about the confirmation hearings," he lied. "They go after everybody in these things. You know they'll bring up the abortions in Guatemala."

They drove a few moments in silence. Out of downtown now, the dark tendrils of willows reached over the narrow road, almost low enough to brush the roof of the car. A light rain had started, and Wyatt turned the wipers onto their lowest setting. Between infrequent swipes of the blade, raindrops collected on the windshield to form amoeba shapes that pulsed brightly with the passing streetlights.

"Daniel?" Ellen paused for a moment as if choosing her words carefully. "What was that page you took during the party?"

"That was Sarah Corbett," Daniel said quickly. He had rehearsed this moment, in case Ellen asked. She was sometimes curious about his patients. She was curious about everything. He didn't wanted to seem cagey. But now as the words spilled out, he wondered if he had said them *too* quickly.

"Who?" His wife seemed to linger on the word. Wyatt realized he had two hands on the wheel now, clenched again.

"A patient."

A patient. That was the worst part of it all. Not merely his marriage vows, but his professional ethics as well. Wyatt squinted through the hastening rain and turned the wipers up a notch.

It had been raining that weekend in Baton Rouge, too. A conference sponsored by Planned Parenthood, he thought grimly. But the whole thing had been happenstance, utterly unplanned.

They'd been staying in the same hotel, an old French colonial with verdigrised wrought-iron rails snaking around the second story. It wouldn't have been out of place on Bourbon Street.

Sarah was in Baton Rouge dealing with her father's estate. Her parents had died a few years before, but despite her father's straightforward will and the poverty of heirs, the meandering course of Louisiana law had required a long effort from his only child. "Southern gothic probate," she'd laughingly called it. Sarah had the soft accent of patrician Louisiana, a lilting dialect in which the word "tomorrow" rhymed with the Italian word *cara*. Other than the car accident that had taken her parents, her life had been soft, too. The family's wealth—not vast, but comfortable—stretched back to the days of sugarcane and cotton, though the old fields were now licensed to oil companies. She had a bright, round face and the kind of easy laugh that goes with assured wealth. She was surprised and glad to see him. It seemed natural, as fellow Lafayettans in the big city, to join her at a restaurant she knew.

The restaurant was expensive, the sort of place that would usually have intimidated Wyatt. It was dark and richly furnished, the chairs covered with some rich fabric. It seemed centuries removed from the stark, fluorescent-lit dining room of the conference center where he and five hundred other delegates had been fed plastic-wrapped sandwiches that afternoon. But Sarah seemed utterly at home there, her skin whitely luminous against her red velvet dress. Her darkly blue eyes gathered glimmers from the blue-and-green stained-glass lamp that sat between them on the rich oakwood table, their sparkle making her seem even younger than her thirty-three years.

"Dr. Wyatt," she said, ignoring his pleas to call him by his first name, "you do remind me of my father?"

Like many women in the south, she always seemed to be asking a question, her voice rising with a tremulous uncertainty at the end of every statement, as if awaiting his confirmation. Wyatt smiled shyly in agreement.

Sarah laughed sweetly when he had trouble reading the menu. Dark restaurants had always upset him. Why make it hard to see unless they wanted to hide the food? he'd always said. But the darkness here felt somehow right. Sarah patiently read the menu for "Dr. Wyatt" from top to bottom in her soft accent, adding her own commentary, and it had made perfect sense to order a bottle of wine.

"She thinks she's pregnant," Wyatt added. "A bit upset about it."

"Is she married?" his wife said.

"Why do you ask?" Wyatt responded, too sharply. *Relax,* he ordered himself.

"Because you said she was upset."

They were almost at home. The Saab turned into the familiar double-lane street. Towering oaks punctuated the median, their broad arms sheltering the car from the rain.

"Of course," Wyatt agreed. "I mean, no, she's not married."

She had known exactly what to say.

In those hours at the restaurant, Wyatt felt like a healer, in his proper role as counselor and confidant, as the velvet mellowness of the wine loosened Sarah's tongue. She was an orphan, alone and away from home in this big city. Her velvet dress seemed almost antebellum in its lushness, as if she were some delicate time traveler trapped outside her proper era. Of course, they went back to their hotel together. And it was only gentlemanly to walk Sarah to her room.

For a moment, in a reflection from steel elevator doors, Wyatt caught a glimpse of himself and his young companion. They did look like father and daughter, he suddenly realized, a distinguished man and his younger charge off to some formal ball. But there was also something electric there, a spark struck by their mismatched ages, by the speckled gray of his mane and the shiny waves of her raven hair, by skin weathered and soft. It was clear from that momentary picture where they were going. What would happen upstairs. Wyatt felt a tug of guilt, but then the doors parted and the picture evaporated. There was no reason for guilt or trepidation. He was simply a friend taking her to her room, a perfect gentleman.

On the seventh floor, Sarah opened her door, a little clumsy with the unfamiliar key, not to mention the effects of that second bottle of wine. She took one step inside the dark room. Wyatt took a step back, straightening himself as one does before bowing, the smile of a pleasant evening's good-bye already on his lips.

Sarah turned to Daniel Wyatt and looked him up and down. Then she reached one hand to her throat, slid her fingers down the white skin there, and unhooked the topmost clasp of the red dress. The velvet parted a little more than an inch, splaying from the weight of her generous breasts, the hooks of the lower clasps growing taut below. And in that one gesture, Wyatt was trapped again by that reflection in the elevator doors. He and Sarah were here as male and female, not just friends, certainly not doctor and patient.

"Daniel," she said, her hand still at her throat, her voice a whisper. "Do please come in."

"Aren't you coming in?" his wife asked.

"The car's knocking again," Wyatt said.

It was true. The Saab shuddered noisily as it cooled on the Wyatts' driveway, some apparently mechanical poltergeist clanking within.

"Well, don't stay out all night." Ellen slammed the door behind her and walked up the path to the front porch. Then she turned and looked back at him. The rain had stopped, but drops on the windshield still prismed the yellow porchlights.

Wyatt felt a cold fear rising in him as Ellen walked back toward the car. Damn, he'd been such a bumbling idiot since Sarah's page. Ellen must know *something*. This is it, then. She's going to ask him. Now is the time to confess.

Or rather, five weeks ago had been the time to confess. He'd tried, too. A whole sleepless night rehearsing the proper words of regret, trying to make it firm and simple, but not too hard on Ellen. He would admit his guilt, promise he would never slip again. He'd even written the speech down on an index card. But there had never been the right time. And he'd burned the card in the kitchen sink one night, carefully washing the black ashes down the drain.

Ellen opened the door for him, and he looked up at her sheepishly.

"Ellen, I'm sorry," he began.

"Don't worry, Daniel. It's okay," she said soothingly. For a moment he didn't understand.

"Most of those hearings go off without a hitch," she continued, smiling. "After all, you're a good man. A hero. The people in this town know it. And I know it. I'm sure the distinguished senators can figure it out."

She gently took his arm and lifted him from the Saab's deep leather seats. Wyatt allowed himself to be led into the warmth of the house. Ellen stood behind her husband and pulled off his rain-dampened jacket. She hung it up and patted his shoulders lovingly.

"Don't let Claire scare you with her feminist paranoia. It'll be a snap."

"Thanks, darling," Wyatt said, and kissed his wife. Why had he strayed? Fourteen years. Why would a man throw away fourteen years?

Ellen giggled. Wyatt realized for the first time that she was just a little drunk. She didn't suspect anything. She was just "tipsy," as she would say tomorrow.

"After all, no one's accusing you of being some sort of Clarence Thomas," she added.

And, giggling, she went upstairs.

Two hours later, when Ellen's breathing had slowed to the rhythms of deep sleep, Wyatt slipped from their bed and softly padded into the hall. He took the stairs slowly, right foot first onto every step like a small child, trying to avoid the usual creaks of the old wood. He moved by memory and instinct through the darkened halls, aware of every sound in the old house.

In his den, where he had practiced medicine at home long ago, he dared to turn on a small desk lamp. The gold leaf binding rows of medical texts glimmered in its light. When he lifted the phone, its dial tone sounded horribly loud.

He muffled the receiver as he punched out the tones of Sarah Corbett's number.

She answered quickly. Sounded as if she'd still been awake.

"I need to meet with you," he said, almost whispering.

"Of course," she said simply.

They were on the line for almost a quarter hour, but exchanged only a few more words. There were long stretches of silence during which they listened to each other breathe.

"I'm sorry."

"I know."

"We'll make it right."

"I know."

"You can count on me. I understand."

When Wyatt hung up, he sat in the comfortable leather chair. From this chair he had counseled the grief-stricken, had dispensed wisdom and good advice. He had probably saved a few lives. Now he thought of Sarah, his mind turning over the medical details. A growing fetus inside, about an inch long. Eventually, the swelling of the belly, the extra sub-cutaneous fat making the face full and lively. The glow that anyone recognizes in a pregnant woman. It would suit Sarah, this transformation.

Wyatt realized with horror that he'd been thinking of Sarah's naked body with affection, almost with desire.

He dropped his head into his hands. This is why doctors don't sleep with their patients, he realized. The clear vision of the healer is compromised by the gaze of the lover.

"Daniel?"

Ellen stood at the door of his office, harsh white hall lights behind her.

"Are you okay?"

"Yes. I'm coming to bed now."

"No point sitting down here," Ellen said.

Wyatt nodded his assent.

"It's too late," she added as they went up the stairs together.

5 | REMEMBRANCE DAY

When Agent Costilla emerged from the shower, he saw the message light flashing on his cell phone. Naked except for a towel around his muscular shoulders, he sat on the rumpled bed and pulled the phone from its recharging cradle with a snap. As the phone connected to his messaging service, he saw mist rising from his shower-heated arm. These Canadians keep their hotel rooms cold enough, he thought. He'd be glad to get back to Washington once Remembrance Day had passed.

"This is A.D. Richards," the familiar voice announced. Costilla imagined the assistant director's weathered face, the phone cord, as it always was, wound through her fingers enough times to make it seem she was wearing a knuckle-duster made of black plastic. "You know the number."

"Short and to the point," Costilla said to himself, pressing the number 1 on his phone. Most people's speed dialers started with their wife or husband's number, he reflected. Or their girlfriend, or maybe their mother. Costilla's started with his boss.

"Richards," she answered.

"Costilla," he said.

"You still up there pissing in the snow?"

"Yes, Assistant Director. The Toronto Hilton, to be exact."

"Well, I need you back in Washington. ASAP."

"That anywhere near Washington, D.C.?"

"Not funny. Nor is this call likely to amuse you, Agent

Costilla. A friend of mine wants a very quiet and very deep background check on the surgeon general nominee."

Costilla removed the phone from his head and whispered a profanity, then jammed it back to his ear.

He could barely contain the contempt in his voice. "A background check? On a *surgeon general*? Shall I check on the postmaster while I'm at it?"

"The friend in question is a senator, Costilla. A Republican senator on the Labor and Human Resources Committee. He's also on the Judiciary Committee. You may have read that the surgeon general nominee admits to having performed abortions. This seems related to your field of expertise."

"Yeah. I'm sure the senator in question would love me to find some dark secret in this baby killer's past," Costilla fumed. "Hell, the poor bastard may even be hit-listed. Maybe I could find his kids' names on-line. But I'm kind of busy up here, Assistant Director. It's November tenth. Tomorrow is Remembrance Day."

"Any action yet?" Richards asked.

"No. But there will be. My killer's due for a hit."

"And you're sure it's going to be up there?"

"Absolutely. 'Tis the season."

Remembrance Day was the Canadian version of Veterans Day, but somehow, that more general name had evoked a darker side from the holiday north of the border. Anti-abortion groups had dubbed it "Remember the Unborn Children Day." Since 1994, an average of one doctor a year in Canada had been shot on or around the holiday. Across the country, OB-GYNS were advised to wear body armor at all times. Even in their homes. After all, Dr. Barnett Slepian had been shot through his living room window.

"It's serious. You should see the mailers going out to warn doctors," Costilla continued. " 'Don't jog. Don't keep a regular schedule. Don't use a parking space marked with your name.' "

"Shit," Assistant Director Richards muttered. For a moment, Costilla could hear genuine anger in her voice. Then her usual dry reserve returned. "And I thought they were all pacifists up there."

"You ever watched a hockey game?"

"I take your point, Costilla. Well, you have until the day after tomorrow. Then I want your ass back in D.C. The confirmation hearings start next week. Assign two of your team to get started today."

Costilla grimaced. He was understaffed as it was. His FACE Task Force was fighting a loosely defined group of terrorists with thousands of active members and hundreds of thousands of sympathizers. But his wasn't a popular crusade. Not with the majority of the Senate, anyway. The Freedom of Access to Clinic Entrances Act had been passed in 1994, back when the Senate majority had been in different hands. Assistant Director Richards had political aspirations, and she knew better than to antagonize the ruling conservatives on this issue. Costilla wasn't even allowed to use the word "terrorist" in his official reports. They were just "an armed group using murder and threats to create terror among those who disagreed with them." Richards might quietly support him, but she hadn't signed off on bringing the whole team to Canada. And now she wanted him back to manage this political errand.

"Let us stay on this for the next two days," he pleaded. "We've got to monitor dozens of websites and chat rooms. It's labor-intensive as hell. Otherwise, we're just reacting."

"*Costilla.*"

"Until the day after tomorrow, then I'll handle the background check personally," he offered. "Even if it means going down to . . ." Where was this guy from?

"Louisiana," Richards supplied.

"I'll go to Louisiana, then."

There was a satisfied pause on the other end of the line, and Costilla realized that Richards had gotten what she'd really wanted.

"All right, Costilla. You've got your two days. But I want some information on this nominee by next Wednesday. I don't care if you have to obtain it from your pro-life friends. You know these hearings; it doesn't have to be a capital crime, just enough so our honorable senator can raise his eyebrows and huff a little for the cameras. Show the folks back home he knows the score. Shit, the guy's gonna get confirmed anyway. Just make the other side look like they tried."

"You got it," Costilla promised. He began to towel himself dry, realized that he'd broken an angry sweat during the conversation. One shower wasted. "Who's the lucky guy, anyway?"

"Some small-town doctor. Happily married, three kids. He'd be a shoo-in if he hadn't messed around with Planned Parenthood."

"So he was asking for trouble."

"Just give me *something*, Costilla. Even if it stays in the raw files for the senator to allude to. Traffic violation. A misdiagnosed hangnail. Anything."

Agent Costilla wondered for a moment if A.D. Richards wanted him on this for a reason she couldn't say. She knew Costilla's sympathies, and had always implicitly shared them. Perhaps she wanted him to find just the right amount of dirt, and no more. Like that touch of virus in a vaccine that immunizes a patient.

If nothing else, he'd be someplace warm.

"Shouldn't be too hard, Assistant Director," Costilla said, kneeling to reach for his pants. "He's from a small town? No problem. Somebody's always ready to talk."

6 | BREAKFAST

"How's Lynn Roderick?" Sheriff Mark Hicks asked the next morning.

"Oh, I reckon she's better than she looks," his daughter, Millie, responded. "She wasn't even concussed. That girl's tough as nails."

Hicks nodded and sipped his coffee.

"If she's as tough as her old man, she'll be fine." But the domestic dispute the night before still bothered him. Both Wayne Roderick and Jack Williams were in jail, but you never knew when a beaten wife would end up going back to her man. Hicks hoped that taking Lynn to WAG to meet with Claire Davis would prevent future abuse, but somehow these stories never seemed to end properly. They just wound along like some soap opera, sometimes spinning through the generations. Mark Hicks sighed. He liked his tales with a beginning, a middle, and an end.

Millie placed the eggs before him with a little curtsy, a habit she had picked up from her mother.

Hicks smiled lovingly at her, wondering at how the early death of his wife, so meaningless and tragic, had resulted in such a daughter. It was almost as if a measure of her mother's wisdom and beauty had somehow passed to Millie that awful day, eight years ago. At sixteen, she'd been a brat; willful, spoiled, angry at the world. But blind tragedy had molded her like a skillful artisan, and at the young age of twenty-four, Millie had achieved an older woman's graces. Hicks suddenly knew that she wouldn't ever marry a man like Wayne Roderick. She was too wise, too mature. And a good thing, too; even the power of the Law wouldn't save the man who touched Mark Hicks's daughter.

"Aren't you joining me?" Hicks asked as Millie started to scrub the frying pan.

"I'm having breakfast with Sarah Corbett."

"I thought it was lunch," he said. He always treasured breakfast with Millie. Since she had become an EMT, their schedules had been at odds, what with her working nights.

"She changed it. She's having lunch with Dr. Wyatt."

"That girl's a hypochondriac," Hicks concluded. Sarah lived next door, in a huge, ill-kept house that was decades older than those in the rest of the neighborhood. Originally, her parents had owned all the land in sight. Morlean Street had been their private drive in the old days. But they'd sold off the estate to a developer, and now their old house was stranded, an island of the Old South surrounded by tract housing and playgrounds.

"What do you mean, Daddy?"

"She was complaining the other day that the dust from those workers was making her ill," Sheriff Hicks explained. Sarah Corbett had recently decided to fix up the old house, which was about time in the Sheriff's humble opinion. But in retreating from the noise and mess of construction, she spent far too much time in the Hickses' kitchen.

"Oh. I think she just likes Dr. Wyatt. She does go on about his nomination."

Hicks's eyebrows raised. "You think there's anything going on between them?"

"*Daddy!*" Millie scolded, lifting her car keys from the cookie jar by the door. "She may think Dr. Wyatt's dreamy. Who doesn't? But Sarah is a southern lady."

"Meaning?"

"Meaning she would have gossiped about it long before now *if* there was anything to gossip about."

Sheriff Hicks chuckled as his daughter kissed him good-bye.

She was right about that. Sarah Corbett was from a good family, but she'd never been able to keep her mouth shut.

"**D**r. Wyatt?" the maître d' greeted him. For a sickening moment, Daniel Wyatt thought the man had recognized him. Was he a former patient? Did the whole town know his face because of the nomination? Then Wyatt's eyes followed the man's arm down to where his index finger rested on the reservation book. Of course, on a weekday at lunchtime the restaurant was almost empty, and he'd foolishly made a reservation in his own name.

"Yes. For two," Wyatt said, his voice dry.

"The other party hasn't arrived yet, sir," the waiter said, and led him to a dark, secluded table. Perfectly discreet. Almost too discreet, in fact. Did the waiter assume that this was a lunchtime assignation? Maybe it was that kind of place. The name of the restaurant was Laissez les Bon Temps Rouler. Good times, indeed.

Sarah had suggested it. The sort of old-world Cajun luxury in which she was so at home. But it was too sensuous for Wyatt. It reminded him too much of his first meal with Sarah, when this nightmare had all started. Was she expecting a reprise?

Wyatt sat and ordered himself to relax. The affair was over. Hadn't even lasted the full three days of the conference. That last night he'd explained to Sarah that it had to end. Fourteen years of marriage came first.

She had seemed to understand. In her soft, polite, almost world-weary way, she'd sadly agreed that it was for the best. Of course, Sarah had suggested just one more night together.

Wyatt had been flattered, but silently shook his head no. And she'd accepted his verdict without another word.

Surely today he could convince Sarah of the right course. Wyatt knew she still looked up to him, and would listen to his advice. She was so soft, so pliable.

She was late. Wyatt looked at the time on his silent pager. Only ten minutes, standard for a southern lady, but the minutes were crawling by, punctuated by the intolerable attentions of the maître d'. Would you prefer another table? This one was fine. Would you care to consider the specials? Not yet. Would you like a glass of wine while waiting? Absolutely not.

"Daniel!" a voice came suddenly from across the room. Wyatt jumped at the sound of his name. Sarah. He rose to greet her.

"It's good to see you," he said. She kissed his cheek. The smell of her perfume evoked a rush of memory, and he sat down heavily.

"Manners, Dr. Wyatt," she said in mock disapproval. Wyatt smiled a feeble apology, realizing that he had plopped himself into his chair before she, the lady, was properly settled. How ungallant.

The waiter appeared, and Sarah ordered a glass of wine. Wyatt nodded his head for the same when asked. Suddenly a drink seemed necessary.

When the ruby-filled glasses came, Sarah lifted hers toward him.

"Congratulations on your nomination."

"Thank you," Wyatt answered. The taste of the wine stirred memories again. The dim lighting, the plush restaurant. Damn, her dress today was red. Not the crushed velvet she'd worn that night, but close enough. Wyatt felt trapped, as if time had jolted back to that weekend, and he would be forced to watch as he again derailed his life.

But that wasn't happening, he reminded himself. He wasn't going anywhere near a hotel room with Sarah Corbett again. He was here to fix this problem, not exacerbate it. Wyatt decided to skip any more small talk. He plunged into the first item on his carefully planned agenda.

"Sarah," he said. "How sure are you?"

Sarah regarded him absently across the table. For an absurd moment, Wyatt thought he might have to be more specific. But then she answered.

"Two home tests. Then I went to my gynecologist. It's confirmed."

Wyatt nodded his head.

"Now—and understand that I have to ask this—are you absolutely sure that it's . . . ?"

"*Really*, Daniel," she said, her blue eyes flashing. "It is certainly yours. Unlike you, I haven't been sleeping with anyone else."

"I'm not sleeping with anyone else," Wyatt insisted.

"You and your wife don't . . . ?" Sarah arched her brows as she said this, and let her pause fill the air.

"No, that's not what I—" Wyatt took a deep breath. "I mean, I can't be 'sleeping with anyone else' because I'm not sleeping with *you*."

A look of sorrow crossed her face, and she shook her head mournfully.

"Oh, I know that, Daniel. I certainly know that."

Wyatt ground the heel of one palm against his forehead. This was not going well at all. He couldn't insult Sarah. A word from her could destroy his life.

"I'm sorry," he said. "But you remember where we stand, don't you?"

"Of course," she answered. She reached across the table and took his sweating hand. "It's our little secret, what happened in Baton Rouge."

Wyatt sighed gratefully. Maybe this was going to work out. In his panic since her page, he had forgotten Sarah's quiet respect for him. Her easy, gentle voice. She was an ally in this unfortunate mess, not his tormentor.

"But," she continued, "our little secret is getting bigger every day."

Sarah placed one hand tenderly on her belly.

"Of course," Wyatt answered, closing his eyes. "You have to understand how awkward this is for me. I never thought . . . I mean, you said you were on the pill."

Sarah nodded. "I did. And I was. But you are a doctor, Daniel. Surely you know . . ."

"Yes. Yes." He knew the failure rate for oral contraceptives. He also knew the numbers on birth-control compliance; an alarming percentage of people who claimed to be using birth control, even in controlled studies, used it intermittently or not at all.

"But this is very delicate. Especially now," he said. He heard a tone of pleading enter his voice. That wasn't wise. He had to be the mentor now. Advising, not begging. He tried to start over.

"You never told your wife, did you?" she interrupted.

The waiter chose that moment to appear. Did you and madam wish to order yet? No, we needed a few more minutes.

"No, I didn't," Wyatt admitted when the waiter's slow gait had carried him to a safe distance. "I couldn't."

Sarah patted his hand again. "Poor dear. I'm sure you tried."

"It's not just my wife. Do you understand? You're a patient under my care. And I slept with you. I could lose my license to practice medicine."

"Oh, Daniel," Sarah whispered, her eyes widening. "I didn't realize that."

He nodded again, biting his lower lip. Sarah's gaze sank to the linen napkin crumpled in her hand.

"People expect so much from doctors, don't they?" she said.

Wyatt began to feel the edge of his panic recede. There it was again, that respect in her voice. That reassurance that she needed his guidance, his wisdom.

He turned his hand under her delicate one and took it in a strong grasp.

"That's the way it's always been," he said. "I'm used to it. But what do *you* want?"

"I think a child should have a father?" she said, her voice rising in a question.

Wyatt nodded in careful agreement.

"And by that I mean, two parents who are married," she continued, still staring downward. "I do want a child, but not outside that union."

Wyatt tried to hide the wave of relief that spread through him. Slowly, surely, he told himself. He wanted to push her to say more, but Wyatt felt as if he were building a house of cards. Any wrong move could cause the whole structure to collapse.

"You're only thirty-three," he said. "A young woman."

She looked up slowly, her eyes wanting more.

"A beautiful young woman," he added.

Finally, she smiled.

"Thank you, Daniel."

"I'll support your decision," he said. "I have a colleague, a fine physician, who can help you." Help us both, he thought.

"I am in your hands, Dr. Wyatt," Sarah said.

They ordered, and the food came quickly.

Sarah soon shook off her solemn mood, and prattled about the restoration she was doing on her house, the home her parents had left her. She'd let the grounds become overgrown, and the kudzu vines that climbed the porch rails had to go. "Positively gothic," she murmured.

As they finished the rich and spicy meal, she ordered her third glass of wine. "I do love wine. I'd hate to give it up. That's one advantage . . ." she began, but trailed off, her eyes staring into the distance.

Wyatt patted her hand. "You have every advantage, Sarah. With all you've been through, you should enjoy yourself."

Sarah beamed back at him.

"Is that doctor's orders, Dr. Wyatt?"

"Absolutely."

The check arrived, and Wyatt paid with the large roll of cash he had brought. He didn't want this meal appearing on his credit card bill. It amazed him that he was thinking this way. How did married men who had affairs—*real* affairs—cope with the complications?

As they walked toward the door, Sarah slipped her arm through his. The bright sunlight outside reminded him that this restaurant wasn't in faraway Baton Rouge, it was in his hometown. He gently disengaged his arm when they reached the door.

"Don't worry, Daniel," she said solemnly. "I promise you it's the truth. I haven't told anyone."

He turned to face her, looked into her blue eyes. That respect was still there, that need for approval. He rested his hands on her shoulders.

"We made the right decision."

"I know," she answered.

Suddenly they were kissing. His mouth responded hungrily to the forceful pressure of her lips, her body insistent against his. He breathed deep the smell of her, mingled with the taste of wine.

Then, amid the whirlwind of sensation, the reality of what was happening rushed over him. He stepped back, a flush rising in his face. "Sarah, we shouldn't . . ."

"It's okay, Daniel." Sarah's lipstick was smudged, but she seemed calm and confident. "Just following your orders. Enjoying myself. Don't worry. I'll call you."

Then she turned from him and went through the door. From inside the restaurant he watched her get into her car, an aging green Cadillac, and drive away.

Wyatt wiped his mouth with the back of his hand, a red stain on his knuckles marking the passage of Sarah's lips. He tried to control the conflicted feelings inside him. The surging lust, the light-headedness of lunchtime wine, the shame of that kiss. And underneath his confusion, the sure knowledge that he was a fool. He looked over his shoulder guiltily. The staff of Laissez les Bon Temps Rouler were nowhere visible; it was hours before dinner patrons would arrive.

He straightened and walked hurriedly to his Saab. As he drove back to his office, Wyatt's pager buzzed against his belt. He glanced at the number. Not Sarah. The office. He realized that he was late for his first afternoon appointment, and drove faster through the light afternoon traffic.

The smell of Sarah's perfume, familiar and haunting, seemed to fill the car. Wyatt rubbed the back of his hand furiously, trying to remove the lipstick stain. It seemed impossible to erase. Finally, he realized the skin had simply reddened from his own abrasion of it.

Wyatt pulled into his marked parking spot and strode into the cool waiting room of his office. Mary, his receptionist, shook a finger at him with a lazy smile.

"There you are, Dr. Wyatt," she drawled. "Me and Mrs. Johnson were getting worried about you."

Abigail Johnson, his one o'clock appointment, looked placidly up from a magazine.

"I was telling her about your nomination," Mary continued. "And how your head hadn't swolen up one bit. But then you go and leave her waiting for twenty *minutes!*"

Mary and Abigail Johnson looked at each other with mock surprise.

"I'm terribly sorry, Mrs. Johnson. Just let me make a quick phone call and I'll be right with you."

Wyatt fled to the safety of his consulting office and picked up the phone. He dialed a number and waited with drumming fingers as it connected and rang.

"Dr. Magley's office."

"This is Dr. Daniel Wyatt. May I speak to Dr. Magley, please."

"Certainly, Dr. Wyatt," the receptionist said alertly. "And congratulations, by the way."

There was a short burst of Mozart as he was put on hold. Then the voice of Ernest Magley came on the line.

"So, what can I do for the new surgeon general? I hope it won't be a character reference," Magley joked.

"No, just a favor. For a friend."

8 | PARADOX

The fog was so dense it seemed to cling to the ground, curling like powdered, wind-borne snow across the highway. At the edge of visibility, the Mercedes's red taillights shimmered into and out of sight, like some ghost car that might be swept away at any moment.

Peter O'Keefe smiled at the appropriateness of that thought.

Then he increased the pressure of his foot on the accelerator, easing his stolen Dodge faster on the lonely highway. There was no point in being subtle in his pursuit. In these conditions, any driver would be focused on the road ahead, not in his rearview mirror.

Within twenty seconds, O'Keefe was close enough to read the Mercedes's vanity plate. It said PARADOX. A very slim pun that the driver shared with the other doctor in his Toronto practice.

Who was it who said that the heart of evil was banal?

Still, it seemed a shame to ruin the pun. But this Remembrance Day night, one of the pair of docs was destined to die. O'Keefe wondered how long the other half would take to order new plates.

On schedule, the Mercedes began to slow. Through the wisps of fog that coiled around the bilingual road signs, O'Keefe saw that he and his unknowing prey were approaching the Rosedale exit. O'Keefe accelerated, sure now that the doctor was definitely headed home. He had practiced this route twice already, once in the daylight and again last night.

Even with the fog, he felt confident that he could stay on course.

The third time's the charm.

The Mercedes slipped away off the exit ramp just as O'Keefe passed him. He forced the reluctant old Dodge up to eighty miles an hour, calmly muttering three Hail Marys in a measured cadence, marking the thirty seconds it would take before the next Rosedale exit appeared. He swung the car down the ramp and into a hard left under the highway, doubling back on the now broad and tree-lined roads.

He drove fast, feeling the familiar surge of adrenaline as the elegant old homes swept past on either side. But even with the hormones of excitement coursing through him, an impossible calm began to take over. A clear sense of purpose quieted his usual rage, the constant torment of living in a world that had forsaken God's law. The incessant pain that was the price of every day's failure to take action against the world's sins would be eased, at least for the next few hours. It had been too long since O'Keefe had last struck a blow for the righteous cause. Too long.

"Thank you, Father, for this moment," he whispered, his right hand leaving the wheel to finger the cold metal of his silenced nine-millimeter.

O'Keefe reached the intersection right on schedule. The Mercedes was just passing through at its careful, leisurely pace. The Dodge turned right against a red light to fall behind it. O'Keefe couldn't remember whether right-on-red was legal here in Toronto, but this late at night on empty streets it wouldn't seem suspicious. Even if the doctor had noticed his pursuer before, he wouldn't realize that the same car was behind him again. O'Keefe had chosen the Dodge for its nondescript appearance. He certainly wasn't fool enough to use vanity plates. He smiled grimly at the thought. KILL4GOD?

But Dr. Gregory M. Blackmun had no such compunction. He freely advertised what he was. A doctor who killed rather than cured. A paradox indeed.

The Mercedes reached a large Colonial house, its two stories alight. O'Keefe rehearsed the names of the occupants of the house: Blackmun's wife, Hillary, two daughters, an infant son. A bay window downstairs flickered dimly with the uncertain flicker-rhythm of television images. Although O'Keefe had driven past the house three times in the last week, once in his own car and twice in the stolen Dodge, the sight of such luxury still made him grit his teeth. What a sick society, he thought, where a mass murderer could be rewarded with such wealth.

The car turned into the mansion's driveway, and its lights were extinguished.

O'Keefe slowed his vehicle, his surreal calm carrying him through a host of reflexes that timed the passage perfectly. His left index finger pressed the button that lowered the passenger window. He switched hands on the wheel and brought up the automatic pistol with his right just as Dr. Blackmun emerged from the car. The porch light backlit the dark form, making a silhouette as distinct as a shooting gallery target.

But just as O'Keefe began the few whispered syllables of his prayer of thanks, the doctor's exposed form leaned back into the car, straining to pull some recalcitrant piece of baggage from the far seat. O'Keefe's foot stabbed out to hit the brake, and the Dodge's bald tires produced a short but distinct screech as the car jerked to a halt.

Dr. Blackmun stood up quickly, a dry-cleaning bag in one hand, and peered through the darkness at O'Keefe's car. For a split second, the two men stared at each other's obscured form, then Blackmun burst into action.

He bolted toward his house, leaving the door of the Mercedes open behind him. Absurdly, he still clung to the dry-cleaning bag, which trailed behind him like a cape, its skin of transparent plastic glimmering in the orange halogen streetlights.

Peter O'Keefe calmly leaned toward the window to widen his field of fire, and uttered the words of celebration.

"Gaudeamus igitur."

Therefore, let us rejoice.

He squeezed off a series of shots at the fleeing form, the silencer rendering them no louder than seven bursts of air from a bicycle pump, continuing to fire as his target spun on the icy walk. The man crumpled to the ground, tangled now in his burden of shirts, plastic, and hangers. O'Keefe stepped from the Dodge, leaving the engine running. Normally, he trusted his marksmanship to take them out. He had never been wrong. But those were head shots, his targets standing still and unaware. This had gotten messy.

It was fortunate that he checked. As O'Keefe strode quickly across the rimy lawn, he heard Blackmun groan. Then, incredibly, the man rose and took a few lurching steps toward the house, a hoarse shout escaping his lips.

The man was wearing body armor, a Remembrance Day precaution. O'Keefe fired twice more, aiming at knee level. The man fell to the ground again, this time making a high, womanly keening sound that proved O'Keefe's bullets had met flesh.

O'Keefe closed the distance between them and put one foot on Blackmun's chest. Even through the bulk of Kevlar and the doctor's heavy winter coat, the moment of physical contact was intense. O'Keefe could feel the man's lungs straining to fill for another scream, the mindless struggling of any organism wounded and in peril. The freezing night air brought O'Keefe's excitement to a new high. Compared to this, his previous killings had been anonymous, impersonal, somehow unreal.

A sudden shaft of light spilled across the lawn. O'Keefe swung his nine-millimeter up toward Blackmun's front door. Hillary Blackmun stared back at him, her eyes not yet adapted to the darkness outside, uncomprehending concern on her face. She was dressed in a nightgown, something thin enough to glow translucent from the house lights behind her.

O'Keefe imagined for a moment what it would be like to shoot her, to tumble her fragile form with few well-aimed shots. His arm shook for a moment with the intensity of the feeling. Then he grabbed hold of himself and swung the pistol back down toward the doctor. Staring into the man's eyes, he loudly uttered the prayer of rejoicing again and squeezed off four shots into Blackmun's skull.

O'Keefe walked quickly back to the Dodge, the cries of his victim's wife cutting into him like a sudden wind in the cold night.

9 | HEARING

"Dr. Wyatt, you were quoted in *The New York Times* as having said that giving drug users free needles lowers their risk of contracting AIDS. As surgeon general of the United States, would you support and encourage federal funding of programs to pass out free needles to *drug addicts*?"

Needle exchanges. Wyatt knew he had an index card for that one. It was somewhere here in the unruly pile of colored cards in front of him. Red for needle exchanges, he reminded himself. No wait, red index cards were parental consent for teenage abortions! Blues were needle exchange. After a few seconds of nervous shuffling, he found three cards, their surface crowded with typewritten bullet points and Claire's tight handwriting. Wyatt's eyes scanned the important points quickly:

more science needed
Shalala, 2/97
local choice!
BUSH ADMIN!!

"Uh, yes," Wyatt began. "Actually, my remarks were in regard to research originally funded by the Bush administration in 1992." That's right, make it bipartisan. "The objective of this research was to discover whether needle exchange programs, carefully managed, could reduce the spread of HIV and other blood-borne diseases. And I believe current research shows that needle exchanges do reduce such risk.

That conclusion was reported to Congress by the secretary of health in 1997."

Wyatt's interrogator leaned closer.

"I see, Dr. Wyatt. But would you support and encourage federal funding of such programs for drug addicts?"

"Well, I'll tell you what I would support," he answered haltingly. "Um, more research is required in order to make sure that such programs do not encourage drug use in our communities. Until that time, federal funds should not be used in that manner." The words left a sour taste in his mouth, although his questioner nodded in agreement.

"But, Dr. Wyatt, your own counsel, seated there with you at that desk, filed for assistance from the state government of Louisiana to fund just such a program."

Wyatt shuffled through the cards, vainly searching for more blues. He remembered that now. But Claire hadn't said a thing about this. It wasn't fair!

"Answer the question, Dr. Wyatt!"

Wyatt threw up his hands.

"Frankly, if the senator would spend less time worrying about needle exchanges and more time exercising, his well-known case of hemorrhoids would probably be less of a pain in the ass!"

Wyatt's tormentor leaned back with a satisfied smile.

"Your point is well taken. But you owe me another dollar."

Wyatt sighed and pulled out his wallet. He found a crumpled one and pushed it across the card table to Claire Davis. She ceremoniously added it to her growing pile. The fluorescent overhead lights of the Women's Advocacy Group break room flayed Wyatt's tired eyes cruelly. He rubbed them with the palms of his hands and wished this was all over.

"The correct answer, of course, is that you believe communities have the right, under the Tenth Amendment to the Constitution, to create their own strategies to deal with this terrible and devastating disease."

"I hate this." Wyatt sighed. As an advocate for women's choice in a conservative region of the country, he'd had to defend himself in the press, and in front of community meetings and government panels. In those forums Wyatt had enjoyed the fight. With Claire at his side, they gave as good as they got. But now that he was a nominee, everything was changed. The firebrand that was Claire Davis now counseled caution and dissembling.

"I should just tell them they'd want their own kids to have clean needles," he said.

"Oh, great strategy."

"What's happened to you, Claire?"

"You'll thank me when you face the real committee. They won't be as pleasant as me."

Wyatt couldn't disagree with that. Claire had downloaded the transcripts of the last two surgeon general confirmation hearings, and Wyatt had read them in disbelief the night before. Claire's questions were terribly close to what had actually been said.

"Tenth Amendment . . . That's states' rights, yeah?" he said, struggling to remember his grade-school civics classes.

"Correct. You can always plead the Tenth with these bastards." Claire sneered. "The Republicans at least have to pretend that they want to free state governments from government control, even if New Jersey decides to pack condoms in the school lunches it gives out. But you had it in front of you. Local choice works for everything. You just have to *concentrate*. What's your problem tonight? Is anything wrong?"

Wyatt sighed. They'd been at it for three hours now. Claire had insisted that they skip dinner after his first few answers hadn't lived up to her expectations. He constantly checked his pager. He had called Sarah today, going over the details of her appointment with Ernest Magley. There had been an all but palpable reluctance on her part. She'd acted like a recalcitrant child being dragged to the doctor, as if it hadn't been her idea in the first place. *Will it hurt, Daniel? Are you sure you'll be there, Daniel?*

He almost wished that Sarah still called him Dr. Wyatt.

When had that changed? Of course. Right before their kiss at Laissez les Bontemps Rouler. What an idiot he'd been. The change from Dr. Wyatt to Daniel seemed unspeakably ominous. He'd half expected her to call back tonight to cancel the appointment, and it was driving him crazy. Claire's mock confirmation hearing wasn't helping.

Not for the first time, Wyatt thought of confessing his affair to Claire. At least he would have an ally in this nightmare. But the thought of her reaction—disgust at his idiocy, horror at what this might do to the nomination—made it impossible to form the words.

"No. Nothing's wrong. Just tired."

"All right, then. Let us now turn to the subject of gun violence."

"Come on, Claire. Are they really going to hit me on gun control? I'm the surgeon general, for crying out loud."

"Not yet you aren't. And yes, they hit Foster and Elders with it."

Claire assumed a southern drawl. Although she was from Louisiana, her undergraduate days at Vassar and postgrad training at NYU Law School had softened her accent until it held only the merest traces of the south. But still, when she wanted to make a point, or sometimes when she'd been drinking, the Louisiana girl slipped out.

"You stated to the *Times-Picayune* in 1999 that gun violence is a public health problem," she drawled. "Is this really an issue for agencies such as the Centers for Disease Control, when other agencies have primary responsibilities in this area? And don't the people of the United States have a right under the Second Amendment to be free of government controls over firearms?"

"You're enjoying being a senator way too much, Claire."

"Did I ever say I would stop at counsel general, or even attorney general?" she countered. "Now answer the question, y'all!"

Wyatt gave up his search for orange index cards and rubbed his eye sockets with his fingers. He decided to wing it.

"Each year, there are over fifty thousand homicides and suicides in our country. That's more Americans dead in one year than were killed in the entire Vietnam War. If cholera were killing that many of us, it would be a signal priority to reduce that number of deaths. In fact, the National Council on Injury Prevention and Control, under the surgeon general's auspices, collects data about firearms injuries. That data can empower people to make decisions that reduce injury to themselves and their children in a way that agrees with their own values."

"My goodness," Claire said softly. "You finally got one right."

She carefully selected a dollar from the pile of crumpled bills and passed it back to Wyatt.

"I guess this is finally sinking in," he said, running his fingers back through his hair. He looked at Claire. It was good to see her smiling. She'd worked herself ragged to prepare him, but this whole thing with Sarah had left him unable to function. It wasn't fair to Claire, after all she'd put into his career.

His pager emitted its sickening beep.

He reached for it with trembling fingers, unclipping the vibrating plastic from his belt. It whirred once more in his hand as he extended it far enough to read with his tired eyes.

Sarah's number.

"I . . . uh . . . It's a patient," he mumbled. "I should call her."

"Duty calls." Claire smiled. "Let's not forget why we got into this business."

Dr. Wyatt looked around uncertainly. There was no phone in the break room. Whatever the rightness of the cause, Claire ran a tight ship.

"Here, you can use the phone bank room."

She led him to a windowless room about fifteen feet square. It was filled with long folding tables, each of which held three telephones. Wyatt remembered coming by during the last school board election, when the Christian Coalition had targeted the Lafayette Independent School District for a takeover. The official issue that sparked WAG's involvement had been sex and AIDS education, which Daniel and Claire had worked to implement almost a decade ago. But Wyatt also considered himself a man of science, and the idea that his three children might learn biology without hearing the name Charles Darwin appalled him. The phone bank was also staffed fourteen hours a day by volunteers who offered HIV and pregnancy counseling. The fact that it was deserted now showed how late Claire had kept him.

"I'll leave you alone, Daniel," she said. "Just got some things to do in my office."

He nodded wearily and sat heavily down, turning the pager over and over in his fingers.

When Claire's footsteps had receded down the hallway, he picked up one of the phones at random.

"Daniel?" Sarah answered. Wyatt swallowed hard. What if it had been someone else calling? What would they make of her answering the phone that way?

"Are you okay?" he asked.

"Yes, I'm sorry. I'm sorry." Her voice sounded small and distant. "It's just that I got scared. I don't know if I'm ready for tomorrow."

Wyatt closed his eyes. In his mind, colored index cards swirled mockingly. Which color was he looking for? White? No. That was mandatory HIV testing. Pink? Partial-birth procedures; surely not relevant here. Ah, yes. Green. The five-hundred-pound gorilla itself: abortion.

Claire's spoon-fed pap roiled in his head as he tried to think of what to say to Sarah. *I sincerely hope that I can use the power of this office to focus on those issues that unite Americans, not those that divide them. To send a message of abstinence and responsibility. To build consensus.*

"Sarah, I thought that we had agreed—"

"I know, but when you're not here I feel so . . . alone."

"I'll be there tomorrow. I'll be with you."

"But tonight has been just . . . ghastly. I keep thinking of the baby. Our baby. It seems like this night will go on forever."

Her voice was higher than usual. Like a child's. Wyatt imagined her alone in her huge old house, surrounded by the relics of her parents' life together. Positively gothic, she called the house. But she loved it there.

"Daniel? I'm just lonely, I suppose."

As Sarah's voice softened, close and intimate in his ear, Wyatt's panic lessened. He had to stop thinking of Sarah as a threat. She was lost and alone, simply another person who needed his care.

"Sarah. Would you like me to come over?"

"Oh, Daniel. Would you?"

Wyatt, his eyes still shut, nodded. Then he said, "I'm leaving here soon. But I can only stay a little while."

"Of course, Daniel. I'll be waiting."

10 | CALL

Claire Davis stood in the doorway and watched Wyatt's Saab pull out of the WAG parking lot and onto the dark, empty streets of downtown Lafayette.

She had known Daniel Wyatt for fifteen years, but she'd never seen him like this. At first she had assumed it was just the pressure of the nomination. Not everyone was cut out for the national stage. But Daniel was a grounded man. The small-town values that were touted in WAG's press releases weren't just a marketing ploy. He genuinely cared about the health of women and children, and if going to Washington would help that cause, then Claire knew in her heart that he was up to the job.

But something had changed in the last week. Perhaps as early as the celebration party. At first he had seemed swept away by the emotion of the event, the outpouring of respect and love. But later in the evening, a haunted look had come into his eyes. As if something were eating at him.

There had been that message on his pager, right before his speech at the celebration party, and the short phone call he'd left to make. After the page tonight, his face had turned white.

Over the last few days, Claire had sifted her memories to figure out what it could be, had all but asked him tonight. But Daniel had decided not to trust her with his secret.

She walked back inside through the metal detector, essential equipment for any family planning office, and the device chirped angrily at the ring of keys she carried.

She ignored the machine's buzzing, concentrating on the keys as she walked down the hall. The small pieces of tape on which the keys' labels had been handwritten were mostly unreadable, some rubbed down to the adhesive backing by constant use.

But Claire knew the key she wanted.

The technical room was small and crowded. It looked like the audiovisual department of some underfunded public school, cluttered with slide projectors and folding projection screens for giving presentations and a host of VCRs in various states of disrepair. A pile of ancient computers filled one corner, dating back to green phosphor screens and modems that you dialed yourself, then hurriedly dropped the phone into a cradle. Claire had tried to donate them to a local school a year ago, but they'd just laughed at the worthless junk. Throwing them away seemed wasteful, though, after the thousands of precious dollars that had been spent on them, so they sat in the corner, waiting like mummies for some distant revivification in a museum of technology.

But not all of the room's contents were junk. Claire sat before a long metal console. Like something from the phone company, it was striped with fader sliders and covered with a Medusa's-head tangle of patch cords. The machine had its own key, of which Claire had the only copy, a piece of circular metal that looked like it went with a kid's pair of skates. She inserted it into a slot next to a set of buttons labeled MONITOR.

The monitor buttons flickered alight. She peered at them a few moments. Her volunteer technical director, a lesbian filmmaker who made the commute from New Orleans every few weeks, had once shown her how this worked.

"Just like a VCR," she repeated the woman's explanation wryly, visualizing the flashing "12:00" above her television at home.

Claire punched a button that looked like "play" on a remote control. Her own voice came from two tiny speakers mounted to either side of the console.

"You've reached the hotline of the Lafayette Women's Advocacy Group. Please hold the line. In order to assure the best information and advice for you, this call may be recorded. Thank you."

A halting electronic voice replaced her own.

"There are . . . twelve . . . current calls."

Claire breathed a sigh of relief. She had remembered correctly. The switchboard cleared itself every morning, sending the recordings off to some backup drive. She wouldn't have to wade through weeks of dramas.

"Sorry, everyone," she said, and pressed a control that looked like two play buttons mating. "I'll try not to listen."

Voices now flowed from the tiny speakers.

"WAG. Can I help you?" That was Henry, one of the few male volunteers.

"I just wanted to ask one thing—" drawled another voice, an older woman.

Claire pressed the advance button again. There was no squeal of tape speeding by, just a soft click, and:

"My baby's been—" God, that voice was young, Claire thought. *Click.*

"My husband just doesn't seem—" You married him. *Click.*

"Is it really true that—" *Click.*

"You damn liberal—" *Click.*

"Is there anyone I can talk to about—" *Click.*

"Daniel?"

Claire's hand paused over the advance button.

"Are you okay?" God, this was it. Daniel Wyatt's voice.

"Yes, I'm sorry. I'm sorry. It's just that I got scared. I don't know if I'm ready for tomorrow."

"Sarah, I thought that we had agreed."

Sarah. Claire racked her brain, calling Daniel's friends to mind. She couldn't remember any Sarah.

"I know, but when you're not here I feel so . . . alone."

When you're not here? she thought. Damn.

Claire stabbed the square button between play and

rewind. The sound cut off. For a moment, an inane thought went through her head. It really *was* just like a VCR.

"What am I doing?" she said aloud. For years, she had instructed her volunteers about the importance of confidentiality. She was Wyatt's *lawyer,* for God's sake. And here she was, spying on him.

But the die had been cast. There was someone in Daniel's life besides his wife, that was growing clear. Normally, that would be his business. But Claire's career was now riding on the confirmation hearing, too.

It most definitely *was* her business.

She shook her head. She'd never figured Daniel for the type to cheat, and to cheat on *Ellen.* That woman would be deadly if she ever found out.

And the voice, the voice of the other woman. She sounded so young, so helpless and in awe of Dr. Daniel Wyatt. Claire decided she might as well see how bad it was.

"In for a penny, in for a pound," Claire muttered, shaking her head. She pushed the play button.

"I'll be there tomorrow. I'll be with you."

"But tonight has been just . . . ghastly. I keep thinking of the baby. Our baby. It seems like this night will go on forever."

What?

Claire clumsily rewound the tape and listened again.

The baby. Our baby.

"Oh, what have you done, Daniel?" Claire moaned.

For a moment, the weight of the words left her unable to think, unable to breathe. For Claire, it felt as if she had been the one Daniel betrayed. The surgeon generalship could be finished. If this Sarah was a patient under Wyatt's care, his practice would be finished, too. Their whole organization would be tainted, and at a time when they were under the spotlight of congressional hearings.

The surgeon general job in Washington would have been perfect to bring their work to a national level. To bring *her* to a national level. And now Wyatt was pissing it all away.

"God," she finally brought herself to say. "Men are fools."

Well, it would be up to her to fix this. Claire knew that.

She picked up the phone, ready to stab out Wyatt's beeper number. She had to demand an explanation now. But she couldn't ignore the machine. Having gone this far, she might as well hear the rest.

The small, young voice came from the speakers again.

"Daniel? I'm just lonely, I suppose."

"Sarah. I could come over, if you need me."

"Oh, Daniel. Would you?"

"I'm leaving here soon. But I can only stay a little while."

"Of course, Daniel. I'll see you soon."

Claire stormed from the technical room. He was headed to this woman's house now! This had to be stopped.

From her office, she punched the speed dial for Wyatt's pager number. When the line connected, she entered her own number. After a moment's silent fury, she added six more digits: 911 911.

11 | EYEWITNESS

Whirling beacons of emergency vehicles filled the sky with a tremulous dome of light, visible from blocks away. Agent Costilla dropped the *Toronto A-to-Z* he'd been reading by penlight onto the passenger seat of his rented Hyundai.

"Northern lights," he muttered to himself. And right on schedule.

Remembrance Day was thirty minutes old.

He followed the auroral display until he reached a cordon of orange plastic cones. A Toronto city policeman held up a gloved hand and gestured for him to turn around. Costilla parked instead.

Costilla's FBI badge got a careful going-over from the cop, but the man let him through. Maybe he'd heard of the FACE Joint Task Force. Maybe Canadians were just used to Yankees butting in.

The corpse wasn't steaming. At this temperature and humidity, that meant the killing had probably happened before midnight, a half hour ago. The shooter wasn't playing by the rules. Perhaps Remembrance Day was becoming a multiday event, like the Super Bowl.

Some of the doctor's clothes had been cut away to reveal body armor. White chalk marked the spots where four slugs had been stopped by the Kevlar. At least the man had been prepared.

The kill shots were to the head. Enough of them to make the doctor unrecognizable. A plainclothes officer was marking fragments of skull with little yellow flags. Judging by the distribution of the bone fragments, the doctor had been lying on his back when he'd been executed.

"Did you find any rounds yet?" he asked the plainclothes officer.

"Yep. Four of them."

"Nine-millimeter?"

The man squinted up at him questioningly. Costilla extended his badge case. Again, a moment of close attention to the Yankee credentials.

"Yep."

Overkill. Head shots. That was the modus operandi Costilla had been following for three years. The shots to the body and knees were new, and probably meant that the victim had spotted the killer before he'd started shooting.

Costilla now saw the Mercedes, its driver's-side door open, the interior light waning as the battery ran dead. The victim knows he's being followed. Makes a run for his house. Castilla's eyes now registered the strewn laundry bags and shirts. Correction: victim doesn't spot the shooter until after he's out of the car.

The plainclothes officer was still eyeing him. Costilla offered his hand.

"Agent Eddie Costilla, FBI. With the Freedom of Access to Clinics Entrances Act Joint Task Force."

"That's a mouthful," the man answered, his handshake firm. "Detective Allen, CSIS."

The man's hands were icy. He must have been out here for a while.

"What do we have besides the rounds, Detective?"

"Footprints in the frost." Allen pointed to a section of lawn surrounded by orange traffic cones. "Medium build, heavy guy."

Costilla nodded. A gun store owner questioned in the New Jersey slaying eight months ago had given the same description.

"Skid marks in the street," Allen added. "Small truck, maybe."

A drive-by. That also fit Costilla's shooter's MO.

"And one more thing," the detective said. "An eyewitness."

The doctor's house had the appearance of a mansion under siege. The place was furnished beautifully, with high, vaulted ceilings and lush carpeting. But it was overfull of forensics people, uniformed officers, and detectives, all escaping the cold. The front door mat was covered with dirt, and cell phones and pagers rang every few seconds.

Allen had said the witness was in the kitchen.

Costilla followed the smell of coffee back to a large, bright kitchen where a fortyish woman, shaking though she was wrapped in a bathrobe and two blankets, was giving a statement.

"God, I must enter her," she was saying.

"Are you sure?" a gray-haired detective seated across from her asked.

"That's what he said," the woman insisted.

She clutched a cup of coffee with both hands. Her cheeks were streaked with tears, but her voice was strong. She was in that zone Costilla had seen before in eyewitnesses to the murder of a loved one. Lucid and strangely self-assured. Past the point of crying.

"He stood there, with one foot on Gregory's chest. And shouted, 'God, I must enter her.' "

"And that's all?"

The woman nodded.

Dios mio, Costilla whispered softly to himself. His shooter had moved to a new level. Before now, the killings had been carried out in an impersonal kind of way. He had driven by, or waited in a parked car on a victim's jogging route. But this time, he had been forced by circumstance to face his victim. He'd come out from his hiding place and run the doctor down. He had touched his prey, planting a foot on his chest as he fired from close range. And now this. Spouting cryptic benedictions as he killed.

Until now, he'd been the worst sort of serial killer. Unknown to his victims, as detached as a Mafia hit man, moving across state and international lines. A man with little to connect him to his victims except the most anonymous of goals: the elimination of their profession. But now he had tasted a more intimate kind of murder, and the result had been this strange imperative: "God, I must enter her." Perhaps he was starting to crack. Whatever demons drove him were taking control, demanding greater involvement with his victims.

Costilla's killer was getting personal.

12 | THE SECOND PAGE

Wyatt's hands shook as he drove the Saab toward its destination.

Why was he doing this? It was already hours later than the time he'd told Ellen he would be home. She could page him at any moment. Or worse, she might call Claire's office. *Oh, yes. He left half an hour ago.*

But on the phone Sarah had sounded so lost, so alone. Wyatt felt a wave of guilt rush over him. He had worried so much about himself and his family, about Ellen and their children, that he hadn't realized what Sarah must have been going through. She was younger than Wyatt, didn't have friends and family around her. And she was the one who was pregnant.

Wyatt had gotten her into this. At least he could be there for her.

At least tonight.

This was Sarah's street. He remembered her address. Just once, he had made a short detour to drive by the old house, a week after their affair. It was as gothic looking as Sarah always said, standing out from the modern, ranch-style homes around it, a full two stories and a sloped roof complete with attic. The lonely railing of a widow's walk topped the structure.

Wyatt brought his car to a halt a couple of houses past Sarah's. The neighborhood was dark at this time of night, porch lights turned off. The cooling Saab shuddered in its usual way, its angry knocking putting the edge back on Wyatt's nerves. He looked around fearfully.

It was awfully late for a house call.

But he'd said that he'd come. And it was just for a few minutes. If he broke his promise now, the fragile strands of respect and trust that bound Sarah to the right choice might be broken. Anything could happen.

He found it impossible to open the car door, however. The thought of the interior light flashing on—revealing him here—brought on Wyatt's shakes again. He felt as he once had as a boy, when he'd snuck out of his bedroom to join his friends for a midnight drive in a car "borrowed" from someone's father. Sneaking out had been easy, but when he returned to his house, an orange dawn threatening on the horizon, he'd been paralyzed. The terror of being caught transfixed him, and he'd waited in the bushes outside, unable to gather the nerve to open his window, until his parents were awake. Then he walked in through the front door and confessed all.

Here, now, Wyatt couldn't move. He wished that he could simply will himself into Sarah's house, into that safety and warmth, without moving through the intervening space.

He did want to see Sarah. He imagined her waiting for him, only a few dozen yards away.

His pager beeped.

Shit! It must be Ellen. *Where are you? Claire said you left half an hour ago!*

Wyatt squinted at the beeper's face. It was too dark in the car to read it. His paralysis broken, he nudged the car door open and the light flashed on.

Not Ellen? Claire. And after her office number was the suffix 911 911.

Wyatt stared uncomprehendingly at the pager. Again those numbers. What could it be now? Claire would never send an alarm like this unless it was something serious. Something to do with the nomination. Or maybe someone was hurt.

He needed a phone. But he couldn't burst in and call from Sarah's. Couldn't talk to Claire from the home of his paramour. The separate spheres of his life simply could not collide like that.

Wyatt started the car again, almost relieved to be shaken out of his indecision. Claire needed him. The long, slow torture of his infidelity might be beyond coping with, but Wyatt had spent a career dealing with emergencies.

He drove off quickly, remembering a gas station only a few blocks away.

Sarah Corbett regarded herself in the mirror.

Her hair was still wet from the shower she'd taken half an hour ago, right after talking to Daniel. Two damp locks clung to her cheeks, raven black against her pale flesh. The dark curls matched the thin strokes of eyeliner she had just applied, her eyes radiantly blue.

She stepped back from the mirror and let her bathrobe slip from her shoulders. She shyly gazed at her luminous form in the soft candlelight. For tonight, she was wearing a white silk negligee that she had bought a month ago, but never worn. Her fingers hesitantly touched its frilled edges, then pulled up its hem to reveal her stomach. It seemed plumper, but only slightly, as it sometimes was after a large meal. Perhaps she was only imagining it. Still, the sight of the pregnant belly framed by the sensuous silk saddened her, and she lifted her waiting dress from a nearby chair and held it across herself.

The delicate teal fibers of the dress seemed to shudder along with the flickering candles that filled her bedroom. Just as they had done in the store, Sarah's eyes caught the color of the dress, flashing almost violet in the dim light.

Slowly, she began to dress herself. Daniel would be here soon.

Downstairs, she lit more candles. The workmen had left a terrible mess today. Sarah simply didn't understand why they couldn't be more careful. This was her home, not some . . . *construction site*. But in the semidarkness, the soft shapes of dropcloth-covered ladders didn't look so awful.

She moved from room to room, touching the familiar furniture and objets d'art displaced by the construction. Here was Papa's favorite chair, covered in cracked red leather and resting on four feet that looked like obstinate fists in the dim light. Here was a bust of Antoine Crozat, a French nobleman, her father had long ago explained, who once held the royal charter to all of Louisiana.

Sarah regarded her darkened fingertips with annoyance. Some dusting would be in order tomorrow.

The old creaky-doored pantry in the kitchen yielded a bottle of wine that looked suitably old and distinguished. Sarah decided she might as well open it while she was waiting.

While she struggled with the corkscrew, she heard the sound of a car passing slowly by outside. She carefully lifted the corner of one curtain to peer out.

It was Daniel's car. He was really here, at her home.

The familiar brown Saab drove past, then settled to a stop just beyond Sheriff Hicks's house. Sarah giggled. If Daniel wanted to be discreet, he'd picked a terrible place to park. Old Mark Hicks kept a watchful eye on everything in the neighborhood.

Sarah turned from the window and pulled the cork from the bottle. She filled two waiting glasses just a hair less than halfway, as her mother had taught her to do, and quickly looked around the living room. Everything was ready, as neat as could be expected given the depredations of the workmen.

Daniel and she needed this time together, she told herself. What they'd had in Baton Rouge was something special. The baby proved that. She felt her stomach, the gesture made painful by the thought of what she had to do.

"You were too soon," she whispered. "But next time, we'll both be ready for you."

Next time.

Sarah Corbett sat, contented as she hadn't been for what seemed like years, and waited for the knock on her door.

"For heaven's sake, Daniel!" Claire's angry voice greeted his anxious hello.

"What is it?" he responded.

"Where are you?"

"I'm . . ." Wyatt strained to read the street signs swinging above the intersection in the soft, warm breeze. "At a gas station."

"Well, go home!" Claire ordered. "Don't you dare go to that woman's house."

Wyatt's mouth formed the first syllables of several words of gibberish, then sputtered to a halt.

"Don't ask me how I know. I just do," Claire continued. "Now go home before you screw everything up. Worse than it already is."

A roaring filled Wyatt's ears. The shame of discovery and exposure choked his throat.

"How did you . . . ?" he managed. "Who told you?"

"Never mind. I just know. I trust that no one else does?"

"No. No one," Wyatt said. "But I told Sarah that I'd see her tonight. I promised."

"Go *home*," Claire ordered. "This has to be fixed, somehow. But if you show up at her house in the middle of the night you're just compromising yourself. Until I say so, you *don't know her*, all right?"

"All right," he feebly repeated.

"Now go home to your wife. I have to think about this." A pause. Then Claire's voice changed, and a note entered it that Wyatt had never heard before; Claire Davis sounded panicked. "Daniel, do you know what you've done?"

"Claire, I'm so sorry."

"In the morning, Daniel."

"Tomorrow she's getting an—"

"In the morning. Good-bye." She broke the connection with a sharp click.

Wyatt dropped the phone back into its metal cradle. He reached for another quarter, dropped it into the slot of the pay phone. He had to call Sarah, tell her he couldn't make it.

His fingers wouldn't dial the number. He was too tired. Another woman yelling at him, another woman disappointed in him. How had it come to this?

Wyatt let the phone drop; it dangled on its end like a hanged man from a gibbet.

He had failed them all. Ellen. Claire. Sarah.

Daniel Wyatt walked the long yards to his car and started it again, and drove tiredly for home.

Sheriff Mark Hicks sat at his window and sipped his coffee.

It tasted wrong. Hicks suspected that Millie was sneaking decaf into the jar of instant they kept in the fridge. He'd been complaining about his stomach, and she was on him to stop drinking so much coffee.

It certainly wasn't caffeine that was keeping him up tonight. It was what he'd seen through the window an hour ago. An unfamiliar car had crept by the house at about eleven, finally slowing to a stop right in front of the kitchen window. It had paused there for almost five minutes, lights off and motor stilled, but the occupant had stayed inside.

Hicks could see that it was a man. The fellow wasn't looking for a certain house or checking out the neighborhood in any way. He sat and stared ahead, once or twice resting his head in his hands. He didn't look like trouble; Hicks was sure of that. Maybe he was just lost or tired or had had too much to drink.

But then the interior light had flashed on, clearly illuminating the man's face for a moment. It was Daniel Wyatt.

Then the car had driven off, in a hurry.

Hicks thought about his conversation with Millie a few days before. Was there something going on between Sarah Corbett and Dr. Wyatt? He'd got a good look at Wyatt in that fleeting moment, and the expression on the man's face stuck with him as he stared out into the dark night.

There in that Saab had been one terrified man. Hicks had seen such faces on the suicidal, on cornered criminals and fleeing perps. Something awful was pursuing Daniel Wyatt; he was a frightened, unlucky, driven man.

A man capable of desperate things.

13 | LET US REJOICE

"Costilla."

"Samuels, here," came Agent Tabitha Samuels's voice from the tiny speaker of his cell phone.

Costilla's hand paused at the ignition switch. He'd been about to turn off the rental car, but even a few minutes without air-conditioning could be brutal. It was, in fact, much warmer here in Lafayette, and his body wasn't adjusted yet to the change. He'd flown the red-eye from Toronto to New Orleans, then a prop plane to Baton Rouge.

"Any presents for me, Chaos?" Costilla asked, using her nickname in the team. While he was stuck down here, a sacrificial lamb offered up to Washington politics, at least his team was still at work on the Toronto slaying.

"We're about halfway through the mirrors," Samuels said. "What a bunch of yahoos. And I don't mean the search engine company."

Costilla frowned in confusion, but said nothing. Agent Samuels frequently made jokes he didn't understand. In the early days of the FBI, all agents were required to have a law degree, proof positive that they were the cream of law enforcement. In the era of Prohibition, agents were accepted with accounting degrees; after all, they'd bagged Al Capone on tax evasion rather than his more dramatic crimes. As forensic science advanced, medical degrees joined the list. And now in this cyber age, computer and mathematics degrees were all the rage.

Tabitha Samuels, all five feet two inches of her, had some

sort of doctorate from Yale that had the word "chaos" in the title; hence her nickname. She'd tried to explain it to Costilla once. It had to do with numbers.

"So what do your mirrors tell you, Chaos? Found anything that looks like our shooter?"

The "mirrors" were photos of antiabortion sites, down loaded every few minutes after the Blackmun slaying. They showed how the sites changed from moment to moment; what postings were added, which were removed.

"Not sure. One of my search algorithms came up with something that I thought you'd want to hear."

"Shoot."

"It's . . . kind of a poem." Agent Samuels cleared her throat.

> *"Let us rejoice.*
> *For another reaper*
> *Has left his coil.*
> *Fallen past all the little ones*
> *Lost, to boil.*
> *Therefore, let us rejoice."*

Something about the laughable quality of the poem gave Costilla a chill. The ineptitude of it, trumpeting a murder with a flood of doggerel.

"When was it posted?"

"Twelve forty-five that night. Seventeen minutes before anything about the murder hit the wires."

"Then that's our man. Trace it."

"It was routed through an anonymous remailer in Finland. I need your authority to start procedures."

"You've got it." It was a long shot, but sometimes an anonymous posting could be traced to its source. It required good luck and cooperation from every country the packet had been remailed through, which meant lots of time, but it could be done.

"Nothing about 'God, I must enter her'?" Costilla asked.

"Next to nothing. A very low-confidence hit on some stuff about God placing the soul in a fertilized ovum, like He's right there with the eyedropper waiting for the lucky sperm," Samuels said. "But that's not the same as 'God, I must enter her.' And it's from old posts on a cobwebsite. I'm designing a search for poetry with the shooter's phrasing."

"Keep working it, Chaos."

"You got it, Costilla. How's Louisiana?"

"Hot and sticky."

"Like my lovers."

"Hey. Don't ask, don't tell, Chaos," Costilla protested. *Maria,* these younger agents were disrespectful. "And don't waste my batteries. I gotta go see a gynecologist."

"Don't ask, don't tell, yourself—Agent Costilla."

"Twelve years, Daniel."

"I've been married fourteen years, actually," Wyatt responded sadly.

"No, I mean *us*," Claire exclaimed. "For twelve years we've worked to create this organization. We practically built it with our bare hands, and you've put everything in jeopardy."

"She'll be there," he repeated.

"I certainly hope so."

"She wants to terminate. I know she does," Wyatt said. In his years of counseling and practicing medicine, he'd seen women who desperately wanted children. He had seen those who weren't sure, and those who were utterly distraught by the thought of life growing within them. It was easy for Wyatt to see where Sarah fell on that continuum. She might want children with a husband one day, but the idea of being a single parent shocked her. As she saw it, having a child was a way of cementing a relationship; outside of marriage it would be a badge of shame.

"After it's done, I don't want you talking to her again."

"That's cruel, Claire."

"Someone will notice, eventually. And at this point, even rumors could sink the nomination."

"Claire, she's a sensitive woman. She needs support right now, and that could drive her over the edge," Wyatt explained. "If I ignore her, eventually she'll find someone else's shoulder to cry on."

Claire turned to him with icy certainty in her voice. "Daniel, let me explain something to you. From what you've told me, there's only one reason why Sarah hasn't started talking yet. She thinks she's in love with you. That's why she's cooperating. She wants you, and she's trying to find a way to be with you again."

Wyatt looked at Claire in stunned silence. Even as she said the words, their truth began to dawn on him, appalling though that was. How was he such a fool that he hadn't seen it?

"If she can get you into a compromising situation, she will," Claire continued. "If she can bring down your marriage, she will."

Daniel Wyatt felt his world collapsing. His family, his nomination, his role as a healer—all of it could be destroyed.

"Then we're sunk," he said, defeated.

"No, we're not. The committee hearings will start Wednesday, the day after tomorrow. They could be over as soon as Friday, and the committee will probably vote on Monday. You could be confirmed by the full Senate late next week. As long as it's after the vote, whatever she says will be old news."

"But, Claire!" Wyatt cried. "What about my marriage?"

"Why should your wife believe her if she decides to go public about this? Why should anyone believe her? Once she isn't carrying your child, she has no proof that you so much as touched her. She's just another celebrity stalker, selling her story to the tabloids for twenty-five grand."

"So you think I should just ignore her, and deny the truth if she starts talking?" he cried in disbelief.

"What's the alternative, Daniel?" Claire leaned across her desk, taking his hands in hers. "Stay her friend, her trusted mentor? Listen to yourself. Do you think that you and Sarah Corbett are going to be confidants, bound together forever by your special secret? Is that what you really want? To stay *that* close to fucking her again?"

Wyatt tried to pull away, but Claire's grip on his hands was iron.

"Well, it doesn't *work that way*," she continued. "As long as you stay involved with her in any way, she'll just want you more. *You* will just want *her* more. And you will slip again, Daniel."

Finally, Claire released him. Wyatt staggered to his feet, needing terribly to escape the room. Claire turned back to look out the window, sadness in her voice.

"Daniel, I'm not saying that this is pretty, or fair. I'm saying it's what you have to do. You're going to do it for your marriage. For your career. For me. Once she has aborted that child, you must make yourself forget her name."

"*Claire.*" Wyatt stopped to clear his throat. The sound of his own voice was painful. Wyatt felt as if Claire's words had dragged something out of him, pulled some sensitive and private portion of his being out into the light and crushed it. But she was right. There was some part of him still holding on to the image of Sarah and Dr. Wyatt reflected in the elevator doors. Some part hoped that the kisses, like the one stolen in that ridiculous restaurant, would go on. It took a long minute for him to speak again.

"Some people will believe her, won't they?" he finally asked.

"Not necessarily. In fact, I'm not sure I believe her."

"What do you mean?" Wyatt said.

"That it's your kid? How the hell do you know? Because she *told* you? We don't even know that she's really pregnant, Daniel."

Wyatt shook his head. He'd never considered that Sarah might be lying. But, of course, how well did he know her? Their relationship consisted of only a few dozen hours together.

"I've hired a private detective," Claire continued. "By the time we find out more about her, you may not believe her yourself."

Wyatt mutely nodded.

"Just don't talk to her once it's done, Daniel. And when you're with her this afternoon, be careful. Just play a game in your mind. Assume that she is recording everything you say. Pretend you're just a doctor there to support a nervous patient. That's all. Period."

Wyatt walked from Claire's office unsteadily. He felt numb, as if he were no longer a participant in this drama. His job was to do as he was told, his answers before the committee scripted, the dimensions of his heart beaten and reshaped like so much tin. He crossed the unbearably hot parking lot in a daze, not realizing he had left his jacket in Claire's office.

As Daniel Wyatt drove for the medical building on the outskirts of town where Sarah Corbett would meet him, his pager chirped in Claire's empty office. Three times he was paged, frantic messages from the office of Dr. Ernest Magley.

The medical building was situated just outside Lafayette Parish. Agent Costilla wondered briefly if there were some zoning law or political reason for its location. Maybe it was just a tax thing.

He found the office of Dr. Ernest Magley in the directory of offices and made his way through hallways that smelled vaguely of hospital. There was an outpatient clinic here, and a host of offices for doctors, therapists, and dentists. A medical mall.

Magley's receptionist asked him to wait a few minutes, and he sat down before a low table scattered with the usual magazines. There were three women in the waiting room. Costilla felt each of them glance at him with slight curiosity. Between his gender and the heavy fabric of his dark winter suit, he felt distinctly out of place. It hadn't helped that the receptionist pronounced his name as if it rhymed with "vanilla."

"Mr. Costilla," the receptionist announced. "Dr. Magley will see you now."

The doctor waited in his consulting room, portly and regal behind a simple metal desk. Agent Costilla noted sourly that the room's shelves were crowded with more insurance and HMO manuals than medical texts.

"Thank you for seeing me on such short notice, Dr. Magley."

"Anything for Daniel," Magley said, smiling broadly. "That is, I assume you're here about Dr. Wyatt's nomination. Right?"

"Yes, Doctor."

"Good. I couldn't think of anything I'd been up to that would interest the FBI!" The doctor laughed and pounded one meaty palm on the desk.

Costilla managed to smile, but wondered for a moment if the man was up to something. His forced jocularity bordered on the bizarre. Perhaps it was merely the combination of unfamiliar southern hospitality and too little sleep.

"I suppose that FBI agents aren't a common sight down here," Costilla said.

"Maybe in New Orleans. Not here in Lafayette, though."

"Well, this is just a routine background check," Costilla said, pulling out his notebook and pen. "If you could just tell me in your own words how you came to know Dr. Wyatt."

"That would be Harvard Medical School. We were roommates, you know?"

"Oh, I hadn't known that, Dr. Magley," Costilla said, although he had. He made a meaningless scribble on his pad as if recording the fact. "How would you describe Dr. Wyatt's career at medical school?"

The interview droned on for almost an hour. If the whole background check went this way, Assistant Director Richards was not going to be happy. Dr. Wyatt was an Eagle Scout. No drugs, no real drinking, not even any pot. Magley seemed to enjoy boasting of his own exploits, but none of them seemed to include young Daniel Wyatt. And Ernest Magley didn't seem like the type who could hide dark secrets, either. He was too busy exaggerating the life story of one Dr. Ernest Magley to be circumspect about the skeletons in anyone else's closet.

It wasn't until the end of the interview that Costilla caught a whiff of something. Magley began glancing at his watch as noon approached. With the subtlest movements of wrist and eyes, he was keeping track of the time. Something was definitely bothering him. His volubility took on a desperate edge. Although Costilla had gotten everything he needed, he deliberately extended the interview, just to see what would happen.

Finally, Costilla guessed that the doctor must simply have patients to see. He was just too polite to ask the FBI agent to leave.

"I'm sorry for taking so much of your time, Dr. Magley," the agent apologized.

"Well, I sure hope I helped you out."

As Dr. Magley rose from the desk to offer his hand, Costilla spotted rings of sweat under his arms. Yet the office was brutally air-conditioned. Clearly, Magley was nervous about something.

Costilla left the office a little puzzled. He paused at the directory of offices, wondering how to follow up his hunch.

Then, in a reflection on the glass that covered the directory's neat columns of stick-on letters, he saw an older man walk past. Costilla turned to watch him recede down the hallway. The man was headed toward Dr. Magley's office.

Costilla followed, peering around the cover of a Coke machine as the man entered Magley's office. When he entered, Costilla walked quickly after him down the hall. He couldn't be the one. It must simply be sleeplessness or the heat. But Costilla had to be sure.

He peeked through the foot-wide glass panel set in Magley's door.

And there he was. Talking to the receptionist, easily recognizable from his photo in the file that had been FedExed to Costilla in Toronto.

Dr. Daniel Wyatt, surgeon general nominee.

Costilla was waiting in his rented car on the medical building parking lot. The car was like an oven. The heat inside climbed along with the blazing sun. Costilla strained to keep awake.

After perhaps twenty minutes, Wyatt appeared outside the medical building. Costilla hunched down against the scalding vinyl of the car's front seat.

Wyatt seemed to be looking for something. He shaded his eyes from the sun and stared out across the parking lot. He stayed outside, intermittently checking his watch, gazing out over the highway. Finally, Wyatt disappeared back into the building. He was gone for the right amount of time to urinate or to make an unanswered phone call. Then he returned to take up his lonely vigil.

Costilla thought of accosting the man, questioning him right then and there. Sometimes the value of surprise was worth the tipping of your hand. But he decided against it. He wanted to see who would arrive, if anyone, and he could always mention this little appointment to Dr. Wyatt later.

After an hour and a half in the sweltering heat, Wyatt got into his car and left.

Whoever he'd been waiting for simply hadn't come.

15 | AGENT

Claire Davis had given up smoking when she was thirty-eight years old.

That was a dividing line for most large scientific studies, between the still-young thirty to thirty-seven grouping and the one Claire now occupied, which stretched from thirty-eight to forty-five. This was the age range when the data were unmistakable, and unavoidable if you were the head of a women's health advocacy group. The charts and graphs on WAG's posters all showed the spike. Here was the time of life when smoking started to kill you.

So, five years ago, Claire had stopped.

She'd tried the patch, but that made her crazy. Her already sharp temper became explosive, as if the flesh-colored square on her arm were dripping vitriol instead of nicotine. The gum was foul, like something rescued from an ashtray. And acupuncture, which many of her friends swore by, somehow didn't work on her. Whatever subtle balance of mind-body-spirit those tiny needles were meant to adjust required some more formidable manipulation in Claire Davis.

Hammers maybe. Jackhammers.

So after the false starts and the failures of all those crutches, Claire had quit the old-fashioned way. Halfway through a filterless Camel, she'd tossed it still burning out the car window, followed by the carton she kept in her glove compartment. And without any announcement or chemical assistance or twelve-step plan, she had never touched another cigarette.

It had been painful. But it was the best kind of pain. Facing the sleepless nights and horrible head spins of craving alone and without sympathy, she had succeeded. She had beaten the thing inside her. And now Claire Davis didn't smoke. So completely had she accomplished her goal that her friends and coworkers had forgotten that she'd once stood puffing away just outside the propped-open WAG office fire door every morning at eleven and at two and four o'clock in the afternoon.

So why was she here now? Why was she suffering the growling wind of a twelve-thousand-BTU air conditioner's rear end, here in this smoker's purgatory? At the age of forty-three, why was she staring at the ground, fingering a pack of matches, hoping to discover a merely half-consumed cigarette lodged in the butt-littered white gravel?

Because Wyatt had just called: Sarah Corbett hadn't shown.

"That bitch," Claire muttered to herself.

Daniel had arrived at Magley's offices ten minutes early, ready to greet Sarah, to guide her safely to the end of this nightmare. But no Sarah Corbett had appeared, and to better rattle Wyatt's nerves, he'd barely missed running into an FBI agent doing a background check. The narrow escape from that coincidental meeting had left Daniel even more paranoid.

Claire shook her head. Why had Magley even told him about the FBI agent? Idiot. They'd been med-school roommates and lifelong friends, so a visit from the feds was purely routine. Why terrify Daniel any more than he already was? Claire was annoyed that Magley was a part of this at all. She still couldn't believe that Wyatt had turned to his old roommate during this crisis and not to her.

If she'd only known, Claire was certain she would have had this problem sorted out by now, somehow. She still hoped to fix the situation.

But that wasn't going to happen until she had a cigarette.

"Smoke?"

The tanned brown hand held a pack of Camels, and that

was all Claire could see at first. She pulled one—filtered, un-fortunately—from the box and struggled with her matches uselessly. Her nervous fingers had worried them ragged.

"Light?"

Claire nodded gratefully and cupped her hands to shield the offered lighter from the angry sirocco of the air condi-tioner's exhaust. That first puff was harsh, and she willed away the urge to cough, but soon the ancient, familiar, and gloriously forbidden taste of nicotine began to fill her.

"Thank you," she said, and blinked as she finally looked at her benefactor.

He was just above her height, compact and powerful in-side his heavy, dark suit. His features had that precise beauty that only small men possess, with a touch of Latin elegance. From some air of confidence about him, she put his age at thirty-five, though he looked younger. His dark hands shielded the lighter as he lit up his own cigarette, his move-ments graceful and controlled.

"Thank you very much," she added.

"You're welcome, Ms. Davis."

"You have me at a disadvantage," Claire said, hearing her voice slip just slightly into its southern mode.

"Agent Eduardo Costilla," the man said. Claire's eyebrows raised. The FBI man. Ernest Magley's description hadn't done him justice. His voice was beautiful, too. When he said his own name, the until-then neutral colors of his accent briefly flared with Hispanic flourish. "Your receptionist told me I'd find you out here."

"And I thought my secret was safe," Claire lamented, re-garding the cigarette between her slim fingers. She wondered who had spotted her on her way out. The whole building must be buzzing with the scandal of it by now.

"They never are," Agent Costilla said.

Claire smiled. "But we like to think we can keep them. You know?"

Costilla nodded.

"I guess you're here about Daniel?" she asked.

"If I could have half an hour or so, I'd like to ask a few questions. You've worked with Dr. Wyatt for . . . ?"

"Twelve years," Claire said, and was instantly horrified to hear the anger in her own voice. She laughed to cover it. "I guess my age is starting to surprise me."

"Age is a gift," Costilla said simply.

"Something your mother says?" Claire asked archly.

Agent Costilla laughed. "My grandmother, actually. At seventy-six."

"Well, I prefer youth," Claire said, stubbing out her cigarette.

Costilla shrugged his shoulders, dropped his own cigarette into the butt-littered gravel. "It's good you know what your preferences are."

"I think lunch is my preference, at this exact moment. Have you eaten?"

They went to a place on Main, where Claire told Agent Costilla about her work with Daniel Wyatt.

Leaving the office behind, she felt the tensions of this awful week begin to recede. It was a pleasure to talk to a stranger about the history of WAG, recounting the struggles of the early days and the excitement of their successes in recent years. Of course, in front of the FBI agent, she had to edit out the dire situation with Sarah Corbett, but excising the events of the last few days was like therapy for Claire. It helped her to remember the reasons she loved her work, and why she was so intent on saving Daniel's career, despite his best efforts to destroy himself.

Eduardo Costilla was a good listener, silent and attentive. His large brown eyes gazed at her with an intensity that many women might have found intimidating, but to Claire was refreshing. As a lawyer, a community leader, and a political force, she knew most men in Lafayette considered her a threat to male privilege. Her power and forcefulness might turn some of them on, but it was the attraction of a sport, a freak, an adolescent fantasy of the dominant woman.

But Eduardo Costilla seemed supremely confident, not the sort of man to be intimidated. His voice was soft and low, projecting a quiet authority. And the subjects of women's rights and women's health didn't make him uncomfortable. In fact, he seemed to be very knowledgeable about the history of the antiabortion movement. His questions about clinic access and harassment, particularly about WAG's security system, revealed an understanding of the daily fear that Claire and her workers faced.

"I noticed that Dr. Ernest Magley's office wasn't very secure," he said in passing.

"When you interviewed him, you probably also noticed that he's mixed in with many other doctors," Claire answered. "The building isn't stigmatized." She shrugged ruefully. "Family planning clinics were a bad idea, I guess. They isolate doctors who perform abortions, and that supplies the pro-life movement with easy targets. Magley's safe because he's integrated; no one thinks of him as an *abortionist*."

Costilla nodded, his eyes narrowing as if registering something new and interesting. Claire was surprised that he'd never heard that lament before. Then she saw the suggestion of a smile on his lips. She wondered what he was thinking.

Damn, she thought, realizing her mistake. Costilla hadn't mentioned the visit to Magley's office before his passing remark. Claire shouldn't have known that Costilla had been there earlier today.

"You've met Ernest Magley?" she added quickly. Costilla's smile broadened. Too late, Claire mentally chastised herself. The last thing she wanted Costilla to know was that Wyatt's friends were calling each other about his interviews. It looked too conspiratorial, as if there were something to hide.

"Oh, yes," Costilla answered. "It was a very interesting visit."

"I doubt that," she said. "Magley's a pompous ass, as far as I'm concerned."

"It wasn't so much Dr. Magley who was interesting," Agent Costilla said. But he left the cryptic remark unexplained.

Claire began to admire the subtlety of the man. Should she ask what he'd meant? Would it reveal too much to innocently inquire? Or was it wiser to feign disinterest?

"What was so fascinating, then?" she asked lightly, taking a chance.

"Just watching the building, after the interview. Seeing who came in and out."

Claire struggled not to gasp. Costilla had seen Wyatt! she realized. Their paths must have crossed outside the clinic. What a disaster.

She nodded and attempted a smile. "Well, I'm glad you're taking time to appreciate the local population." Despite her calm demeanor, Claire's mind reeled as she wondered what Costilla must be thinking.

Perhaps it wasn't so bad. Wyatt was Magley's friend. Showing up at Magley's office didn't necessarily mean anything. Actually, it could have been worse, Claire realized, suddenly thankful that Sarah Corbett had skipped the appointment.

"I have no complaints about the locals," he said, smiling.

Claire ordered herself to relax. Whatever his suspicions, Costilla didn't have anything to go on. As she had reminded Wyatt, the committee would probably be voting on Monday. He could be confirmed by the end of next week. This FBI agent might be clever, but there wasn't time for him to make trouble.

But it wouldn't hurt to distract him, just a bit.

"Agent Costilla," she said. "I'm sure the locals have no complaints about you, either. How does dinner sound?"

His long lashes blinked just once, and then he answered, "That sounds very hospitable."

On the way back to the office, all four windows rolled down to air the smoke from the cigarette burning in her hand, Claire had an idea. It grew as she drove, refining itself as her deft mind probed the possible complications.

She pulled into the WAG parking lot at top speed, almost certain that she had hit upon an answer. Claire looked at the remainder of cigarette in her hand. Nicotine again, after five long years. She knew now that quitting again would be just as hard as the first time. But at least her transgression had given her a spark of inspiration. Or perhaps it was the very stimulating Eduardo Costilla. She shrugged and threw the butt out the window.

When she reached her office, she slammed the door and brought her computer on-line. After a few moments, she found the site she needed, and read with growing confidence for the next half hour. Then she turned to the phone, forming the conversation in her mind before she picked up the receiver.

"Hello?" a woman's voice answered.

"Hello. Are you alone?"

"Is that you, Claire?"

"Yes it is. Do you have a moment? We have a problem here, and I think you could help."

Wyatt watched his three children get ready with equal measures of affection and despair.

The oldest, Kenny, was dressed as some sort of Indian. Although the pageant tonight was a Thanksgiving festival, he had insisted on wearing what he called "war paint"; his cheeks were striped with three shades of Ellen's lipstick. The middle child, Clarise, was a Pilgrim girl, as precious as diamonds in her black dress and white lace bonnet. Dexter, the youngest, was not part of the pageant, but had been swept up in the preparations. In his insistent way, he had managed to convince Ellen that he needed war paint, too. It was smudged already, making Dexter look like the victim of too many affectionate aunts.

Daniel Wyatt watched his three children swoop into and out of the living room, each for a moment ready to go, then wandering off before the others could be assembled, while Wyatt himself jangled his car keys in a fruitless sign of impatience. Ellen, who had dressed the kids, was shouting from upstairs that she was almost ready. There was a warmth and familiarity to the frenetic scene that filled Wyatt with abject sadness. He felt like a ghost, observing them all through some scrim of irrevocable loss, powerless to participate.

He'd tried to reach Sarah. Was she all right? Why hadn't she come to Magley's office? But there'd been no answer. Magley was terrified after his interview with the FBI agent, and kept muttering things about perjury and conspiracy. Even if Sarah changed her mind again, Wyatt doubted that Ernest would agree to perform the abortion. The man was convinced that some sort of Ken Starr would soon be setting up shop in Lafayette, subpoenaing Wyatt's friends and acquaintances with abandon. And Claire hadn't been at her office all afternoon either, his one confidante with a clear head about all this mysteriously gone.

So Wyatt stood there, desperate and alone, as he watched his family members attempt to organize themselves. He had so much to lose. If only he could reach back in time and erase that one weekend. Claire was right, of course; part of him still wanted Sarah—or at least that jolt of vicarious youth their short affair had made him feel. But standing here amid these preparations, it was easy to see what that desire amounted to: the empty vanity of an aging, insecure man.

The nomination didn't matter. The work didn't matter. If only he could salvage these moments with his family.

Ellen appeared and started down the stairs. She looked beautiful, radiantly flush with the exertions of the last hour. Daniel smiled a little sheepishly, putting the car keys back into his pocket. The living room was empty of Wyatt children, and his one, simple task remained unaccomplished.

But, as if their mother were a magnet, the three kids were drawn to the front door, appearing from various directions over the next thirty seconds.

"Everybody ready?" Ellen asked.

Wyatt opened the door and held it while the company trooped out.

The phone rang.

"Let the machine get it," Ellen ordered. Wyatt slammed the door on the noise and followed them to the minivan. The sound of the ringing phone reverberated in his mind, though. Was it Sarah, calling to say she had reconsidered? Claire, with some solution to this mess? The FBI?

Wyatt stopped in his tracks.

"Wait," he said. "My wallet!"

Ignoring Ellen's expression, he turned on one heel and headed back toward the house. As he fumbled with his key in the front door, he heard one last arrested ring from the phone, the beginning of the outgoing message.

Finally, the door relented, and he was inside. He ran toward the kitchen as Sarah's voice began booming through the house.

"Daniel, I know I'm not supposed to call you there. But it doesn't matter anymore."

Wyatt faced the phone machine without a clue how to make it stop. Why was it so *loud*? It was ensconced in an incomprehensible matrix of phone and power cords.

"I can't go on pretending like this. I just want to have your—"

Wyatt pulled the machine's plug from the outlet. The noise stopped immediately, leaving only the sound of his tortured gasping.

Ellen's voice came from the front door.

"Daniel? We have to go *now*!"

"Can't find my wallet!"

"Then leave it," Ellen said. She was in the kitchen now, staring at him with disbelief. "The kids have to be there half an hour early, or they won't be allowed to participate."

"Just go, then," he said. "I'll take the Saab. Really, I just need a few minutes."

"Who called?" she asked.

"Just the office. It was nothing."

Ellen looked at Daniel across the kitchen. For a moment her eyes seemed bright and sharp, as if she were about to cry. Then she smiled, calm returning to her face.

"Okay, then. See you there."

Half an hour.

Wyatt stared at the answering machine. How to erase the message? When he plugged the machine back in, the message light was not blinking. But Wyatt vaguely understood that the message was still there on the tape until someone called and taped over it. Was there an erase button? He couldn't see one. Perhaps he should go to a pay phone and leave a long message, erasing the entire tape. But what message? Heavy breathing?

He pulled the tape out and dropped it to the floor, crushing it under one heel. He put the crumpled remains into one pocket.

He raced the Saab down side streets, avoiding the route Ellen and the kids would be taking. At a strip mall near the school, he pulled into the parking lot beside a Radio Shack.

"I need a tape for an answering machine."

"What kind?"

"Kind?" There were different kinds? "Just a tape."

The kid in the Radio Shack sighed and pointed down at a glass case. Next to watches, cell phones, and a neat row of miniature flashlights was a shelf of tapes. They were branded: Sony, Panasonic, Maxell. They ranged from normal audio-tape size to one no bigger than a book of matches.

Wyatt sighed, pulled the crushed tape from his pocket, and dropped it onto the glass.

"One like this."

The kid gave the broken tape a poke with one finger, as if it were a dead frog he'd discovered on the highway, then lifted the cracked plastic to inspect it. He reached down into the case and produced a duplicate.

Wyatt dropped ten dollars on the case and said, "Is this enough?" And fled.

Fifteen minutes.

Not enough time to go back home and still make it to the school. He couldn't be late. But after it was over, he would be leaving in the Saab. It would be easy to get home before Ellen and the kids. Wyatt just hoped he could replace the tape and record another outgoing message in time.

Wyatt reached the school with five minutes to spare. Other parents and children were still arriving, and he joined the crowds milling around the auditorium entrance. He had just enough cash to pay the three dollars for a ticket. Inside the buzzing auditorium, he spotted his wife and war-painted Dexter, an empty seat beside them. His space.

Ellen smiled at him a bit primly as he came down the row. He felt like a tardy schoolchild, but Ellen held his hand as the lights went down. In the darkness, Wyatt's fingers crept into his pocket to feel the newly purchased tape. He hoped the kid at Radio Shack had been right.

The pageant was slow torture. After the mad dash of the last half hour, being trapped in that seat was unbearable. Now that the emergency was over, the full realization of what had occurred began to eat at him. Sarah's words played over and over in Wyatt's mind.

It doesn't matter anymore.

Wyatt closed his eyes. If only he had made it to her house last night. That's all she had wanted. Some company at a sad, lonely time. Sarah didn't have what Daniel Wyatt had. What Ellen Wyatt had.

I can't go on like this.

There weren't going to be any more pages, any more secret messages, Wyatt realized. Now Sarah was striking directly at him, phoning his home. Leaving messages for his wife, his children, to hear. Next time he wouldn't be there to intercept her words. How could he stop her? Wyatt was hers to destroy.

I'm going to have your . . .

Sarah's last words buzzed inside his head, losing meaning like some mantra repeated for hours on end. She was really going to go through with it, bringing a life into this world just for . . . For what? Out of spite? Jealousy? Because she wanted something she couldn't have?

Whatever her reasons, Sarah had made her choice.

It was over.

As the pageant went on, a quiet feeling slowly began to replace Wyatt's panic. Relief, in the form of a feeling of solemn defeat, overtook the pounding of his heart. The starving Pilgrims were befriended and taught how to eat gourds and plant their corn with rotten fish as fertilizer, and Wyatt felt the hope within him start to die. The chances that this would all work out, or that some bond, some secret alliance, would last between him and Sarah, quietly expired. A delegation of Indians, Kenny alone among them daubed with war paint, presented the Pilgrims with paper turkeys, plastic pumpkins, and drawings of corn.

Wyatt sighed as it finally ended. The Pilgrims and the Indians were allies now. He had lost everything.

Ellen kept Dexter while Daniel went to retrieve Kenny and Clarise backstage. Excited children, still in costume and some still in character, milled around his legs. He found Clarise and lauded her efforts, then found Kenny and told him he was great. He swallowed as he praised his children, wondering if such a simple parental duty would feel like this, guilty and saddening, from now on.

"Where's Mom?" they asked.

"Out in the parking lot with Dexter."

The three of them wound their way through the crowd of actors and spectators, Daniel with one hand softly resting on his daughter's bonneted head. When they spotted Ellen talking with another parent, Kenny raced forward.

Wyatt stopped suddenly, the panic rising in him again.

The person with Ellen wasn't another parent. Not yet, anyway.

Ellen was talking to Sarah Corbett.

Not here, he thought.

Ellen hated any hint of gossip, any trace of scandal. And here was Sarah Corbett, in front of friends, other parents, their children. For a moment, Wyatt felt nothing but a stab of hatred for her. What had he done to deserve this?

But then his hopelessness returned, a blissful numbness as he walked toward the two women.

Ellen gathered up Kenny and kissed him, adjusting his headdress and showering him with praise. Then Clarise arrived and demanded her share of attention. Ellen lifted her up and rubbed noses with her, laughing.

Ellen didn't know. Not yet.

Sarah smiled shyly at Daniel, one finger at her lips for a split second.

How cruel, Wyatt thought in those moments as Ellen and the two older kids discussed the play while he, Sarah, and Dexter patiently waited.

Sarah was giving him hope again.

"Did you know Sarah's nephew goes to school here?" Ellen said.

"No, I didn't," Wyatt answered. He turned to Sarah, the only child of her dead parents. "But how did you know Ellen?"

"Oh, I saw her sitting with you. I just wanted to say hi, and give my congratulations again."

"Sarah's offered to watch the kids while we're in Washington this week," Ellen said, hoisting Dexter into the air.

"They're staying with their grandparents," Daniel answered.

"But it's kind of her to *offer*," Ellen corrected him.

"Oh, I need the practice," Sarah said, one hand on her belly. "I'm expecting," she explained to Ellen.

"How kind of you. I'm sure our three little ones would be great practice, but I would never want to impose."

"No imposition at all. It would be my pleasure. Anytime."

"Well, I'll have to get your number from Daniel."

Ellen winked at Wyatt, proud of herself for not betraying her husband's confidences. She must have remembered Sarah's name from the car ride the other night.

The wind blew colder as they talked, and a few drops of rain began to fall. Kenny began a rain dance.

"Your dance is a bit late," Ellen scolded, one palm out to catch the rain.

"Oh, and I walked here," Sarah lamented. "I live just up the road," she added to Ellen.

"Well, fortunately we're here in two cars," Ellen said. "Daniel would be happy to give you a ride home."

"No. It's not far. I'll just get going before it gets too bad."

Wyatt thought of the tape in his pocket, the empty answering machine at home. He considered the fact that Sarah lived miles from here. It would take him ages to get her home. But he was long past being a participant in this affair. He felt Ellen's sharp eyes upon him, compelling him to be the gentleman.

"I insist," he said.

The rain grew heavy even as they waited in the line of cars departing the parking lot. In this weather, any chance of beating Ellen home with daredevil driving was gone. Wyatt leaned back and watched the windshield wipers streak the red taillights of the car in front of him.

"Are you mad at me?" Sarah ventured timidly beside him.

"*Mad* at you?" Wyatt said. He shook his head. Sarah was worried that he was angry. "I'm way past anything like that. I'm . . . just sad."

"Oh, Dr. Wyatt," she said softly. "Then we're both sad."

Wyatt found himself nodding, listening to the whoosh of the windshield wipers. He wondered if there were words to stop the inevitable. Words that could make her understand what she was doing.

"Do you know what almost happened tonight?" he said, keeping his voice even.

"I suppose so. I'm so sorry, Daniel. I shouldn't have called your house."

"What if Ellen had heard you? Or my kids?"

"I just couldn't stand to page you, Daniel. I couldn't stand to wait by the phone, hoping you'd call me. It was just too gothic."

"What?"

"What if I'd paged you, and you didn't call back? I couldn't stand it."

Wyatt clenched the wheel, peering through the thick blanket of rain.

"I would have called," he said finally.

"But you didn't," Sarah countered.

Wyatt nodded. "I know. I'm sorry."

They drove silently for a while. The muffled rushing noise of the Saab's tires was somehow soothing, like waves on a distant seashore barely heard. The warm cocoon of the car helped Wyatt relax. The solemn calm of his hopelessness returned. He hated lying, all this had at least taught him that. And Sarah was someone he didn't have to lie to anymore.

They pulled up beside Sarah's house.

"I did come here last night," Wyatt said.

"I know."

"I wanted to see you. But when I got here, I couldn't get out of the car." He turned to her. "Tonight, you saw what I have. That's my life, that woman and those three kids."

"And what about *my* life?" Sarah cried. "Do you ever think about that, Daniel? I refuse to accept that your life is more important than mine. And I have a child now, too."

Wyatt was silenced by her outburst. But he lifted one hand from the wheel and gently took her wrist. She looked at his hand on her arm, and a sob burst from her.

"You don't need a child to make your life important," he said softly.

"But you didn't come," she answered.

There it was, the flat truth. He had betrayed Sarah, as he had betrayed Ellen, as he had betrayed Claire. The new, hopeless Daniel Wyatt simply nodded his head.

"I know. And you needed me last night. I was wrong."

"Oh, Daniel," Sarah sobbed. "I'm sorry."

They sat for a while longer in silence.

"I don't know," Sarah said finally.

Wyatt felt something stir at the edges of his awareness. Not again, he thought.

"I mean," she continued. "I don't know what to do about it."

He shook his head. What was she saying now?

"I want this child, but not without a father."

There it was, growing in him once more, ready to torture him all over again. Wyatt couldn't stand to hear any more.

"I should head home," he said.

"But I need to see you again."

He nodded. "Certainly. When I get back from Washington on Friday I'll call you."

"And this time, you'll come when you say you will?"

"I promise. This time I'll come."

"Okay, then."

He smiled at Sarah, looked past her at the slackening rain. "Do you need an umbrella?"

"Not yet, silly," she answered. "You've still got to drive me back to that school."

"But . . ."

"You don't really think I walked all that way, do you?" Sarah laughed and squeezed his hand. "Come on. Let's go get my car."

They drove back to the school in silence. Sarah seemed happy, as if everything she wanted had been somehow obtained with this meeting. And Wyatt was too cautious to speak, certain that one wrong word could shatter the spell of her contentment. The dreaded feeling was stronger now, slowly taking fragile form in his chest, already displacing that calm and quiet sea of loss, of desperation that had almost captured him tonight.

Hope. Daniel Wyatt felt a ray of hope.

Mark Hicks recognized the car this time. Even in the heavy rain, the brown Saab was definitely the same one that had cruised by the other night. Dr. Daniel Wyatt's car.

Millie hadn't left for work yet. She was in the kitchen, making coffee.

"Make sure that's got caffeine in it, Millie," Hicks ordered.

"Do you want to stay up all night, Daddy?" she yelled back.

"Maybe," he muttered.

"Well, maybe you do," she said, entering the room with two steaming mugs in hand. "But some of us have to live with your grumpy old self in the morning."

Hicks snorted good-naturedly and took the coffee from her. He tasted it carefully. Now, that was real coffee. She must have made the good stuff for her night on call at the hospital.

"You'd be surprised at what I get up to here late at night."

"Oh, I'm sure," Millie said.

"Why, just looking out this window, I see quite a lot."

"Such as?" Millie asked.

"Well, last night I saw Dr. Wyatt drive past Sarah's house. He pulled up right here and waited for five whole minutes."

Millie scowled. "Lying is sinful, Daddy."

"I ain't lying."

Millie peered closely at her father. "Waiting for what?" she said cautiously, still not sure if he was pulling her leg.

"I don't know. After five minutes he just up and drove away. Are you sure that Sarah never said anything about the two of them?"

"Cross my heart, Daddy. Are *you* sure it was Dr. Wyatt?"

"Yep. Just as sure as I am that his car's sitting out there now."

"Go on!" Millie shouted, but she deposited her coffee mug on an end table by the couch and sprang to the window. "Mark Hicks, now I know you're lying! How can you see anything in this rain?"

"This old dog still hunts, Millie," he answered. "I know that's the car. Now, I'm not saying that Daniel Wyatt is in it. Might be Ellen Wyatt sitting there, after all."

Millie still peered out the window, straining to see. "Well, if you're not lying, I can't *wait* to tell this bit of news down at the hospital," she announced.

"Be careful who you talk to about it," Sheriff Hicks cautioned. "When I saw Dr. Wyatt out there the other night, he looked pretty riled up. But maybe you could find out if anybody knows anything. Just be careful as to how you ask."

Millie frowned. "Hey, Daddy?"

"Yeah?"

"Rain's clearing up a little. And it does look like Dr. Wyatt in there."

"Hell, Millie, your eyes are sure better than mine."

"But he ain't alone, Daddy," she added.

Millie pulled herself away from the window. "Goodness. Now that I can see something, I almost feel like I'm *spying*."

Her father felt no such compunction. He leaned closer to the window. "Ain't peeping if you're looking out of your own house," he explained. "Who's in there with him?"

Millie didn't look out the window again. She put one hand to her cheek and shook her head slowly.

"Well, Daddy, I'd say that was Sarah Corbett."

17 | VASSAR GIRL

Agent Costilla's sleep was penetrated by the sound of his cell phone. It woke him more quickly than any alarm clock, and he was fully alert in an instant. In the darkness, his fingers probed the nightstand for the device, the shapes of an unfamiliar room coming into focus around him.

"Costilla."

"Richards." His boss's voice emerged from the tiny speaker harshly.

Costilla rubbed his eyes, then looked at his phone's display. Almost nine. He had overslept.

"How's Louisiana?" she asked.

"Hot. Friendly people."

"Wonderful. Find anything on the good doctor yet?"

"Not yet. But I'm working on a few angles."

He heard a snort on Richards's end. "Well, I hope so, Costilla. May I remind you that it's Tuesday. The hearings start on Wednesday. By then I need something to feed my senator."

"I think I may have something. I don't know what it is exactly yet, but it's something." Costilla ground his teeth, tasting the inside of his mouth. He hoped he was right, that he was onto something. Today he was headed to the hospital where Dr. Wyatt worked. Hospitals were obligingly full of professional jealousies, bored workers, and juicy rumors. Maybe someone there would know why Wyatt had been at Ernest Magley's office yesterday, and whom he had meant to meet there.

"Just see that you do," Richards commanded. "By the way, have you met Wyatt's partner yet?"

"Partner?"

"A lawyer named Claire Davis."

"Ah, yes," Costilla said, lowering his voice a bit. "Yesterday. She was very helpful."

"Well, my senator has been talking to some of his pals in the good-old-boy network. It seems there are rumors about Miss Davis."

"Rumors?"

"It seems that everyone from Lafayette to Baton Rouge knows she's a lesbian."

"I see," Costilla said.

"Obviously, that's nothing to hang Wyatt with. But if my senator could get a little confirmation, maybe he can talk about stuff 'coming in over the transom.' Maybe rile Wyatt a little. Maybe just amuse the boys back home. You got me?"

Costilla sighed. "Got you."

"Good memory. It's no big deal. Just the way the game is played. So check it out, will you?"

"I'll get right on it, boss."

Richards hung up. Costilla shook his head and leaned back into the warmth of the bed. He was an early riser, but this morning he didn't feel quite like moving yet. His gaze moved slowly around the room, tracing the line of a rolltop desk across from him, its myriad pigeonholes resembling a hundred eyes in the early morning shadows.

A hand moved tentatively across his chest, and the warm form next to him began to stir.

"What time is it?"

"Nine."

"Shit," Claire said with little conviction.

"We had a late night."

"So I remember," she assured him. "There was wine involved. And grim tales of Canada. And much discussion of Daniel Wyatt."

She rose onto her elbows.

"And something about . . . having sex?"

He smiled. "If memory serves."

She kissed him, and tasted faintly and appealingly of wine.

"Who was that?" she asked.

"My boss."

"Anything important?"

Her hand slid down his chest and belly now, her nails tracing a slow, spiraling pattern. Claire genuinely liked him, Costilla was sure, but she wasn't above probing for information about his end of the Wyatt nomination.

"Maybe something you could help me with."

"Certainly."

"One of the distinguished senators on the committee had a question about you."

"About me?" Claire's hand paused for a second, then continued its ministrations.

"He was under the impression that you were a lesbian," Costilla explained.

Claire giggled. "Vassar girl, remember? Well, what's your expert opinion?"

"I would say that the senator is laboring under a misunderstanding."

Claire looked at him with slightly narrowed eyes, still questioning.

"Either that," Costilla added, "or *I'm* laboring under a misunderstanding."

"Young man," she answered. "Your labors have not yet begun."

She wrapped her arms around him and shifted her hips until her weight pressed down upon him. Costilla heard the cell phone thunk to the floor from his hand.

The hospital could wait.

When Claire arrived at WAG, Wyatt was already there. His bags were waiting in one corner of her office. His plane tickets were in one hand, and he was nervously drumming on her desk with the other.

"Sorry I'm late."

He looked at his watch.

"You've got two whole hours."

"But I'm supposed to be there an hour before the flight time."

Claire rolled her eyes. She had traveled enough with Daniel to know how fastidious he could be. He left an extra half hour for traffic to the airport, at least an hour for check-in, and another fifteen minutes "just in case." Claire herself arrived ten minutes before the plane left. She had almost half a million air miles, and she'd never missed a flight.

"Well, I'll make this short, then," she said. "First of all, I think Sarah's telling the truth."

Daniel nodded. "I was getting pretty sure of that."

"For one thing, she definitely is pregnant. Here's a copy of the test from her OB-GYN's files." Claire placed the folder on her desk. Wyatt looked at it with horror. Confidential medical records, acquired illegally. Claire dropped the offending document back into her desk drawer. "Forget you saw that. My private investigator went a little overboard. I just wanted to know if Sarah was lying. Believe me, I told him to return the originals."

Claire wondered what the investigator, an ex-cop, would do with them. Probably just get rid of them the easy way.

"As far as your being the father," she continued, "my detective didn't find anything. No boyfriends, no lover in Baton Rouge, not even a one-night stand in the last six months."

"Did he hear anything about . . ."

"About you?" Claire asked. "Just the barest of rumors, and he knew where to look. But no, she hasn't been blabbing."

"She's about to start," Wyatt said simply.

"What?"

"She called my house last night. Tried to leave a message. Then she showed up at my kids' school, lied about having a nephew there. She met Ellen."

Claire closed her eyes. Counted to five.

"So she's stalking you," Claire said carefully. "That's not necessarily a bad thing."

"What?" Wyatt cried.

"Daniel, all we have to do is get to next Friday. You'll be confirmed by then." She waved aside Wyatt's objections. "My detective did find something. A few years ago Sarah Corbett was on probation. She made two false claims in a deposition about her father's estate. She's a perjurer."

"Really?"

"She has a history of lying. Lying to enrich herself, Daniel. So she's been stalking you, trying to extort money with these claims of a pregnancy. It's your word against hers. A pillar of the community against an unstable, perjurous woman who is desperate for attention."

"*Claire,*" Wyatt started.

"Daniel, we *have* to do this. Look at what she's doing to you. She could destroy your life. You know that. What do you think she wants?"

Wyatt looked out the window, a picture of dejection, his plane tickets to Washington still clutched in his hands.

"She wants me," he said.

Claire smiled. Wyatt had finally gotten it. He understood what he was up against. "So, Daniel, ask yourself, what do *you* want?"

He looked at her, confused.

She continued, reaching across the desk to hold his wrist. "Do you want your marriage to continue? Do you want Ellen to keep looking at you as a hero? Do you want to live in the same house as your children, watching them grow every day? To go to Washington and take our work to every woman and man in this country?"

Claire dropped Wyatt's hand suddenly, as if it were a distasteful thing.

"Or do you want to be Sarah Corbett's lover? An outcast, living with an unstable younger woman, wondering what your children are doing today."

Wyatt looked at her with cold eyes. She realized in that moment that she had torn something, damaged some part of the respect and love between her and Daniel Wyatt. But it had to be done.

"You know what I want," he said.

"Tell me."

"My life back."

"Then you have to do this my way. This isn't some romantic secret between you and Sarah; it's a war."

"She'll win," he said. "In the second trimester she can have a paternity test done."

"Only if she's pregnant."

Claire reached into her desk drawer and pulled out a laminated box covered in multilingual labeling. She placed it on the desk between them, and watched as recognition bloomed in Daniel's eyes.

"Where did you get that?"

"From an organization in New York, two years ago, back when we were all so fed up with FDA stalling. It was unsolicited."

"It's illegal for you to have it. You're not a doctor, Claire."

"But you are!" she said. "Besides, it's hardly a dangerous

drug. It's been available in Europe for years. And you know damn well that using RU-486 is safer than bringing a pregnancy to full term."

Daniel nodded. It was the old truth of which pro-choice forces had so often tried to remind people. Pregnancy was a dangerous business, more likely to be fatal than any form of abortion or birth control.

"What are you suggesting I do with that?"

"I talked with Ellen yesterday afternoon. I told her that the hearings might stretch into a second week. So after Friday, I suggested you go away for the weekend. Somewhere alone."

Daniel looked puzzled.

"I have an idea; call Sarah—ask her to go away with you. Tell her that you and she need to work things out. Just you and her, Daniel. No Ernest Magley, no metal table in a doctor's office, no prying eyes. A private decision, made between two adults without government or small-town moralists or even the United States Senate looking on. You were right, Daniel. She wants you. And right now, she wants you to do this with her, to do this *for* her."

Claire felt the power of her words. She saw Wyatt respond to them, something like hope dawning on his face. This wasn't just another political speech; this what what they both believed. People should be free to make their own decisions quietly, without the forces of society bearing down on them, when it came to having a child. This was the promise of RU-486.

Daniel nodded his head calmly. He picked up the box, turning it sideways to check the open date, scanned the label with doctorly care.

"I hope she'll do it," he said.

"She has every right," Claire said. "So do you."

He looked at her, perhaps puzzled by that last remark. But then he glanced at his plane ticket and then his watch.

"My God, I've got to go."

"You'll make it easily. And I'll be in D.C. by noon tomorrow, right at your side."

She smiled, and Daniel smiled back. They shook hands. Wyatt took his bags and left her office.

Claire leaned back, dropping the RU-486 back into her desk drawer. She locked it, sealing the drug and her just-purchased carton of Camel filterless from prying eyes. She took a deep breath. Finally, some control again.

It turned out that Sarah Corbett's number was listed. Claire rehearsed the reason for the call in case WAG's phone records were ever pulled. Wyatt had just told her about the encounter at the school, and she was calling as his lawyer to see what game Sarah was playing.

"Hello?" Recognizing the voice, Claire wondered if she herself had sounded so young at thirty-three. Or ever.

"This is Claire Davis. I work with Dr. Wyatt."

"Oh." A little taken aback, nervous. Perfect. "Hello."

"Daniel's told me a lot about you. Daniel and I are very close. He shares everything with me." Claire let that hang for a moment. "I'd like to meet with you, if that's possible. He's out of town right now, but there's something he thinks you and I should discuss."

"I, uh, would like that very much?" An unsure little southern girl, Claire thought, always asking, never saying.

"That's wonderful, Sarah. I'm leaving for Washington rather late tonight. For Daniel's confirmation hearing. But I'll be back Thursday night. Would Friday morning be all right?"

"Certainly," Sarah answered, sounding impressed that she was being squeezed in among the senators.

"How about ten A.M.? At your house?" Claire asked, her finger marking the address in the phone book.

"Yes, of course."

"I'm looking forward to meeting you."

"**M**ay I ask you, Dr. Wyatt, some rather detailed questions about the funding of foreign nongovernmental organizations by U.S. taxpayers?"

"Certainly, Senator," Wyatt answered. "In this age of jet travel and international epidemics, the surgeon general's job certainly doesn't stop at this country's borders. What would you like to know?"

"Well, as you may well already be aware, it is a matter of U.S. law that no federal aid shall go, directly or indirectly, to foreign organizations that practice or promote abortion."

"Yes, Senator. Since 1999." The man on television looked carefully at notes before him. "Although some prohibitions on international funding of abortion go back to 1973."

"Your facts are correct, Dr. Wyatt. The law is clear," the senator continued. "And we have all been assured that you are a man of the law."

Even on the cheap television's blurry screen, Peter O'Keefe noted the predatory gleam in the senator's eye. Dr. Daniel Wyatt, a man of the law? Not God's law. He was a murderer, a baby killer. The papers all said he had performed abortions in Guatemala, when he was working with the Peace Corps back in the 1970s. No one on the committee had mentioned it yet, but O'Keefe knew they were saving it for a big finish.

"You get him," Peter O'Keefe coaxed the television set at the other end of his hotel room.

"I would certainly not allow monies from the CDC or

other agencies under the surgeon general's control to contra-
vene the law on this matter," the murderer on the screen was
saying.

"What would be your opinion, then, on so-called menstrual regulation?"

Dr. Wyatt shuffled his notes a bit, as if looking for something, but then put them aside. He certainly looked the part
of country doctor, O'Keefe thought. His gray hair and handsome face seemed so trustworthy and kind.

"As Lucifer was beautiful," O'Keefe muttered to himself.

Wyatt folded his hands and surveyed the senators with a
professorial air.

"In some countries where abortion is illegal, women who
have missed their menstrual period undergo a procedure
called menstrual regulation. It involves aspirating the lining
of the uterus."

"Isn't that a form of abortion, Doctor?"

"Only if the woman is pregnant, Senator."

"Well, if she's missing her period, isn't she pregnant,
Doctor?"

Through the television's speaker, uncomfortable laughter
could be heard in the room. The senator tried his best to
looked genuinely perplexed.

"There are other conditions that result in suspension of
the menstrual cycle, Senator. Malnutrition, disease, any
number of other factors may contribute."

"But aren't *some* of these women pregnant, Doctor?" the
senator asked.

"It isn't customary in these countries to require a pregnancy test prior to menstrual regulation, Senator. So it's not
actually known if they are pregnant or not. And under their
laws, one is not legally pregnant unless one has been tested."

The senator looked aghast. "Are you saying that it takes a
test to make a woman pregnant, Doctor?"

Daniel Wyatt smiled and leaned forward into the microphone. "If I remember my medical training correctly, that is
not what it takes."

Finally, the hearing room exploded with laughter, expelling the discomfort that had been building in the exchange. Wyatt leaned back, looking satisfied.

"I concede to your expertise on that point, Dr. Wyatt," the senator answered, anxious to get in on the joke.

"What a buffoon!" O'Keefe hissed. Once again, Wyatt had defused a line of questioning. Every time they started to close in on one of his liberal, self-deluding euphemisms for murder, he turned them aside with humor. Jokes! As if government-funded murder were some screwball comedy. Only his second day of questioning, and Wyatt was gaining in political savvy before O'Keefe's eyes. Someone was coaching him very well indeed. A man like this could go far in Washington.

The senator continued with the questioning, but now there was a smile on his face. He and Dr. Wyatt were both men of the world, his smirk seemed to say. As if they both appreciated the sophistry of their verbal sparring, like Jesuits or medieval theologians.

"Do you think that these kinds of procedures should be funded by the United States taxpayers?" he asked.

"Well, as you have so kindly said, I am a man of the law. At the moment, they are not abortions under local law or custom."

"This is U.S. law we're talking about here, Doctor."

Wyatt removed his glasses.

"Under U.S. foreign aid laws, medical procedures are defined by the local government, unless the Agency for International Development specifically makes a determination to the contrary."

"Doctor, do you think that the AID should make such a determination? Shouldn't they just be honest? If abortions are being performed, shouldn't funding be cut off?"

"Well, in this case, the women have not been tested. We may suspect that *some* women are pregnant, but we don't know if any *particular* woman is pregnant. So the AID would have to make a finding that an abortion could be performed on a woman who has *not* been tested, and may not be pregnant. In other words, the United States government would be saying that uterine aspiration is abortion, even if it is performed on a woman who is not pregnant."

The senator laughed and shook his head. "Well, I'm sure that this is all too complicated for me."

"It *is* difficult, Senator. Fortunately, the agency in question is not under the auspices of the surgeon general," Wyatt added, and leaned back in satisfaction.

He was running circles around them, O'Keefe thought. More proof that it was pointless to put one's faith in politicians.

"You've got a majority," O'Keefe muttered. "Just declare the man a murderer and throw him out on his ear."

He patted the nine-millimeter that lay on the bed next to him. Now here was something you could trust. The weapon had never jammed or misfired, and in a steady hand it seldom missed. He fingered the cool steel, comforted by its solidity, as undeniable as God's word.

O'Keefe didn't feel the urge to use the weapon again, though. Not yet. His execution of Gregory Blackmun had sated him for the time being. But watching Daniel Wyatt these last two days was rekindling the fires inside him. The injustice of such a man being called to the nation's capital, to become the voice for doctors eveywhere, was appalling.

Or perhaps, Peter O'Keefe thought, his own need to take up arms for the righteous cause was growing more frequent, like an addiction that required ever-greater doses of a drug to quell. That moment when O'Keefe had touched Gregory Blackmun, standing over him in the cold and unbearably clear air, had somehow quickened his desire for justice.

O'Keefe's cause was immense, compelling, as sovereign as God's word. A few murderers here and there were just kindling to the fire that must come.

Perhaps next time Peter O'Keefe's fever would consume something more extraordinary than one lonely doctor.

Agent Costilla wondered what his boss would think of him, lying here on his hotel bed watching television in the middle of the afternoon. She would scream, of course. She was screaming already, with the hearings in their second day and him with nothing to show for his deep and quiet background check.

Costilla felt he had earned this little rest, however. Finally, he had accomplished a small but key victory.

And besides, Wyatt's hearings were under way. Costilla hadn't caught them yesterday, but now he wanted to get a sense of the man he was investigating. As an added bonus, Claire would be testifying later. Costilla could just see her in the long shots of Wyatt, behind the doctor and to his right. Costilla fondly touched the sore spot on his shoulder, felt the tiny ridges that formed an arc in the shape of human teeth. He couldn't wait to see the committee tangle with her.

"It *is* difficult, Senator. Fortunately, the agency in question is not under the auspices of the surgeon general," Wyatt was saying. He and one of the senators were in some hairsplitting match about foreign aid. Wyatt was giving as good as he got, taking advantage of the conservative old men who always seemed boyishly uncomfortable about discussing women's issues. When the senator had said "menstrual regulation" earlier, he'd had the sour face of a good old boy forced to attempt a word in Swahili.

A member of the minority took over. As the other side had made some points off the good doctor, it was time for the liberals on the panel to throw him some soft pitches.

"Returning to the issue of foreign aid, Doctor."

"Certainly, Senator."

"Is it the case that the procedure we were discussing . . ."

"Uterine aspiration, the application of suction to the lining of the—"

"Ah, yes," the senator interrupted uncomfortably. At least masculine unease wasn't limited to conservatives. "It is the case that this procedure has some medical benefits outside of abortion. Am I correct?"

"Absolutely."

"So, not every occurrence of the procedure would necessarily signal an abortion."

"Not at all."

"And what about other means of menstrual regulation? What about mifepristone, or RU-486?"

Costilla sat up in bed, suddenly alert. For an instant, a change had come over Wyatt's face. One moment, he'd been so confident, assured by the power of his arguments, the unassailability of his expertise. The next, he seemed to be frozen, as if transfixed by something terrifying in the middle distance.

But now Wyatt was back, nodding his head to cover the lapse.

"Yes, uh, mifepristone is sometimes used in developing countries by women who aren't yet sure if they are preg—"

"Excuse me, Doctor," the senator interrupted. "I meant to ask if mifepristone might have some medical value *other than* for abortion."

"Oh, yes," Wyatt stuttered. Phew, Costilla thought. Here the guys on Wyatt's side finally throw him a softball and he blows it.

Wyatt cleared his throat and started again. "Drugs such as RU-486 have been shown to be beneficial for breast cancer patients, for patients with fibroid tumors, Cushing's syndrome. It's even possible that RU-486 could be used to induce labor during a problematic delivery."

"So to assume that the use of these drugs by a nongovernmental organization necessarily denotes the practice of abortion would be foolish, would it not?" the senator continued, leading Wyatt by the hand now. "An organization might purchase RU-486 for use in treating breast cancer, as you just said."

"It could be used for any number of things," Wyatt said. "Besides, a drug like RU-486 is safer than taking a pregnancy to full term."

There was a gasp in the hearing room just audible on the television. The senator squinted at Wyatt, obviously wondering how he could have said something so utterly stupid. Wyatt had just implied that the medical value of RU-486 was termination for its own sake, an escape from the rigors of pregnancy. What was he thinking?

The senator put his glasses on and turned quickly to some notes in his hand. He left the subject as quickly as possible, hoping that some of those present might not have heard the doctor's remark. Wyatt looked confused still, as if aware that he had blundered, but not sure exactly how.

Costilla contemplated the exchange. Was Wyatt simply tired? Had his early success made him giddy?

Or was it something else?

Costilla's mind turned to his small success today. It had taken two days of interviews, sifting through the multitude of doctors, nurses, interns, and residents, even EMTs with whom Wyatt had worked. But slowly, something had taken shape. A rumor. One that had to be teased out so slowly, it was almost as if it were only just now spreading through the hospital, taking wing in the last two days. And hardly anyone gave it any credence. For most of them it was just a bone to throw to the persistent FBI agent who refused to go away. Everyone was fiercely loyal to Dr. Daniel Wyatt, couldn't believe a word of ill about him. Besides, they'd only heard the rumor since the nomination, so it must have been fabricated by some envious rival. But newly minted or not, the rumor was there. An affair of some sort. Not proven, not enough to hang him with. The ideal pocket scandal to throw back to A.D. Richards and her senator so Costilla could leave this small town and get back to his real work.

But to escape purgatory, he had needed one crucial detail.

Late this morning, finally, Costilla's tenacity had paid off. He had broken through the silence, the feigned ignorance, the shrugged shoulders.

Finally, after three long days of interviews, Agent Costilla had a name.

20 | DEPARTURE

The brief cold front that had eased through Lafayette in the middle of the week was gone, and Sarah Corbett decided to wear a sundress for her meeting with Claire Davis.

She had watched Ms. Davis on television the day before. The senators, who had been awfully polite to Daniel, weren't quite so pleasant to Claire Davis. One had consistently called WAG an abortion clinic, even when Ms. Davis had reminded him umpteen times that they never performed any medical procedures whatsoever, only provided information and assistance to . . .

Sarah frowned as she stood contemplating the contents of the huge closet that her mother's wardrobe had once occupied. She supposed that WAG provided assistance to people like her. Single mothers. Sarah shook that unfortunate thought out of her head. Those sorts of labels didn't really apply to her. Women of education and independent means weren't the sort of people who needed WAG's help. Sarah hardly expected Claire Davis to arrive with a handful of brochures about low birth weight and the importance of prenatal care. Such things were for women who couldn't take care of themselves, who didn't know who the father of their child was, or whose partners had disappeared. That didn't apply to Sarah, who knew exactly where her man was. In Washington, D.C., on television.

Claire Davis was not coming here with brochures. Obviously, she knew about Sarah's relationship with Daniel. Sarah smiled at that thought. It was about time that Daniel began to tell his friends about her. Secrecy in front of all those awful senators was one thing, watching the hearings had shown her the need for that, but among close friends, discretion at some point turned into dishonesty.

She selected a dress, bright yellow with a sunburst in orange over her chest and belly, and pulled it over her head.

Downstairs, she put the kettle on. It was almost ten, and she suspected that Claire Davis was the sort of person who was always right on time.

Claire parked around the corner. Not so much to hide her car as to give herself a short walk before she arrived at Sarah Corbett's. She needed a smoke, and she didn't want her car smelling of cigarettes.

She pulled out a Camel as she rounded the corner, checking the street number written on a Post-it stuck to the pack. With one hand, she bent a match and brought it alight while its base was still anchored in the matchbook; the old skills were all coming back.

One house stood out on the street of low, ranch-style homes. It was a looming two stories, built of dark brick that seemed funereal beside the brightly painted aluminum siding of the surrounding homes. Claire checked her cigarette pack again to confirm the number. Of course, this misfit was Sarah Corbett's house.

She dropped the Camel and ground it into pulp, then headed up the overgrown walk.

Sarah Corbett, it turned out, was actually quite beautiful.

Claire guessed that she looked better here in the flesh than in photographs. She was a tall woman, her face full and round, her mouth large and generous. And her eyes were a steely blue that reflected the grays in the morning sky. She opened the door with a warm smile, one hand extended.

"Hello, Ms. Davis. It's so nice to meet you."

Sarah's voice was beautiful, too, a husky alto with an Old South accent. As she had on the phone, Sarah sounded young, the slightest nervous tremor inflecting each word

with uncertainty. Claire smiled inwardly. Sarah had empha-
sized the "Ms." just enough to suggest, "Yes, I'm a feminist,
too."

"Hello, Sarah," Claire said, taking the offered hand. Sarah's
grip was surprisingly strong. "You can call me Claire."

"I must say, you look just like you do on television."

Claire laughed as they went through the door. Two people
at the office had said the same thing.

"Well, I suppose C-SPAN only adds five pounds."

Sarah looked back at Claire a bit quizzically.

The morning sun was just beginning to reach the interior
of the house, bringing the dark wood furniture and floors to
life. Claire stopped with surprise next to a desk strangely
placed to one side of the foyer.

"This is lovely," she said, running her hands across the
closed rolltop.

"That was my father's. He took great pride in everything.
He wrote all his correspondence by hand at that desk. I
moved it there from the study. He was a fastidious man. He'd
be shocked by the mess."

Claire now saw the workman's bench that explained the
odd placement of the furniture.

"Let's go into the dining room, which has so far been
spared the ravages of redecoration," Sarah suggested, sounding like a girl playing at hostess. "Would you like some coffee,
Ms. Davis?"

"Coffee would be perfect."

Claire Davis was much more interesting than Ellen Wyatt,
Sarah found herself thinking as she stepped into the kitchen.

The woman had such presence and assurance, a sense of
command in her gestures and voice. She certainly had told
those senators a thing or two.

Sarah placed two spoonfuls of instant into each of the
lovely old porcelain cups decorated with tiny green leaves
around their rims. Only two cups in the set left without
chips or cracks, she thought sadly.

Then Sarah picked up the jar of instant and frowned. Why hadn't she gotten real coffee for Ms. Davis? She shrugged, doubting she could even remember how to make the stuff.

She brought the coffee into the dining room and placed a cup before Claire Davis.

"Thank you, Sarah."

"Well, I'm just so glad that you're visiting, Ms. Davis."

"I am, too. Oh, do you have any sugar?"

"Of course!" Sarah said, and headed back into the kitchen. "How could I have forgotten?" she called over her shoulder.

Sugar in hand, she returned. After Ms. Davis added a tiny spoonful to her coffee, Sarah followed her lead.

Claire took one sip and said, "I'm not only Daniel's lawyer and partner, I'm his closest friend. I'm here to talk to you about your relationship with him."

Sarah found that she could only nod, thinking, My, but this woman was direct. Having never told even her closest friends about her affair, Sarah found it strange to hear the words coming out of the mouth of someone she hardly knew.

"This must have been very hard for you, Sarah," Ms. Davis continued. "I know that Daniel hasn't always been able to tell you how he feels. But you must try to understand what all of this is like for him."

Sarah nodded agreement, still unable to speak.

"Daniel has worked a long time to get where he is today. His position in this community, his work at WAG, and his family—all these are terribly important to him. And now, of course, he's been appointed to the highest medical post in Washington."

"Yes," Sarah finally managed. "I am so happy for him."

"But I think that there's something else in his life, too."

Sarah blinked, unsure what the other woman meant. To cover her confusion, she took a sip of her coffee. It wasn't very good. She'd put too much instant in.

"And that something is you," Ms. Davis finished.

It took a moment for the statement to penetrate. Sarah felt a flush of heat rise to her face, and her words rushed out.

"Oh, do you really think so?" she stammered. "I mean, I *knew* there was something between us, but Daniel seems so distant, almost as if he's afraid of me. And when he didn't come here, the night before I was supposed to . . ."

Claire nodded, and closed her eyes.

"That was my fault, I'm afraid. I didn't know then what I know now, Sarah."

"What do you mean, Ms. Davis?"

"He wanted to come. He got all the way to that curb out there."

"Oh, yes, I know. I saw him."

Claire put one hand on Sarah's, which was quivering.

Sarah wrapped her hands around the warm cup and sipped as she listened.

"I didn't know who you were. I suspected that you were just trying to set him up. So I told him to stay away from you. That's what lawyers do. But I've talked to him about you since, and I think that what you two have is worth . . . exploring."

"Oh, Claire!" Sarah exclaimed. A rush of relief came over her. Finally, someone who was on her side.

"You and Daniel met at a very difficult time," Claire continued. "You know that. You watched us on television, so you can see what those men in Washington want to do to him."

Sarah swallowed and nodded again.

"And your pregnancy makes things even more complicated."

Sarah shook her head. "But, Claire, if it weren't for my pregnancy, I don't think I would have ever seen Daniel again. Not alone, as a friend. Perhaps not ever. After what happened in Baton Rouge, he didn't want to keep seeing me. And I just accepted it. I did. But when I found out I was carrying his child, it brought us back together."

"Is that what you really think?"

Sarah blinked. "I'm sorry?"

"You shouldn't believe that your pregnancy is something that changed Daniel's mind. Or that this child is the key to what you two have. That's selling yourself short. You're a beautiful young woman. Daniel respects you, loves you, desires you. It's just that men need time, especially after they make such a strong and sudden connection. They need time alone to work things out."

Claire took her hand again.

"You probably needed time as well. And yes, the fact of your pregnancy brought you together again. It put you back in contact. But it isn't the *reason* why you and Daniel . . . have what you have."

Sarah felt tears rising behind her eyes. She could see that Claire Davis understood the importance of what she and Daniel had, somehow, even though Daniel himself was unsure. She clutched Claire's hand.

"You don't know what this means to me, Claire. I've been completely alone with this."

"You aren't alone. Daniel is with you, in spirit."

Sarah nodded. Perhaps Claire was right about his reluctance. It was only natural. He was a man, a married man. He had more to lose than Sarah.

"What should I do, Claire?"

Claire released her hand and leaned back, pausing thoughtfully.

"I think that you and Daniel need time together, time away from all this."

"That sounds . . . wonderful. But how could we do that?"

"Daniel is coming back from Washington after the hearings end today. But he's not going to stay in Lafayette. He's headed to the Gulf Coast tonight, to a beach house where he can spend some time away from all this. He needs rest after the confirmation hearings. And . . . can you keep a secret?"

Sarah nodded solemnly.

"He asked me to tell you that he wants you to join him there."

Agent Costilla looked at the list of remaining Sarahs in his hand.

Sarah Cable.
Sarah Carver.
Sarah Coble.
Sarah Corbett.
Sarah Culver.

The game of gossip had played a cruel trick on him. There was no Sarah Quarter in the Lafayette phone book. And his check of unlisted numbers hadn't given him a Sarah Quarter or Quartermaine or any other variant. He'd spent yesterday evening calling every family in the greater Lafayette area with either name and asking for Sarah. No luck.

Costilla thanked his stars that he hadn't forwarded the rumour to A.D. Richards before checking it out. But he needed something for Richards, so he hadn't given up, expanding his search through the Q's and into other letters. Even when Claire Davis had called him last night after her return from Washington, Costilla's fear of A.D. Richards had overwhelmed temptation, and he'd worked the phones. Now Costilla was down to these five names, culled from the C's of the Lafayette phone book.

He looked at his watch. Almost noon. The hearings would wrap up early today, so it was probably already too late. Maybe just enough time to get a call in to Richards. Costilla imagined an aide handing a folded note to one of the senators, a moment of high drama when Wyatt was asked, "Do you know a women named Sarah . . ." He began dialing.

Sarah Cable wasn't home. He left his cell number on her machine.

Sarah Carver didn't believe he was from the FBI, and no, she hadn't heard of Dr. Daniel Wyatt.

Sarah Coble was at least eighty years old.

When Sarah Corbett answered, she sounded rushed.

"Ms. Corbett? This is Agent Eduardo Costilla of the Federal Bureau of Investigation."

"Yes?"

"I was calling about a Dr. Daniel Wyatt."

A long pause. "Who did you say you were?"

"Agent Eduardo Costilla, FBI."

"Well, I'm sure I don't know what you're talking about?" As usual, her statement ended as a question.

"Dr. Daniel Wyatt. Do you know him?"

"Daniel?" Sarah Corbett paused again. She was breathing hard into the phone. "I'm not sure I . . . Listen, I'm sorry, sir, but I'm just on my way out the door. I have to go to the Gulf Coast today, rather unexpectedly."

"Ms. Corbett, if you could just answer a few questions."

"I'm sorry. I have to go."

She hung up on him.

Her house was across town. Costilla made it there in half an hour, pushing his rented car hard through the heavy Friday traffic. When he reached her street, he found the house easily. It looked like a house from back east, more Cape Cod than southern.

He rang the doorbell.

No one answered.

He peered through the bay windows beside the door. No lights were on inside, but someone might be upstairs. He rang again.

Then Costilla noticed a woman watching him from the front porch of the house next door. She was about thirty, and tall with dark straight hair. He waved at her, hoping she knew the whereabouts of her neighbor.

The woman didn't wave back. Instead, she walked quickly down to a car parked between the two houses.

"Pardon me, miss," Costilla called.

She didn't hear him. Or at any rate, she didn't stop. The Cadillac pulled away, its tires skidding just a bit as it accelerated.

Costilla sighed, and walked across the unkempt lawn to the other house. Taped to the door was a note.

Millie—
Had to go to the coast.
Don't worry.
See you Sunday night.
  Love,
  Sarah

Costilla replaced the note carefully, shaking his head. There it was. He was too late.

Well, it was none of his business anyway. Probably not the business of the U.S. Senate either.

His cell phone rang. He grimaced when he saw the Caller ID.

"Costilla."

"Richards. So time's up. Really up. What do you got for me?"

Costilla looked down the street in the direction the Cadillac had disappeared. Sarah Corbett was long gone.

"Sorry, Assistant Director, but I got *nada*."

21 | BEACH

Wyatt kissed his wife good-bye at the Hertz counter in New Orleans International. Ellen was taking the Saab back to Lafayette, picking up the kids en route. She said she understood completely. After the three days of testimony, anyone would need some time on his own to recover.

"I won't even call you, Daniel," she assured him.

Claire had arranged the car. A FedEx package was waiting at Hertz, with house keys and directions. The bulging envelope also contained a small, familiar pharmaceuticals box. Wyatt turned it over in his hands, staring at it dolefully.

He took a deep breath and headed for the car.

Driving usually cleared his mind, but this afternoon an endless inquisition was taking place inside his head. Some of the questions that tortured him he'd actually had to answer, some Claire had prepared him for though they'd never been asked, others seemed to be spontaneously generated in some part of his mind still whirling from the hearings. The accusatory stares of the committee still pursued him, echoing within Wyatt like the memory of witnessing a sudden and ferocious fight between strangers on the street.

"Dr. Wyatt, you have admitted performing abortions. What message do you think your confirmation to the surgeon generalship would send to young women making a choice whether or not to bring their pregnancies to full term?"

"Is it possible, Dr. Wyatt, that you performed abortions in Guatemala, but never in the United States, simply because you believe that the life of an unborn in the developing world is worth less than a fetus in our own country?"

"Dr. Wyatt, you state that taking RU-486 is safer than bringing even a healthy pregnancy to full term. Would you recommend to your patients that they terminate their pregnancies in order to avoid the natural risks of childbirth?"

"As you must know from your work with children, Dr. Wyatt, one of the most reliable predictors of children's health is a stable, two-parent environment. As surgeon general, what would you say to those fathers who abandon their families, however fleetingly, for the momentary thrills of an illicit affair?"

By the time the road began to parallel the Gulf Coast, the sea hidden by scrubby dunes, the sky was glowering. A single huge mass of cirrus clouds hung to the south, fringed with the wan, yellow light of the invisible afternoon sun.

Wyatt found the house easily enough. It stood a hundred feet or so from the shore, each of its thick wooden supports surrounded by a skirt of sand. At extremely high tides, or when the hurricane surges that occasionally made it this far west pulled the sea up onto the land, the gulf waters certainly lapped at the base of the structure. The walls of the house showed the effects of weathering at any one of a dozen different stages, the result of much repair of its shingles over the years. Wyatt reflected that living on beaches, sandbars, and small islands was further evidence, if such was needed, of human hubris, the vain assumption that man could regulate and control nature.

Inside, Wyatt found evidence that a housekeeper or caretaker had been on the premises earlier that day. The sheets were crisp, the refrigerator stocked, even a few bottles of wine had been set on the kitchen table. Wyatt took a cold beer and went out onto the deck, watching the ocean turn gray as the light faded.

The phone rang.

Perhaps it was Sarah. Calling to report a simple road accident, an emergency, some reason she wouldn't be coming. Perhaps some deliberately feeble excuse, tacitly revealing that she had suddenly realized the futility of continuing her relationship—if that's even what it was—with Daniel Wyatt.

"Hello?"

"It's me." *Claire.*

"She's not here yet."

"I know. Sarah said she was leaving just after noon. She'll be there soon, though."

Wyatt swallowed his stray, self-indulgent hopes of a reprieve.

"I've got the drugs, Claire," he said.

"Well, I guess the rest is in your hands," she answered. "Be supportive and gentle. Don't be too pushy. This is a woman who more than anything wants to be with you."

"I know . . . I have such a hard time expressing my feelings, but I know you're right. This is the best way for everyone."

There was a pause, a long chain of seconds marked by the pulsing of the waves. "I can hear the sea," Claire said softly.

"I'll finish this, Claire. We'll get to Washington."

"All right, then." Another pause, as if they were both reflecting on their shared history, wondering how all their hard work and idealism had come down to this.

"Good luck, Daniel."

"See you on Monday."

Sarah Corbett arrived just before the sun set, her old Cadillac negotiating the gravel drive with angry pops and growls.

"Daniel!" she cried, as if his presence there were some unexpected bonus rather than the reason for her own visit. She stepped from the car and they embraced. As always, the feeling of Sarah in his arms surprised him. She was so much taller than Ellen, so much more substantial. Her hands met at the small of his back, and she pressed herself against him hard.

He realized that he wanted to kiss her, but he pulled away.

"It's good to see you, Sarah."

Wyatt carried her luggage, two absurdly large suitcases, into the house. He had already taken possession of one of the two bedrooms, and he put her bags in the other.

"This is simply marvelous," she announced, drifting from the kitchen into the living room, her hands lingering on this or that piece of furniture. She stopped before the floor-to-ceiling windows that faced the Gulf and gasped.

"Oh, my." She shook her head.

"Let's go out on the deck," Wyatt suggested. "Would you like a beer?"

"Now, Dr. Wyatt! In my condition?"

A jolt went through Wyatt. That's it, he thought. She was set on having the child. But then she grinned, her voice lilting higher to show that she'd been teasing him.

"Well, I suppose I could handle one bottle . . . if it's doctor's orders?"

He smiled thinly and went back inside, splashing some cold water onto his face from the kitchen faucet. It was pointless trying to read his fate in every word Sarah said. Nothing was decided yet. The choice would be made later, when he'd had a chance to explain how the drug worked. Claire was right, it was in his hands. He pulled two beers from the refrigerator, along with two glasses, and joined Sarah on the deck.

"You're so wonderful to think of this, Daniel."

"It was Claire, really," he started, then wondered if that was the right thing to say.

"Oh, yes," Sarah agreed enthusiastically. "She was very helpful. I think that she and I are going to be friends."

Wyatt nodded mutely, and worked at balancing the glasses on the deck's thin wooden rail. He poured the beers carefully, avoiding Sarah's gaze.

"You're such a doctor, Dr. Wyatt."

His confusion must have shown on his face.

"You move so elegantly, so precisely. It is certainly a pleasure to watch you."

Wyatt smiled and handed her a glass. They toasted, the touching glasses making a delicate sound against the rage of the sea. The waves roiled under Wyatt's gaze, cold and gray, their white tops foaming up and foaming out. To the south-west, the sunset shone red beneath the mass of dark clouds.

"Look at me?" Sarah asked simply. "I don't feel as if you've looked at me." Her tone wasn't demanding, merely a bit confused.

Wyatt turned and looked at her.

She was beautiful. Her eyes caught the steely hue of the water, turning a deep and mournful gray. Her smile appeared unforced and open, widening as she placed her hands on his shoulders.

"I am so glad to be here, Daniel," she said. "You're mar-velous to invite me."

"I'm glad you came," he said.

Her arm slid around his waist, and the two stood facing the sea, sharing their bodies' warmth in the cool ocean breeze.

Wyatt felt himself start to relax. They were alone out here, as far from Lafayette as they'd been that weekend in Baton Rouge. Sarah adored him, trusted him, perhaps even loved him. True, her purpose in coming to this beach house was very different from his own. But at least they could face this decision together.

They made dinner together.

Sarah was charmingly helpless in the kitchen. She called on Wyatt to open the cans of tomato sauce, and deferred to his expertise when it came time to determine if the pasta was cooked enough. But Daniel enjoyed himself, the inquisitorial voices in his head finally vanquished by Sarah's buoyant company and the better part of a bottle of wine.

By the end of dinner, he felt ready to face the task of ask-ing Sarah to abort her child.

They returned to the deck, where a brilliant half-moon showed through the thinning clouds. Sarah was bundled in one of Daniel's coats. (She had brought nothing for the cold. What was in those two suitcases? he wondered.) They sipped the last of the wine and listened to the ocean.

"Sarah, we should talk about this child," he said simply.

"Our child," she responded.

"Yes, our child," Daniel agreed.

The moon broke free at last, lighting a glittering path across the surface of the sea.

"I've thought about it, I really have. Not just as your friend or doctor, Sarah, but as a parent. A parent of this child."

Her hand grew tighter in his. She leaned into him.

"When you first told me that you were pregnant, you said that you thought a child should have two parents. Including a father who could be there for his child, all the time."

"Oh, yes, Daniel. And I still think so."

Wyatt nodded. "Well, I agree with you, of course. But where you and I are now, I couldn't be a full-time parent. Not yet."

She pulled away from him, but just a bit, a telltale shifting of her weight.

"Not yet?" she asked.

Wyatt waited for the courage to speak. He allowed the close warmth of Sarah, the smell of her, to work its power over him. For a moment, he permitted his fantasies free rein, and let the demands of lust inside him take full purchase. Her beauty would tempt most men, he knew, and the cold and clear sea air seemed to urge him to succumb to his need for a wilder and fuller experience than his day-to-day existence offered. To the dreamer, Wyatt thought, real life is the dream.

He felt himself sliding helplessly into the vision that he had carefully constructed since that weekend in Baton Rouge. In this fantasy, he saw himself throw away everything—wife, children, career—in exchange for the embrace of his young lover. For her awestruck gaze, her radiant blue eyes, her generous body.

And in that state, weakened as he was by desire, he was able to dissemble with a conviction he could never have achieved in his ordinary state of consciousness, to lie not coldly, but with deep-felt tenderness in his heart.

"You and I have something special, Sarah. And I believe that we'll have it for a long time. But right now, what we have is under siege from all directions. It's not just the fact that I have a wife and family. There's my career to consider. You're a patient. I broke my oath. And, of course, those people in Washington want to destroy me."

He pulled her closer.

"I can't imagine any two people with more to overcome," he continued. "But I think we're strong enough. Wise enough to keep what we have safe, to protect it. If we are very careful."

"Oh, Daniel," she said, her voice barely audible.

"And one day, Sarah, when we're on the other side of these dangers, there will be room for a child. Our child."

"Our child," she said. He felt her hand move, pulling aside her coat and coming to rest on her belly.

"But I don't want you going to that office outside Lafayette," Wyatt said. "I don't want you in another man's hands, on some metal table."

Suddenly she froze.

"What do you mean, Daniel?"

"Sarah, my beautiful Sarah, let me show you something."

Inside, seated across the small wooden kitchen table from Sarah, Daniel solemnly showed her the RU-486. At this moment, he was a doctor, the nerves that usually plagued him in Sarah's presence subsumed under the force of his professional authority. His voice stayed steady and low, as if he were a high priest describing some profound and ancient ritual to an acolyte. He explained the compond mifepristone itself, how it worked by breaking down the lining of the uterine walls, which had grown thick and full for the nourishment of the fetus. Then he showed her the prostaglandin, a muscle contractant that was taken twelve to seventy-two hours after the mifepristone, which helped force the leftover material from the body, the lining of the uterus expelled just as it was every month. Like a normal menstrual period, he explained. He opened the package, revealing the innocuous-looking pills.

"They look as harmless as aspirin," Sarah said, turning the white, smooth tablets over in one hand.

"I suppose they do," he agreed.

Sarah nodded, the patient listening carefully to her doctor.

"Almost a quarter of pregnancies end in an event much like this. And most women never even notice when that happens," he said. "That's because the fetus right now is only about an inch long."

"The fetus," Sarah repeated.

Dr. Wyatt folded his hands. "The fetus that could *become* a child," he said. "But only if you choose that path. I'll be here either way."

"You will, Daniel?"

He nodded solemnly.

Sarah picked up the pills again. Her eyes went from one to the other, a little unsurely.

"Those three are mifepristone," he reminded her gently. "You take them first."

She put the pills down, shook her head.

"Not just this moment," she said. "I didn't know that you . . ."

Wyatt felt the calmness of his professional demeanor waver a little. If she would just take the pills, this nightmare would all be over. But he forced himself back to the role of doctor, mentor, healer.

"I just wanted to give you this choice again, Sarah," he said. "I don't want fear to make your decision. I wanted to explain all this to you so that you could make an informed decision."

Sarah nodded, and Wyatt realized that there were tears in her eyes. Idiot! he thought to himself. He had gone too far too fast, pulling her inside and parading these drugs before her. Just when she was beginning to trust him, to trust in their future together.

But then she was smiling, reaching for him.

"Thank you, Daniel. Really. Thank you for putting the decision in my hands."

Sarah stood and took two steps toward him, and they embraced. She cradled his head against the warmth of her bosom, then lifted him from the chair. Their mouths met, lips brushing and then opening hungrily. Wyatt felt his hands grasping her, reaching under her sweater to feel the smooth, broad expanse of her back, the ridge of spine, the soft orbs of her generous breasts.

The scent of her overwhelmed Daniel, vanquishing his pretense of clinical detachment and firing the passion he remembered from Baton Rouge. The world of his fantasy flooded over him, and suddenly the woman in his arms was no longer an obstacle in his path but a goal to reach for.

"Come to bed," she said, and he hastily complied.

Afterward, Sarah lay in Daniel's arms and stared at the ceiling.

One of her hands rested on her stomach. Occasionally, she let it slide a few inches up or down, as light as a breeze against the flesh of her belly. She imagined a life in which this child was permitted to come to term, the natural outgrowth of her and Daniel's first encounter, the pure and simple lust that had ruled them that weekend. But then she thought of the pain the child would cause Daniel; the newspapers, his family, even the esteemed gentlemen of the Senate pointing at her and her bastard child. The name Sarah Corbett would become some sort of dire warning against the dangers of a wanton woman.

And if she let the child go?

Would Daniel really stay with her? She felt the warm reality of the body next to her. Their lovemaking had been desperate and frantic, the passion rising suddenly and overwhelmingly in the kitchen. The strength of their emotional connection, so long obstructed by a wall of suspicion and regrets, had burst forth in an unstoppable wave. She felt it now, the bond between them, the sharing of longing and desire and something sweet and fragile yet fierce and demanding. She had to trust it.

But her hand stirred of its own accord, sending a warm sensation through her belly. As if the child were calling to her. What if she aborted the fetus, and Daniel found himself feeling betrayed? What if behind his enlightened, eminently reasonable facade, Daniel secretly wanted her to keep the child? Wanted to protect and nurture it as fiercely as he did his three children already born? Perhaps if she made this choice to abort the child—no, not child, *fetus*—that fragile bond between Daniel and her would be broken.

What should I do? she asked the unborn life inside her.

She could just step out of bed and go into the kitchen. Swallow the pills with a glass of wine.

No. Not yet, she thought. Not in these precious minutes after their lovemaking. There was still time for her to decide. Later tonight, or tomorrow.

Her choice.

Daniel Wyatt listened to his young lover breathe deeply next to him. Occasionally, she would stir, but she seemed to be asleep, and Wyatt felt alone in the privacy of his thoughts.

Here he was in bed with her, his body spent from their passion. Is this what had been in his mind all along, from the moment Claire had broached her idea of a weekend alone? Daniel supposed that some animal part of him had always focused on this possibility above all else, those shuddering moments of bliss inside Sarah. But now he felt like a betrayer again. Not just of Ellen, but of the woman next to him.

He had gone along with Sarah's overtures to convince her that she would still have a hold over him, regardless of the fate of her fetus. That they would still be together, however secretly. But in thinking that he was lying to Sarah, whom had he really deceived? He knew that he had succumbed because he simply couldn't stop himself. There was a connection between them, a passion that any real opportunity would ignite. He wanted Sarah Corbett. Always had.

Daniel wondered if Sarah would take the pills. Had sleeping with her been the way to influence her choice? Or would she now start to think of them as a couple, with every right to raise their own child? What would she do?

Frustration gripped him as he lay there helplessly. How had his life become dependent on the whim of this woman? Didn't he have the right to make any choices himself? He wondered for a moment whether the mifepristone had any taste if it was mixed with some food or drink. If he was to slip the drug to her, would she even know the difference? He indulged the fantasy guiltily, imagining an end to all this trouble. . . .

The thoughts tumbled in his head, as the inquisition in the Senate had tumbled that afternoon. Over and over, until at the edge of consciousness, he thought he felt Sarah slip out of the bed.

And then he was asleep.

22 | CONFIRMATION

"The nomination of Dr. Daniel Wyatt for surgeon general passed its first hurdle today when the Senate Labor and Human Resources Committee voted five to two in favor of Dr. Wyatt. The full Senate is expected to confirm the nomination later this week. The two senators who voted in the negative cited their concerns about Dr. Wyatt's service in the Peace Corps, during which he performed . . ."

The last words were drowned out by the boisterous cheers that swept through the offices of WAG. The strains of National Public Radio had filled Claire's head all morning, following her inescapably across the archipelago of portable radios her staff had brought in for the day of the vote. No one wanted to miss the moment the news was announced. Although the White House had called with good news on Friday, confident of at least two Republicans and all the Democrats on the committee, Claire felt a rush of relief as the vote was confirmed. Her liaison in the administration was predicting seventy votes or more in the full Senate, but more important, the story was now off the front page. With the committee hearings over, the confirmation of Daniel Wyatt was business as usual, no more explosive than approving the appointment of some ambassador to some third-world country.

She headed back to her office, shaking hands and accepting hugs along the way. Daniel was at her door, looking a bit lost amid the throng. Almost all the volunteers had come in today to share in his victory. But when Wyatt saw Claire, his smile faded for a moment, replaced by the hangdog expression he had worn all morning.

Daniel did not know if Sarah had taken the pills. She had gone as far as holding them in her hand, but after that first night, she'd declined to talk about it.

Daniel hadn't described the weekend to Claire in detail, but she knew that Wyatt had slept with Sarah again. Claire shook her head. She should have known that would happen, out there alone on the gulf shore, and should have guessed that Sarah might take it as a sign that her relationship with Daniel was going to continue. It had been a risky proposition, and now it was looking as if rather than defusing her fears it was going to confirm them.

Confirm. Claire smiled grimly at the word.

She forced her smile back on for the troops.

Claire walked through the throng, which parted respectfully for her, and embraced Daniel.

"We've made it. It's okay," she said.

Someone took a picture.

"I hope so," he said softly, a beaten look on his face.

A cake was wheeled out. The word CONGRATULATIONS stretched across it in sugary letters. There was more applause, a pile of paper plates was produced, and Dr. Wyatt set to work cutting dozens of pieces. As cries of "a *really* small one for me" rose up through the room, Claire watched the surgeonlike precision of Wyatt's hands. Somehow, the sight comforted her. No matter what she'd done in the last week, how many lines she'd crossed, it would be a waste to let those hands go unused, slowly losing their skills, never healing again. A terrible waste.

"If you'll excuse me, there's something I have to do."

Claire Davis went to make a call.

The news of Dr. Wyatt's success in the committee vote flashed across a small AP newswire window in one corner of Agent Tabitha Samuels's screen.

She turned to Costilla, who hovered over her shoulder. "Isn't that your man in Louisiana?"

"Yes, Chaos, that's my man."

"Well, congratulations, Dr. Wyatt," Chaos said, her fingers never slowing as she scrolled down the hits her latest algorithm had produced.

Agent Costilla wondered how she could scan the words so quickly. She read and discarded each highlighted block of text in less than a second, as if the search for Blackmun's murderer were some sort of manic video game. The team was going back into the past now, digging into defunct cobwebsites in the hope of finding posts that had coincided with the shooter's other murders. Unfortunately, the key word in the murderer's poem was "rejoice." In the vast world circumscribed by religious fervor and God's Word, it was what Chaos called a "highly nonselective search parameter."

In other words, a very big net in which they were trying to catch a very particular fish. Chaos was working toward an algorithm that would pare down the results to something manageable. Of course, at her superhuman speed, thousands of hits was a manageable number.

For some reason, no search result had ever come up with the words "God, I must enter her." Costilla was starting to wonder if that hadn't been a bad lead produced by a traumatized witness.

Costilla's head was ringing from watching Chaos work, but after his Friday-night dressing down by A.D. Richards, he was glad to have a job at all. He'd flown back after the hearings had concluded, preferring to face his boss's wrath sooner rather than later. Costilla hadn't even mentioned the Sarah Corbett rumor to Richards. It was too little to go on, and in any case it was too late at this point.

Now things were back to normal. He was working on solving murders, not ruining reputations. So, why not congratulations to the good doctor?

"Check this out!" cried Chaos.

Costilla blinked and scanned the small block of text her mouse pointer hovered over.

This injury against justice,
This devourer of the helpless,
This scourge of the little ones,
Has fallen.
Therefore, let us all rejoice.

Costilla checked the date and immediately recognized it. Back in 1995, two weeks and a day after the first hit that bore the shooter's MO, an abortion provider in rural Kansas had been wounded in a drive-by.

"Damn," muttered Chaos. " 'Let us *all* rejoice!' No wonder we didn't hit it right away. And he's not rhyming yet, you'll notice."

"What's this site?"

"Message board archives of the White Power website ring."

"Website ring?"

"A ring is a loose confederation of websites with the same theme. They're all linked together in a big virtual circle jerk. *Star Wars* fans have one, Goths, transgendered people—PEZ dispenser collectors, would you believe? You name it, there's a ring."

Chaos's fingers clacked for a few moments. "Unfortunately, these archives are shared, so I don't know which site was the origin of this post. It could be any site on the ring."

"How many sites are we talking about, Samuels?"

"White Power? On the Internet? About a zillion. Those guys have total-loser free time on their hands."

"Shit," Costilla said. "This guy's leaving us messages, just handing us clues, and we can't do anything with them."

He rubbed his temples. Finding the origin of the first poem Chaos had discovered had proven impossible. But now they had a trail again, leading straight into that other arm of the extreme right: White Power. This could be the break they'd needed. White Power organizations were carefully tracked by the FBI and a host of private watchdog groups. If they could discover which organization this poem was related to, Costilla and his team might well have a list of names to start with.

Chaos sat back. "This is from back in 1995," she said. "Dinosaur times. There was a whole lot less Internet back then."

"Meaning?"

"Meaning I can eliminate any site built after 1995."

"You're a genius, Chaos," Costilla said. "Do some history homework. Find out which of these sites has been around that long."

"You got it."

Costilla smiled. At last he had something concrete, a clue that might lead him out of the thicket of the Internet, in which every place was linked to every other place like some tangled brier patch, and every statement concealed by layers of anonymity. Unlike Internet chat communities, White Power groups lived out in the real world. They had headquarters made of bricks and mortar, and addresses without *.org* in them. You could meet them face-to-face.

Agent Costilla felt like he'd been chasing a ghost these last two years, a creature who took corporeal form only for those few minutes he needed to kill, then slipped back into the mists of the Internet. But now, for the first time, there was a chance of finding the man behind the ghost.

Costilla straightened, feeling the muscles in his back ache from his long vigil over Chaos's shoulder. He knew what he needed to do.

"Keep it up, Tabitha," he said. "I think I'm due for a trip to the shooting range."

"The nomination of Lafayette surgeon Dr. Daniel Wyatt was sent to the full Senate today by a five-to-two committee vote, with a recommendation to confirm."

Mark Hicks watched carefully, though the eleven o'clock

news was merely repeating what he'd heard all day. He had thought the local station would provide more details, but it was the same story in almost exactly the same words.

Hicks looked out the window at Sarah Corbett's house and wondered if all his suspicions had proven to be unfounded. That morning on his way to work, he'd seen Ellen Wyatt strolling up the walk of the Corbett house. She had her youngest kid in tow, and had been fixing to leave him there with Sarah for the day. He felt sheepish about his peeping now. If Sarah Corbett were baby-sitting for the Wyatts, it might explain the comings and goings of Dr. Wyatt to and from her house. True, he'd never noticed the kids with Daniel, but as Hicks reviewed in his mind what he had in fact seen, it didn't amount to very much. His eyes weren't what they used to be, and maybe he'd been wrong about the troubled expression on Dr. Wyatt's face that first night, and his imagination had supplied the rest.

Hicks realized that he had stirred up gossip at the hospital by telling Millie all about it. Even the FBI agent who'd been poking his nose around town had gotten wind of the story, it seemed. Just goes to show, he thought, nothing good comes of telling tales. That's why the Law had no truck with rumors, just hard facts.

"Peeking again, Daddy?" Millie asked as she swept into the room wearing a fresh set of bright blue scrubs.

"No, I've sworn off peeking," he announced, and turned resolutely from the window. "Caused enough trouble already."

"Now, I don't think it was such a disaster, Daddy," Millie said, attempting to comfort him.

"What would you call it?" he complained. "I'm spreading rumors about the most prominent citizen in town, just when he's been called up to Washington."

"Well, where does that leave me, thank you very much?" she said.

"You were just repeating what I told you," he countered. "It's all my fault. Hell, that FBI man could've taken the whole thing seriously. Imagine the trouble that would've caused Dr. Wyatt."

"Well, I wouldn't worry about that FBI man," she said mischievously. "He was awfully cute, but I think he was misinformed."

"I thought you said you didn't talk to him."

"I said no such thing," Millie said. "I just said that I never mentioned Sarah Corbett's name to him. I may have mentioned some other Sarah's name, though. I'm not quite sure."

"Millie, what are you saying?" Mark Hicks exclaimed. "Did you lie to a federal law enforcement official? Why, that's—"

"I did not *lie*," Millie explained. "I just got one little name a little bit wrong. You know how vague rumors can be, Daddy."

Hicks sputtered for another moment and then found himself laughing. He pulled himself from the deep chair and hugged his daughter.

"Well, Millie," he said. "It looks like you fixed what your daddy broke, then."

"You're very welcome," she answered, curtsying. "But I'll tell you, I'm not so sure you were wrong. There's something more than baby-sitting going on between those two. I just don't think it's the business of the FBI."

"Or us, either," Hicks finished. He sat back down heavily. "Do you think we've got any coffee?"

Millie rolled her eyes. "Yes, I would love to make you some, Daddy."

"With caffeine in it."

Millie turned back to her father and began a retort, but was cut off by a sudden and insistent ringing of the doorbell.

"Who on earth is that?" she said.

Hicks followed his daughter to the door. It was mighty late, and whoever was pumping the doorbell was having a wild time of it. Hicks hadn't even heard a car pull up to the house.

Millie yanked the door open.

Standing there was Sarah Corbett, wearing a white sundress. Her face was deathly pale, her hands reaching out for Millie as she stumbled forward.

And in a long swath below her waist, almost black in the darkness of the front porch, her dress was streaked with blood.

23 | EMERGENCY ROOM

"**L**et's get her to my car!" Sheriff Hicks shouted to his daughter. "We'll need the siren."

Millie opened the rear door of the SUV and jumped in, then pulled Sarah in after her. Hicks noticed that Millie's fresh hospital scrubs were already covered in blood.

"Grab my first-aid bag, Daddy!"

Hicks slammed the door and ran to his daughter's car. The bag was there on the front seat. He was momentarily grateful that folks in Lafayette still left their doors unlocked. He reached in for the bag, then jogged back to the SUV. He settled himself in the driver's seat and reached down for the red light. Once it was planted on his dash, Hicks started the car and rolled out of the driveway onto the dark and empty street.

"I need my kit, Daddy."

Hicks slowed as he reached the first intersection and passed the bag back to Millie. Out on the main street, he let the siren rip.

"She's lost a lot of blood," Millie reported. Hicks heard the sound of a sphygmomanometer being pumped, the hiss of its release.

"Oh, Sarah," Millie said, sounding terrified. "Her blood pressure's way too low, Daddy. Sarah? Can you hear me?"

Hicks barely heard Sarah's soft voice over the pulsing siren.

"Millie?"

"Sarah, I need you to listen to me for a minute. I need you to listen real good."

"Okay?" Sarah answered.

"Honey, you're bleeding from your birth canal. You're bleeding something fierce. Now I need you to tell me something. And you've got to tell me the truth. Hear?"

"Okay, Millie," Sarah said. She sounded contented, almost dreamy.

"Are you pregnant, Sarah?"

There was a pause. Hicks forced himself to keep his eyes on the road. He'd driven this route a hundred times to pick Millie up from work. He'd driven it the day Millie was born. And he'd come this way, speeding like a madman but all for nothing, the day his wife had died.

"Are you pregnant, Sarah? Answer me."

The lights of the hospital, a much taller structure than the surrounding houses, were just visible on the horizon. In the light mist that had settled over Lafayette as night had fallen, the building seemed to emit a faint aura. It was orange, the color of the bright towers that lit its parking lot.

"Are you pregnant, honey? You've got to tell me."

"Yes?" Sarah responded.

Hicks slowed for a moment to check both ways before plowing through a red light. He'd hardly seen another car in the ten-minute trip. As he sped up again, the sheriff risked a look back at his daughter.

Their eyes met for the length of one red flash from the pulsing dashboard light.

"Oh, Daddy," Millie said, then bent back to care for her patient.

Hicks was about to go in search of coffee when the doctor stepped into the waiting room.

"Is her family here yet?"

Hicks shook his head ruefully. He'd been trying to figure out whom to call.

"Her parents are dead. She's got no sisters or brothers," he answered. "I know she's got an aunt somewhere. Baton Rouge, probably. But I don't have a name."

"Who's the father?"

Hicks started to speak, then clenched his jaw. "I don't have any idea," he answered.

The doctor shrugged and looked down at his clipboard.

"We may have a next of kin on file. Once we find the file, that is. For some reason, her medical records are missing."

"How is she?" Hicks ventured.

"She's lost the baby."

Hicks swallowed. He knew the pain of losing a child. His own wife had gone through two miscarriages before Millie was born. That was one of the many things that made his daughter so precious to him.

Millie came through the swinging double doors. Her blue scrubs were streaked with blood, as was her face. As she peeled the thin plastic gloves from her hands, Hicks could see that there was blood on their insides as well as outsides.

She looked forlorn and wounded, standing there, and Hicks gathered her into a hug. Her hands hovered over his back for a moment, as if reluctant to bloody his shirt, then clutched him with a terrible strength.

"Oh, Daddy," she sobbed. "She never told me she was pregnant."

Still cradling his daughter, Hicks turned to the doctor.

"But she'll be all right?"

"We can't tell without her records. We're trying to figure out what caused the hemorrhaging. Did you know her parents?"

"Yes."

"Was either of them a hemophiliac? Or did they have any kind of problems with bleeding?" the doctor asked.

Hicks racked his brain. Somewhere in the mists of his memory, there was something about the aunt in Baton Rouge, her mother's sister. A rare and obscure medical condition.

Hicks gave up. He was too old to think back that far.

"Maybe. I don't know."

"Well, it's unlikely. This may have been caused by an infection. Or it may just have happened. Sarah seems to have stopped bleeding for the moment. She'll be fine if she doesn't start again."

"Thank God," Hicks said softly.

"I guess you and Millie are next of kin for the moment," the doctor said. "We're running some blood work to see what caused the hemorrhaging. Until we get results, I don't know what you can do."

Millie released her father and stepped back from him.

"You go on home, Daddy."

"Are you all right?" Hicks had seen his daughter tend the brutally wounded, the dying. He had never seen her so overwhelmed.

"I'm fine, Daddy. I'm just so sorry for Sarah. That she never told me. That she was so alone."

"Maybe not as alone as we thought, Millie."

She peered up at him, then nodded. She put one finger to her lips for a fleeting moment, a sign for silence. The gesture left a small mark of blood on her chin.

Hicks nodded back. This was not the time to start spreading more rumors.

"I'll be here when she wakes up, Daddy. You go on home now."

"All right," he agreed. Maybe he could call some of the boys at the station. Dig up the name of Sarah's aunt.

He walked down the hall. Suddenly he was bone tired.

Maybe tomorrow they could start to untangle all this. Tonight he was going to get some sleep.

24 | VISIT

Daniel Wyatt entered Claire's office ashen-faced and out of breath.

Davis sighed and looked up from the vellum sheets on her desk, on which were drawn the floor plans of the surgeon general's office. The administration was confident enough about the full Senate vote to send them to her. Claire made a mental note to herself to keep her own counsel general's office a fair distance from Daniel's. He had a habit of bursting in with bad news instead of calling. She wondered if he thought his phone was bugged.

"She's had a miscarriage," Wyatt said.

"Close the door," Claire ordered softly. Daniel did so.

He sat in her visitor's chair, leaning forward with hands clenched together at his chin.

"I got a call from Lafayette General this morning," he began. "I'm listed as her primary-care physician down there. Apparently, she came in last night, bleeding badly."

"And she's lost the baby?" Claire asked, trying to keep any trace of hopefulness from her voice.

Daniel nodded. "Sarah's preliminary blood work showed some sort of coagulation problem. They don't know exactly what yet. She might have platelet problems, or she might have . . ."

"Taken the drug? You gave her . . . *handed* her the pills at the beach house, didn't you?"

Wyatt swallowed. "RU-486 causes excessive bleeding in about one in ten thousand cases," he recited carefully. "Or maybe she was predisposed. But I never looked at her medical records with this in mind."

His eyes darted back and forth, as if seeking enemies in the room.

"I should have been more careful. I wasn't a very good doctor about all this. That's why physicians aren't supposed to—"

"Daniel," Claire interrupted. "Is she okay?"

"She's stopped bleeding."

"And she's going to recover?"

He thought for a moment, then nodded. "There's no reason to think she won't. Unless she really has some sort of coagulation disorder."

"Like being a hemophiliac?"

"Hemophilia is X-linked and recessive. True hemophilia is limited pretty much to men. But there are other, less well-known, less common disorders."

"Would that have been in her records?" Claire asked. She hoped Daniel didn't ask to see the records. She had burned the copies three days before. Hopefully, her private investigator had returned the originals to Lafayette General by now.

"Probably not," Daniel admitted. "It's the sort of thing that doesn't show up until an accident, or an event like this."

"So this isn't your fault, is it? This is just a one-in-ten-thousand chance."

"No, I suppose not," he admitted. "And she may have just had a miscarriage."

Daniel was calmer now, willing to be led down a reasonable path. Claire leaned back in her chair, finally allowing the wave of relief that had been building in her to wash over her. This unfortunate matter was finally coming to a close.

"The timing, Daniel," she said. "It's too close to be a coincidence."

He looked at her with sudden wariness. "What do you mean?"

"I'm just saying that I don't think this is a natural miscarriage. I think she took the pills."

"But I told her to take the prostaglandin a day or two after the mifepristone," he said. "Her reaction occurred Monday night. She hasn't been back long enough."

Claire shook her head. "She might have taken the mifepristone out at the beach house. Maybe she didn't tell you."

"Why not?"

"She didn't want to tell you."

"What are you saying? She knew what I wanted. I was practically begging her. . . ."

"She didn't want you to see her end the pregnancy. Sarah wanted this to be a private moment. That's why she never showed up at Magley's office."

Wyatt blinked his eyes, stunned for a moment at Claire's words. He put one hand to his brow and began to shake his head slowly.

"But it's what I wanted."

"And it's what she wanted, too, Daniel," Claire reassured him. "But it was her choice, finally. A woman's choice. That's the point of this drug, Daniel, to get the power out of a man's hands."

Wyatt took a deep breath, his head still cocked to one side, as if in confusion.

"She wanted this to just happen, as if it were natural. Sarah realized that this pregnancy was a huge problem, a mistake, a disaster for you both. But because of her upbringing she couldn't admit what she had to do. She hid it from you. Maybe even from herself."

Daniel nodded.

"Just remember," Claire continued. "Your relationship is over now. Just accept this event as you would have a natural miscarriage."

"Which it may have been," Wyatt said weakly. "Possibly."

"Are you going to see her?" Claire asked.

"Yes. I suppose I would go see any patient under these circumstances."

"Good answer," Claire said, pleased that Daniel was finally

accepting the reality of the situation. He had to let go of Sarah Corbett. Some part of him had fallen in love with Sarah—they both knew that—but the time for male midlife-crisis fantasies was over.

"I'll see her this afternoon," he said a bit hesitantly, as if needing confirmation.

Claire nodded. "Just remember, she may not want to talk about what she's done. She may even want you to think that this was natural, simply a coincidence. God's will rather than her own."

"Okay."

"As of now, you have to be completely professional," she explained. "It's time to play doctor, Dr. Wyatt. Not lover, not mentor, not special friend."

She saw Daniel's hesitation before he agreed. But he knew she was right, and he nodded in capitulation. Claire realized with satisfaction that it would be a long time before he doubted her word again or kept secrets from her. If this sad affair had taught Wyatt anything, it was that he could trust Claire Davis to make things right.

"Daniel," Sarah Corbett said, her voice soft and hopeful.

Wyatt had worn his white coat for this visit. He gave Sarah a warm smile and walked to the end of her bed. His eyes swept across her chart without really seeing the data, but outwardly he gave the impression of doctorly reserve.

"How are you, Sarah?"

"Oh, Daniel," she said. "I'm so sorry. I can't believe what's happened."

"It's okay, Sarah," he assured her. He crossed the space between them, stood to the side of her bed. "Miscarriages happen more often than you'd think. People just don't talk about it. As far as we know, this won't affect your chances of having another child."

"I see, Daniel," she answered slowly. "I'm so glad."

Wyatt suddenly saw the glassiness of her eyes, realized

what it meant. Sarah was under sedation. He checked the chart again. Between the sedatives they had Sarah on and her physical weakness caused by blood loss, he doubted anything he said would upset her. Her usually bright face seemed dull and tired.

Wyatt kept up his role of visiting doctor. Maybe this was the kindest way to introduce her to the nature and limits of their new relationship, the blow cushioned by the mild sedatives in her system. Perhaps by the time she went home, their affair would seem like a bad dream.

"I'm very sorry about this, Sarah. I'm very sorry for your loss."

She just looked at him.

"Call me if there's anything you need."

"Of course, Dr. Wyatt," she answered.

"And, since you've lost a lot of blood, you should make sure to get a lot of iron. They're giving you supplements now, but you should watch your diet in the days ahead."

"Oh, Daniel," she murmured. One of her white hands slid slowly across the sheets and up to her chest, and her head fell to one side.

"You're very tired, I suppose. I'll let you rest."

Sarah didn't answer.

As Dr. Wyatt left the room, he felt a crushing weight of guilt settle upon him. This was how he was leaving his lover, Sarah Corbett. In a hospital bed, under the care of strangers. He had seduced her, had impregnated her . . .

And now he was leaving her behind.

Daniel imagined an IV stand trailing him down the hospital halls, a needle in his arm delivering a slow and measured drip of calmness, of quietude, of detachment. He couldn't let the feelings in his heart carry him away now, couldn't afford to run back to Sarah Corbett's side. That was the disaster he and Claire had worked so hard to forestall, yet still it tempted him: Daniel and Sarah together, at the price of everything else he had.

But he made it into the sunlight, and even in late November the heat of the relentless Louisiana sun soaked his medical coat with sweat before Wyatt made it to his car.

And when he closed the Saab's door behind him, he felt free.

Millie Hicks left her father at about 11:00 P.M., sitting in his usual chair and drinking his usual cup of coffee.

Her slow program of weaning Mark Hicks from strong coffee was finally showing results. He was now convinced that fifty-fifty caffeinated and decaf was the real thing, and only complained when Millie went to quarter strength. He'd even managed to fall asleep in his chair last night. She'd found him there in the morning just after her shift had ended, still facing the window as if keeping his vigil on Sarah Corbett's place. But he hadn't seen anything in the last two days; Sarah was still at Lafayette General, and no one had dropped by her house.

Millie had spent much of her last two shifts looking in on Sarah Corbett. Lafayette General wasn't a big city hospital, understaffed and in a constant state of emergency. Another EMT had offered to take her shifts on the truck. Between visits with Sarah, Millie found herself running errands like a resident. It didn't have the charge of being on the front line, but Sarah needed her now.

Sarah had yet to talk much about her miscarriage. The first night, she'd woken up screaming every few hours, until they'd put her on mild sedation. Millie had spent most of her shifts holding her hand while Sarah moaned quietly, repeating again and again, "I'm sorry."

Millie hadn't even dared to mention Daniel Wyatt's name.

When Millie checked in, the night nurse immediately pulled her aside.

"Dr. Arnistead wants to talk to you right away. His office."

Millie went straight to the doctor's office. He was the attending physician who had treated Sarah on her first night in the hospital. Arnistead was only thirty-two, but he was well regarded by the residents and doctors at Lafayette.

Millie braced herself before entering his office. When the hospital finally succeeded in contacting Sarah's aunt in Baton Rouge, they had confirmed a family history of coagulation disorders. Millie just hoped the terrible bleeding hadn't started again.

Dr. Arnistead looked up from a file and gestured for her to sit. He seemed more puzzled than alarmed, and Millie allowed herself a measure of relief.

"We got Sarah's blood work back from New Orleans," he said, shaking his head. "It's not what I expected at all. Just like our workup here, there are disorders in a few of the coagulation factors."

Millie nodded. After the first rounds of testing at the Lafayette lab, Arnistead had sent a sample to Tulane Medical for further work.

"But the other things they found are . . . disturbing."

Millie looked at him questioningly.

"Tulane didn't think that the coagulation anomalies would have accounted for that much bleeding, not without some other factor present," Dr. Arnistead continued. "So they performed some specific assays. I don't like what they found. It seems unlikely that the results could be from natural causes. The hormonal elevation was almost certainly the result of ingesting mifepristone and prostaglandin."

The words swirled in Millie's head for a moment before they found purchase. Then the realization of what the doctor was saying took hold.

"You mean, she took RU-486?"

"That's what it looks like," he confirmed.

Millie sat back. "She had an abortion? I had no idea. But that's legal now, right?"

"Only under a doctor's care. But when Dr. Wyatt came by to look in on Sarah, he didn't mention it. He would have known."

"Maybe she went to an out-of-town doctor," Millie said. "To hide what she was doing."

"Well, she should have had a follow-up exam. That's the law. It looks like somebody dropped the ball." Arnistead lowered his eyes. "Unless she took it herself, without telling anyone."

Millie shook her head. How could Sarah have gotten hold of a controlled drug on her own?

"Have you talked to her? Asked her about this yet?"

Arnistead shook his head. He must have been waiting for Millie to come on shift.

"Let's go, then," Millie said.

Sarah was awake, more lucid than Millie had seen her since she entered the hospital. She smiled thinly when Millie and Arnistead came into her room. Dr. Arnistead ushered away the nurse who'd been taking Sarah's temperature. Millie was glad the other bed in the room was empty.

"Hey there, Sarah."

"It's nice to see you, Millie," Sarah said. "Doctor."

"Sarah, we have the results from your blood work back from Tulane," Arnistead said. "There're a couple of things we don't understand."

"What do you mean?"

"This is a rather delicate matter, Sarah," Dr. Arnistead began. "There's a question of possible malpractice."

"Malpractice?" Sarah's hand went to her belly.

"Nothing to worry about at this point," Millie interrupted. "We just want you to know about possible side effects."

"Side effects of what? I don't understand."

Dr. Arnistead held up the blood-work file. "We found traces of mifepristone and prostaglandin in your blood,

Sarah. Those are the two elements of RU-486, the abortion drug."

Sarah looked at him, blinking her eyes as if she didn't understand.

Millie went to the side of the bed and took one of Sarah's hands. The hand was trembling, and seemed small and cold.

"You didn't do anything wrong, Sarah," she said. "But the doctor who gave you these drugs to take may have—"

"I didn't take any drug!" Sarah suddenly shouted. "I wanted this baby more than anything!"

Millie clenched Sarah's hand. "Listen, Sarah. It's okay if you—"

"It's not okay!" Sarah cried. "I told you, I wanted this baby. I would never do anything to hurt my child!" Sarah tore her hand from Millie and held it to her face. Her body was racked by a low sob.

Dr. Arnistead took a step back from the bed, as if recoiling from a sudden realization. He looked at Millie, and their eyes locked for a moment. Millie shook her head. What was in her mind seemed unthinkable. But she turned back to the weeping woman now curled up in the bed.

"Sarah? Could someone have *given* you this drug... without your knowing about it?"

Sarah's tearful blue eyes shown brightly as she peered up at Millie.

"I don't know?" she said. Then Sarah looked at Dr. Arnistead.

Arnistead took another step backward, shaking his head. Had he heard the rumors? Millie wondered.

"Let me talk to her," she asked him, and he nodded and left the room with a few quick and anxious steps.

Mark Hicks stared out the window at Sarah Corbett's darkened house. He and his family had lived a few dozen feet from the Corbetts for more than twenty years. Sarah had been in this kitchen at least a thousand times, gossiping with

Millie over coffee or lunch. And yet he and Millie hadn't known she was pregnant. Hadn't even been sure if Sarah was having an affair.

It made you wonder, Hicks thought as he looked down the street, what was happening in all those other dark houses. All those gray places, hidden from the harsh light of the Law, where families did terrible things to each other, husbands betraying wives, parents maltreating their children. Lafayette was a good town filled with God-fearing people. But Hicks didn't doubt that every street had its secrets.

The phone rang.

"It's Millie," his daughter's voice announced. She sounded upset.

"What's wrong? Is Sarah okay?"

"Well, she's much better. The bleeding has stopped, and she's awake and alert. But it's not okay. Not at all."

"What's wrong with her?"

"It looks like she took some sort of drug."

"Damn," was all he could say. Good people like the Corbetts, and their daughter was taking drugs.

"But not a recreational drug, Daddy," his daughter continued. "It was an abortifacient. An abortion drug."

"You mean, she did this to herself?" Hicks asked.

"That's just it, Daddy. She says she didn't. So someone else must have."

As Millie explained the blood tests and their irrefutable results, the worried frown on Hicks's face grew deeper. If Sarah was telling the truth, someone had slipped her a drug without her consent. Someone had killed her unborn child. Someone had committed a crime.

Hicks rose, looked toward the bedroom where his gun and badge waited in their bedside drawer. Sarah's pregnancy was no longer hanging suspended in that gray area, that hidden place of private betrayals. It was now a matter for the Law.

"Millie," he asked, "did she tell you finally? Did she say who the father was?"

"I'll give you one guess."

Hicks nodded.

"I'll be right down."

"Daniel Wyatt and I first made love on October second."

Mark Hicks nodded solemnly. There was something almost formal about Sarah's slow confession. Even in her hospital nightgown, she had an air of dignity. The deliberate and grave way in which she chose her words made her seem like a defeated general calmly discussing the conditions of peace after some battle that he had lost.

Sarah also seemed relieved. Hicks's intuition told him that she hadn't told anyone else about the affair. But she must know that rumors were flying now. This was her chance to set the record straight.

"I learned that I was carrying Dr. Wyatt's child four weeks later," she said. "And I told him about it a few days after that."

That kind of formality disturbed Hicks. The way she called the father of her child "Dr. Wyatt" instead of "Daniel." This had been an affair between patient and doctor, he reminded himself. A breach of medical ethics at the very least.

"When was the last time you saw Dr. Wyatt, Sarah?" he asked.

"Last weekend," she said softly. "Sunday night, I guess."

Hicks exchanged a meaningful look with his daughter. She nodded almost imperceptibly. If he had slipped her the RU-486, that was within the time frame to have caused her miscarriage on Monday night.

"You saw him after you got back from the coast?" Millie asked.

"No," Sarah said, shaking her head sadly. "We were at the Gulf Coast together. All weekend, just Daniel and me."

Hicks whistled softly. From what Sarah had said so far, Millie had gotten the impression that the affair had been a short fling. But from the glimpses he'd caught out his window, Hicks knew it was more complicated than that.

"Sarah, do think Dr. Wyatt could have slipped you anything last weekend? Any kind of pill, or powder?"

Sarah shook her head. "He never gave me anything to take, no."

"But did he give you something to drink or eat?"

Sarah's hands clenched, bunching the hospital bedsheets into a worried mass at her belly.

"We . . . we made dinner together, both nights. We drank a bottle of wine. Well, I guess we drank, too."

Millie looked at her father and nodded again. "That's good enough," she said. "The dosage of either stage of RU-486 would be innocuous enough to dissolve in a glass of wine."

"Oh, but Dr. Wyatt would never . . ."

"Sarah, I'm not saying he did or didn't. But we can't know unless we investigate this. And for that to happen, you have to decide to press charges."

"Press charges?"

Hicks let his voice grow firm, setting his jaw as he spoke. He wasn't talking as a friend anymore, but in the voice he assumed as an agent of the Law.

"If Dr. Wyatt gave you a pill without your consent, he's committed a serious crime. He may very well have killed your baby. His own child. In my book, that's a crime. Maybe even murder, but I'd have to run that by the county D.A."

"No, not Daniel," Sarah said. "He's a good man."

"Well, whether he's a good man or not, we've got to find out who did this to you. I'd like to take an official statement."

Sarah turned to Millie, a sudden look of horror in her eyes.

"No!" she cried. "This isn't what I wanted! This is crazy. I just wanted someone to know what happened, to know who the father was. I just wanted someone to *listen*."

Millie gathered Sarah into a hug, shushing her and holding tight.

"It's okay, Sarah. It's fine," she said. Over Sarah's shoulder, her eyes flashed at her father. "Just you wait outside, Daddy."

"Now, Millie, I'm just saying—"

"Outside—now!" she commanded, and Mark Hicks felt himself backing away, propelled out the door and into the hall. He was dumbfounded by the sudden anger in Millie's voice. He was just trying to follow the dictates of the law here. If a crime had been committed, it had to be investigated. More surprising, though, was the effect Millie's words had had on him. It had been a long time since anyone spoke to Mark Hicks that way. Not since his wife had died, in fact.

Hicks leaned against the wall in the hallway, troubled by everything that had happened in the last few weeks.

"Hey, Sheriff! They said you was here."

Hicks looked tiredly up to see Tom Jenkins striding down the hall.

"Hey there, Tom. What brings you to the hospital?"

"We had old Jack Vremy in the car, and he up and banged hisself against the divider. Damn near broke his nose."

Tom's smirk sent an unpleasant feeling up Sheriff Hicks's spine.

"Let's hope old Jack tells it the same way, Tom," he said gruffly.

Tom put two hands up defensively. "It wasn't nothing like that, Sheriff. He just was just leaning up to get his handcuffs straightened and Ray came to too quick a stop. Wasn't nothing but an accident, and Jack'll tell you the same."

Hicks waved the deputy's protests away. The man didn't have a cruel streak that Hicks had ever seen. And both the deputies knew that Mark Hicks didn't tolerate brutality on his force.

"Whatever you say, Tom. I'm just in a bad mood tonight."

"You here to visit Sarah Corbett?" Jenkins ventured. "She all right?"

Hicks nodded. "She's okay. But something pretty unbelievable happened to that little girl."

Tom looked at him questioningly. Hicks realized that he needed to figure out how to proceed with this matter, and in order to do that he needed a cup of coffee something fierce.

"Tom, it looks like this case might require a criminal investigation," Hicks said. "I'm going to need you and Ray to check some things out. But you're gonna have to be real quiet about it."

Tom touched one finger to his lips. "You know me, boss. I hear a lot of things, but I don't repeat 'em."

Hicks nodded. This wasn't like spreading gossip, he reassured himself. This was one lawman talking to another.

"All right, then. Let's go get us some coffee. You aren't going to believe what I'm about to tell you."

27 | DISTRICT ATTORNEY

Riley Mills's phone rang at a quarter past midnight, pulling his attention from a beautifully translucent glass of twenty-one-year-old Springbank. Mills had been drinking Talisker most of the evening, slowly consuming the remaining third of a bottle he'd bought on his last trip to New Orleans. When it was emptied, he felt he needed one more shot, something fiery to take him to unconsciousness. The light brown of the Springbank had been calling to him all night, so Mills decided to indulge himself. The bottle had cost over a hundred dollars of his district attorney's salary, and his outrage at realizing that the precious glass could have been interrupted—at this time of night!—brought an angry demon out of Mills's usually easygoing state of inebriation.

"What is it?" he snapped into the phone.

"Uh, sir? It's Tom Jenkins."

Tom Jenkins? A mental picture of the lanky red-haired deputy enraged Riley Mills further. "What the hell are you calling me for? Do you know what time it is?"

"Uh, yessir. But you're going to thank me for this one."

"Jenkins, you sorry-ass piece of shit, I'm going to thank you not to call me at home. Try my office tomorrow. Hear?"

"Tomorrow might be too late, sir," Jenkins said.

The man's persistence momentarily gave Mills pause. Normally, Tom Jenkins ran like a whipped cur at the first sign of his superiors' displeasure.

"What the hell is it?" he asked, sitting heavily back into his drinking chair.

"Sir, this one's going to put you in the governor's mansion. It's unbelievable."

Mills rolled his eyes, then turned them longingly back to the Springbank. It was so potent, he could smell the stuff from here: dense peat, a salty measure of the sea, and fire.

"The last one was a piece of shit, Jenkins. Remember Augusto Martínez? Fifty kilograms, you said, and we tore his crappy house apart for a five-ounce bag of crack."

"This ain't drugs, Mr. Mills. It's murder."

"The governor's mansion on a murder, Tom?" Mills scoffed. "Who's the victim?"

"A child. An unborn child, murdered by its father, when the mother wanted to bring it to term."

Riley Mills blinked, still scowling, his face showing the beginnings of interest. His mind, never really dulled by whiskey, perhaps just a bit slower than usual, turned the deputy's words over. Maybe there was something here.

"A forced abortion? There a kidnapping angle?" Kidnapping could tip the whole thing to a death penalty.

"Nope. He used that abortion pill. RV-468, or whatever it's called. Done slipped it to her in a glass of wine. But that ain't the best part. Guess who the perp is."

"I know this gentleman?" Riley asked. Through some deep-seated political reflex that no amount of alcohol could dim, a list of local community leaders instantly sprang to Riley Mills's mind. He mentally marked those whom he knew were having affairs, categorizing each by party affiliation and position. Scenarios cascaded through his thoughts, how the power structure would shift were he to take down this or that member of the mayor's staff, the parish police jury, the Lafayette Chamber of Commerce. But the effort soon overwhelmed his tired brain.

"Just tell me, Tom."

He heard Jenkins swallow before speaking. "The suspect is Dr. Daniel Wyatt."

Despite the warm glow of the evening's whiskey in his belly, Riley Mills felt goose bumps break out along his arms.

Dr. Daniel Wyatt, surgeon general nominee, pillar of the community, and foremost abortion advocate in Lafayette Parish. And now murderer of an unborn child.

"Are you sure?" he demanded.

"I got it straight from Sheriff Hicks."

A chuckle, then a laugh escaped Mills's lips. He could see the headlines: ABORTION DOCTOR SLAYS OWN BABY. MURDERER-GENERAL ON CALL FOR BABY KILLING. And, of course, that always popular tabloid sobriquet: DR. DEATH.

Even better, Riley Mills realized, Wyatt was the partner of one Claire Davis, that liberal-bitch-dyke lawyer who had caused so much trouble these last few years. This was Mills's chance to take her and that whole Women's Advocacy Group all the way down. Those harridans had been spreading their phone bank work into all kinds of issues since Wyatt had become a national figure; they'd even taken a few shots at Mills himself during the last district attorney election. A conservative law-and-order candidate like him was always in their sights.

Well, now they would pay.

"Tom, you better be damn sure about this."

"I'm sure as shit. The woman's a patient here at Lafayette General. They done tested her and know she was slipped the drug. And she was a patient of Wyatt's."

Perfect. A breach of medical ethics along with murder.

Mills grabbed his glass of precious whiskey and downed it in one, feeling the fire sear his throat and blaze rampant in his chest.

The governor's mansion? Shoot, that was only the beginning. This wasn't just a means of local revenge, he realized with the sudden clarity wrought by adrenaline. This was a way to embarrass the president of the United States for his liberal appointments. This would rock the administration for the months a trial would last. Mills would be a national figure by the time it was all over.

"There's only one problem, Mr. Mills."

The district attorney pulled himself from his reverie.

"What's that, Deputy Jenkins?"

"The mother—the only witness, if you know what I mean—she's been kind of reluctant to talk to the sheriff. She's still kind of in love or something with this Dr. Wyatt. Doesn't want to get dragged into all of this."

Mills scowled. What kind of woman must she be? he thought. To love the killer of her own child? That just showed what the world was coming to, with abortion pills that made murderers of mothers. Well, that only made the lesson of this case stronger.

"Tom, I believe that self-abortion is still illegal in this state," Mills said sarcastically. "Like it is in every state."

"Uh, yes, sir. I know," Jenkins blathered. "But I'm not sure if Sheriff Hicks is going to go after her. You see, the woman is Sarah Corbett. Her folks was good people, real close to him."

Mills stood, a motion that served to stoke the furnace in his belly, its vapors rising like a plume of fire into his head. He was speechless for a moment until the rush of it tapered off.

"I don't give a damn what Hicks wants," he exclaimed when his equilibrium was fully restored. "We're going to hit this little lady like a ton of bricks tomorrow morning. She'll give us a statement unless she wants to face a charge of self-induced abortion. Maybe I'll throw in manslaughter for good measure."

"Yes, sir! Should I stay here at the hospital?"

"Just go about your business, Tom. Don't give away that you told me anything."

"But I got you a good one, didn't I, Mr. Mills?"

"Yes, Tom, you did. I ain't going to forget it neither. But right now I've got to drink myself some coffee and make a few calls."

Mills hung up. As he lurched toward the kitchen, his wide body brushed against the table that held the bottle of Springbank. The slender column of glass spun on its base for a moment, its circuit as slow as the final gyrations of a child's top, then tipped and fell to the carpeted floor. The improperly replaced cork popped out, and the bottle's precious contents began to gurgle into a brown, spreading stain.

At the kitchen door, Mills turned at the sound and directed a vague, drunken glare at the unfolding disaster. But he smiled, then barked a laugh, and he headed for the coffeemaker. The good Lord giveth, and He taketh away.

Governor? Bullshit.

Riley Mills was thinking U.S. senator . . . for starters.

28 | STATEMENT

"**W**hat do you mean, I can't have a warrant?"

Despite his rage, Riley Mills took time to appreciate the expression on Assistant D.A. Morrisey's face. Whenever he began to yell, Morrisey's jaw worked and her lips disappeared, and she looked something like a cat trying to chew its own tongue off.

"Hicks's affidavit is speculation. The judge said it doesn't amount to probable cause, and he's not going to issue a search warrant involving a doctor that's not letter perfect."

"This is a crime committed by a doctor, dammit!" Mills cried. Watson was an elected judge, but served a parish district that always went Republican. It was practically an appointed seat, and he knew better than to antagonize Riley Mills. How dare he refuse to issue a warrant?

"Not by the doctors treating Corbett at Lafayette General," she explained. "We can't grab her records without her say-so. Especially since we haven't even asked her."

"This might be a conspiracy, you know!" Mills said. "We didn't hear a damn thing from these doctors when they found evidence of a crime. Got it all secondhand."

"Shhh!" came the sharp retort of the duty nurse, who had been glaring in a sleep-deprived way at Mills and his assistants since they'd arrived.

A.D.A. Morrisey dared to smirk. The remonstrances of the nurse had given her unusual courage.

"Fine," she hissed in a stage whisper, "you want to indict every doctor who's treated Sarah Corbett since she's been here, you've got a conspiracy. I'll take that back to the judge."

Mills swore and stalked down the hospital corridor, getting some distance from the team he'd brought with him. They knew better than to follow. He needed a moment alone to think. Here they were, about to burst in on Sarah Corbett, using surprise to their advantage to obtain a statement from her, and they had nothing to surprise her with. If a pet judge like Watson wasn't going to give a simple blood test to them, Mills didn't like his chances with any of this in open court.

The district attorney wondered for a moment if this case was going to be the jackpot he'd thought it would be. The fact that the issue of doctor-patient privilege was looming reminded him of the tricky terrain he was entering. It was a crime committed within a woman's body; that was where the investigation had to start. But one false step, one scream from Sarah Corbett, and every woman in the state would be calling for Mills's blood. He stopped in his tracks and shook his head, clearing the cobwebs left by last night's whiskey.

No. This was no time to be squeamish. He had investigated hideous, disgusting crimes before. Mills had seen what violence could do to the body of a woman. And he had seen what the images of that violence could do to the public, the media, the voters. Once the facts were known, once they'd been released to the public in exactly the right way, the heinousness of this crime would be obvious to all. It was all a matter of properly telling the story.

If he could manage that, it would be Daniel Wyatt's blood they'd be demanding, no matter what Sarah Corbett wanted.

But before he could begin to tell his tale, he had to know the story himself.

Mills noticed a blue binder stuffed full of papers lying abandoned at the edge of an unattended nurses' station. On the top page was written a complicated-looking table of numbers in fine print, covered with an illegible scrawl of annotations in red and black ink.

Mills looked up and down the hall. Despite the traffic of

staff arriving for the early morning shift, no one seemed to be watching him. He lifted the binder from the desk, noting with satisfaction that it was embossed with the Lafayette General seal. He walked confidently back toward his team, a smile on his face.

He waved the binder at Kathleen Morrisey.

"Sarah Corbett's medical records," he said. "At least, that's what we're going to tell her."

Sarah lay in bed, watching the slow creep of the rising sun move the shadows of the blinds' slats. The hospital room had assumed a sort of comforting familiarity, and she was almost sad she would be leaving today. Mostly, she dreaded going home. The dark and lonely house, full of dust and memories, and worse, the resumption of real life, suddenly an empty prospect.

Millie had been called away the night before, only an hour or so into her shift. Sarah had tried to stay awake for her return, but the little pink pills the doctors had prescribed made that impossible. She'd slept all night, dreaming of rowing a boat. The dream was long and uneventful, an endless, unimportant struggle against a tide that thwarted her efforts no matter what direction she tried to take the small craft. And now the sunlight heralded a return to an existence just as pointless, as directionless.

Sarah now wished she'd told the truth to Millie about what had happened at the beach house. But she couldn't even bear to admit that she and Daniel had made love again. It had been so private and special, and had seemed the start of something more real, more lasting than their first weekend.

But now it didn't seem that way at all. It was so humiliating, to have shown up on the Hickses' doorstep, bleeding that way. Like a raped woman, like some cast-off, broken thing.

She closed her eyes and let her hand stroke her belly again.

"I'm so sorry," she said. "I should have protected you. I guess I wasn't much of a mother."

The murmurs and footsteps of a small group impinged upon her consciousness. Sarah opened her eyes sleepily, expecting to see the doctor and his passel of students on their morning rounds. She was surprised to discover a grotesquely fat man, hat in hands over his chest, smiling softly down at her.

"Oh, excuse me," she said. "I guess I dozed off."

"No, ma'am. Excuse me for disturbing you. If I'd known you were asleep, I wouldn't have come by."

"I'm sorry, but I don't—"

The man extended his hand. The fingers were as round and pink as hot dogs, Sarah thought.

"Riley Mills, ma'am."

Still bemused, she offered her hand, and he took it gently and held on.

"It is just so terrible what's happened, Miss Corbett. I can't begin to tell you how sorry I am."

Sarah smiled. She wondered who this man was, and who the silent people with him were. But the words were good to hear.

Riley Mills released her hand from his moist grip and clenched his hat with two angry fists. "An awful thing has happened to you and your baby."

Sarah nodded. "Yes."

"First of all, is there anything that you need . . . May I call you Sarah?"

She tried to focus her mind on the question, but the sedatives made the task impossible. What did she need? Daniel, beside her right now? Her child back? Some means of invisibly eradicating all traces of everything that had happened in the last two months?

"I'm sorry," she said. She had said that a lot in the the last three days, and in her current confusion it came easily to her lips.

"Now, Sarah," the fat man said, easing some of his weight down onto the edge of her bed. It wasn't quite sitting, which his girth and the narrow bed wouldn't have allowed, but Sarah felt a shifting of springs and mattress as if someone had gotten into bed with her. "This is not your fault. You don't need to apologize."

Sarah closed her eyes. Nodded.

"Sarah, something wicked happened to your baby." At the last word, his voice shook a little, and he cleared his throat. "Your poor child never had a chance to live and breathe. To grow up, to have children of its own. You never even got to see your baby, Sarah. And something should be done about that."

Now that her eyes were closed, Riley Mills's voice was pleasant to listen to. It rose and fell in a slow Cajun cadence, compelling her to nod agreement at the end of every sentence. She was tired, always tired now, as if the awful bleeding had carried off some vital spark. It was good to retreat while others acted, spoke, decided.

"Now, I am the district attorney for this parish. That makes it my job to make sure something is done about this terrible crime."

Something about the words shook Sarah from her daze. She opened her eyes.

"District attorney?"

Riley Mills nodded his head solemnly.

"I represent the people of this parish, Sarah. I do the talking for them, I guess. And sometimes that means I speak for people who can't speak for themselves. Like your baby."

The man stood up and gestured to one of the people who had come in with him. Sarah had almost forgotten they were there.

"This here is Bill Harper. He's a stenographer for the parish of Lafayette. I'd like to ask you some questions, while he's listening, so that we can start to find out what happened to you and your poor baby."

Bill Harper smiled at her, and pulled a machine from a battered leather case.

Sarah felt she should say something. She didn't like the sound of all this. But it was easier to let the others keep talking.

"Now, when did you first know you were pregnant, Sarah?" asked Mills.

"About three weeks ago."

"And you knew you were pregnant because a doctor told you so?"

"Yes."

"What was the name of this doctor, Sarah?"

"Dr. Thomas Bartholdt."

Riley Mills looked down at her in puzzlement. He put out his hand, and a woman in the group handed him a thick folder. Mills opened it and leafed through the pages for a moment.

"Now, that's not your usual doctor, is it?"

"Well, no," Sarah said. "But Dr. Bartholdt is my OB-GYN."

Riley Mills planted a fat finger on a page and again nodded.

"Of course. I see now. Now, who was the father of your baby, Sarah?"

"Dr. Daniel Wyatt." The words just slipped out. It felt good to say them out loud, just as it had with Millie. To proclaim them to this representative of the people.

"Now, did Dr. Wyatt know that you were pregnant?"

"Yes. I told him right away."

"What did he say about that?"

"I . . ." she started, then faltered. "He was upset."

"And why was that?"

"Because he was married. Because I was his patient."

"What did he want you to do about your baby, Sarah?"

"He asked if I wanted to . . . get an abortion."

"And did you?"

Sarah's head started to spin a little. This was already her longest, most coherent conversation since coming to the hospital. It was tiring to talk to this man, but it would also take effort to resist his questions.

"No. I decided not to. I decided that I wanted the baby."

"That's right, Sarah. You wanted that baby, didn't you?"

"Yes."

"Now, when was the last time you saw Dr. Wyatt?"

"Sunday," she said softly.

"Where did you see him?"

"We were at a beach house together. We spent the weekend there."

"Now, think carefully, Sarah," Riley Mills said, leaning close. "Did Dr. Wyatt give you anything to drink or eat while you were there?"

"Wait," Sarah said. "I don't think this is—"

"Did he give you something to drink? Some wine?"

"Yes, I suppose," she answered. "He gave me orange juice one morning. But why . . ."

The fat man lifted the blue folder again, scanning the papers. Sarah saw the words "Lafayette Hospital" printed on its front.

"Now, Sarah . . ." Mills squinted at the documents in his hand. "It says here that your doctors found some drugs in your blood. Do you take drugs, Sarah?"

"No, I don't."

"Of course you don't, Sarah. I bet you haven't ever taken drugs. But it says here that this was some kind of abortion drug. A drug that kills babies inside their mother. And this drug was in your bloodstream, Sarah."

Sarah closed her eyes again. This was all wrong. This man didn't know what had gone on between her and Daniel. She wished she could just stop talking, and that the man would go away.

"Have you ever heard of this drug, Sarah?"

She nodded.

"Who told you about it?"

"I don't know."

"You don't know?" he repeated. There was a long, uncomfortable pause that stretched on until Sarah couldn't stand it any longer.

"Maybe I just heard about it. On the news or something."

"Did Dr. Wyatt ever tell you about this drug?"

"I don't know."

"Now, Sarah. Somehow you took this drug. This drug that killed your baby. It says here that it just flushed your baby right out of you. Like taking a scrub brush to dirty dishes."

"I'm sorry, but I don't know," she said pleadingly. "Monday night, I just started bleeding. That's all."

"Sarah. Did you know that this drug is dangerous?"

Sarah's breath caught. She opened her eyes and looked at Riley Mills questioningly.

"Dangerous?"

"Using it is very serious business," Mills said, waving the blue folder again. "A doctor has to be registered to give it to you. And it can kill the mother as well as the child. Did you know that?"

The hot feeling of a sudden flush came over Sarah, almost if she were about to faint. She tried to remember. Daniel hadn't said anything about the RU-486 being dangerous. It had came in a box, marked like regular medicine a doctor would give you.

"Sarah?" Mills pressed her. "Do you use dangerous drugs?"

A wave of shame passed over her. Here she was in this bed, drained of life, being questioned like some drug addict.

What had Daniel Wyatt done to her? What had all her trust earned her? She didn't have a baby anymore, and Daniel wasn't here, either. And now, in her flimsy hospital gown, she had found out that his drugs could have killed her. Daniel Wyatt had taken her for a ride, she decided. Taken her child, her life, and her dignity.

"Okay," she said. "What do you want to know?"

Riley Mills smiled.

"Maybe we should start over, Sarah. Where did you say this beach house was?"

"I want a seal on that house," Mills instructed A.D.A. Morrisey as the team left the hospital. "It's a crime scene. Even Jack Watson should be able to see that. Thank god it's in Vermilion Parish. I'd hate to lose this little old case over an issue of jurisdiction."

"Shouldn't be a problem, sir."

"Now we have enough for a search warrant for Wyatt's offices. Computers, records, everything."

"Yes, sir," Morrisey said.

"And the offices of the Women's Advocacy Group. Let's see what we can do with Claire Davis. Am I missing anything?"

"Well, I'm not sure about Corbett's statement, Riley."

"What do you mean, Kathleen?"

"She might try to go back on some of this. We might have to put some pressure on her again. We don't have anything on her without her records. Not even a charge of self-abortion."

Mills looked at the thick blue folder still clutched in his hand. Sarah Corbett had believed they were the real thing, but the trick wouldn't work with a jury. He paused to drop the folder into a trash can just outside the hospital.

"I don't give a damn about Sarah Corbett. I want Daniel Wyatt."

Kathleen Morrisey nodded, but didn't seem convinced. "It's just that . . . she doesn't want you to hang her man. She's lost her child already."

"By the time I'm through with Daniel Wyatt, won't nobody want him. Case closed. Let's get a warrant for the bastard."

"What's the charge?"

"Let's see. We've got motive, opportunity, and means. And we've got a child, a dead child. What do you think?"

Morrisey looked at him unsurely.

Mills laughed. "Sounds like textbook murder to me."

29 | WARRANTS

Claire stayed home that Friday, wanting to escape the celebration that would erupt at WAG when the full Senate voted. She needed to savor the victory alone, to untangle the conflicting emotions it would bring. Her joy was lessened by the knowledge that she had compromised her principles, thrown them to the wind to overcome the unexpected obstacles that fate had put in her path. Claire knew that she should be horrified by the actions she had taken in this affair. But years of being in the crosshairs, of metal detectors and bomb threats, of half the right-wing politicians in the state using her as a cautionary tale for a woman with too much power, had left her with a sharpened sense of survival. Sometimes her own reactions scared her. When WAG was under attack, when legislation, proposed or enacted, threatened the right of a woman to choose, she acted against her enemies without hesitation or remorse.

As Claire lay in bed, she thought that this was how soldiers drafted in wartime felt when, after months under fire, they awoke one morning and realized that they were no longer farm boys, factory workers, or seminary students—they were killers.

She got up and treated herself to a late breakfast, watching C-SPAN throughout the morning. The legislative work proceeded in a flurry of activity as Congress prepared to recess before Thanksgiving. She observed the proceedings with a sharper eye, now that she and Daniel would be going to Washington. Confirmation hearings weren't the only time the surgeon general was called to testify before Congress; there were reports, crises, advice sought on pending legislation.

Besides, Claire thought, once she got to Washington, there would be many opportunities opening up before her. She wouldn't always be the counsel general for Dr. Daniel Wyatt. Perhaps one day she would seek confirmation before the Senate herself.

She punched her remote control to bring up the time on the television. The Senate was running thirty minutes behind the schedule the administration liaison had sent her yesterday. But at this rate they'd still confirm Daniel before breaking for the day in the early afternoon.

The phone rang.

"Davis."

"Claire, this is Andrea Hutchinson."

Claire sat up in bed. Hutchinson was the administration's point person on the nomination. The woman's voice sounded strained.

"Yes."

"There's a problem."

No, Claire silently mouthed. Not now.

"Anything major?"

"We're not sure. The Republican leadership is postponing the vote."

"But the session's almost over. It'll be weeks if they don't vote before adjournment."

"I know. And the outgoing SG is leaving office next week. Frankly, we don't know what's going on. But it sounds like they've got something."

"Like what?"

"Something big. Now, Claire, you've been a pleasure to work with. A lot of us thought that Dr. Wyatt was a risky nomination, but you prepared him for the hearing perfectly."

"Thank you," Claire said, trying to keep the rising panic she felt from her voice.

"And we're willing to support Daniel if there's a problem.

We're not going to bail out on him, his support from women's groups is too strong for that. But we need to know what's going on."

Claire's mind spun. She very much wanted to prove herself to Hutchinson. And if she could handle this crisis, keeping the White House happy while she forestalled any problems, her star would rise. If only she knew exactly what the holdup was about.

But what to say? The trick was to keep this manageable. Should she admit the affair with Sarah? No, that was too much. Perhaps, Claire thought, she should say she'd heard rumors of an affair, but didn't believe them. God, but what if it was something else entirely? She didn't want the administration sniffing around Lafayette during what could be weeks between now and the confirmation, looking for a Sarah Corbett. Things were still too sensitive.

The whole stall could be a Republican trick, anyway, a last attempt to get a man they had desperately sought to find grounds against to reject.

After a few seconds of frantic thought, Claire decided to hold the fort.

"I wish I knew what the problem was, Andrea," she said. "I've been over Daniel's life story about a hundred times in the last two months. I wish I had something to throw you. But he's just not the kind of guy to have secrets."

"So you're in the dark, too?"

"Absolutely."

"Is Dr. Wyatt in?"

"No, Miss Davis, he left early today. He's probably home by now."

"Thanks." Claire hung up. She was still dressing as she spoke, cursing herself for taking the morning off. The holdup on the Senate vote felt like retribution for her self-indulgence.

She applied her makeup quickly, trying to remain calm. Should she call Sarah at the hospital, find out if she'd been talking? No, Claire decided. Any contact with Sarah Corbett now would just complicate things. If Daniel's affair was blowing up, then for the record she didn't know Sarah.

If only the vote had been yesterday, she lamented.

The phone rang again.

"Damn," she said, then answered.

"Claire!" It was Molly Rovine, the receptionist at WAG.

The panic in the woman's voice sent a chill through Claire. "What is it?"

"There are these men here," Molly said. "Sheriff's department. They have a search warrant."

"What the hell?" Claire Davis cried.

"They just showed up. They're about to start. What should I do?"

Claire took a deep breath. Her anxiety, her nerves, her fear for Daniel all evaporated. The fighting reflexes honed in over a decade of Louisiana politics responded instinctively and instantly. She placed the phone down for a moment as her fingers leaped to grab her keys, pager, cigarettes. Whatever this was about, someone had just made a big mistake.

She lifted the phone to her mouth and said carefully, "Molly, if they have a warrant, you can't stop them. But let me talk to the officer in charge."

A few moments later, the voice of a policeman came on the phone.

"This is Claire Davis. I'm the head of WAG and a lawyer. I've instructed Molly to cooperate. However, I must advise you that there are attorney-client-privileged documents in the office that you have no right to seize."

The young-sounding officer began to speak, but Claire interrupted.

"I'm on my way over. I'll be there in a few minutes. Perhaps it would be better if you waited until I arrived."

She hung up without waiting for an answer.

When Daniel Wyatt arrived at his home, Ellen and Dexter were on the front porch. At the sound of the car, Dexter looked up from some metal construction that glimmered in the high, early afternoon sun. The child waved at his father, then turned back to the interlocking arms of aluminum and brightly colored plastic, then looked at Daniel again, as if a little unsure where to direct his attention. Wyatt watched Ellen observe this moment of childish indecision, and smiled as, with a few words, she urged Dexter to rise and run toward his father.

Wyatt scooped the boy up. Dexter was the last of his children he could lift into the air without eliciting protest. He spun the boy once, then carried him back to the porch at a trot. Dexter extended his arms to transform his journey into a flight, making a jet engine sound through pursed lips.

Ellen took a step down to kiss Daniel as he reached the porch, and immediately Dexter's arms waved for her. The two parents transferred the child, and Ellen sat him down with a grunt of complaint. He went back to his metal creation, sifting through the unused pieces for some new extension.

With every unspoken action in this simple coming-home ritual, Wyatt felt his heart grow larger. He was glad he'd left the office early today, not even bothering to watch the Senate vote. The other two kids would be home soon, and the weekend seemed to stretch out as long as summer before him.

His pager went off.

Wyatt shook his head and smiled at Ellen. When he glanced at the little box and saw Claire's office number, he returned it to his belt. He had no intention of answering the call, wanting the wordless magic of his return home to continue. Daniel Wyatt felt as if he were home for the first time in two months. The simple familiarity of it, the rightness of everything, moved him as nothing in life ever moved him before.

Besides, the purpose of Claire's page was probably just to congratulate him on his final confirmation. And since the committee's endorsement, victory in the full Senate was a foregone conclusion. Wyatt decided to celebrate the simple joys around him.

He reached out and touched Ellen's arm, and she drew him in for a kiss.

The two cars pulled up together in front of the house, the tires of one of them scrunching against the curb. Dexter saw them first, making a surpised little noise as their doors opened and disgorged five men in uniform and one in a suit and tie. Daniel pulled himself from Ellen's embrace and turned to face them. Sheriff Mark Hicks was leading the group across his lawn.

"Hey there, Mark," Wyatt said, not sure what to make of this unexpected intrusion.

"Dr. Wyatt, Ellen," Sheriff Hicks greeted them with a touch of his hat brim. Then he faced Ellen. "Ma'am, do you mind if I talk to your husband for just a minute?"

"Not at all, Sheriff," Ellen answered, and gathered Dexter up. The boy protested for a moment, but was placated by some promise that Wyatt couldn't hear. Wyatt's ears were buzzing, his vision losing focus at its edges. He couldn't imagine why the sheriff had come.

"Dr. Daniel Wyatt," Sheriff Hicks said, his voice suddenly flat and mechanical, "I have here a warrant for your arrest."

Two of the deputies moved to either side of the stunned doctor. They took his elbows in firm grips.

"Arrest?" Daniel was stunned speechless.

There was a flash of silver to one side, the sun catching metal in a deputy's hands. Wyatt looked down. The jingle of handcuffs confirmed what his eyes couldn't believe.

"The charges are furnishing medicine without a medical necessity, and murder in the first degree."

"Murder?" Wyatt cried. He felt the cool rings of the hand-cuffs slip around his wrists, the short, metal rasp as they contracted. "Mark, what is this?"

"Dr. Wyatt, I have to inform you of your rights. You have the right to remain silent . . ."

Somehow, the familiar words of the Miranda rights struck Wyatt with awful force. On television and in movies, they signaled the apprehension of the criminal, the end of the

...e, the shift from police detection to courtroom maneu-
...ring. And, as if they were a magic spell, the intoning of the
familiar words rendered him powerless, deflated, voiceless.

By default, Daniel Wyatt opted for his right to remain
silent.

They led him to one of the cars and protected his head as
they pushed him awkwardly into the backseat. He looked
back at his house searchingly, and glimpsed Ellen in one of
the windows, watching her husband be arrested as a criminal. Her face was expressionless, and he saw her speaking un-
hurriedly into the phone.

Then the car door closed.

Before he was driven away, the remaining three deputies
and the man in the suit arrayed themselves before the door
of his home and knocked. A piece of paper was presented to
Ellen, another ritual performed, and the men filed in.

They were going to search his house as well.

And Daniel Wyatt realized that nothing would be private
for him again. Anywhere. Ever.

"Your warrant doesn't cover these records, Deputy."

"Ma'am, you'll have to talk to that lady over there," the
spotty-faced boy said to Claire Davis for the tenth time.

"Well, just you leave them here, and I'll do that." She
smiled at the boy with the expression of forced politeness
that seemed to render him paralyzed with terror, placing a
firm hand on his bony shoulder, and turned to approach Assistant District Attorney Kathleen Morissey again.

"Kathleen."

"What now, Claire?"

"Those boxes over there contain records of rape victim
assistance services. When WAG volunteers meet victims at
the hospital, they keep written and sometimes photographic
records of medical conditions with the highest confidentiality. If those aren't covered by patient privilege, I don't know
what is. If your men so much as open one of them, the head-

line on this tomorrow will be 'Police Paw Through Pictures of Battered Women.' A national story, I would guess."

"Now, Claire," Morrisey answered, a tone of ironic deference in her voice. "You and I both know that won't be the headline tomorrow. The headline tomorrow is going to be about Daniel Wyatt. Only way you're going to change that would be to shoot the president, I reckon."

Davis glared at her adversary. This search was all a pointless fishing expedition. Did D.A. Mills really think she would leave anything they would want lying around the WAG offices? It was almost an insult. Claire never left anything to chance. She had taken care of this unthinkable possibility the moment Sarah Corbett had headed toward the beach house to meet Daniel. The remaining RU-486 was long gone, destroyed. Still, Claire felt it was her duty to keep WAG's records out of Mills's grubby hands. There was no telling how a megalomaniac like him might use other people's secrets. Besides, she didn't want WAG's work to come to a screeching halt.

Morrisey looked the boxes over and took a picture with the Instamatic she had brought. "All right, I'll take your word for it on these records. But it'll be an obstruction charge if you're lying."

Claire waved the comment off and walked back to her office.

"Did he call?" she asked her secretary.

The woman shook her head.

"Damn." Why wasn't Daniel answering his pager?

Claire restlessly moved through the offices, stopping to upbraid two deputies who were mishandling a computer. Damn, Riley was really out to get her. Even if his case fell apart, this search had already caused thousands of dollars' worth of damage.

"This warrant doesn't cover general records, boys," she said. "Just anything to do with Dr. Daniel Wyatt."

"Well, how do we know what kind of records are on this computer, ma'am?" one asked.

"I'm telling you."

"You'll have to talk to—"

"A.D.A. Morrisey, I know," Claire finished. She went to find the Assistant D.A. again, contemplating a one-day lifting of the ban on smoking in the WAG offices.

Suddenly her eyes caught two deputies in the tech room, and she stopped in her tracks. The two men were carefully packing a set of small magnetic tapes into a cardboard box.

"You can't have those," she said with a dry voice.

"Miss Davis, these are recordings of phone calls. The warrant specifically includes all phone records and recordings."

He was right. It was one part of the warrant that was unambiguous. And the tapes in the deputies' hands were definitely the backup tapes from the phone bank. The tapes were created automatically every night when the control board cleared itself. Claire felt her heart sink. On one of those tapes was Daniel's conversation with Sarah Corbett, which had occurred the night before she was to have had an abortion. Claire struggled to remember what the two had said exactly. God, Daniel didn't even know he'd been recorded. Claire had never told him how she knew about the affair.

Where was Daniel, anyway? Morrisey wouldn't answer her questions about the D.A. office's plans for him. Were they looking for an indictment? Did they have enough to arrest? She couldn't imagine that they had anything but rumors and supposition fueled by Riley's political ambitions.

But with the tape recording of that conversation, they would have a lot more. Fortunately, it was hidden among thousands of calls. Perhaps they wouldn't have the manpower to listen to all of them. With that thought, Claire had an idea.

She went back to the deputies, who were waiting obediently by the computer.

"Take it," she said.

"Okay, ma'am."

"Go ahead and take them all. In fact, I've got some more computers you should get."

"Ma'am?"

Claire led the unsure deputy to the tech room and pointed at the stack of old computers that she had never brought herself to throw away.

"Dr. Wyatt used one of those in the last few months. I can't remember which. You'd better take them all. Oh, and those boxes of records over there, too." She gestured to the battered women files she had kept Morrisey from taking a few minutes before.

The deputy raised his eyebrows, but set his men to work collecting the records.

Claire piled on more and more, withdrawing every objection to the search's parameters she'd made so far. If they wanted evidence, they could have it. Enough to choke on. By the time she was through, the taped conversation between Sarah and Daniel would be a needle in a haystack.

"Claire!"

It was her secretary, waving at Claire from outside her office.

"It's Ellen Wyatt."

Claire crossed the room at a run, tore the phone from the woman's hand.

"Ellen?"

"They've arrested Daniel."

"Good God. For what?"

"I don't know. They just came to the house and—"

"All right. I'll be downtown in a few minutes. Don't worry, Ellen, I'll handle this. Daniel's going to be fine."

As Claire Davis moved through the WAG offices, the figures of deputies and shocked volunteers on either side of her turned into a blur. Daniel, pillar of the community, surgeon general nominee, healer, had been arrested. There was only one explanation.

Sarah Corbett had talked.

Claire reached the doors of the building and whis through the metal detectors, which the deputies switched off when they arrived. The sight of the park outside filled her with new feeling of dread. The realization of how bad this situation had become finally hit Claire Davis with full force.

Reporters filled the walkway outside the building.

Dozens of them.

30 | MEDIA CIRCUS

"Of course, there is no truth at all to these charges. They are a blatant and reprehensible attempt by the right wing to take political revenge on a pillar of this community. The anti-choice forces in this country have proclaimed that Dr. Daniel Wyatt is their mortal enemy. Once they discovered that they couldn't win on the Senate floor, they chose to attack him personally with these outrageous charges. This is a witch hunt, pure and simple."

Father David John watched the screen of his television with growing disbelief. Could it be true? As hard as he had fought against Daniel Wyatt's confirmation, he found it hard to believe that the burgeoning story could really be the truth. A father taking the life of his unborn child through subterfuge, reaching into the womb of a young woman to commit murder.

What if this Corbett woman were really telling the truth? To think that such a monster could have been the surgeon general of the United States.

Father David crossed himself.

The image of Claire Davis on the television was replaced by that of a newscaster. Dr. Wyatt would be arraigned tomorrow in Louisiana. He released a deep sigh. Lafayette, was it? He looked out of his window at the snow that had just begun to fall over New York City. At least it would be warm down there. Perhaps his rheumatism would clear up, Father David thought. Catholics for Life might be encamped in Louisiana for a long while.

He shook himself from the thoughts and took a step toward the phone. He had to get the troops assembled.

Before Father David's hand could reach the receiver, the phone rang.

"Are you watching?" his second-in-command's excited voice asked.

"Yes, I am."

"It's going to be a real media circus down there, Father David."

"I know, Peter."

"Can you imagine? A father taking his own child's life, without the consent of the mother? It's a criminal abortion that no one can possibly defend."

Father David listened to his lieutenant's impassioned words indulgently. Peter was so very intense. The younger man's fury intensified whenever he wasn't actively fighting for the righteous cause. Father David let him rant; it was good for him to get it all out.

David alone among the leadership of Catholics for Life knew of Father Peter's past: before he had seen the light, Peter had been a member of a racist Christian organization, one that advocated the use of violence to bring about its goals. Despite his new understanding of Scripture, he was still an overly aggressive young man.

Finally, Peter seemed to run out of steam.

"All right, then," Father David said. "Start working the phone tree. We'll be headed down late tomorrow."

"Yes, Father!"

David smiled at Father Peter's enthusiasm. It was God's will that Peter rejoin the mainstream Church. Sometimes passion was necessary. It was good to have a young man working with him, for whom the fight was still a fierce battle of good against evil. Not that Father David had lost his faith in the righteous cause. No, abortion was still the foremost abomination in the developed world, a hideous blight on creation. But in his old age, he could no longer muster the energy that Peter brought to the war each and every day.

"Gaudeamus igitur!"

"Yes, Peter," Father David said. "Into battle again."

The old priest allowed himself another smile.

Peter O'Keefe was a good man.

"This is a witch hunt, pure and simple. And we have no intention of backing down. Despite any reports to the contrary, we are not withdrawing from the nomination. Daniel Wyatt will be the next surgeon general of the United States of America."

Lynn Neuman watched Claire Davis's performance with admiration, but shook her head for the sake of those watching the television with her.

"What a disaster," Neuman said flatly.

"Fuck, I worked the phone banks for that guy, trying to get people to call their senators," one of her assistants lamented.

"Do you think it's true?" another asked.

"No way. It's some kind of right-wing plot," opined a third.

"That's what you said about the blue dress."

"That whole *thing* was a right-wing plot."

Lynn Neuman turned to the group of women who had gathered in her hotel room to watch the exploding story and silenced them with a look.

"Here's what I learned from my years in politics," Neuman said. "We have to assume the worst. Sure, be the voice of reason at first; presumed innocent until proven guilty. But we have to be prepared to hang this guy if any of this turns out to be true. And every time any reporter asks for the official line, start with these words: 'If this is true, it's one of the most heinous crimes I can imagine.' Make sure that's the first sentence from your mouth."

Neuman's sharp eyes surveyed her lieutenants, the young and telegenic spokespeople for Women for Choice. In a way, it was fortunate that they were all together at this disastrous moment. Normally, these women would be scattered across the country. But this week they had been brought together for a conference in Boston.

"Don't let the right wing express more indignation on this than us," Neuman continued. "Keep reminding the press that we are not pro-abortion, we are pro-choice. And it's a *woman*'s choice we're talking about. No man, whether he's a father, a governor, a senator, or even the fucking surgeon general, gets to make this choice for us. Ever. Period."

"But what if Wyatt's been railroaded?" someone asked.

"Then we make him the martyr of the century. If he's been framed, no one will remember that we didn't stick up for him. And frankly, that's not the scenario I'm worried about. If this is true, he'll be the poster boy for making RU-486 illegal again. And keeping it that way for the next hundred years."

A distressed murmur went through the room. Lynn Neuman had seen this before. There was no more difficult a crisis in a life in politics than the one that followed the discovery that a man you had worked hard for has betrayed you. But it happened every time, all the way back to the suffragists who had worked for emancipation, and had been assured that once the slaves had their rights, women were sure to follow. Sixty years later, of course.

But there was no time for shock or dismay. The WFC conference was wrapping up tomorrow, with Lynn Neuman giving the keynote address. It would be a good opportunity to make sure the rank and file stayed in line.

"My God, you're right. We've got to get back to Washington."

Neuman lit a cigarette. Nonsmoking room, her ass.

"We're not going to Washington." She pointed her cigarette at one of the women. "Get us flights to Lafayette. We're leaving tomorrow, an hour after the keynote."

Again, a murmur of surprise.

"Every right-wing, anti-choice nut in the world is going to be there within a few days. Do you think we're going to let them have all the fun? Let's go kick some Cajun ass."

A few smiles answered her fighting words. Good. For the moment, this disaster hadn't killed their spirit. This circus was going to galvanize national opinion, and WFC had to be in the middle of it. Every disaster was an opportunity, as long as you kept your head.

Lynn Neuman dismissed her troops with a wave of her hand.

"Now get going. I have a speech to rewrite."

". . . We are not withdrawing from the nomination. Daniel Wyatt will be the next surgeon general of the United States of America. I'm sure the Senate of the United States can see through false accusations motivated by the worst sort of partisan politics. Reason will prevail."

Agent Eduardo Costilla shook his head with amazement. Claire Davis certainly wasn't going down without a fight. His eyes traced the line of her jaw with quiet longing. A formidable woman. She might even have a chance of saving Wyatt, he thought. She'd definitely distracted a certain FBI agent from finding out the truth about Sarah Corbett.

Costilla sat back as the television's image returned to the anchor. He'd caught Claire's curbside performance three times now on CNN.

The FBI agent surveyed the walls of his study, which were decorated with pictures of crime scenes, bombed clinics, vandalized hospitals. No pictures of friends or family, he noted ruefully. Costilla felt as listless as the corpses who stared out at him from the walls.

Assistant Director Richards was not going to be happy that he'd missed this tidbit about Wyatt. Not happy at all. But behind his annoyance at knowing he'd been had by Claire Davis, Costilla was allowing himself to feel a measure of anticipation.

Lafayette, Louisiana, was about to become a media circus of unbelievable proportions. Crazies from left, right, and center were about to descend upon the small city, which for the next few months would surely be a lightning rod for the whole abortion issue.

Eduardo Costilla smiled. There was no way his shooter could resist a magnet like that. He and his team had to get down to Louisiana. The only trick was convincing A.D. Richards.

He picked up his phone, speed-dialed Agent Samuels's home number.

"Yo, Costilla," she answered. "You watching?"

"You bet, Chaos."

"How'd you miss this one, Cost?"

"I almost got it, Chaos. But it drove away in a green Cadillac."

"Too bad."

Costilla smiled. "But I have a feeling this little do in Lafayette might be irresistible to our man. How do you like Cajun food?"

"The hotter the better."

"So let's change our search parameters a bit. We've got to convince Richards that out shooter will be down there."

"Way ahead of you. But I'll tell you, chat about this Wyatt guy is burning up the boards. I'm going to need some pretty specific terms, or we're going to be getting about a million hits an hour."

"You'll know it when you see it, Chaos. I have faith in you."

She made a grumbling noise. But already Costilla could hear the clattering of a keyboard on her end of the line.

"Let us rejoice, Costilla."

"See you tomorrow, Tabitha."

He hung up, turning his attention back to the news. Already, the pundits were weighing in. A panel had convened on *Crossfire*, and even with the sound off, Costilla could identify the feminist, the Operation Rescue spokesman, the Republican senator, the medical expert, and the defense-attorney-turned-talking-head.

It had started.

Costilla reached for the remote to bring the sound back up, but the phone rang again. The Caller ID told him the bad news. Assistant Director Richards, demanding an explanation.

Agent Costilla groaned, and reached for the phone.

31 | PRISONER

When Claire Davis had gone off to college at seventeen years of age, she had insisted on taking her cat with her. The pet couldn't fly in the aircraft's cabin, and was relegated to the nether regions of the plane, boxed like so much freight. Sadly, the one piece of her luggage that went astray on that traumatic day was the one containing Thurgood.

The cat eventually arrived at JFK Airport, where Claire had encamped to wait for him, twelve hours late. The drugs that were meant to ensure a quiescent trip had worn off by then, and Thurgood had been trying to escape his small cage. Two claws were torn free from one paw and blood and urine fouled the carrier. With his usually fluffy fur matted and wet, Thurgood looked half his normal size.

When this pathetic creature was presented to Claire by nervous airline officials, she took one look at it and declared that they had found the wrong animal. This was not her cat. Only the metal tag on his collar finally convinced Claire that this feline wreck was indeed her Thurgood.

When Davis finally located her client, Daniel Wyatt, in the labyrinth of holding cells beneath Lafayette Central Station, she found herself, at least momentarily, back in that terrible situation. Despite the familiar gray hair and the usual unfashionably wide tie, she was unable to recognize the man who for more than a decade had been her partner. He looked wrung out, defeated, abject, and his eyes were dull, as if some long-broken homeless man had been hired to perform some shabby impersonation of Daniel Wyatt. He looked like a lost cat.

For a long moment, she was unable to say anything. An unfamiliar emotion arose in her, precluding speech, thought, and even her desire for revenge on Riley Mills. Claire Davis felt only regret.

"Daniel," she finally managed. "I'm so sorry. Sorry that I ever suggested any of this."

Wyatt's eyes rose from the floor to look at her, and he shook his head slowly, like some weary animal conserving its final supplies of energy.

"No. Everything that's happened has been my fault. From that first weekend onward. I betrayed you. I betrayed everyone."

Claire closed her eyes. She refused to hear this. "Daniel, I should never have suggested the RU-486. That was a mistake. Sarah wasn't ready. I should have known she'd pull something like this."

"Claire . . ."

"She was obviously unstable. She might have been fine if she'd just aborted normally, hadn't wound up in the hospital. And if only Riley Mills hadn't gotten hold of her."

Claire took a step closer, put one hand on a bar of the cell, and looked around. They'd placed Wyatt in his own cell; he and Claire were a hundred feet away from the prisoners who had whistled at her as she'd been led down, and the policeman who had escorted her had backed off. They were alone in this godforsaken hole in the ground. Even if the police were recording this, it was covered by attorney-client privilege, she reminded herself.

But still, she whispered her next words.

"She did take the pills herself, right? You didn't slip them to her?"

Wyatt looked up at Claire with a vacant stare.

"I'm sorry. I'm sorry," she said, covering her face with one hand. "I should never have asked that. It was a crazy question. You would never—"

"Don't apologize, Claire," he said. "Don't apologize for anything. Just tell me, how long am I going to be here?"

By an act of sheer will, Claire turned back to her client. It was time to stop being foolish, she told herself. Act like a lawyer, dammit.

"Not long, if I have anything to do with it," she stated flatly. "We won't be able to see a judge tomorrow, or Sunday either. So you're spending the weekend here. But you'll be out after arraignment Monday."

"Monday?" Wyatt cried.

"You're the victim of a typical prosecution ploy. Being arrested on a Friday. But we should be able to make bail quickly."

"How much will it be?"

"With your connections in the community? We'll be able to keep it manageable. One good thing about being a national figure, you're hardly a flight risk."

Pain crossed his face, and Claire winced.

"I'm sorry, Daniel. I shouldn't have said that."

"No," he said, shaking his head, "I should have realized. Thank God there's no CNN to watch down here. But I was thinking of Ellen." Wyatt dropped his head into his hands.

Poor Ellen, thought Claire. The slightest rumor was like acid in the face to this woman, and here she was, the cheated-on wife in a national soap opera.

"I'll go see her, Daniel. I'll make sure she has everything she needs."

He nodded mutely. His back straightened, and some of his old strength seemed to return to his eyes. Claire decided to tell him the rest. "So here's the bad news. Judge Thibodeaux has decided that this case is of national interest, you being the surgeon general nominee and all."

"Am I still?" Wyatt asked in wonderment.

"Damn straight. The White House is privately asking for you to withdraw. Not an admission of guilt, of course, just until things get sorted out. Yeah, right. I told them to fuck themselves, for the moment."

"Whatever you think is best," Wyatt answered. "But what's the bad news?"

"I checked with the court clerk. As your case is of national interest, Judge Thibodeaux's allowing television cameras into the courtroom."

"Damn," Wyatt exclaimed. "So what am I up against, in the long run?"

"According to the news, they have the packaging for the RU-486. Apparently, the box was found discarded in a trash can close to the beach house, but not on the property. There's a slight chance that it won't be admissible, as it was found outside the area covered by the warrant. If the RU-486 packaging is thrown out, they've got next to nothing."

Daniel nodded agreement. He'd learned enough about the law during his training as a doctor to know that.

"But if the box is admitted, we may have trouble. Even if we get the jury to understand that Sarah took the drug herself, they'll probably believe that you provided her with it. Now, I can argue that RU-486 has been approved, et cetera, and is safe. But you didn't go by the book, and unfortunately, Sarah was a one-in-a-million bad reaction. I'm not hopeful, unless we can exclude so much evidence that the jury doubts that the affair happened at all."

"I won't deny the affair," Wyatt announced.

"You may not have to," Claire answered. "If this comes to trial, one of our most difficult decisions is whether or not you'll take the stand. But we won't face that choice until we see the prosecution's evidence."

He seemed surprised for a moment, then a look of resignation came over his face. It was something that clients had to overcome, the realization that they were no longer in control of their own destiny. Once they were inside the maw of the justice system, their fate was in the hands of their lawyer.

"Unlawful practice of medicine," Wyatt said sadly.

"Furnishing medicine without a medical necessity," Claire corrected. "That's hardly likely to get you sent to prison,

Daniel." Then she realized his meaning. With a guilty verdict on that charge, he would almost certainly lose his medical license. A healer no more.

But the resigned expression on Wyatt's face faded, became something darker still.

"But, Claire, I'm facing murder. I can't believe this."

"That charge is ridiculous, Daniel. That's also for the press. Mills is bucking for the governor's office, and he thinks a trip to the Supreme Court will get him there."

"The Supreme Court?"

"Try to understand, Daniel. Even if the jury believes that you drugged Sarah Corbett against her will, that's an abortion, and in the first trimester. Now, if a mother can abort her child at that stage legally, it can't be murder if the father does it. In order to get a murder conviction to stick, Mills would have to get a reversal of *Roe* v. *Wade*."

Wyatt's eyes widened in horror. "You mean, this case could bring down *Roe*?"

Claire gripped the iron bars with both hands.

"Not a chance, Daniel. I'm going to pound that point from the opening statements on. If you are convicted of murder, then precedent will be set that every woman in this country who gets an abortion is a murderess. If I have even one pro-choice juror, you can kiss that charge good-bye."

"Kiss it good-bye?" Wyatt asked. "My marriage is already destroyed, and now I'm facing a murder charge. None of this is just going to disappear, Claire."

She sighed.

"Now try to get some sleep," Claire ordered. "I'm going to meet with the district attorney right now. I know it sounds crazy, but try to relax over the next two days. I don't want you looking like shit for your arraignment. It'll be your first time in this case in front of the cameras."

Wyatt smiled ruefully. "But not the last."

"No. Not the last," she agreed. "Just remember, don't say anything about the case to anyone but me; our conversations are privileged. If you have visitors, just assume it's being recorded. And watch out for other prisoners. They'll cooperate with the prosecution in order to get a lighter sentence, even just better food."

He looked at her fearfully. Claire realized that her warnings were scaring him. Well, he had to know.

"And don't worry. We're going to win this case," she added.

Suddenly Daniel stood and grasped her hands through the bars.

"You know, I didn't do it, Claire. I really didn't. Sarah must have taken the pills herself. I would never have given her anything against her will."

The pleading in his eyes was terrible, they burned like a drug addict denied his fix. Claire bit her lip to keep from showing the pain of his iron grip.

"I know, Daniel. I know," she said.

He released her, and sat heavily back down. Claire Davis turned and walked away from the cell, not looking back. Her mind still spun from the ferocity of his proclamation of innocence, his desperation to be believed.

She only wished she could convince him that she really did believe him.

District Attorney Riley Mills had the pleasure of seeing Claire Davis enter his office, her face distorted with anger and frustration.

Hidden for a moment in his crowd of staff members, he watched Davis storm toward the receptionist. Her face was flushed, as if she'd run the whole way here, and her eyes were bright with a kind of animal fury. That Claire Davis was quite a woman, Mills found himself thinking. It would be a joy to destroy her and Wyatt together.

She reached the receptionist and began making demands. The man seemed to crumble under the ferocity of her attack. Mills stepped forward and tapped her on the back.

"Excuse me, Counselor Davis. But are you here about a Dr. Daniel Wyatt, by any chance?"

At the sound of his voice, Claire turned to face Mills with hatred in her eyes. "This is outrageous. Do you think you can prosecute morality?"

"This is not about morality, Ms. Davis. Taking a life is murder, as I see it. I'm prosecuting a crime to see that justice is done."

"You have an agenda, Riley," Davis spat, "and it doesn't have anything to do with justice. Just by bringing these charges, you're destroying a man's life."

"The only life destroyed was that of Sarah Corbett's baby," he countered. "And that's murder."

"That charge is absurd," Davis argued. "Listen, let's at least agree on a reasonable bail. So my client doesn't have to spend the weekend in jail."

"I'm going to object to any bail being set. This man's a menace to society."

Claire Davis shook her head in disbelief. "You know Wyatt's not a flight risk. And obviously he's not a danger to anyone."

"Make your arguments to the judge," Mills said flatly.

"I will. And I'll move that all the charges against my client be dropped. You haven't got enough to hold him."

Riley Mills looked into Claire Davis's eyes malignly and let his southern accent reach its maximum drawl.

"Oh, but I believe I do, Miss Davis." He raised one hand to tick off his points. "I have a statement from Sarah Corbett, explaining Dr. Wyatt's unceasing demands of her to get an abortion against her will, and detailing their assignation at a remote beach house. We have eyewitnesses that put Daniel Wyatt on the scene down at the beach house, and other witnesses who have seen Corbett and Wyatt together on several occasions here in Lafayette. I have traces of an abortifacient drug in Sarah Corbett's bloodstream."

"That's nothing," Davis said. "Maybe they had an affair, and maybe they even discussed whether Sarah should exercise her legal right to an abortion. But what difference does it make if they went to a beach house or not? Sarah Corbett could have given herself that RU . . . whatever drug it was. Anyone could have."

Mills smiled at her misstep.

"But Sarah Corbett says she didn't take any drugs at all," Riley Mills intoned with barely supposed glee. "Not in her whole life. And here's the best part: the packaging for the drug was found in the trash at the beach house. And guess whose fingerprints were on it?"

Mills watched with pleasure as Claire Davis's eyes narrowed with horror at this last news. He knew he'd scored with that one. She had expected no connection between Wyatt and the physical evidence, only the most wildly circumstantial case. The box that had once contained the abortion drugs was powerful evidence in its own right, but with Wyatt's fingerprints on it, it was damning. It seemed strange, though, what they had found in that box. But Riley Mills wasn't about to give that particular bit of information to Claire Davis just yet. She would have to wait until discovery.

Claire smiled cruelly, and for a moment Mills felt a twinge of nerves at the sight of those sharp teeth. Such a woman did make one nervous.

When Daniel Wyatt awoke the next morning, he experienced a brief lapse of memory.

For a moment, his situation seemed completely incomprehensible. He did not know why he was in jail, and the concept of jail was itself outside of his mind's reach. The bars, concrete floor, and hard bed of his cell seemed merely strange and depressing, like the plumbing in some impoverished foreign country. He was hungry, but the feeling was completely unfamiliar, as if the gnawing in his gut was an odd symptom of a new strain of flu. And for those few confused moments, he didn't remember how much trouble Daniel Wyatt was in, for he didn't realize completely that he was Daniel Wyatt.

But slowly and with a thudding feeling of inevitability the pieces of his life fell together in his mind. The facts solidified around him until they were as undeniable as the walls of his cell. He was Dr. Daniel Wyatt, prisoner, object of national scorn, accused murderer.

Two guards collected him, shackling his ankles and hands. They led him upstairs, where a man in a jailer's uniform met them.

"Dr. Wyatt? You have a visitor. Your wife. Would you like to see her?"

"Yes."

They took Wyatt to a small room, no bigger than a cubicle. One of the guards pushed him into a chair. Wyatt began to realize what being a prisoner was all about. The shambling gait forced by the chains, the constant escort. Every movement of his body seemed to be an extension of someone else's will.

He faced a glass partition, a telephone in front of him. After a moment, the door on the other side of the glass opened and Ellen came in. Her eyes were red and swollen from crying. They exchanged a painful glance, and lifted their respective phones. Her voice seemed distant and frail, as if she were calling from Australia, separated by a long and tiring voyage.

"What's going on, Daniel? How could you be arrested for murder?"

"That's the question I've been asking myself, Ellen. Claire says it's crazy."

"*Is* it crazy?"

"Yes," he replied.

"Daniel, I'm so humiliated. The news says you got a patient pregnant. Daniel," she cried. "How could you do this?"

Wyatt tried to answer, tried to admit his infidelity. But as it had done so many times before, the truth somehow became unspeakable. He strained to say it, but his mouth wouldn't form the words. The medical term for the impairment of the power to speak or comprehend words came to mind—"aphasia." How wonderful, he thought, that he could remember a Latin term he'd learned twenty years before, but couldn't say that simplest word in English: "yes."

So he nodded.

Ellen lowered her face into her hands and sobbed once, a horrible, racking sound that cut Daniel to his soul. He looked away from her, unable to bear the sight of her tears.

Then he remembered what Claire had told him. The phone call was being recorded, and was admissible in court.

He swallowed. Say nothing about the incident, he ordered himself.

"Ellen," he said. "I can't tell you any more about this right now. I just want you to know I love you and I feel horrible to have hurt you this way. Now, dear, tell me how the kids are handling it all."

"They want to know why," she said. "Why their daddy isn't home. Dexter saw them take you, Daniel."

Wyatt took a breath, his hands beginning to tremble in their shackles.

"I think it's best if I take them away from all this," Ellen said. "Up to Opelousas, to stay with my parents."

Daniel nodded, though he dreaded what he knew would probably go on there. That small town, with its vicious rumors and petty thinking. Ellen and the children would be prisoners in her parents' house.

"But you've got to come back for the trial," he pleaded. "I don't know if I can stand this without you. Ellen, I'm so sorry."

She looked away from him.

"I'll need my family," she said.

"But you're *my* family," he protested, his hands straining against the bonds under the table.

She shook her head. "I don't know, Daniel. I just feel numb. You have been my whole life and suddenly nothing is what I thought it was. I need some time away from here, Daniel. Please understand. I just have to get away."

Ellen rose, and one of the guards opened the door for her.

"Ellen," Wyatt pleaded. "Will you ever be able to forgive me?"

She looked down at him, her red eyes suddenly fierce.

"I don't know."

Ellen Wyatt turned and was gone, and they took him back to his cell.

Monday morning came, eventually.

Before they took Wyatt out the door, he was briefly unshackled. A heavy, dark green object was placed over his head, and he briefly panicked. For a moment, he thought it was some sort of restraint, as confining as a straitjacket. Then his head came through, and he found his arms free, and he realized what the garment was. A bulletproof vest.

"Lot of crazies showing up in town, Dr. Wyatt," one of the

guards grunted as he adjusted the weighty vest. "Wouldn't want you to get shot now, would we?"

"Speak for yourself," Wyatt answered.

The guards grinned appreciatively at his brief foray into gallows humor. Wyatt wondered for a moment how he had been able to make the joke at all. Perhaps such humor was some sort of natural reaction to despair, a sad but necessary replacement for hope.

A phalanx of policemen surrounded him for his brief moment of exposure in the street behind the police station. The walk was blinding and deafening, punctuated by flashes from cameras, shouted questions, a boom microphone that swung at his head like some flailing inorganic tentacle. Then he was inside the darkness of a van with heavy grilled windows.

"Where are we going?" he asked, suddenly unsure.

"The courthouse," came a terse answer.

Wyatt leaned back and reflected on this. They were traveling all of three blocks. He wondered if everything that was once simple—talking to his wife, going a few blocks, walking out a door—would from now on be fraught with terror and difficulty.

The media gauntlet was repeated a few minutes later. This time, Wyatt was able to look around. He spotted satellite vans from every news outlet in the country. A horde of reporters, protesters, onlookers. He couldn't believe they were all here for him. But the surge of sound and movement that swept through the crowd of media people behind the courthouse was undeniable.

Wyatt realized that this was how most Americans would see him for the first time, shackled and in a bright orange jumpsuit. Later, in the courtroom, he would wear a suit and tie, he supposed, but for now he was a marked man.

Daniel Wyatt was, as Claire had always promised, a national figure.

He was taken to a courtroom, where again the spectators reacted to his entrance, although this time with a sudden hush, like a moment of embarrassed silence at a party. Claire Davis and the prosecutor, a fat, pink man, sat at either side of a podium. Claire smiled at him.

Wyatt looked at his old friend. Claire looked far better today than she had looked on Friday night. At least one of them had gotten some sleep. Her hair was impeccably styled, her makeup far more elaborate than usual, and the dark blue suit she wore looked new. And more, she all but glowed with an intensity, an energy Daniel remembered from their old days of fighting zoning boards, regulatory commissions, even the state legislature. This was Claire in her element, the political animal. Her eyes were on fire.

My God, Wyatt thought, Claire Davis, Esq., was actually enjoying herself.

The arraignment went by quickly, a ritual in which the charges were read again. Then came the subject of bail.

The fat man, Prosecutor Mills, began his argument.

"Your Honor, the crime is of a very heinous nature, and the evidence is overwhelming. The accused has considerable assets, which could be used to aid flight. The People request that the defendant be held without bail."

"Your Honor," Claire began. "The Eighth Amendment—"

"Does not require that bail be set," Mills interrupted. "Only that if it *is* set, that it not be excessive."

"If I may," Claire said sharply to the prosecutor, then turned to the judge. "There is no likelihood of the defendant fleeing, as he is now a person of national prominence and easily recognizable. His assets are here and his family is deeply rooted in the community. In addition, the allegations are of an isolated nature. It is hardly likely that he would be a danger to the public. And, as a doctor, he has a number of patients who are under continuing care."

"I hope none of these patients is pregnant, Your Honor!" the prosecutor interrupted.

"Your Honor, those sorts of remarks are completely inappropriate. . . ."

The argument went on for a few minutes. Wyatt searched

the spectators for Ellen's face. The benches of the courtroom held people taking notes, interested onlookers, and a few spectators who glared back at Wyatt with obvious hatred. But his wife, the one he desperately wanted to see, wasn't among the crowd.

Bail was set at one million dollars. The sum made Wyatt's head swim, but he understood vaguely that his home would be put up for most of the amount. Another piece of his life entangled in this affair.

Finally, it was time to enter his plea. Wyatt was called to rise, his heart racing as the judge glared down at him.

"Do you waive formal reading of the complaint and advisement of constitutional rights?"

Wyatt turned toward Claire, unsure. She nodded.

"Yes, Your Honor," he managed.

"To the charges in the complaint, how do you plead?"

Wyatt had thought of this moment over the last two days, and had been afraid that his voice might shake, that he would panic, and forever brand himself as guilty in the eyes of the world. But the words came easily, and his voice did not betray him.

"Your Honor, I am not guilty."

33 | SIEGE

Sheriff Mark Hicks drove down Main Street slowly, watching the unfolding invasion of his town with growing doubts. What had he started here? Had his simple attempt to enforce the law really caused all this? All Hicks had wanted was straight answers from Sarah Corbett, and a low-key investigation into what had happened to her baby, and now all of Lafayette seemed to be under seige.

Damn that Tom Jenkins! He had no more sense than a doorknob, and about as much loyalty as a snake. But Hicks blamed himself more than anyone. Even as exhausted as he'd been that night, he should have realized that he shouldn't involve Jenkins.

Talk always gets you into trouble, Hicks thought.

Well, now there was plenty of talk for everyone in the whole United States. This Daniel Wyatt affair was filling up just about every channel on television. Worse, it was filling up the streets of Lafayette with satellite trucks and TV reporters doing stand-ups in front of the courthouse and the town hall, and it was filling up Mark Hicks's jail with demonstrators. Already, he and his men (minus Tom Jenkins, who was pulling desk duty in the bowels of the station house) had made two dozen arrests.

Only a little more than twenty-four hours since Daniel Wyatt had been arrested, and the crazies were arriving by the busload. There were anti-abortion demonstrators like Operation Rescue and Life Dynamics, women's groups—some of whom had come to see that Wyatt got a fair trial, some to see him hang—men's rights groups who thought Daniel Wyatt was some kind of hero, and some crazies who seemed to be, well, just crazy. Turned on by the circus itself, these last wore costumes, shouted senseless slogans, and performed whenever a camera was pointed at them.

Demonstrating for the sake of demonstration. What was the world coming to?

Now the FBI was on hand, too. Hicks pulled up in front of the new Hyatt that towered over this block of Main, realizing he was late for his meeting with the FBI agents. Traffic was all screwed up, but Hicks figured that was the least of his worries.

The Hyatt's lobby was filled with people. Most didn't look like the lawbreaking type, at least. Most wore suits. Reporters and political people, Hicks guessed. There was even a group of priests in one corner, their pile of luggage marked with a sign that read CATHOLICS FOR LIFE. Hicks hoped he wouldn't be arresting any of them. The line at check-in was getting longer by the minute, so Hicks pushed through and showed his badge to the harried young woman at the desk.

"I'm here to see FBI Agent Costilla."

She blinked, then tapped away at her computer.

"Honeymoon suite."

"Pardon me?"

"They're in the honeymoon suite. Top floor."

Hicks shook his head and walked toward the elevator, shaking his head. The Federal Bureau of Investigation, and they were headquartered in the honeymoon suite? Didn't that just beat all?

Sheriff Hicks had to knock twice before the door to the suite swung open, and for a moment, he thought he'd entered the wrong room.

The woman who opened the door certainly didn't look like any FBI agent Hicks had seen before. She was in her early twenties, only about five-three in her heels, and she wore a smart leather jacket in the cold of the hotel's air-condition-ing. Her hair was dyed a shocking red, and her makeup un-der her eyes was heavy and black against her pale skin.

She looked Hicks up and down and turned from him back to the room, announcing him with the words "It's not the pizza. Looks like a local tin carrier."

The young woman let the door swing open for him, walk-ing back to the large table in the middle of the room. It was covered with computer equipment and a tangle of cables and power strips. A man rose from the table and crossed to where Hicks stood. The sheriff recognized Agent Costilla. The man hadn't been around for the first background check on Dr. Wyatt, before the nomination, but had showed up later, ask-ing about Sarah Corbett.

Costilla's eyes followed the young woman's return to the computer table with an indulgent half smile. "Sorry about the introduction, Sheriff. We were hoping you were pizza."

"I see," Hicks managed as he entered. The large room was decorated in pinks and reds, with lacy curtains and a gilt-framed mirror for newlyweds to admire themselves in. Hicks wondered if the bathtub was heart-shaped. "Your de-livery's probably caught in traffic. Sorry I'm late myself, Agent Costilla."

The compact Hispanic agent looked distractedly at his watch. Millie was right, he *was* a good-looking man.

"*Costilla*," the young woman corrected his pronunciation as she typed at the largest computer on the table. "Like tor-*tilla*."

"That is Agent Samuels," Costilla said. "And Agents Stan-ton and Watson," he added, gesturing to two men who were setting up a folding table by the room's large window. "This is Sheriff Hicks."

"Nice to meet you," Agent Samuels said, smiling but not looking up from her screen. The other two just grunted.

"Well," Hicks said, a little overawed by the strange room and its occupants, "I'm just glad you folks are here. I'm hav-ing a little trouble keeping this town in one piece. There's too many people here, and too much emotion about this case. I can't imagine what's going to happen when the trial starts."

"Sheriff, I'm afraid we're not here to help you with crowd control," Costilla explained. "My team and I are here after one of the Bureau's Most Wanted."

Hicks raised his eyebrows and let out a sigh. This was just what he needed right now, some sort of master criminal in his town.

"This man is number six on the Bureau's list, and number one on mine."

"What's he wanted for?"

"A string of five murders and attempted murders, all abortion doctors. He's normally a shooter. Prefers it personal. But he has bombed a clinic. Did a good job of it, too. Two bombs, not one," Costilla said. "Timed thirty minutes apart. The first one was just to draw a crowd."

"My God," Hicks said. "Do you think he's going to try to kill Daniel Wyatt?"

"Absolutely."

Hicks rubbed the back of his neck and sighed.

"Well, do you have a name for this fellow?"

"No," Costilla said flatly.

"What's the description, then?"

"Not much of a physical description, really. Just a white male, twenty to fifty, average build."

Hicks let out a low whistle. "That's not much to go on."

"We know some things, though," Costilla said. The agent stared out the window at the street below. It was getting dark, but Lafeyette was still bustling with cars and pedestrians.

Costilla turned toward Hicks.

"This killer is a very religious man. He's working from a sense of duty, a passionate commitment to rid the world of abortion. He thinks that God's will is driving him. And whatever's in his head is relentless. He needs to kill, can't stand to exist unless he purifies himself with the ritual of committing murder. He's like an addict needing a fix. And as far as we can tell, his addiction is getting worse."

Hicks looked down to the darkening street. There were hundreds of people within his view, probably thousands headed into town. Damn. He had complained all day that Lafayette was filling up with crazies, but to learn that one of them was *really* crazy chilled Mark Hicks to his marrow.

"Well, we've got Dr. Wyatt's house under guard. And we put him in a vest for his court appearances."

Costilla shook his head.

"I don't know if a couple of deputies outside his house is going to do it. I'm going to post one of my own men down there at all times."

Hicks winced at the words "a couple of deputies." Right now, it was just Roy Scopes down at the Wyatts'.

"Do you know if Dr. Wyatt has an alarm system?" Costilla asked.

"No, sir. I couldn't tell you for sure. But I don't know hardly anyone in Lafayette who does. He lives in a real nice neighborhood, after all."

Costilla shook his head. "All right. We're going to have to get some equipment in there. I want the place alarmed, and I want to be able to record incoming calls. Can you set up a meeting between me and Wyatt?"

"Well, sure. But you'd probably better talk to his lawyer first. She won't want anyone fooling around in his house without a warrant, I'll bet you."

The FBI agent looked at Hicks with sudden interest. "His lawyer? Is that Claire Davis?"

"Yeah. You know her?"

"I met her last time I was out here. Last week."

"I'll get you her number," Hicks offered.

"Thanks. You do that."

With those words, Costilla turned back to the computer table and began poking inexpertly at one of the keyboards. Sheriff Hicks realized that he had been dismissed from the agent's mind. The encounter with the FBI agents had disturbed him, made him comprehend how out of his control this whole thing had become.

He planted his hat back on his head.

"Just one more thing, Agent Costilla," he ventured.

"Yes?"

"What makes you so sure that your man's down here? You got any real evidence that he's after Dr. Wyatt?"

Costilla smiled slowly.

" 'He took her child, before it breathed at all. God's will defiled, now the sky must fall,' " the man chanted.

"What does all that mean?" Hicks said, hearing annoyance finally creeping into his own voice. He'd had about enough of these city slickers coming into his town, giving orders and acting crazy.

"It means he'll be here. There's something he needs that he can't get anywhere else. He wants to make the whole world listen to him, and the world he cares about is gathering here, right now."

"He wants to kill Dr. Wyatt to get attention?"

Costilla shook his head. "Frankly, Sheriff, I think he's changed tactics. One man's life isn't enough anymore."

Hicks swallowed, and waited for the agent to say more.

"I hope I'm wrong," Costilla continued. "But I think that this time he's very hungry. And the only thing that will satisfy him is a massacre."

"I don't have time to see anyone!" Claire Davis barked as she pushed past her secretary.

Molly looked hurt, but this was no time to worry about feelings. It was Monday morning before the long Thanksgiving weekend closed down the courts for five days, and Judge Thibodeaux would be hearing pretrial motions at ten. Claire thought she had an outside chance to exclude the RU-486 packaging from evidence. It had been found in an area that was clearly not part of the beach house property and wasn't covered by the search warrant. In fact, the box had been found closer to another house than to the one where Daniel and Sarah had stayed. This was her one chance to end this quickly.

Without the physical evidence of RU-486 linked to Daniel Wyatt's fingerprints, the prosecution's already circumstantial case would begin to crumble.

"Not even the FBI?" came a voice from inside Claire's office.

She pulled up short at the sight of the man sitting in her visitor's chair. Agent Eduardo Costilla leaned back to look at her, as comfortable as when she'd last seen him in his hotel-room bed. Claire took time to shrug at Molly, then closed the door.

"What brings you into town, Agent Costilla?" she said, sitting at her desk.

"It's good to see you, too, Claire," he returned.

She allowed herself to smile. It was good to see him. In

this last awful week, Claire had forgotten how handsome he was, how his low voice and soft accent could entrance her. She noticed the unlit cigarette he worried in the fingers of one hand.

"Here to tempt me with bad habits again?" she asked.

"I'm afraid not. But I wish I was."

Claire leaned back, getting comfortable but keeping one eye on the clock over Eduardo's head. She decided to allow herself five minutes of conversation with this pleasurable man. Then a troubling thought struck her. Was Costilla here to testify for the prosecution?

"Just dropping by to help destroy my client, I suppose."

Costilla looked surprised. Claire regretted the words as soon as she said them. They had come out sounding unexpectedly bitter.

"I'm sorry," she said. "Not enough sleep. And maybe the feeling that the whole world is out to get me."

He shook his head.

"Don't worry. I don't regret anything that happened here, Claire. Digging into Wyatt's personal life wasn't my idea of a plum assignment. Although I suppose if the FBI had found Sarah Corbett, this whole thing might have been handled a little differently."

Claire's mind swam for a moment as she entertained the maybes of that possible turn of events. Then she cleared her head with an act of will. It was a pointless exercise, trying to reconfigure the past. She allowed herself to feel guiltily glad that this new nightmare had at least one redeeming feature. It had brought Eduardo Costilla back into town.

"Then why are you here?" she asked.

Costilla leaned forward and placed the unlit cigarette on the desk in front of Claire, then reached into his pocket to produce a book of matches.

"I'm here to save Dr. Daniel Wyatt."

"From charges of murder?" she asked hopefully.

"From being murdered."

Claire Davis reached for the cigarette.

* * *

She was on time, although the conversation with Costilla had taken longer than five minutes.

Claire watched the throngs of protesters that she passed on her way to the courthouse with new attentiveness. She'd managed to block the demonstrators out over the weekend, to imagine them as mere obstacles, impediments to getting up and down the courthouse steps. But now that she knew one of those angry faces was planning to kill Daniel Wyatt, their earnest placards and pictures of fetuses at the bottom of trash cans seemed far more threatening.

Her team was waiting outside the courtroom. More than a few of her staff at WAG had quit over the last two days, tearful phone calls coming at all hours of the weekend as the media pilloried Wyatt. But the women she most trusted and needed had remained loyal. In a very small, very private meeting with them, she had explained the entire situation, that Sarah Corbett had taken the drugs of her own free will, and was being manipulated by a small-town prosecutor for his own political ends. This was the story that Claire intended to sell the public as well, whatever legal maneuverings she would employ to help her client. In any case, this case was bigger than any act of betrayal they might feel Daniel Wyatt had perpetuated. The future of not just WAG, but of *Roe* v. *Wade* and all it had guaranteed for women's lives over the last three decades was at stake.

Davis had also received offers of legal and financial help in the defense. She supposed every defendant on the national stage elicited sympathy from someone, somewhere, no matter how heinously their crime was portrayed. Disturbingly, the largest offer had come from a radical fathers' rights group. She had checked their website, and discovered that they were hailing Daniel Wyatt as a hero for taking the power of abortion into his own hands. If a woman can unilaterally decide to end her child's life, they argued, why can't a man?

A group with that particular philosophy was not exactly a natural ally for Claire and WAG, but she had quietly accepted the money. She knew the prosecution wasn't going to want for resources.

Despite her late arrival, Judge Thibodeaux kept her and Mills waiting for another few minutes. She had requested a meeting in Thibodeaux's chambers before going into open court. Finally, she and Mills, with one assistant each, were ushered into the judge's chambers. As always, she found the small, linoleum-floored office unequal to its grand name. It looked more like a large broom closet with a desk than a chamber.

"Judge," she said once they were all seated, "some of the evidence we will be discussing today is highly prejudicial. If broadcast on television, it may be heard by potential jurors, whatever your eventual ruling."

"I understand your fears, Counselor," the judge said. "But trials are public. These motions will be heard in open court."

Claire swallowed. The box of RU-486 would be a graphic on every national television news show tonight. Once it aired, the White House would pull the plug, no matter how hard she pleaded. Claire finally began to realize what should have been obvious from the start: Wyatt's nomination was history, no matter what happened in this case.

He was presumed guilty already, and would pay the price with his career.

In open court, they started with her objections to the evidence seized near the beach house, namely the packaging for RU-486.

"The beach house is believed to be the crime scene," Mills explained. "I hope relevance is not the issue."

"The issue, as my motion states, is of a constitutional nature," Claire said. "The search warrant covered only the beach house and did not extend to its grounds.

"As you can see in my motion, Your Honor, the garbage receptacle where the RU-486 packaging was found is on the grounds of the beach house, not inside. It was not covered by the warrant," she said flatly.

"Your Honor, the box was discarded in a trash can next to a public walk. This trash can is used by passersby, thus no warrant at all is required to search it. Daniel Wyatt had no expectation of privacy covering what was in effect a public facility. It's unambiguous."

Claire squirmed. She'd known this motion was a long shot, but she had to keep trying. The entire case could turn on the box that had held, in effect, the "murder weapon."

"But the evidence was found in a trash can on a path used by passersby on their way to the beach," she explained. "The box could have been deposited there by anyone."

Riley Mills let out a low chuckle. "But, Ms. Davis, your client's fingerprints were found on the box. Do you think those fingerprints were also deposited there by some random passerby?"

"Ms. Davis, your arguments do not go to the admissibility of the evidence," Thibodeaux said. "Merely to the weight the jury might give it. You can explain to the jury where the box was found. They can use their common sense to determine why the good doctor's fingerprints might be on it. The motion is denied; the evidence will be received."

Claire nodded, quietly smoldering inside.

"I would also like to protest a lack of discovery on the part of the D.A.'s office, with regard to tests performed on the box," she announced.

"Tests?" the judge asked.

It was Mills's turn to look uncomfortable. "Well, we are having the box tested to see if there was any residue from the drug," he explained.

"Your Honor," Claire insisted, narrowing her eyes at the judge. "The defense demands that the evidence be made available for testing by our own experts."

"This is our evidence, Your Honor," Mills complained. "The results were inconclusive, so we're having them done again."

"Inconclusive? Or exculpatory?" Claire asked.

"We have a right to retest this evidence with more sophisticated means than the local laboratory," Mills complained.

"Your Honor, the prosecution doesn't like the results they got, and they're going elsewhere to try to get what they're looking for. We demand to know what the status of the testing is to date, and to have access to the lab reports."

Thibodeaux's face held a look of unease. The laws of discovery allowed the defense to have access to whatever evidence the prosecution was able to come up with. Thibodeaux would have to demand that Mills reveal what his lab had found.

"Mr. Mills," the judge said. "What sort of result are we talking about?"

"The local lab believes that the results were probably the result of contamination," Mills explained. "Materials from somewhere else in the lab must have wound up in the testing apparatus, as far as I understand it."

"What sort of materials, Riley?" Claire asked.

"It doesn't matter," he said. "They're doing the tests again. This time at a laboratory with more sophisticated equipment than the state lab."

"If they're going to do it again, then just tell us, Mr. Mills!" Claire demanded. "Your Honor, how many times are they going to be allowed to test the same evidence? Are you going to let them continue to look for a lab that will yield the results they want?"

Judge Thibodeaux cleared his throat again, and his voice took on an unsure note. "Just tell us, Mr. Mills," he asked.

"Is that a ruling?" Claire demanded.

"Well, yes, then!" the judge exclaimed. "Tell us what they found."

Mills glared at the judge for a moment, then replaced the expression with an injured shrug.

"Well, the box definitely showed traces of mifepristone and prostaglandin. But it also contained traces of a substance called, I believe, salicylic acid," he said.

"Salicylic acid?" Thibodeaux repeated.

Claire leaned back into her chair. "Isn't there a more common name for that substance, Mr. Mills?"

Mills sat silent for a moment, perhaps sizing up his chances of willing this all away by magic. But he sighed and put up his hands.

"As I said, they think it was just a mix-up, and they're running the test again. But what they also believed to be in the box were traces of . . . aspirin."

"Aspirin?" Judge Thibodeaux asked.

Claire smiled, watching as Riley Mills struggled to keep himself calm. He was probably cursing himself for testing the box. The packaging, clearly marked as RU-486, would probably have been enough for the jury. It was the old prosecutor's instinct, however: belt and suspenders.

But at least this once, she'd caught Riley Mills with his pants down.

35 | THANKSGIVING

Daniel Wyatt watched with growing awe as the young, red-haired woman installed the machines that were supposed to protect him. When she had first come to the door, Agent Tabitha Samuels had seemed insecure, almost shy as she introduced herself. The FBI man with her had brought in the bulging cases of electronics and, without a word, returned to his vigil in the car outside. As she started to unpack the cases, running her hands over the sleek plastic forms of cameras, transmitters, motion detectors, and other devices that she hadn't bothered to explain, Agent Samuels seemed to grow more confident. She fitted lenses into the cameras, put together delicate microphones with tiny screwdrivers that she pulled from a plastic case in her breast pocket, and ran the cables that now reached every room of the empty house.

She looked quietly happy in her silent work, as completely fixated and strangely innocent as an autistic child.

The house was quiet, with Ellen and the kids gone. In his first hours of freedom, Wyatt had answered the phone every time it rang, thinking it might be Ellen. In each case it was only media people asking for interviews, along with a few crazies and the occasional death threat. Finally, he'd just allowed the phone to ring, filling two days with its screeching. After Agent Samuels had arrived and worked through a few unanswered calls playing out their interminable summonses—the answering machine's tape was, of course, full—she had shown him how to unplug the phone from the wall. He thanked her, and wondered why he hadn't done this himself. The silence was a relief, but now it seemed almost sad, the utter quiet of his home.

Now he watched across the kitchen table as Agent Samuels's graceful fingers fitted an antenna no bigger than a butterfly onto the top of a small TV. She avoided his gaze, and he wondered if she thought he was the monster the press was making him out to be. Perhaps she simply preferred the company of her machines.

Wyatt sighed and reached for the phone again, plugging its cord into the wall socket. He lifted the receiver and dialed the number for Ellen's parents for the twelfth time that day. He counted the rings, sure that again they wouldn't answer.

"Hello?" came a wary voice. His mother-in-law.

"It's me, Daniel," he said hurriedly.

Click.

He looked at the receiver in shock. They'd been disconnected, or maybe . . .

Wyatt dialed again. The phone rang ten times.

"Hello." Ellen's father, Harold.

"It's me, Daniel."

"Yeah." The man's voice was flat, hostile. Daniel tried to think of what to say. How to explain. Words failed him.

"Is Ellen there?"

"Nope. She isn't in."

Wyatt could hear instantly that Harold was lying. The forced, rehearsed words came one by one from his mouth. Wyatt felt his blood pressure rise. He wanted to shout at his father-in-law, to tell him to get his damn wife on the phone. . . .

"Can you just—" he started, his suddenly dry voice cracking. He swallowed. "Could you ask her to call me . . . when she gets in."

"I'll do that."

"Thank you, Harold," he said, and hung up.

Daniel Wyatt reached back to the wall and unplugged the phone. Ellen wasn't going to call. Wyatt realized that he was alone now. His friends, his patients, his family were gone. All that was left was Claire and this strange FBI woman. Her red hair was cut in a short bob, and Wyatt thought he saw the mark of an old piercing on one side of her nose.

Agent Samuels looked up from her work. She regarded Wyatt for a moment, narrowing her eyes. Thankfully, her gaze was not filled with pity. But her interest was disturbingly cool, her look reminiscent of that one might give an insect caught under a glass.

Then she smiled.

She pushed a button on the television, and a grainy black-and-white image flickered into being. Agent Samuels turned the TV toward him.

"You're on."

Wyatt leaned forward and squinted. His eyes managed to resolve the picture, and he saw that he was, indeed, on the little screen. He waved one arm in the air experimentally, and the white blob waved back at him. He tried to orient himself, turning around a bit stupidly to find the camera.

Agent Samuels pointed one red fingernail at the transom above the door to the living room. Wyatt found the small camera, a lifeless and still eye staring down at him.

She stood on tiptoes, holding the television in one hand, and reached up to nudge the camera a bit to one side. Now it covered the door that led from the kitchen out to the backyard. The woman seemed satisfied with her adjustment. She put the television on the table and walked from the room without a word. Wyatt heard the rattle of her cases in the living room.

He looked at his own kitchen on the screen. A white little world, as stark as some prison cell. He realized that once Samuels left, he would be alone.

Claire had told him that she was traveling to New Orleans tomorrow, meeting with some legal experts about the implications of the case on *Roe*. Then she was going to her parents' house in Miami for the long weekend. The number of protesters had lessened in town the last two days. Probably most of them were also headed home for the holidays. But the circus would start up again on Monday.

Agent Samuels came back into the kitchen, the much-lightened cases over her shoulders.

"All done," she said, and walked toward the door. She picked up the little TV and placed it in a bag. "Costilla asked me to tell you that an agent will be posted outside at all times. That's over and above the sheriff's men out there. If you go anywhere, you got to tell us *and* them. Your doors are all under video cameras, and it's all being taped. So don't walk around naked. You've got motion detectors in the garage and in the kids' rooms. Just stay out of there."

She opened the kitchen door and stepped out into the darkness, the warm air and sound of cicadas rushing in.

Agent Samuels turned back to Wyatt and favored him with a shy smile.

"And have yourself a happy Thanksgiving, Dr. Wyatt."

"Thanks. You, too," he managed.

She let the door swing shut, and Wyatt felt the silence wrap around him.

Father Peter O'Keefe watched the red-haired woman leave. She waved as she walked past the plainclothesman (was he FBI? was she?) who waited in the car in front of Daniel Wyatt's house. The woman ignored the sheriff's deputy who was parked on one side of the house, got into her car, and drove off.

O'Keefe lowered the binoculars and chewed his lip. She'd been in there for hours installing security and surveillance equipment. The place must be wrapped up pretty tight by now. Getting in would be a trick. Of course, there were always ways for a determined man to get the job done. The window shades were drawn, but one could still tell the room in which Wyatt was located in the otherwise empty house;

there were shifting shadows against the shades as he moved around. With a sufficiently powerful and indiscriminately wide-ranging weapon, O'Keefe could fill a large area with bullets and hope for the best. From a hundred feet away, the large bay windows would allow a wide field of fire into the living room.

Of course, there was also the martyr approach. Wearing body armor, an assassin could charge the house and gain entry before either of the two men guarding Wyatt could respond. Wyatt would be dead before they reached the door. There would be little chance of escape for such a man, but a new trial, focusing on the same issues, would simply replace the current one. The new defendant, Wyatt's killer, would be on television every day for months at least. And one less baby killer would walk the earth.

O'Keefe considered the U.S. mail. He had used explosives before, though never anything as sophisticated as a letter bomb. He doubted that Wyatt would be stupid enough to open anything very large himself. But O'Keefe knew of websites that contained detailed plans for building lethal devices no bigger than a manila envelope.

Ultimately, though, this was all speculation. O'Keefe had decided not to kill Daniel Wyatt. Not yet, anyway. This trial was bigger than one man, was about more than the fate of a single murderer. This unfolding drama in Lafayette was a challenge to O'Keefe's imagination, it tested the magnitude of his faith. He would have to think, and pray, before he knew how to send the message that was needed. This business was all just getting started, really, and it was pointless to rush himself. O'Keefe felt the itch inside, that old craving to act for the benefit of the righteous cause. He wanted to reach out and talk to Dr. Daniel Wyatt, to know the man's evil firsthand. That contact would nurture O'Keefe's need for vengeance, feed his competence as a warrior in the cause of truth, make him an actor who was as large as the stage on which the future event would be enacted.

This would be his ultimate act of rejoicing.

O'Keefe was sure that when his plans were realized, the whole world would notice, and all God's children would learn God's lesson.

PART TWO

Riley Mills scanned the sheet of paper that A.D.A. Morrisey had just put before him and chuckled.

A woman's right to choose to terminate a pregnancy allows her greater autonomy in determining the course of her life.

   (Strongly Agree, Agree, Not Sure, Disagree, Strongly Disagree)

A man is more likely to succeed at a long-term career because men are better able to balance attention to work with the needs of a family.

   (Strongly Agree, Agree, Not Sure, Disagree, Strongly Disagree)

A mother of an unborn child should always consult with the father before terminating a pregnancy . . .

"You taken the quiz yet, Morrisey?" Mills asked, grinning.

His assistant snatched the paper back and glared at him.

"No. But fifty-seven prospective jurors have. The defense is tabulating the results now," she said angrily.

Mills rose from his desk and stretched his arms.

"Well, more power to 'em," he proclaimed. "And to their precious computers."

"Riley!" Morrisey cried. "I can't understand why this doesn't bother you. The defense is going to know the abortion politics of every prospective juror right down to the tiniest detail, and you don't even want to look at this?"

Mills turned his back on his assistant and stared out the

window of his courthouse office. The number of protesters had increased since the beginning of jury selection, the effects of near-constant human habitation beginning to show on the park across the street from the courthouse.

"We've got to get twelve jurors on our side, Riley," Morrisey continued. "They only need one. Don't you think we should have put together a questionnaire of our own?"

"Morrisey," Mills said, "this isn't some election for city hall we're running here. This is a murder trial. This is justice, not some focus group trying out new breakfast cereals. I've been picking juries for twenty years. Never used a computer, never used an expert or a questionnaire. I use my eyes, Morrisey. And I use my gut."

He sat back down, leaned back, and closed his eyes.

"Now, Morrisey, I know this is going to be different from the usual jury trial. But it's also different from the usual abortion debate, isn't it? No matter what these questionnaires are telling Claire Davis, abortion is a political issue only when a woman chooses it, not when it's forced upon her. Forced on her like rape, Morrisey. That's the story we're gonna tell. I don't care if you pick the jury straight from the ACLU mailing list, there ain't gonna be one woman on it who doesn't wake up screaming one night, dreaming that Daniel Wyatt tried to sneak into her body. I guarantee it."

He opened his eyes and grinned.

"Never thought I'd see the day when a prosecutor would want twelve women on his jury. How about that?" He chuckled.

"Riley, don't you think it would be good if we had a few pro-life jurors among these twelve angry women?"

"Maybe. Maybe not. I know Davis'll pound the *Roe* argument into the ground every chance she gets. 'A murder conviction for Daniel Wyatt is a murder charge for every woman who exercises her right to choose.' She's gonna say it, there's nothing we can do about it. But I have a feeling that if we tell this story right, there'll even be some pro-choicers out there taking a second look at abortion by the time we're through."

Morrisey scowled.

"All right, Riley. You pick 'em with your gut if you want. But even if we have to use all our strikes, let's get the hard-core feminists off the panel."

He nodded his head. "Fair enough. I'd just as soon not have to look at 'em. But give me eight or nine women, and I'll have everything I need."

"You think Davis will strike Catholics?" Morrisey asked.

"Maybe. She won't want any over forty years old, I'd reckon," he answered. "Give me four or five Catholics, maybe. I don't want too many, though. If they start making this a religious thing, they'll back some agnostic son of a bitch into the corner and he'll hold out on us. What I want is a nice, balanced jury that can all get angry together. Just give me a representative group of Daniel Wyatt's Lafayette neighbors. Those are the folks he betrayed, Morrisey."

The A.D.A. smiled.

"A jury of his peers?"

"That's right, darlin'. Just what the Constitution ordered."

Claire watched the statistical program making its final run before she headed out to the voir dire, her first chance to meet the jurors face-to-face.

For the tenth time today, the white dots on the screen started in their little cluster at the center and then began to jiggle, spreading out toward its edges like grains of rice dropped onto a vibrating surface. Each juror was a dot, a grain of rice, and the location of each showed that juror's political position on a two-dimensional spectrum, based on the questionnaires they'd filled out. In the upper right were the Libertarians, who believed that the government should have as little to do with their lives as possible. They wanted no help from the government, and little governance. No federal health insurance, but the right to have an abortion if they wanted. The Social Conservatives were lower right. Strong governance, but no particular handouts. Or, more specifically, no federal health care and no right to an abortion. Lower left were the Populists. They wanted federal health care and strong moral guidance from the government. That is, no abortions allowed with your free health care. And on the upper left were the true Liberals. Health care for all. Abortion on demand.

She watched the grains move, rendering subtle shades of gray between these cartoon oversimplifications. Claire had run the data all night, choosing different meanings for the graph's two axes. Sometimes up represented naked freedom, sometimes personal responsibility; sometimes left was wealth redistribution, sometimes a religious belief in a helping hand. By now Claire Davis was starting to know those fifty-seven grains of rice pretty well, in some ways better than they knew themselves. A picture was starting to form in her mind, of how each of her jurors would respond to any political issue, of how they would be inclined to negotiate almost any situation involving a man and a woman and the powers of the state. It recounted an old human story in new guise, this software. The oldest process of politics: people explaining what they thought was acceptable for a community to demand of its members.

Claire's fingers gripped a new list of questions. These were the ones she hadn't bothered to put on the questionnaire. What are your hobbies? What do you do with your spare time? What have your kids learned lately in school? Questions that would reveal nothing to a computer but would help her see exactly what kind of people they were. What was important to them.

Claire just hoped she could spot the subtle clues that people gave about themselves in the voir dire. She knew her opponent was more skilled with jury selection than she. He was a specialist with jury trials, whereas Claire had tried only a few in her career. But she also knew that Mills relied upon a firm belief in black-and-white reality, in absolute wrong and right. Like any storyteller, he succeeded because he believed his tale himself, completely and unquestioningly. Riley Mills lived in a world where any situation was simple and straightforward, and facts were facts.

But Claire Davis knew that this case was more complicated than that. She wasn't sure yet exactly how or when they would happen, but she guessed that Riley Mills wouldn't be ready for the surprises this case would bring.

Sarah Corbett watched the jury selection closely, the awful fascination of the unbearably long process slowly gripping her.

These twelve people, once they had been chosen, were to have such power. They could set free Daniel Wyatt, the man who had killed her child, just pat him on the back and out he'd go, his innocence established irreversibly. Or they could find him guilty of murder, a heinous crime. That might even mean life in prison, which to a man like Daniel Wyatt would be as bad as the death penalty. In effect, the jurors held the power of life and death. They were all such ordinary people, too. It looked as if fifty-seven bystanders had been taken off the thronged streets outside the courthouse.

Sarah could tell that many of them recognized her. After a few hours of hearing the same questions repeated again and again, they became bored, despite the solemnity of the proceedings, and their eyes would wander across the room. Until they found her, that is. Then they would hover uncertainly, then stare intently, or perhaps look away with embarrassment when they realized who she was.

Everyone in town seemed to recognize Sarah Corbett now. She was famous. The looks she got weren't exactly hostile, but Sarah was still unsure exactly what the suddenly narrowed eyes or embarrassed smiles meant. Was it pity? Was she Sarah Corbett, the innocent victim of the most sensational crime in recent memory? Or was it the distaste that a pathetic and abused woman might engender, particularly one who was not just a victim but a perpetrator, a home wrecker, as well. Perhaps it was a strange envy for her un-earned celebrity? Images of her had flooded the media for the last two months, in magazines and newspapers, in the short glimpses captured by the cameras that tracked the trial's participants in and out of the courthouse.

Or was it simply anger? The inhabitants of Lafayette had seen their town overtaken by the media and the mobs of protesters. Sarah wished she could explain to them, to every-one, that this was not what she had wanted. All she'd wanted was to be a mom. All she had desired was a little more recog-nition from the father of her child. Certainly not this.

Sarah watched intently as the two lawyers talked to the jurors. The district attorney was full of Old South humor and heavy-handed gallantry. His jokes all sounded as if he'd used them a million times, although you laughed at him po-litely, as you would laugh at an old uncle who thought he was funny. Claire Davis seemed a bit nervous, but the younger prospective jurors seemed more comfortable with her than they did with Riley Mills. When Claire talked to them, she would sometimes drop the stage voice she used when addressing the whole court, and ask a simple question about kids or television, or how working as a juror on a long trial would affect their marriage. And underneath her jitters Claire still had that confidence, that hard glamour that had so entranced Sarah on the one morning they had met face-to-face.

Sarah wondered why she had lied to the D.A. about Claire Davis. Perhaps it was the way he had asked questions about Claire. He was terribly nasty. Riley Mills seemed to want to implicate her in all of this, to put her on trial as well as Daniel. Did Claire Davis know about the affair? Had she tried to convince Sarah to get an abortion? Had she offered Sarah money or anything else to abort the child? But Sarah hadn't told Mills how Claire had come to her house to set up the trip to the beach house. She hadn't mentioned the visit at all.

Sarah thought that this was the right thing to do. It was

the least she could do. She didn't want Ms. Davis to be a defendant at this trial. Claire hadn't done anything but try to understand. And Daniel certainly needed a good lawyer to defend him.

One thing Sarah couldn't believe was how terribly the newspapers and people on TV were treating Dr. Wyatt. They called him a great manipulator, as if his relationship with Sarah were some sort of game he'd been playing. As if she couldn't control her own mind. They always referred to her as the "much younger Sarah Corbett," although she was almost thirty-four, for heaven's sake. They hadn't seen how confused and frightened Daniel Wyatt had been during the last two months. Whatever he had done, he didn't deserve life in prison.

Now that the first terrible week after the miscarriage was over, Sarah had had time to think. She was past being angry at Daniel Wyatt, and certainly hoped that nothing too terrible happened to him. In a way, she supposed that she was still in love with him. Maybe the tests were wrong. Maybe it had simply been a mistake. Her mind raced sometimes as she lay in her bed unable to sleep, trying to find some way out of all this.

Once, Sarah had brought up the possibility of dropping the charges to Riley Mills's assistant, Kathleen Morrisey. The woman had hushed her up, said they weren't her charges to drop. The case now belonged to the People of Louisiana. Then A.D.A. Morrisey had explained about perjury, and what it meant to change your story in a court of law. Well, Sarah had heard of perjury before, unfortunately.

The jury began to fill. An older black woman was empaneled first. Sarah had expected her to be chosen. Everyone had seemed to like her frank, funny answers to the two lawyers' and the judge's questions. Then a white woman who had three kids at home. A young guy with a strong Cajun accent was the first man. Picking these three accounted for about twenty of the prospective jurors, and the judge ordered the court to start getting another batch ready for tomorrow.

Despite the care with which they'd been chosen, they still looked so . . . ordinary, considering the power they would wield. The power to set Daniel free, the power to end his life.

Sarah sighed to herself. Maybe there was something she could say that would help him, that could lessen this terrible ordeal, just a little. She couldn't think of what it would be, not yet anyway.

But maybe it would come to her, one of these sleepless nights, and then everything would be all right.

Opening arguments.

Claire Davis carefully took another drink from the bottle beside her. Her tongue seemed bone dry the moment the water passed over it, like some miracle substance out of a diaper ad. She was careful not to drink too much, though. This bottle had to last the morning, and there was no telling how long Riley Mills's opening statement was going to take.

She looked down at her notes. Suddenly the short, choppy paragraphs and bullet points seemed inadequate, amateurish. Why hadn't she stuck to the legal side of this and hired a seasoned pro to work the jury? Was her hubris going to cost Daniel Wyatt his freedom? She was painfully aware of Daniel sitting next to her, his hands clenched, though she'd told him several times not to show any nervousness when the jury was in the box.

Her eyes scanned the twelve members of the panel, and Claire wondered how great a defeat they represented. Eight women. Normally, females were the natural allies of the defense, at least according to courtroom common wisdom, but for this case everyone was saying they would go with the prosecution, as often happened when the charge was rape. Claire Davis wasn't so sure, though. She suspected that the same reason that women usually favored defendants—a tendency to see morality as nuanced, ethics as situational and flexible—would apply here as well. Of course, if D.A. Mills could convince them that Daniel Wyatt had definitely drugged Sarah Corbett and aborted her child, Claire would have eight very angry women to contend with. But she suspected that the facts of the case weren't going to read so simply. Sarah might have taken the drug herself, and then, faced with the bloodstained truth of what she had done, erased the event from her memory. Women weren't only prone to seeing mitigating factors when it came to the perpetration of a crime, they were also more attuned to the ways the subjective mind of an alleged victim could create a new reality.

The jury also had five blacks, three of the women and two of the four men, all of them in their forties and fifties. Claire knew from her political experience that blacks were generally more pro-choice than whites, the result of their long alliance with the Democratic Party, but their nominal support, especially among those who were religious, was undercut by a greater discomfort about abortion. All of the five African-Americans on the jury had tested high in their religious convictions. Of course, if Claire could make an effective case for believing that Wyatt was under attack by conservative political forces, she felt that would resonate with the black jurors.

Of the seven whites, five were Catholic. She had removed a number of strong Catholic believers with her preemptory strikes, the limited number of jurors she was allowed to take off the panel without stating a reason. She still wasn't sure how to sell the case to anyone who was strongly anti-choice, who thought of RU-486 as an abomination, and who might even regard Wyatt's adultery as a crime in itself. But Louisiana was the most Catholic state in the nation, and Claire supposed that five of twelve wasn't the disaster it could have been.

Her great hope on the jury, in case one of the charges (hopefully not murder) came down to a single holdout, was the one Protestant white woman on the jury. Peggy Fontenot was only twenty-five years old, college-educated, and was living with a man she wasn't married to. From the questionnaire, she seemed adamantly pro-choice. Claire wondered why Riley Mills hadn't used a strike to get her off the jury. Indeed, in the voir dire it almost seemed as if Mills had devel-

oped something of a crush on the woman. Maybe he just
wanted a pretty face on the jury, and assumed he could
charm her with his southern wiles.

There was no overestimating men's ability to be guided by
their dicks, it seemed.

Mills began his opening statement, reminding the jurors,
as he had several times at the voir dire, that he represented
the People of Louisiana. Claire wondered if she should turn
that around on him. In her career, she represented the people, too. Only she did it one at a time.

As the prosecution's case unfolded, Claire soon realized
how Riley Mills was going to play this. He argued his case as
if the lesser charge—furnishing medicine without a medical
necessity—was an afterthought. He was going for the big
one. Nothing else mattered.

"There are three basic steps to proving a murder case," he
explained. "Motive, opportunity, and intent. And the evidence that the People intend to produce will support each of
these three parts, and will show you how they fit together to
form unshakable proof that Dr. Daniel Wyatt committed
murder in the first degree.

"First: motive. What did Dr. Wyatt have to gain by killing
the child inside Sarah Corbett? Well, for one thing, he was a
married man," Mills proclaimed as if this were some unexpected revelation.

"He had been married for fourteen years, and he had
three kids. By the time he knew of the pregnancy, he had become a public figure. Imagine what would happen if suddenly everybody knew about Sarah. Not only was Dr. Wyatt
having an affair with Sarah Corbett, but she was bearing his
child. His adultery was about to bear a bitter fruit that would
make it not only obvious, but also scientifically undeniable
that the child was his. Don't forget, you can lie about sleeping with someone, but you can't deny a paternity test. Blood
will tell, ladies and gentlemen of the jury. Blood will tell."

Mills paused, letting the melodramatic effects of his
telling sink in. The jury was already caught by his masterful

delivery, a few of them shaking their heads along with him. Claire realized Mills was giving the impression that a paternity test had in fact been performed, linking Wyatt with the child. She wondered if she should object, but willed herself to be patient. She didn't want to seem overly combative at this early stage. Claire made a note to point out in her own opening that no paternity test had ever been given. The tiny fetus had been found amid the blood and uterine lining, but discarded as medical waste as a matter of course. No genetic test could link Wyatt to the fetus Sarah had carried.

"Surely such a public humiliation would destroy this man's marriage," Mills continued. "Would cost him his home, his family, his standing in the community. His good name."

Mills let the irony of the last two words resonate in the courtroom a bit before he continued.

"Dr. Wyatt had also been recently appointed to a high post in the government, the evidence will show. This was the culmination of all his life's work. A chance to go to Washington, to work closely with our president to bring his beliefs to the entire nation."

Mills shook his head to punctuate the words. As Claire suspected, the DA was going to use every opportunity to make the administration squirm. When it had become clear that the case was going to trial, they had withdrawn Daniel's nomination, of course. But the White House was still on the burner as long as reports of this case were leading every newscast. Claire knew that her promising career in Washington was as likely to happen now as an August snowstorm in New Orleans.

"And his third motive was to protect his practice. As a doctor, he was sworn to uphold a code of ethics that forbids doctors from taking advantage . . . from having sexual relations with their patients. Not only his reputation, not only his new job with the administration, but his very livelihood was dependent on no one finding out about his relationship with Sarah Corbett. Motive indeed."

Mills took a deep breath.

"Number two: opportunity."

There was a stir in the courtroom. Claire wondered how many in the audience, seduced by the drama of Mills's tale, had forgotten that there were two more points to go.

"Now, we aren't talking here about a gun, that makes a terrible noise when you fire it. Or a bank robbery, where you've got to haul off a truckful of money. We're talking about very small pills, no bigger than aspirin."

Riley held up something in his hand toward the jury. Claire thought of objecting again, as it might be argued that Mills was presenting actual evidence in his opening statement. Then she realized that it was just his empty fingers in the air, describing the size of the pills. A few of the older jurors leaned forward, as if trying to see what he held. A nice technique, Claire thought, creating reality out of thin air.

"These RU-486 pills are almost invisible. The expert evidence will show that it's hard to taste them. You could crush one into powder and put into a drink and the person you served the drink to wouldn't know it! You will see that Dr. Wyatt had a close relationship with Sarah Corbett, very close indeed. Her testimony will show that he was with her for a whole weekend. They made meals together. Dr. Wyatt brought her wine to drink."

He let the last words roll out slowly. Dr. Wyatt the seducer, the snake in the garden. Claire circled one of her notes a few times, reminding herself to explain that RU-486 required two precisely timed doses, not just one. Mills was making it sound like dosing someone would be the simplest thing in the world. Every little bit of difficulty in committing the crime would help build that precious measure of reasonable doubt.

Mills talked for a while about the state's evidence. The witnesses, the box with Wyatt's fingerprints. But he seemed not to want to bore the jury with dates and facts. He was too good a storyteller.

Riley Mills soon turned back to his theme of opportunity. "The evidence will show that Dr. Wyatt arranged to be alone with Sarah Corbett for an entire weekend. Plenty of time, plenty of opportunity to deliver the drug to an unwitting party.

"And don't forget that Daniel Wyatt is a doctor. He is experienced with giving people drugs, he knows how they work. His expertise isn't merely that of general physician, either. As we look at his career, we will see a special interest in abortion, even a *political* interest."

Riley Mills swung his ample frame as he addressed the court, letting his gaze fall on the defense table and Claire Davis in particular. She forced herself to return his gaze without emotion. So, that would be part of his strategy, too. To impugn not only Daniel, but his and Claire's work with WAG. As far as Riley was concerned, Daniel's crime was a natural outgrowth of his consorting with liberal, abortion-loving feminists and all they represented.

"And finally, intent."

Mills closed the distance between himself and the jury with a single step. He lowered his voice, as if to address each of them separately.

"Ladies and gentlemen of the jury, once all the evidence is in, there won't be any doubt about what his intentions were. Dr. Daniel Wyatt wanted to kill Sarah's child. His own child. You will see that the tests performed on Sarah Corbett's blood showed amounts of these drugs that could only have been intended to cause an abortion. Now, it has been claimed by some folks—folks who want these drugs placed into every pregnant woman's hands—that they might help treat certain diseases. But those claims have never been proven, and the drug RU-486 has never been proven to have *any positive effects*. More importantly, Sarah Corbett didn't have any diseases. No, she didn't. The evidence will show that Sarah Corbett was a healthy young woman with a healthy baby inside her."

He looked over at the defense table, his eyes spearing Wyatt.

"Healthy, until Dr. Daniel Wyatt took it upon himself to end her pregnancy. To kill her child."

His voice broke on the last words. Claire couldn't help marveling at his mastery of rhetorical effects.

"Now, the defense will try to tell you that this isn't murder. They'll say, 'Mothers terminate their pregnancies all the time. Is *that* murder? Maybe if a mother's allowed to do it, a father should be, too.' But don't be confused."

Mills swung around toward the jury. He was looking straight at Peggy Fontenot, Claire realized.

"Not any man has that right," he continued. "No man has the right to make this choice for a woman."

Claire Davis suddenly realized why Riley Mills had left Peggy Fontenot, a young, pro-choice woman, on the jury. She was his token liberal. Mills felt she would be angered by the crime Daniel Wyatt had allegedly committed, convinced with all the rest of them, and that she would put her stamp of approval on a murder conviction. The rest of the jury would look to her to say it was okay.

Claire could smell it in the courtroom already, the sympathy for Sarah Corbett, the animosity toward Daniel Wyatt. Mills was getting the job done in his opening statement, for God's sake. What could she have done? When should she have objected?

"What would you call it?" Mills asked, looking straight at the jury. "What would you call the crime, if, with premeditation and purpose, a man killed the child living within you? A child you desperately wanted?"

He shook his head woefully.

"We will hear expert testimony. We will see pictures of what such a child of eight weeks would have looked like. Tiny hands, feet, ears. A brain. Even a beating heart."

Fuck, thought Claire. Mills hadn't mentioned any pictures of fetuses in his discovery. She made a note. Another one for the judge.

"So what would you call this crime?" he asked again. "Understand what this man has done, completely against the will of the mother. He has killed a child."

Mills moved slowly, ponderously toward the prosecution's side of the courtroom, headed for his chair as if weary from his exertions on behalf of the People of Louisiana.

"There's just one name for it," he said. "Murder."

And he sat heavily down.

Claire felt the gasp in the courtroom, the appreciation for the gravity of the charges, for Mills's virtuoso performance.

"Ms. Davis." Judge Thibodeaux addressed her. "Would you prefer to begin your opening statement now? Or wait until after recess?"

Claire knew she should start immediately. She didn't want the jurors pondering Mills's words during a long lunch break, the narrative he had delivered so masterfully cementing in their minds. But she didn't have the strength to begin just yet. She was still reeling from the damage Mills had already done. She needed an hour to collect herself.

She knew it was a mistake, and cursed herself for her weakness, but she said, "Your Honor, defense will be glad to make its opening statement after a recess."

Thibodeaux nodded somberly, and dismissed the court.

Once the jury was out of sight, Claire shook her head. This wasn't good.

She'd said only one sentence so far in the case, and it had been the wrong one.

Riley Mills returned to the courtroom still flush with the excitement of delivering his opening statement. His staff had assured him that it had been one of his best performances. He was also a bit flush from the three shots of seventeen-year-old Bowmore whiskey he'd rewarded himself with. There wasn't much more to do today. Claire Davis had appeared crushed by his opening, and Mills doubted that she could even come up with anything worth objecting to.

He took a long look at the jury as the court assembled itself for the defense's opening statement. They had their grave faces on, as juries always did the first few days of a trial, before the boring part started. But these jurists looked graver than usual. Mills knew he had moved them, had made them see the depths of this crime. The women appeared to be particularly angry. As Claire Davis stood and prepared to deliver her statement, there was a palpable sense of hostility toward her. Normally, a female defense attorney brought out the understanding side of female jurors, but in this case, Davis ran the risk of appearing as a traitor to her gender.

As she began, Riley Mills could detect something in Davis's voice that he'd never heard there before. She was nervous.

"You've listened to the district attorney's opening statement," she said, gesturing toward the prosecution table with one long arm. "And I'm sure you will agree with me that he tells his story very well. I doubt very much that I'll be able to meet his standard of dramatic delivery."

Mills frowned. What was she up to? This false modesty wasn't going to save Daniel Wyatt. Was she playing to the media? Already apologizing for an unwinnable case?

"But in our system of justice, the defense doesn't necessarily have to tell a story. My job isn't to come up with a different or a better drama than the one Riley Mills is acting out for you. My job is much less exciting: to point out the holes in what he's telling you. Not the dramatic holes, of course. We all agree how exciting Riley Mills is to listen to. Just the factual holes. My job is to make you notice what's missing in his story."

Davis was using his name a lot, Riley Mills realized. So, her defense was going to focus on him personally. The old saying: If the facts are on your side, argue the facts. If the law is on your side, argue the law. If neither is on your side, pound the other lawyer.

"Let's look at the prosecution's case and see what's missing, shall we?" Davis continued.

"Motive. Riley Mills asks you to assume that Sarah Corbett's child was actually fathered by Dr. Daniel Wyatt.

"Mr. Mills talked in his opening statement about paternity tests, but none was ever given to Sarah. When Sarah Corbett went to the hospital, no tests were done on the fetus. Why not? Because they didn't keep the fetus. Genetic tests on that fetus might have shown that Wyatt was not the father. But the fetus is missing."

There was dead silence in the courtroom. Mills chewed his lower lip. Davis was on thin ice here. The whole subject was an uncomfortable one. Mills didn't want to get into a discussion over how doctors routinely threw away miscarried fetuses as medical waste. He didn't want the hospital witnesses talking about how tiny it was, so insubstantial that they'd barely been able to find it among all the blood and other discharge. This contradicted Mills's argument that the fetus was a fully formed human being.

But her line of argument revealed what sort of case Claire Davis was going to present, hitting the prosecution from every conceivable angle rather than presenting a coherent theory. Like the old lawyer joke: That's not a dog bite. Besides, my client's dog doesn't bite. Besides, my client doesn't have a dog!

"But," Claire Davis continued, "Riley Mills might argue that it stands to reason if a man and woman are having an affair, sooner or later the woman will become pregnant with the man's child. But were Daniel Wyatt and Sarah Corbett having an affair? Where are the love letters? Where are the presents shared between lovers? Where are the hotel bills? Where are the friends who knew about it? They're all *missing*."

She shrugged again.

"Riley Mills will bring forth eyewitnesses to testify that Dr. Wyatt and Sarah Corbett were seen together at various places. But they were friends. He was her doctor. She even baby-sat for his children. You will have to ask yourself, Can any of these witnesses be sure that they were having an affair?"

Claire Davis let the question hover unanswered in the air.

Mills noticed that she hadn't added the misplaced medical records to her litany of things missing. It was odd, those records disappearing. He wondered if Davis knew what had happened to them. Perhaps that's why she hadn't commented on them directly; lawyerly ethics wouldn't allow her to mention them if she'd somehow, even inadvertently, caused their disappearance.

"Now let's talk about opportunity."

She held up her hand, as Mills remembered he had done, holding a tiny and imaginary object.

"The 'murder weapon' in this supposed murder case is a few small pills. These pills, of course, no longer exist. They're missing, too. What traces of them still exist? Riley Mills will bring forward expert witnesses who will explain how some of the chemicals from these pills were found in Sarah Corbett's bloodstream. But these experts can't tell you how those chemicals got there. You can't be sure if these chemicals came from a pill, or from some medication accidentally given to Sarah Corbett in the hospital. Or if they came from contamination of her blood after it was taken from her body. These chemicals could even have occurred in her blood naturally. Unfortunately, we can't repeat the tests, because by now the substances have been cleaned out of her body.

"We don't even know if this drug or any other drug caused Sarah Corbett's miscarriage, if that's what it was. Fully a quarter of all pregnancies end naturally that way."

Davis turned to face the jury full-on now. She was hitting her stride, finally, trying to build up reasonable doubt from every direction.

"But this is the most important point. No one can tell you for certain that Daniel Wyatt gave Sarah Corbett these pills. When talking about opportunity, Riley Mills spoke of how easy it was to give someone RU-486. That's right. It's easy. You don't have to be a doctor. Anyone could have slipped them into her food, into her drink. And, of course, Sarah Corbett could have taken them herself. We don't have any eyewitnesses to what happened. Those eyewitnesses are missing."

Mills smirked. The box of RU-486 with Daniel Wyatt's fingerprints was going to make short work of that argument. He should have talked about it more in his opening, he realized. Perhaps Claire Davis was right, and he'd let himself get too involved with the drama of the crime. He had assumed that Davis would argue the *Roe* v. *Wade* angle, the terrible precedent that this case might set. But she was going for acquittal. That was all right with Mills. He could argue the facts if he needed to.

"So what do we have in this murder case?" Davis continued. "We have no eyewitnesses to the crime. The alleged victim, Sarah Corbett, doesn't even claim to know when the crime happened. Indeed, we can't be sure if she was pregnant with Wyatt's child at all. The alleged murder weapon can't be found either. We have to infer its existence from a few arcane tests of Sarah Corbett's blood, tests that can't be repeated.

This entire case is based on supposition after supposition, assumption upon assumption, guess upon guess.

"And what about the prosecution's most important charge? Murder in the first degree?"

Here it comes, thought Mills. He could see Davis picking out Peggy Fontenot in the box.

"Even if you believe the story that Riley Mills has told us here today, there's one last question. Even if you *believe* that Sarah Corbett was pregnant and that Daniel Wyatt was the father, and *assume* that he gave her the drugs, a question remains. Is that murder?"

Claire Davis stepped back from the box to include the entire jury in her gaze.

"If, as the Supreme Court has held, a mother can terminate her pregnancy without breaking the law, why can't a father? Or, to put it another way, if this court finds Daniel Wyatt guilty of murder, then what happens to those women who exercise their own right to choose over the next few years? What happens to their protection? What happens to *Roe* versus *Wade*?"

The defense attorney sat down, the questioning look still on her face. Mills tried to understand the expressions of the jurors, but Davis's short opening statement had left some confusion on their faces.

If nothing else, Claire Davis had halted the prosecution's momentum for a while. The emotions that these issues raised were still powerful, and could easily distract a jury. Mills realized that he would have to build his case slowly and carefully. But overall, it had been a good day.

Outside the courtroom, A.D.A. Morrisey asked her boss how he thought Davis's statement had gone.

"It was a mess," Mills said, shaking his head. There was no point in showing any doubt in front of his staff. "All over the place. One minute she's casting doubt on whether the child was Wyatt's, the next minute she's arguing for a father's right to choose."

"Yeah, I suppose so," Morrisey agreed. "But I thought Davis had something going when she was banging her 'missing' drum. I've always thought we were a little short on physical evidence, Riley. But her closing was weak. She practically turned around and admitted our case, just questioned whether it was murder." Morrisey shook her head. "She should save the *Roe* stuff for the appeals court."

"Nope, she wants to win here and now, Morrisey," Mills said. "That's Claire's weakness in this case. It's not just saving Daniel Wyatt that's important to her, she wants to save something bigger. Her career, her precious advocacy group, a woman's right to choose. She can't allow herself to fail. So she's biting off more than she can chew."

Mills scratched his head. "Of course, that could make her dangerous."

"How do you mean, Riley?" Morrisey asked.

"Well, we used to say that in a bacon-and-eggs breakfast, the chicken is an interested party, but the pig is totally committed."

Morrisey looked confused.

"Claire Davis's bacon is on the plate," Riley explained. "She's totally committed, and that makes her dangerous. Let's not underestimate her."

"You're not turning chicken on me, are you, Riley?"

Mills chuckled.

"Nope. But I want to go back over the case, witness by witness. Let's make sure there aren't any missing links for Claire Davis to point out. For one thing, we haven't been through all the evidence seized from WAG yet."

"Damn, Riley, there's roomfuls of it."

"Well, get the boys back on it," he ordered. "And let's put this paternity issue to rest with our witnesses tomorrow. We've got to spell out every step of the affair to the jury, otherwise we'll have Davis arguing for immaculate conception."

"Fine with me, Riley," Morrisey agreed. "I never liked hanging too much of this case on Sarah Corbett's say-so, anyway. Davis is sure to mention that old perjury conviction of hers."

"That's from years ago," Mills protested.

"Maybe so, but something about that girl just makes me nervous."

"She'll hold up. After hearing Claire Davis say she didn't even sleep with Wyatt, Sarah'll have something to prove. She'll hang Daniel Wyatt yet."

"Riley?" Morrisey asked, then turned her voice to a whisper. "You don't think Corbett could've taken those drugs herself, do you?"

"Morrisey," Mills answered, the usual steel returning to his voice. "Don't let Davis confuse you. Wyatt did it. He's guilty as sin."

Mills pulled a comb from his pocket and pulled it through his thinning hair. There were cameras on the courthouse steps, and he wanted to give a sound bite on his way out.

"This case isn't so complicated once you get ahold of it," he assured his assistant. "This is murder, pure and simple."

Daniel Wyatt stared at the postcard in his hand.

On one side was a photograph, a crowded beach re-touched with garish colors that turned the sky purple and flesh yellow. He wondered for a moment if Ellen wasn't in-dulging in satire, referring to the beach house that was the scene of his alleged crime. But that sort of gesture didn't seem like Ellen. She had simply grabbed the first postcard she could find, and on the back side jotted a note in her neat, flourishless handwriting.

Plug in your phone. I'll call you.

For the hundredth time that evening, Daniel checked his watch. The short missive from his wife gave a time, which was five minutes from now. Wyatt had been sitting here for thirty minutes, waiting and staring at the phone jack. He wanted to just plug the phone in, but he'd done so earlier and it had rung almost instantly. The media, requesting an interview.

Better than a death threat, he supposed.

Wyatt looked up at the little TV camera that covered the kitchen door. Sometimes he imagined that these cameras and motion detectors the FBI had installed were actually broadcasting. Like the cameras in the courtroom, they were capturing the grim, lonely hours of his life for all to see. Fame, or at least notoriety, was apparently a part of the pun-ishment for his crimes, to be served concurrently with trial, and for some indeterminate amount of time afterward, regardless of the verdict. Would people always know him? Wyatt wondered. He spent the next few minutes trying to remember the faces from the media trials of the last decade or so. If he ran into the Menendez brothers, would he recognize them? What about Claus von Bülow?

Finally, with a minute to spare, Wyatt reached for the phone cord and popped it into the wall.

Then he sat, the phone in his lap, counting the last sixty seconds.

On forty-three, it rang.

"Hello," he answered, bracing himself for whoever was on the line—an angry anti-abortion tirade, the friendly voice of the associate producer of some talk show . . .

"Daniel."

"Ellen," he gasped. The sound of his wife's voice, such an ordinary thing only two months ago, was suddenly a luxury too precious to be believed.

"How are you, Daniel?"

"I'm . . ." Having waited all day for this conversation, Wyatt found himself unable to answer this simplest of questions. The reflex answers—okay, fine, great—were all patently absurd. But he could hardly impose his suffering on Ellen.

"I'm lonely," he managed.

"I'm sorry about that. The kids miss you."

"God, I miss them, too," Wyatt said.

"I'm just telling them that you've got work to do. But they don't understand why they had to change schools. I think Kenny knows something. Some kid at school here must have told him."

"I'm so sorry," Wyatt said. "You know, I tried to protect you, all of you. That's why I . . . lied."

There was silence from the other end of the line.

"But I'm okay," he said, trying to sound strong.

"I'm glad one of us is," Ellen answered. Her voice had grown suddenly hard, resentment and humiliation welling up inside her.

"I can't sleep anymore, Daniel. I'm taking my mother's Valium. And I never leave the house; I can't face the stares."

She sobbed once, and the sound broke Wyatt's heart. He tried to say something, but couldn't force his mouth to work.

"I can't stand it when my friends call here," Ellen continued. "They try to say nice things, but I know what they're thinking."

"Ellen, you have nothing to be ashamed of. This was my fault, all mine. Your friends miss you. You should come back home."

"And face TV cameras every day?"

"But the kids need to see their father."

There was a long pause.

"I'll try," she said finally. "I will try. I don't know if I have the strength, though."

Daniel Wyatt looked at the small camera that peered down at him. Security devices everywhere he looked. Two men outside, guarding his worthless life. Who was he to bring his family into such danger? What a greedy, selfish, arrogant man.

"Ellen," Wyatt said. "Just come."

"Good-bye, Daniel," she said, and the line went dead.

Wyatt hung the phone up, found himself completely exhausted.

Almost instantly, it rang again. Wyatt was filled with an irrational joy. Was it Ellen? Calling back to say yes, she was coming?

He lifted the receiver to his ear.

"Ellen?"

"So, at last I can talk to you." A man's voice, low and menacing.

"Pardon me?"

"I want you to know that I'm watching you. I've been watching you."

Another crank. Wyatt knew he should just hang up. But the dark, insinuating voice angered him. He'd wanted it so much to be Ellen, and here was this moron trying to sound threatening. For a moment, the voice on the phone represented all the sad protesters who harassed him on the courthouse steps every day.

"Listen," Wyatt snapped. "You don't scare me. You're just some loser with too much time on his hands."

"Compared with what you are, Wyatt? A child killer?"

"You don't know what I am," Wyatt said with conviction. "You don't know the choices I've had to make, or what I've been through. Frankly, you don't have the imagination to even begin—"

"The kitchen," the voice calmly interrupted. "You're standing in the kitchen."

A cold finger of doubt traced a line down Wyatt's spine.

"To hell with you," he shouted, walking from the kitchen.

"Now the living room," the voice continued, as soft and careful as an announcer covering a golf tournament. "You're right by the stairs."

Wyatt froze, one hand on the banister. He looked out the bay windows of the living room into the utter darkness, which was suddenly alive with an invisible presence, a piercing stare that the blackness seemed to return to him.

"Don't worry, Dr. Wyatt," the voice said. "I don't want to hurt you. Not yet. You are too perfect in your evil, too pure. A textbook example . . . in a lesson I'm still preparing."

Wyatt sat down heavily at the bottom of the stairs. Hang up, he ordered himself. But it was as if the low, calm voice had hypnotized him.

"By the time I come for you, the whole world's eyes will be upon you, and many will rejoice."

Rejoice, Wyatt thought. This was the man Costilla had warned him about. What had the FBI agent told him to do?

Run. Get upstairs and hit one of the panic buttons, small transmitters distributed throughout the house that would alert the FBI agent outside. But the thought of going deeper into the house, of being cornered in some room upstairs, was too horrifying. He stood, the black eyes of the living room windows lancing through him, but didn't know where to run.

"Men like you have killed so many, Wyatt," the voice continued. "Many must die in answer."

Wyatt had a moment of pure animal panic, and, as if the earth were shaking, only one thought went through his head: *Get outside.*

He threw the phone down and lunged for the door. The three heavy locks resisted his panicked fingers for just a moment, but then the door was open. He ran down the walk toward the FBI agent's car. Wyatt felt a hundred imaginary bullets pierce him from the darkness. Costilla had said the man was an expert shot. The FBI agent's surprised face looked up at him through the car windows. The car's door opened, the agent pulling a gun.

"He was on the phone . . ." Wyatt said breathlessly. "He's close. He could see me."

The agent pushed Wyatt into the car with the words "Stay down."

Wyatt crouched, his face pressed against the vinyl seats, waiting for the blaze of gunfire. He heard the FBI agent on his cell phone. The arrival of the sheriff's deputy. Then, five minutes later, more and more cars, their sirens wailing, their radios crackling.

Another primitive feeling slowly replaced the terror that had forced Wyatt out of his house. A need for safety. Safety in numbers. He sat up, head in his hands, listening to the authorities arrive and reestablish order.

They were here to save his life, Wyatt thought gratefully. Then he shook his head.

What life?

Don't worry, Dr. Wyatt. I don't want to hurt you. Not yet. You are too perfect in your evil, too pure. A textbook example . . . in a lesson I'm still preparing.

The harsh breathing in the background didn't match the words. That must be Wyatt hyperventilating with panic.

By the time I come for you, the whole world's eyes will be upon you, and many will rejoice.

The sound of a car passing on the caller's end. He's definitely outside, looking in.

Men like you have killed so many, Wyatt. Many must die in answer.

Agent Eduardo Costilla pushed the stop button and rewound the tape for what must have been the fiftieth time.

Tabitha Samuels glared at him, her dark eyes reflecting the light from the computer screen before her.

"By the time I strangle you, Costilla, the whole world's eyes will be upon me, and many will rejoice," she said, her voice a gruff imitation of the shooter's. "But no one more than I."

Costilla ignored the young agent and played the tape again. She groaned, mouthing the now familiar dialogue between the doctor and the serial murderer.

This was his voice, Costilla thought. Finally, a piece of the man himself, not just lifeless digital spoor. True, Samuels's sharp ear had identified some sort of effects box, altering the voice a bit. They'd never make a positive ID from this tape.

But after three years of trailing a phantom, it was good to hear him actually speak.

Of course, the words themselves were not so encouraging.

"Many must die," Costilla said to himself when the tape ended again.

"That would probably be due to the fact that 'men like you have killed so many,' " Samuels parroted.

"Sounds like a bombing, Chaos," Costilla said.

"That would go with our White Power hit," Chaos agreed. "By my count, those boys still have twenty pounds of C-4 to spread around."

Costilla shivered. Chaos had traced the old posting on the White Power ring to a small but well-armed militia called the Soldiers of Christ. In 1995, they had been suspected of hijacking a military convoy headed for Fort Dix with a load of arms and munitions. Among various outdated artillery shells and a few small arms, they had gotten away with thirty-four pounds of C-4 explosives.

The Bureau of Alcohol, Tobacco and Firearms had raided their headquarters a few months later, discovering twelve pounds of the stolen explosives and arresting most of the group's membership. Those few who remained at large were suspected in the bombing of a black church in North Carolina, which the FBI believed accounted for one pound of the stolen explosives not yet recovered. Costilla's shooter had bombed one clinic back in 1997, also with C-4. Maybe a pound.

So that left twenty pounds to go.

"Many must die," Costilla repeated.

"You bet," Agent Samuels agreed. "Twenty pounds of C-4? That's any square block of Lafayette, Louisiana, in splinters."

"I didn't know explosives was your thing, Chaos," Costilla said. Her distaste for guns was well known on the team. She was altogether an unusual FBI agent.

"I have spent the last three weeks up to my butt in White Power websites, Agent Costilla," she explained. "At this point

I could build you a pipe bomb out of baking soda and a used-up toilet-paper roll."

"That's sounds deadly, Chaos. Remind me to check under my bed tonight."

"Oh, I would never hurt you, Costilla. Not yet." Chaos stared at him through lids heavy with boredom. "You are too perfect in your evil. Too pure."

"Not yet," Costilla mused, returning his eyes to the transcript of the tape.

He rose, pulling his jacket from the chair behind him. Chaos was right. He had to get out of this room. He'd heard the tape enough times.

Costilla felt that if he heard the voice, he could recognize it, regardless of the effects the killer had used to disguise himself. He pulled a piece of paper from his legal pad, a list of all the pro-life protest groups here in Lafayette. There had been a lull during the preparations for the trial, but now that the show had begun, the population of Lafayette was at a new high.

Costilla stabbed out a number on his cell phone.

"Sheriff's office," a young voice answered.

"This is Agent Costilla. Is Sheriff Hicks there?"

Hicks had wanted to go along on this round of interviews. The sheriff thought he could bring order to the town if he met personally with each of the protest groups. Costilla couldn't think of a reason to deny the request. The local tin might bring a little local wisdom to the case. And at least Costilla wouldn't get lost.

"Hicks here," the phone's speaker drawled.

"This is Agent Costilla, Sheriff. Are you ready to roll?"

"You bet," the older man answered jocularly. "I was thinking you'd gone and left me behind."

Sheriff Hicks found working with Agent Costilla strange. His own job was so very different from the FBI agent's.

As a county sheriff, he worked hundreds of cases a year,

most of them so small that most people would probably just call them incidents. Every day and night there were a few fist-fights, burglaries, domestic disputes, and what-have-you spread over the county. Individual policemen handled most of them, but Hicks was always on call. For one thing, most people in town knew and trusted him. In the majority of these cases, no arrest was made, so Hicks often served as a mediator. He was like a roving judge, making sure that complaints were heard and conflicts resolved as painlessly as possible, making sure that the Law had a voice when problems arose. The days blurred into one another, an endless succession of small issues clamoring for attention.

But Agent Costilla's attention was as narrow as Hicks's was wide. For the last three years, the man had trailed a single killer. When Costilla spoke of his unnamed quarry, he grew grimly passionate, as if the murderer were an old friend who had betrayed him, not just some anonymous nutcase.

"Until now, this guy was strictly low profile," Costilla said as they rode the elevator up from the lobby where they had met. "He was invisible until his hit. You couldn't predict where he'd be. But now he's practically begging for attention. He's working up to something big. With a lot of these guys, the kill is almost sexual. I suppose my shooter has finally discovered the joys of foreplay."

Hicks tried unsuccessfully to chuckle at the disturbing comparison, but Costilla didn't look like he was joking.

"He's readying himself for his final act," Costilla said darkly.

"Well, I'm sure you'll catch him before he does whatever he's planning," Hicks said encouragingly. The elevator stopped. Hicks was happy to have the grim conversation interrupted.

The overcrowded Hyatt Hotel was not only headquarters for the FBI but for two of the pro-life groups in town, a small organization from New York called Catholics for Life and a much larger group called Operation Rescue.

"Let's talk to Catholics for Life first," Costilla had suggested. "Get them out of the way. They're all Catholic priests, so I doubt they're going to know anything about our bomber."

Sheriff Hicks nodded. The FBI agent knew this world better than he. Hicks figured that Costilla was a Catholic himself, now that he thought of it, being Hispanic and from back east.

Costilla rapped on the door of the room of Father David John, the head of Catholics for Life. A few moments passed, and the FBI agent knocked again.

"Well, his second-in-command's just next door," Costilla said, reading from his notes. "Father Peter O'Keefe."

They tried that door, and, after a long wait, a sleepy-looking priest answered their knock.

"Yes?" the priest said.

"I'm sorry, Father," Costilla said. Hicks noticed a note of deference in his voice. The FBI agent was definitely Catholic. "We were looking for Father David, but he's not in his room."

Hicks smelled a strong scent of coffee wafting from the room. It made his stomach growl a bit. He'd been drinking far more than usual now that his town was under siege.

"I'm Sheriff Mark Hicks and this here is FBI Agent Eduardo Costilla," Hicks explained. The priest nodded.

"Father David's at the hotel restaurant," Father O'Keefe explained. "I'd be glad to get him. We could meet you in the lobby in ten minutes."

"Certainly, Father. Take your time," Costilla said.

"You have to understand, Agent Costilla," Father David was saying. "For some of these people, this is a war. A holy war. So they feel they have the right to commit crimes in fighting it. They think that they're following God's law, not man's. But, of course, none of our group would break the law."

"We've been concerned about violence ourselves," Father O'Keefe added. "When you have this many people together, there are always a few who stray from the path of peace. It's sad but unavoidable."

"I understand what you're saying, Fathers," Costilla responded. The FBI agent had listened pretty patiently, Hicks thought, considering how well he knew the ground the two priests were covering. "We just wanted to know if you've seen anyone here, encountered anyone who you specifically thought could be a threat to public safety."

Father David closed his eyes, shaking his head softly. "I haven't met anyone who has advocated violence, Agent Costilla. My interests are far more spiritual. No one has discussed it in any way with me, at least outside of the sacred bounds of the confessional."

Hicks raised an eyebrow. *The sacred bounds of the confessional?* So someone *had* talked to the old priest. But he could never say more than he had just said. Confessions to a priest were protected even from subpoena.

"I see, Father," Costilla said.

"Perhaps I have something that would help you," Father O'Keefe offered. "Have you heard of an organization called Soldiers of Christ?"

Hicks didn't remember the name from the list, but Costilla straightened up in his seat like a hound spotting a hare.

"Yes," he said. "But I didn't know they still existed."

"I wouldn't know," O'Keefe admitted. "But there was a man I met the other day. We got into something of a discussion. He claimed that he had once belonged to this organization. He said some terrible things about Dr. Wyatt. About what he wanted to do to him."

Father O'Keefe shook his head, as if the memory of the man's threats was painful and disturbing.

"Did you get his name?" Costilla asked.

"It was Bartlett. I don't remember his first name. He just came down from some rallies in Canada, he said."

"Canada?" Costilla asked. Hicks could see the wheels churning in the FBI agent's mind.

"I believe so," Father O'Keefe said. "Yes. Canada was it."

"Thank you both," Costilla said, standing. He glanced once at Hicks, and headed for the hotel door.

"My," Father David exclaimed, "your partner seems in a hurry, suddenly."

"I suppose so," Hicks replied, looking at Father O'Keefe. "It looks like you knew exactly what to say."

Father O'Keefe smiled, and Hicks tipped his hat to the two priests. Costilla was already halfway to the car, the sheriff realized with a grimace. And damned if he hadn't wanted to get some coffee at the hotel restaurant before they moved on.

41 | EYEWITNESSES

The first day of witness testimony began with Sarah Corbett's OB-GYN at Lafayette General. They discussed the pregnancy test she had taken in early November.

The man was nervous but wholly believable, responding to the district attorney's questions with a politeness that seemed almost exaggerated. Mills took him slowly through the pregnancy test itself, its reliability and the simplicity of its use, and made sure he identified Sarah Corbett from across the room. The doctor was old but sharp-witted, and there was no point in trying to make him look senile.

That was fine with Claire Davis. She had never hoped to cast any real doubt about Sarah actually having been pregnant. Witnesses in the emergency room had seen the tiny fetus before it had been discarded. But doubt was a funny thing. Once a jury got it in their minds, it could spread all over a case. What Claire had sought to do in her opening statement was to start the jury thinking skeptically. The case against Daniel Wyatt had a lot of steps, a great deal of supposition, perhaps enough to make a jury uncomfortable. If Claire could somehow combine that discomfort with unease about the charge of murder itself, perhaps she could win a friendly verdict.

Claire had watched the news networks the night before. The consensus seemed to be that Riley Mills had won the first day. Her statement had been too scattershot, too disorganized compared with his sweeping histrionics. But the talking heads would always prefer the storyteller to the factual and skeptical plodder that Claire intended to make herself over the next few weeks.

When time for her cross-examination came, she made it short.

"Dr. Bartholdt, did Sarah Corbett ever discuss with you who the father of her child was?"

"No, she didn't."

"And she never mentioned Dr. Daniel Wyatt?"

"No, ma'am."

"But Dr. Wyatt was her primary care physician at that time, correct?"

"Yes, he was."

"And you know Dr. Wyatt personally, don't you?"

"I suppose so. Everyone at the hospital knows him."

"So, if Dr. Wyatt was the father, mightn't she have mentioned that fact to you?"

"Objection!" came Riley Mills's voice. "Calls for speculation."

"Withdrawn," Claire said before Thibodeaux had a chance to rule. There was no point in getting him into the habit of siding with Mills.

"Now," she continued, "how did Sarah take the news that she was pregnant?"

"She was upset."

"Unhappy? In tears?"

"Yes, I suppose she cried," Dr. Bartholdt said, closing his eyes as he remembered. "She kept saying, 'Why me?' "

" 'Why me?' " Claire repeated. "No, that doesn't sound like a happy mother."

"Objection."

"Sustained. Next question."

Claire didn't let the interruption halt her momentum. "And did she talk with you about having the child?"

"Pardon me?"

"Did she ask how she should change her diet? About prenatal care. About getting more tests to make sure the baby was developing properly?"

"No," Bartholdt said, sighing more perfectly than Claire could ever have coached him to do. "She just left."

Next up was Dr. Ernest Magley, looking pale and terrified.

Mills took him through the appointment that Wyatt had helped Sarah Corbett make, the one she hadn't shown up for. The testimony kept Claire on the edge of her seat. If there was any part of this case that might suddenly collapse, Magley was it. Daniel hadn't actually told him whose the child was, but he must have known. The doctor seemed extremely edgy on the stand, and Mills kept reminding the jury in various ways that he and Wyatt were friends, did everything but call Magley a hostile witness. It would be hard to get anything positive out of the cross-examination. The jury could easily assume that Magley was protecting Wyatt.

"And did Sarah Corbett show up for this appointment?" Mills was asking.

"No, she didn't."

"Did Dr. Wyatt show up for the appointment?"

"He did."

This was the most damaging part of Magley's testimony: that Wyatt, and not Sarah, had showed up on that fateful afternoon. But there was no way Magley could lie. Too many people had seen Wyatt at the medical building.

"Wasn't that unusual? For a physician to come to an appointment with a patient?"

"Not really," a sweating Magley managed. "Maybe most doctors wouldn't come for such an appointment. But Dr. Wyatt is an old-fashioned doctor, and has very close relationships with all his patients. And Sarah was very upset about the whole thing. He was just there to hold her hand."

"Upset about the abortion?" Mills asked.

"About the pregnancy. She just wasn't happy with it. That's why she wanted an abortion." Magley's downcast eyes sought out his old friend at the defense table.

"But she didn't show," Riley reminded the courtroom.

"No."

"Did she ever call to explain?"

"No."

"Did she call to reschedule?"

"No, she didn't."

"Did you or your secretary attempt to call her?" Mills asked.

"No. Since Daniel was her doctor, I assumed he would call her and find out what had happened."

"Sounds like Dr. Wyatt and Sarah were very close."

"They were friends," Magley insisted doggedly. "He was her doctor."

"Dr. Magley . . ." Claire began her cross. "Did Sarah Corbett ever tell you who the father of the child was?"

"No, I'm afraid not," Magley answered heartily. With Mills out of his face, he had regained some of his usual arrogance.

"Did Dr. Wyatt ever tell you who the father of the child was?"

"No, he didn't."

"Did Dr. Wyatt ever mention that he knew who the father of Sarah Corbett's child was?"

"No. I don't think he knew," Magley said. "I'm not sure that Sarah even knew."

There was a sudden silence in the courtroom. Dammit, Claire thought. Magley was overreaching. Mills was going to pounce on this during redirect.

"No further questions, Your Honor."

"Dr. Magley, you stated that you thought Sarah didn't know who the father of her child was. Is that right?" Mills asked. He had used his option of further direct examination after hearing Magley's answers to Claire's questions.

Magley was sweating again.

"I said that I wasn't *sure* if she knew," Magley answered meekly.

"How many times did you meet with Sarah Corbett?"

"I never met her, actually."

"Never met her. How many times did you speak with her?"

"Just once. When she set up the appointment."

"How long was this conversation?" Mills asked.

"About five minutes."

"And during this five-minute conversation, you decided that Sarah didn't know who the father of her child was?"

"I wasn't sure that she did. I mean, she was unmarried, and was upset. A lot of women don't know," Magley blathered.

Mills shook his head and sat down. Claire didn't bother to recross, her heart sinking as Magley walked from the witness stand. He rejoined the audience with a broad smile, as if he had helped Daniel's cause. The pompous idiot had insulted Sarah Corbett needlessly, alienating everyone in the courtroom, and in the bargain he'd managed to look like the defense had coached him to do so.

That afternoon, the D.A. called two waiters from a downtown restaurant.

Claire cast a wary glance at Daniel. The whole tactic of denying the affair made him nervous. He'd walked around for two months frightened that someone would find out about him and Sarah. Now that everyone knew about the two of them, it must be painful to watch his lawyer try to hide it all over again.

Claire was impressed that the prosecution team had found the waiters. Certainly, there were rumors all over town now. A lot of people claimed to have friends who'd seen Lafayette's most famous adulterers together, but there were few actual witnesses to the affair. After all, Sarah and Daniel had been together only a few times.

The waiters' testimony wasn't particularly damaging. Mills tried to make something of the restaurant's name, Laissez les Bon Temps Rouler, but the two old Cajuns hadn't seen anything romantic happen. In Claire's cross-examinations, she went for repetition, asking each a long list of questions.

Had they seen the two kissing, holding hands, touching each other? The steady stream of "no, no, no" from the two plain-spoken old Cajuns seemed to resonate in the courtroom. Perhaps her strategy could work, subjecting Mills's prosecution to death by a thousand cuts.

Wyatt looked relieved when the second of the two men was let go from the stand. He had told Claire about the kiss in the doorway of the restaurant, but she'd already read the waiters' statements. They hadn't seen it.

Mills's next witness was a fish-and-game warden who had seen Wyatt and Sarah at the beach house together. This was the trickiest part of denying the affair. There really wasn't a plausible explanation for a married doctor and his patient being out of town together for a weekend. But Claire noted with satisfaction that the warden had been moved up in Mills's schedule. Apparently, the prosecutor felt he needed to establish the affair beyond doubt before starting with the physical evidence.

The warden identified Sarah and Daniel convincingly, so Claire's cross-examination was fairly simple. As with the earlier witnesses, she elicited a steady stream of negatives from the man.

"Mr. Aston, you saw Dr. Wyatt and Sarah Corbett only once that weekend, correct? On Saturday morning?"

"That's right, ma'am."

"And were they kissing?"

"No. Just walking together."

"Not holding hands? Or touching each other in any way?" she asked, raising her eyebrows.

"No, ma'am. Not that I remember."

"And you didn't see either of them again the whole weekend?"

"No."

"So, as far as you know, they might have only been on that beach a few minutes?"

"I wouldn't know, ma'am."

Riley Mills's redirect was equally simple.

"Warden Aston, did you drive here today?" he asked.

"Yes, sir."

"How long did that take you?"

"Three hours."

"Three hours?" Mills raised his eyebrows and took his seat at the table, his point unspoken. No man and woman would drive three hours just for a short walk on the beach.

It didn't matter, Claire told herself. All that she wanted was a little doubt at every stage, each witness adding just a bit of uncertainty to the structure that Riley Mills was building. That would leave the jurors open to doubt at the end, when Claire made them ask the really difficult questions.

How many times did you meet with Sarah Corbett?
I never met her, actually.
Never met her. How many times did you speak with her?
Just once. When she set up the appointment.
How long was this conversation?
About five minutes.

Five minutes, thought Peter O'Keefe. Five minutes to arrange the murder of a child. The sight of Ernest Magley on his hotel-room television screen disgusted him. This fat and fatuous man, so sure of himself in the witness box. Here he was, accused of no crime himself, a witness for the prosecution, no less.

But how many unborn had Ernest Magley killed?

Daniel Wyatt was a murderer, O'Keefe was sure of that beyond any precious reasonable doubt, but Wyatt was, in a way, a pure and understandable form of evil. He had performed a handful of abortions in Guatemala and he had slain Sarah Corbett's baby. One could count his victims, imagine their faces.

This Ernest Magley, on the other hand, was an abortionist by trade. Court TV had profiled him before his testimony had begun, explaining that he had started his practice fifteen years ago. How many unborn children had he killed in that time? O'Keefe wondered. His office was one of the gas chambers of this holocaust. In a just and righteous world, the trial of Daniel Wyatt would be a quiet affair, a few days to dispose of a vile, self-interested criminal. But the trial of monsters like Dr. Ernest Magley would be another Nuremberg, the lists of their victims' names read for days on end . . .

But Magley was being portrayed as a bystander, a somewhat buffoonish walk-on character in the ever-expanding cast of this trial. Nothing more.

Peter O'Keefe shook his head. Even here in the Wyatt case, when this insane society had been forced to recognize what an abomination abortion was, simple common sense was turned on its head. The occasional murderer was a national scandal, and the fiend with the blood of hundreds on his hands was a harmless figure of fun.

O'Keefe still hadn't settled on his plan for Wyatt. He was waiting for a sign before that crucial epic step could be taken, justice rendered before the eyes of the world. The itch, the need for action was growing, though. O'Keefe knew that God would give him the sign, soon enough. But was he strong enough to bear waiting for it?

The smiling face of Magley distracted O'Keefe from his anxious reverie.

I wasn't sure that she did. I mean, she was unmarried, and was upset. A lot of women don't know, Magley's image said.

What a babbling fool, O'Keefe thought. What a perfect example of unknowing evil. A warm feeling grew in his stomach, a familiar desire returning, plans forming.

Perhaps there was a way to slake this thirst for vengeance, to make the waiting tolerable while he prepared for his grand gesture.

Of course, it was obvious. This Ernest Magley was no mere bystander; he was part of the Lord's plan. He would provide a valuable lesson while Wyatt's fate remained undecided. And the fate of Dr. Magley would be a way to focus even more attention on the trial.

O'Keefe smiled. He had already managed to distract the FBI by uttering Steve Bartlett's name. Perhaps he could use Magley to misdirect them even more.

Father Peter O'Keefe crouched by his bed, pulled a small

suitcase from underneath it. He carefully unlocked its hasps and pulled it open. The rich smell of coffee grounds filled his nostrils—the explosives were packed in the pungent roast to confuse bomb-sniffing dogs. But O'Keefe's sharp nose could smell the tang of C-4 beneath the coffee.

It smelled like heaven.

Riley Mills had decided that this morning's questioning would fall to A.D.A. Morrisey.

As much as Mills wanted the world to see this case as a battle between him and Claire Davis, he didn't want the women on the jury to interpret the struggle as male versus female. Besides, the forensic evidence that some of the witnesses today were to offer was scientifically complex, and frankly over his head. He also suspected that in her cross, Claire Davis was going to talk about the discarded fetus, and he trusted Morrisey to handle that delicate issue better than he could.

They had decided to start with Dr. Mark Arnistead, the attending physician who had treated Sarah Corbett when she'd come into the emergency room.

"The patient was hemorrhaging heavily from the birth canal," Arnistead explained. "And she held herself . . . there"—one hand on his lower belly—"and said, 'My baby.'"

The young doctor swallowed, and Mills smiled to himself. This fellow was a perfect witness. A youthful, attractive physician with absolutely serious delivery, but suffering from just a touch of nerves that made him seem vulnerable, a little wounded by the tragedy he'd seen unfold. Mills wouldn't be surprised if half the women on the jury had fallen in love with him already.

"Her blood pressure was very low. We stabilized her and I ordered a transfusion."

"Was the bleeding consistent with a patient who was losing her child?" Morrisey asked. She and Mills had decided to avoid the word "miscarriage," although that technically was what had happened, whether brought on by the drug or not. The word sounded too much like a natural event.

"Yes. In pregnancy, the lining of the uterus is built up in a process called decidualization. The blood supply to the uterine wall increases. In the sort of termination that Sarah Corbett experienced, the uterine lining has broken down and is expelled. So, yes. There's bleeding."

"But the bleeding wasn't the usual amount for a natural . . . termination, correct?" Morrisey asked.

"That's right," Dr. Arnistead said. "We suspected that Sarah had some sort of coagulation problem. But we couldn't find her medical records. We didn't have contact with any family members, so we couldn't easily check for hereditary problems. I decided to order extensive testing of her coagulation factors from Tulane Medical."

Morrisey nodded, and gave the doctor over to Claire Davis's tender mercies. The court would hear directly from the Tulane blood technician later that day.

"Dr. Arnistead . . ." Claire Davis began her cross-examination. "You said that Sarah Corbett was bleeding heavily when she entered the emergency room."

"Yes. In a termination like the one she was experiencing, the uterine walls are discharged."

"And you found a fetus among this discharged material, correct?"

"Yes."

"Could you describe this fetus to the jury?"

"Well, it seemed to be at about eight or nine weeks. A fetus at that stage of pregnancy is about an inch long."

"An inch," Claire Davis said slowly. "Could you see its arms? Legs?"

Arnistead looked uncomfortable. Mills was glad he didn't have to do redirect on this whole gruesome issue.

"Well, I can't recall. It was somewhat damaged, basically

just a lump of tissue. You see, adults are about seventy-five percent water, but early fetuses are more than ninety percent water. They are very insubstantial, in other words. Easy to damage."

Riley Mills sighed. He knew that Claire Davis would eventually have more experts on the stand to make this same point about how little there is to an early-term fetus. These courtroom pros would give the whole pro-choice song and dance about lack of brain function, sex differentiation, and viability. Mills had his own experts from the other side lined up. That was for later in the trial. But getting this charismatic young doctor, a prosecution witness, to proclaim the physical insignificance of the fetus was a coup for the defense.

"Dr. Arnistead," Davis continued, "often in a miscarriage, women don't find the fetus at all, correct?"

"Yes. But I wouldn't call this a miscarriage. The word 'miscarriage' usually refers to a natural event."

Claire Davis took a few steps away from the witness stand and regarded the young doctor critically, as if losing a bit of respect for him. Mills had to admit, Davis was getting better all the time.

"In the emergency room, did you have any reason to believe that this wasn't a natural event?"

"Well, no. Not at that point."

"So, except for the excessive bleeding, this could have been a normal miscarriage."

"Yes. That's what we thought it was, except for the bleeding."

"Now, does RU-486 cause life-threatening bleeding?" Davis asked.

"Uh, not that I know of," the doctor answered.

Mills frowned, annoyed. Again, Claire Davis was getting these answers from his witness instead of her own pet experts. Riley Mills wished that the young man would just plead ignorance and get off the stand.

"Are you aware that of the first one hundred thousand

women who used RU-486 in France, only five have suffered any ill effects whatsoever?"

"Your Honor." Morrisey beat Mills to the punch. "This question is outside the witness's area of expertise."

Judge Thibodeaux looked questioningly at Dr. Arnistead, who shrugged his shoulders. "I guess I don't know much about it."

"Sustained."

"Well, then, Dr. Arnistead," Davis said, shaking her head as if further frustrated with the young man's lack of competence, "is it true that you never thought about RU-486 that night, based on the condition of Sarah Corbett?"

"It never crossed my mind."

The blood expert from Tulane Medical was next.

Again, Mills was glad he'd left this morning's testimony to Morrisey. It was all fiendishly complicated. The chain of inference that the lab technician had followed from her initial tests to the assays that had ultimately detected mifepristone and prostaglandin was a long and winding one. Mills had tried to follow it when the technician, a fortyish woman with graying hair, had briefed him and Morrisey, but it was beyond him.

But Morrisey seemed to grasp it, could spit out the ten-syllable words as easily as the expert. They talked about the way that RU-486 worked, how it blocked the receptors of a molecule inside the uterus, preventing the progesterone that would be present naturally in a pregnant female from being produced. The questioning ranged from heat-shock proteins to DNA transcription, but somehow Morrisey kept the whole explanation from becoming mumbo jumbo. They started with the witness's first suspicions that a drug had heightened the levels of certain hormones in Sarah's system, interfering with her blood's ability to coagulate. The technician explained how one test result had led to another in a chain of inference. It had taken a day before she'd begun to suspect what had actually occurred. The patient's chart should have shown if a woman had taken RU-486.

Mills began to realize how easily this could have escaped a less diligent technician. There was certainly no straightforward test for RU-486; the woman had, like a persistent prosecutor, built a circumstantial case, a structure of indirect observations that suggested the presence of excess mifepristone and prostaglandin in Sarah's blood.

"So how sure are you that Sarah Corbett took or was given RU-486?"

"Absolutely sure," the woman answered simply.

Claire's cross began with a simple question.

"Can you actually produce the chemicals found in Sarah's blood?"

"Produce them?"

"Can you show them to me?"

"Only indirectly. The tests show that they were there."

"Indirectly."

The woman nodded her head. "Almost all medical tests work that way. That's the nature of medical science. Observations are indirect because the things we are looking for are very small and very well hidden. For example, the test for HIV doesn't detect the actual AIDS virus. It detects the antibodies that the body creates to fight the virus. And yet it's a very accurate test. The most common test for pregnancy doesn't find the fetus. It detects a change in the Beta BCG hormone that shows us that the body has started to move through the natural changes into pregnancy.

"When you look through an electron microscope, you aren't using your own eyes. All you see are shapes on a little TV screen, you're not really seeing cells and molecules, just representations of them. It's not a direct observation.

"But these aren't guesses," the technician explained, addressing the jury directly. She had an earnestness in her voice, the passionate need to explain of a scientist whose expertise has been called into question. "Indirect observation is the way that we know lots of things. We see smoke, we know that there's a fire. When we treat a man who says he's been shot, we don't always find the bullet in him. But we know from powder burns, from the entry and exit wounds, from the internal damage he's suffered that, yes, he *has* been shot.

"What I found is very simple. Sarah Corbett was given or took both stages of RU-486, at some time over the seventy-two hours prior to her admission to Lafayette General Hospital, with the correct timing and dosage to cause a miscarriage of her child."

Mills was happy to see that Claire Davis didn't bother with any more questions. Here, finally, was a witness who was absolutely certain.

"**W**e're going to lose, aren't we?" Daniel Wyatt said dejectedly.

Claire Davis took a drag from her cigarette and let the precious smoke stew in her lungs for a few seconds before answering. Being a smoking courtroom lawyer had gotten considerably more difficult in the five years since she'd quit. Back in her days as a public defender, smoking in the courthouse had been relegated to a few dingy rooms, but at least it was possible to manage the odd cigarette in the short breaks that constantly interrupted every trial. But these days, between the absolute ban on smoking in public buildings and the gauntlet of reporters that surrounded the courthouse, it was nearly impossible. This was Claire's first cigarette since breakfast.

After a moment, she reluctantly exhaled.

"No, we are definitely not going to lose," she answered. "It just feels that way. So far, it's all been the prosecution's presentation. That's the way it works: they attack, we respond. We haven't even begun to defend you, Daniel. We've got expert witnesses to come who are going to call into question their tests, their forensics, every piece of physical evidence. And then we've got the whole father's rights angle. If Mills gets you for Murder One, every mother who aborts is at risk of being charged with the same crime. There are four or five jurors on that panel who will not convict on the murder count for that reason alone. We've got Sarah Corbett's perjury charge, for God's sake."

Daniel moaned quietly from the passenger seat. They were headed back to his house, Claire's car bracketed by a three-car police escort.

"I hope you're not going to rake Sarah over the coals," he said.

"Daniel, I am not going to rake anyone over anything. This isn't some hell-bent rape defense, bringing out her past sexual conduct and saying she dresses like a slut, all right?"

Claire angrily stabbed out a cigarette. Despite her words to the contrary, the case had not gone well today. But as she'd said to Wyatt, she had not yet begun to fight. The last thing she needed was Daniel going soft on her.

She lit another cigarette, took a deep drag.

"But you have to understand one thing," she said after releasing the smoke. "Your life is at stake here, your career, everything. And the sole witness against you is an admitted perjurer. That fact alone could introduce reasonable doubt. It's not a rumor, not some slander against Sarah, not some deep dark secret. It's a matter of record, and it's my job to make sure the jury knows about it."

Wyatt sat in unhappy silence.

They turned onto his street, the red evening sky broken by the arched oaks that lined its median.

"Daniel," Claire said, her voice softening, "I will get you off. We both know you didn't do this."

"Thank you," he said softly. "Sometimes I wonder myself. I mean, how could Sarah have taken those pills, and then accuse me?"

Claire shook her head furiously as she drove. It was not good for Daniel to start thinking along these lines.

"She's an isolated, insecure woman, Daniel. She was torn between what she wanted—namely, you—and what she knew had to happen, what was best for all concerned— namely, an abortion. These polar opposites confused her. It's like a witch trial, Daniel. In the hands of a determined, manipulative prosecutor like Riley Mills, Sarah might claim the devil himself slipped her those pills."

Wyatt sighed. His mind would never be at rest on this issue, Claire realized, until a jury found him not guilty.

Well, it was her job to make sure that happened.

At least while he worried about the case, he wasn't thinking about Costilla's shooter. Wyatt seemed strangely unafraid after the incident of a few nights before. Claire hoped he wasn't succumbing to fatalism. A defendant with a death wish would be more than she could handle.

They turned into Wyatt's driveway, waited as two policemen from the escort checked the house.

"Claire, do you want to come in?" Daniel asked. "I mean, there's more about the case I'd like to discuss."

"Sorry, Daniel," she answered. "We've got such a limited time, and there's so much more to do for the case. And despite all this, WAG marches on."

He nodded, accepting her refusal quietly.

"Don't worry," she said. "You'll walk away from this. In every sense. Agent Costilla went over the security arrangements with me. There are five men out here now. You won't be getting any more visits from that nutcase."

"Claire, it's not fear of getting shot," Daniel explained. "It's being alone that's so hard for me right now."

She looked up at the large Georgian house with its windows all brightly lit up. The times she'd had dinner there, the three kids had filled it with noise and energy. It must seem terribly empty now.

"I'm sorry, Daniel. I just don't have time," she said softly. "I have a case to win."

He nodded and opened his door, grunting with the weight of the bulletproof vest as he pulled himself from the car. A plainclothes officer and a sheriff's deputy shielded Wyatt as he made his way to the door. Claire waited for a moment, watching as the shades in the house went down, one by one, protection against snipers.

Claire Davis shook her head, and, in a sudden hurry, pulled out of the driveway and drove for home.

* * *

The talking heads on CNN had changed their opinion of her, Claire realized.

She was getting high marks now, for her persistence in poking holes in Mills's case, her smooth handling of the disparate themes of her defense.

Damn, she thought guiltily. This case was giving her more exposure than being counsel for Surgeon General Daniel Wyatt could ever have done.

She sorted through her mail, the television a comforting drone in the background. Obvious hate mail went in one pile. Somebody had posted her home address on the Internet, and a handful of letters arrived every day to chastise her for her betrayal of her gender, the unborn, and God's law.

There were also invitations from the media, requests for interviews from all the major information surveyors. She'd stopped answering her phone, so they had resorted to letters. She discarded them one by one, again feeling guilty that her newfound fame had been won at Daniel's expense. There would be plenty of time for playing celebrity when this was all over.

Finally, she regarded the large package by the door. It was about the size of a coffeepot. There was no return address, but the postmark was from in town. Claire sat down and looked at the package, lighting another cigarette.

She knew what Eduardo Costilla would say. He had warned her of this in his soft-spoken, serious way. Don't open anything you're not a hundred percent sure of, not even a puffy envelope. A bomb big enough to blind you permanently can weigh no more than an ounce.

Claire scanned her mind for any innocent explanation. She could think of none, but that hardly meant that this was a bomb. She sighed. Is this what her sudden celebrity would reduce her to? Being afraid of her mail?

The box had some heft, maybe five pounds. If it was a bomb, it was a pretty serious one. Claire cursed and shook the thought from her head. She was being paranoid. If you were afraid, the terrorists had already won.

Here goes nothing.

In one furious action, she ripped the brown paper from the box and pulled it open. Packing peanuts covered whatever the box held. She reached inside, her spine tingling as if she were plunging her hand into a box of live snakes.

Smooth glass met her touch. It was a large jar of some kind.

Claire smiled. This was probably some of Molly's peach preserves, which she sent to her WAG colleagues every Christmas.

The smile faded as she pulled the glass jar from the box.

Staring blankly at her through the glass, coiled in red-tinged brine, was a human fetus.

By the time Agent Costilla burst through Claire Davis's door, the anger that had sped with him across town had turned to a cold fury. He hardly noticed that Claire flinched before him as he flew past her and strode to her living room.

Costilla pulled a plastic glove from his pocket and yanked it on with a snap. He saw the box, a few Styrofoam pellets strewn around it. When he hefted it carefully with his gloved hand, it felt empty. There was probably nothing more in it, but Costilla held the box at arm's length and poked through the remaining packing material with a pen.

The jar was sitting on Claire's rolltop desk. He inspected it from all sides, moving around the desk to avoid touching it. Then he turned it around slowly with the gloved hand. The fetus was real.

He carefully popped the metal hinge. My God, he thought. It was a canning jar, just as Claire had said in her phone call. He leaned forward to smell the contents of the jar. Formaldehyde.

Claire was watching him, a look of surprise on her face. He realized how he must look, sniffing at the dead fetus.

"Well, it's not nitroglycerin," he said by way of explanation.

In answer, she slowly closed her eyes.

"No. It didn't blow up," she said quietly. "But I suppose I was foolish."

The morguelike smell of formaldehyde had begun to creep through the room, and Costilla resealed the jar. Claire's face was pale. Costilla's anger faded. It was pointless railing at her now.

He took a step forward and raised his hands to grasp her shoulders. Eyes still closed, she leaned her weight against him, arms lifeless at her sides. Costilla held her tightly, one hand in the small of her back, another cradling her head.

"The first year WAG was open," she began softly, "someone sent a dead cat to us."

Costilla ran his fingers through Claire's hair once. He hadn't slept with her since returning to Lafayette. They both realized that reporters were following her, at least some of the time. They certainly didn't want to add another sideshow to Wyatt's trial.

"We couldn't figure out the meaning, you know?" she continued. "Was it supposed to be a feminist hellcat? A dead *pussy*? As hate mail goes, it didn't quite make sense. It wasn't meaningful. Just hateful."

Costilla swallowed. Although they hadn't slept together, they had found reasons to see each other, to discuss Wyatt's safety or to share information about local anti-abortion groups. It felt good, in a way, exercising a professional control, keeping that intense passion at bay. But he had missed holding her.

"But I couldn't help wondering," she said. "Had they killed it just to send to us? Strangled a neighborhood stray? I couldn't stop asking, had this cat died for my sins?"

She pulled back a bit, brought her hands up to grasp his shoulders. There were tears in her eyes, but no trace of weeping in her voice.

"We buried it, but not before we gave it a name. Just like anti-abortion groups sometimes do with the fetuses they dig out of clinic disposal areas. The ritual of burial, to put a soul to rest, to comfort the living."

"Are you all right?" Costilla asked. It almost scared him, to see her so wounded, so quietly sad.

She nodded, lightly rubbing her fingertips against the stubble on his chin. "I'm fine. They only make me stronger, these people."

Costilla looked over his shoulder at the small body in its transparent container. From sheer force of habit, he listed to himself the various tests he could order. Fingerprints would show up well on the glass, or perhaps be preserved under the clear tape that covered the mailing label. The paper of the box could be traced to a manufacturer. Costilla wondered if the fetus's DNA could be sequenced. But where would that lead?

"I just need one thing, Eduardo," she said.

"What, Claire?"

"Don't leave," she said. "Stay here tonight."

He kissed her, the easiest way to answer.

This was the day that Claire Davis had been dreading. She could only hope that it would be over quickly.

The prosecution was calling its forensics team from the beach house investigation. They would give hard, physical evidence, of the sort that had been missing from the case so far. But even here, she reminded herself, she had her ace in the hole.

Riley Mills took over the inquisitorial duties again, having given A.D.A. Morrisey her token day in the sun. He brought his folksy style back to the courtroom, and Claire wondered if some of the jurors had missed him during the long day of technical testimony about blood work and coagulation factors that had ended the first week of the trial.

She hoped that by attacking the prosecution's case from every possible angle, from Sarah's pregnancy to the love affair between her and Daniel, Mills would be forced to slow his case down to a crawl. She wanted him to bore the jury as he tried to cover all the bases, while she swept in for short and succinct cross-examinations, raising a low level of doubt throughout the proceedings. In her closing statement, she intended to hint at a conspiracy against Daniel Wyatt by the right-wing forces opposed to his nomination, creating just enough suspicion that a few pro-choicers on the jury would see this case as a deliberately engineered threat to *Roe*.

But today the forensic evidence would be hard to argue with.

"Whose fingerprints did this extensive investigation discover?" Mills asked chummily. He was old friends with the county's forensic scientists. Had asked them these same questions in this very courtroom for years.

"There were several unknown sets of latents, probably due to the fact that the beach house was rented to a different set of people almost every weekend. We found the cleaning woman's fingerprints throughout the house, and a number of latent sets matching Sarah Corbett and the defendant, Daniel Wyatt."

"Sarah Corbett and Daniel Wyatt," Mills repeated. He looked meaningfully at the jurors. Claire heard Daniel take a sharp breath beside her, and furiously willed him to be silent.

"And were any of these fingerprints found on glassware?"

"Yes. Some of the best sets we got were from a pair of wineglasses."

Claire wondered how this whole case would differ if only the cleaning woman had gotten to the house before Mills's team. She cleaned on Fridays, just before the new weekend guests arrived. She had shown up ready to start cleaning only thirty minutes after the forensics team had begun their work. Just an hour earlier, Claire thought furiously, as if she could will that small change in history.

"Wineglasses?" Riley Mills repeated. He was milking the moment for all it was worth.

"That's right. Wineglasses."

"And was there any residue in these glasses?"

"Yes. Red wine."

"Mr. Carter." Claire started her cross. "Latent fingerprints are impossible to date, aren't they."

The forensics expert sighed, a blank look on his face, as if he were searching for a stock answer to this stock question. He had already explained the mechanics of latent fingerprint retrieval to Mills in the direct. Claire wondered how many times in his long career he'd explained these facts, to how many hundreds of jurors.

"Yes. The oils left behind by the fingers break down eventually, though."

Claire nodded her head. "So, you know that the fingerprints were left that weekend."

"Well, not really," Carter admitted.

"I see. They could have been left before that weekend?"

"Yes."

"But you know that these fingerprints were left, say, in the last month?" she continued.

"Not for certain. Although the glasses would probably have been washed since then."

"Does washing a glass always remove fingerprints?"

"Usually." His voice was smaller. Claire realized that she intimidated this quiet forensicist. Something about her made him nervous. She pressed her point fearlessly now.

"Usually. But not always. Mr. Carter, can you state beyond any doubt that you are certain these fingerprints were left . . . in the last year?"

"Not really," he answered meekly. "Some fingerprints last more than a year. Not often, though."

She nodded, then turned away from the witness dismissively.

"Oh, one more question," she said, pausing on her way to the defense table. "Did you test the residue of the red wine you found, to see if anything had been added to it?"

"Uh, yes we did."

"You tested for any drugs, any toxins that might have been added to the wine?" she continued.

"Yes."

"Did you find anything?"

"No. Just red wine," the man admitted.

"Just red wine," she repeated, turning meaningfully toward the jury just as Riley Mills had done. It was a small victory, but it felt good.

After lunch came the box.

Riley Mills had gone to town on this, as his only piece of

evidence that linked Dr. Daniel Wyatt to the "murder weapon." He had called an outside lab technician to testify about the fingerprints. He'd also brought in a representative from the FDA to testify about the labeling. The sample box Claire had given Wyatt had been the original Ronssel-Uclaf version of the drug, the one used in Europe. The woman could read the French instructions, which Mills made a big deal about. He had her excerpt phrases from the contraindications out loud to the jury in both the original and in English. Like the warnings on any type of medicine, the label was full of dire statements about every possible side effect. Claire made a note to remind her experts to discuss the safety of RU-486. She would have to pound the point that it was safer than going through a normal pregnancy. Statistically safer than a cross-country drive, safer than having one's wisdom teeth out under general anesthesia, safer than a lot of things.

But Mills did manage to establish what the box was for. RU-486, no question. Claire's chance was in her cross-examination, when she brought up the "anomalous" results that both tests of the box had revealed about its contents.

"You tested this empty box, quite specifically attempting to find traces of mifepristone or prostaglandin, correct?"

Of course, Riley Mills had already taken the man through this revelation, trying to take the wind from her sails, but repetition wouldn't hurt.

"Yes. We found minute traces of both."

"But you found something else?"

"Yes, traces of aspirin."

Claire had waited for this moment all day, but still managed to look shocked. "Aspirin?"

"Yes."

"What kind?"

"Pardon me?" he asked.

"What kind? Bayer? Children's aspirin? Chewable?"

She got the laugh she wanted, and Thibodeaux rapped his gavel lightly once. Perfect. The moment would be cemented in the jurors' minds now.

Aspirin.

"I'm not sure," the technician answered. He didn't rise to the bait. He was that smoothest of expert witnesses, giving his evidence with a somber neutrality.

"It was just plain old salicylic acid," he said. "There's no real difference between one brand and another. Not when there are only traces."

"Just plain old *aspirin*," she said, relishing the word. "So, this box might have been used for a demonstration at some point. And contained a harmless pill instead of the real thing?"

"I wouldn't know about that," he answered flatly.

Claire shrugged for the jury.

"But here's something you might know about. When this result was first obtained, District Attorney Mills suggested that it might have been the result of an error," she said, concern in her voice.

"It's not very likely. Aspirin is not a substance used in testing."

"Would such an error be possible?"

"Anything's possible, I suppose. We tested the box twice, to make sure. But there could have been contamination. Labs make mistakes."

"Labs make mistakes . . ." Claire repeated, nodding her head sagely.

She let those words linger in the air, and returned to her seat.

The day hadn't been so awful after all.

The noise sounded as if it had come from right outside the window.

Sarah Corbett listened carefully. Nothing. She closed the book she had been reading with a snap, then sighed. Reading wasn't the word for what she'd been doing. Her eyes had been skimming the page, but she couldn't remember anything about the last few chapters.

Sarah peeked out the window. The front lawn was empty.

Perhaps it hadn't been anything. Sheriff Hicks had been a godsend these last few weeks, making sure that no reporters hung around the house, keeping them off her lawn. They bitched about their rights and about freedom of the press, but he'd made it his business to keep Morlean Street free from the effects of the trial.

Sarah often wondered, though, if having reporters stationed outside at all hours would be so bad. Sometimes, late at night, the dead silence was worse than any number of trespassers.

A knock on the door made her start. She lifted the shade next to her chair and peered out at the form on her doorstep.

"Millie!" she whispered with relief.

Sarah leaped up and opened the door. Millie was in her scrubs. It was about ten-thirty, so she'd be going to the hospital soon.

"Hey, Sarah."

"Hey, Millie. What have you got there?"

Millie put her fingers to her lips and slipped inside.

"We can't let Daddy see these or he'll want to keep them all for himself."

She peeled back the tinfoil covering the dish. A small puff of steam escaped through the opening, and Sarah saw the rich darkness of fresh brownies.

"Oh, Millie! You are terrible. A downright bad influence."

Millie beamed and shut the door behind her. The two stole into the kitchen, trying to stay quiet, as if Mark Hicks were just upstairs listening for their footsteps.

"A knife," Millie commanded in a whisper, and Sarah quietly rifled through her drawers and produced one.

They sat in conspiratorial silence, eating the rich, dark brownies one after the other.

"These are just awful," Sarah opined.

"Aren't they?" Millie giggled. "I just about can't stand to eat them."

"Terrible," Sarah added, the word muffled by the cake in her mouth.

"But hey, I'll need the sugar rush to get me though my shift tonight. I watched too much TV today. Again."

Sarah simply nodded.

"Can you believe that Claire Davis?" Millie continued. "Acting like she never heard of fingerprints before."

"Well, I suppose she's just doing her job," Sarah said.

Millie rolled her eyes.

"She's supposed to create doubt, you know," Sarah continued. She had watched the defense attorney carefully over the last few days. She was still in awe of Claire, even when Ms. Davis, as she still thought of her, seemed to suggest that Sarah hadn't been pregnant at all. There was something compelling about her performance, her unwillingness to accept even the simplest facts of the prosecution's case. She was like one of those ancient philosophers who refused to believe anything existed unless you could prove it to them, even if their own eyes told them so.

"Anyway, this whole mess isn't her fault," Sarah finished. "If only I'd kept my big mouth shut. . . ."

"Now don't you start on that again," Millie scolded.

"But this isn't what I wanted," Sarah moaned, a brownie forgotten in her hand. "None of this. All I wanted was my baby. All I wanted was a little bit more from Daniel. Not a murder trial."

Millie held her hand across the table.

"Now, honey," she said firmly. "That's nonsense. You didn't start all this. You got hurt, terribly. That man went way past all moral decency."

"But look at what's happened to the town, Millie," Sarah said, her voice starting to break. "Sometimes I wish I could just make everything go back the way it was."

Millie shushed her, but Sarah shook her head.

"It's never going to be the same, is it? Never."

"Well," Millie answered, "I suppose I can't argue with you there, honey."

Sarah looked up at her through tear-streaked mascara.

"Just do your part, Sarah," Millie said. "And it'll all be over soon enough."

Sarah nodded. Just do her part, that's what her daddy had always said. But she still prayed that there was some way to make this all better.

Daniel Wyatt sat and watched the television, pushing at the uninspiring food in front of him. He sighed. Here it was, almost eleven o'clock, and he was still looking at his dinner.

The plate rattled as he carried it from the living room into the kitchen. Ellen had never let her family eat in front of the TV, and Wyatt did so only guiltily. He was careful never to leave any evidence of his transgressions in the living room, as if Ellen might return at any moment.

Wyatt passed under the camera in the kitchen without noticing it. He had become unaware of the security devices and their winking red lights that stared at him from every corner. He no longer thought about the guards in his house. They were simply a fact of life. Like gravity, they were undeniable and inescapable, but you didn't think much about them.

He returned to the living room and began to flip through channels.

Suddenly an image appeared on the screen that brought his restless fingers to a halt.

It was some sort of ultrasound imagery, showing a well-developed fetus in the womb. A pair of forceps appeared, bright and gigantic in the monochrome view, grasping at the fetal head like a raptor's talons.

The fetus seemed to recoil, its tiny arms raised in defiance against the metal jaws of the forceps. But they were inescapable. The music rose, ominous and terrible, as the forceps closed on the fetus's head and began to pull. The tiny fetus opened its mouth.

Wyatt was stunned.

How could they be showing this? Here and now? He'd seen it before, of course. Anyone involved in abortion rights knew this piece of propaganda well. *Silent Scream*, made by an abortion-provider-turned-pro-life-activist, Robert Nathanson. The film, much of it misleading, all of it mercilessly heavy-handed, had almost single-handedly created the modern pro-life movement in the United States. It was dynamite.

Wyatt looked at the red glowing number on his cable box. The local public access channel. Someone had rented time to show this.

He ran to the kitchen, plugged in the phone.

"Claire?"

"I know," she said. "Molly already called me. We'll be talking with the judge about it tomorrow."

"But how can they do this? What if someone on the jury sees it?"

"Daniel. We'll handle it."

"God, Claire. Remember when we were forced to sit through parts of it at that state legislators' meeting? You remember how it stirred them up against us?"

"Listen, Daniel," Claire said sharply. "No one's forcing you to sit through it now. Change the channel. Better yet, go to bed."

"But—"

"Turn it off," she ordered. "We will handle it tomorrow."

Hanging up and then unplugging the phone, Wyatt walked back into the living room. The ghastly image still flickered on the screen, coloring the whole room an infernal red.

He sat heavily down and raised the remote to change it, to turn it off.

But he couldn't bring himself to press the button.

Daniel Wyatt watched the rest of the film—he realized he'd never seen it in its entirety—in quiet fascination and horror.

The usual media crowd on the courthouse steps buzzed with a new question the next morning. Riley Mills was ready for it, having been warned in an early morning phone call from A.D.A. Morrisey.

"District Attorney Mills, what impact do you think the showing of *Silent Scream* will have on the case?"

"Do you think the defense will call for a mistrial?"

"Do you plan to ask for an injunction against local access cable?"

"Mr. Mills, do you think the jury should be sequestered?"

Warned or not, Mills hadn't expected anything quite this ferocious.

"Having never seen the film myself, I don't know what you all are talking about," he proclaimed to the crowd of press and cameras. "This is a matter for the judge to decide upon."

Sequestration? *Mistrial?* He couldn't see what all the fuss was about. Maybe this was just the inevitable heat created by having too many reporters in one place with not enough news to report. In a case like this, every little thing that happened outside the courtroom was bound to set off alarms.

Once the judge was seated, Claire Davis made her motion before the jury was in the box. Judge Thibodeaux, who looked more grim up on the bench than Mills had ever seen him, listened to her with evident agreement.

"Your Honor," she began, "a grossly prejudicial film was aired on local access cable last night. As a piece of propaganda, it takes an inflammatory stand on one of the core questions of this case, explicitly referring to abortion as murder several times. It also directly attacks doctors who perform abortion. My client might as well have been named a mass murderer. It's unthinkable that this trial should be allowed to continue under these prejudicial conditions."

Mills shook his head. Davis was calling for a mistrial. And Thibodeaux wasn't laughing her off. The district attorney wondered if the pressure was getting to the young judge. This was a hell of a case even when things were going smoothly, and now Thibodeaux had his first tough call.

"Your Honor," Mills said, standing and holding his hands up helplessly. "The People have not had time to review this so-called piece of propaganda. Let's not rush into anything here."

"I saw part of the film last night myself," the judge said gravely. "And I share the concerns of defense counsel. I trust that the prosecution did not know of this airing in advance?"

Mills stared back at the glowering judge in shock. What the hell was Thibodeaux asking him?

"Your Honor, I assure you that my office has nothing to do with the scheduling of television shows. To suggest that I . . ." Mills shook his head. "Again, I repeat that the People haven't seen this movie. I would like to ask for a recess so that the prosecution can understand what everyone's so upset about!"

"I intend to take a recess, Counselor," Thibodeaux announced. "You can use the time as you see fit. I intend to spend the morning in chambers asking each and every juror in private if they saw the film. And I intend to excuse all those who did. There will also be proceedings at a later date to determine if any officer of this court had anything to do with the film being shown. And it will be a grave matter indeed if they have."

Thibodeaux directed this last threat straight at Mills.

Riley Mills threw up his hands. Thibodeaux was accusing *him* of this chicanery. Damn, just what kind of a two-bit prosecutor did Thibodeaux think he was? Why would he pull something like this? Couldn't that idiot judge see that Mills was winning this case on the merits?

"Certainly, Your Honor," he said. "But let me assure you—"

"Court is adjourned," Thibodeaux interrupted him, his gavel ending the sentence with a loud and angry crack.

"Well, what are we looking at as far as alternates?" the D.A. asked. When he argued a case, Mills was always preternaturally aware of the twelve people in the box who mattered. The four alternates were almost invisible.

Morrisey shook her head. "Not good. With only four alternates, we could be looking at a mistrial. If five jurors saw the film, that's it. If four have, we're going to be on pins and needles."

Mills nodded. With a long trial like this, one of the twelve jurors almost always got sick or had a family crisis, or just couldn't hack it and asked the judge to be dismissed.

"Even worse," Morrisey continued, "the first and third alternates are men. So we're likely to lose a woman from the jury. And I think we're looking at sequestration from here on out."

"Damn," Mills spat. He hated to see a jury sequestered in a complicated case like this. It made them unpredictable, made them want to reach a verdict quickly so that they could get back to their lives. One resolute holdout against the murder charge, and the rest might settle for the lesser counts.

Davis's strategy had already lengthened the trial beyond the normal duration of such a case. Her cross-examinations were short, but poked enough holes that redirect was often necessary. And when the defense began its case, Davis had a host of expert witnesses on the schedule. If the jury was short on alternates and patience, Mills might be forced to rush. He didn't want to tire the jury before Sarah Corbett, the central figure of the case, had taken the stand.

* * *

Late in the afternoon, the bailiff came to collect them. The judge's interviews with the sixteen jurors and alternates were over.

"The damage is less than it could have been." Judge Thibodeaux addressed the open courtroom.

"Only two of the jurors have seen the film. The rest have fortunately been spared that sensationalistic experience. These two jurors will be dismissed, and the first two alternates empaneled. In addition, I intend to grant the request of defense counsel. The jury will be sequestered from this point onward."

Mills sighed. Not the disaster it could have been. With two alternates remaining, the chance of running out of jurors was small.

Then the judge named the two jurors who would be excused, and Mills had to force himself not to laugh out loud.

Both were men.

"What are the odds on that?" Morrisey muttered, shaking her head with a smile.

The first two alternates included a man and a woman. There were now nine women on the jury, a net gain of one.

Riley Mills took a quick glance at Claire Davis when court was adjourned for the day. Her face was expressionless, but Mills knew what she must be thinking. When bad luck compounded a bad case, it could be hard to believe that God wasn't on the other side.

"I'll tell you one thing, Cost, this guy Steve Bartlett puts the 'pro-life' back in 'prolific.' He's got more screen names than a thirteen-year-old boy in the *Hustler* chatroom."

Costilla leaned back toward Agent Samuels, precariously shoulder-cradling his cell phone as he reached for the print-out she offered. He was still on hold with the Virginia FBI lab. Costilla hated being on hold, and he was glad for the distraction. The lab had said that they would have the results on the fetus package back today, but Costilla was trapped in a Muzak-scored maze of transfers and excuses.

He looked at the list in his hand as a syrupy "Send in the Clowns" played in his ear. Agent Chaos was right about one thing. Steve Bartlett was known by many names: MadDog, SkinYrHead, FagKllr, 2Amend . . . Then there were a dozen or so street aliases—Able Stevens, Arnold Bart, Rex Barner—ordinary names that Bartlett used on fake credit cards, to rent cars, or to buy guns.

"Are you sure these are all him, Chaos?" he asked Samuels.

"Yep. The Soldiers of Christ aren't what I'd call criminal geniuses. He's not very careful about hiding his aliases."

"Except when he's writing his 'rejoice' poetry? You never traced those poems to Steve Bartlett."

"Cost, I don't think this is the same guy," Chaos said. "Different style."

"Is that a literary opinion?" Costilla said, smirking.

"No. An on-line opinion. He's got a different . . . *presence* on the—"

Costilla waved the younger agent quiet. The Muzak on his cell phone had just cut off.

"Agent Costilla?" came a voice.

"Yes."

"All right. I've got that information you wanted."

"Finally."

"First the bad news. Only one set of latents on the glass. They match the ones you sent in."

Costilla swore. He'd provided Claire's fingerprints to the lab, knowing that they would show up on the jar. She'd taken a perverse thrill in being fingerprinted, he'd noticed.

"Can't find any other prints at all," the man continued. "We pulled out the mailing label, even checked the packing nuts. Whoever put it together was in gloves from start to finish."

"So what *do* you have for me?"

"The cardboard stock came from a company in Burlington, Alabama. Pretty small operation, probably doesn't sell its product out of the state. Of course, you know boxes. They get mailed, get reused."

"Is that it?" Costilla asked, exasperated. Cardboard stock. He'd been waiting two days for *this*.

"I'm afraid so. There's nothing we can do with the, uh . . . body."

Costilla hung up.

"Santa Maria, *Madre de Dios*," he swore, then breathed deep to gather his thoughts. "Chaos, where did you say Bartlett's last known location was?"

"Niceville, Alabama. Population, twelve hundred and eighty."

Costilla whistled. In Lafayette for two months, and all he had to show for it was one voice-altered tape and two shitty leads. But at least the leads matched.

"All right," Costilla said. "Get the team together. Bartlett's here in Lafayette, and he's our man. Chaos, get a copy of this alias list to everyone. We're going door-to-door, hotel by hotel, until we find this guy."

BOX   309

"I've got a photograph from the old Soldiers of Christ FBI file," Samuels added.

Costilla nodded his head. Perfect. He could feel the noose closing around his man, finally, after three years. He had known that the Wyatt trial would provide an irresistible lure.

The suite's phone rang. It was Sheriff Hicks.

"How's it going, Agent Costilla?"

"Good. We're getting close."

"You said you needed a man from my department?" Hicks sounded anxious to help.

"Yeah. We think we know who our man is, and he's associated with a group that specializes in C-4 bombings. I wanted to station a man to watch for signs of explosives preparation."

"Station him where?" Hicks asked.

"The county dump," Costilla said. "To watch for remnants of any bomb-making process. We'd be glad to tell him what to look for."

"Sounds like a pretty thankless job, especially in this heat," Sheriff Hicks observed. "Dump's overflowing, what with all these visitors in town."

"I know, Sheriff," Costilla agreed tiredly. He'd doubted Hicks would pull one of his men for dump duty with all the protesters in town. Well, it had been worth a try. "I'd put one of my team on it, but I'll need every man I can get to canvass for this bomber. Maybe if you could just—"

"Don't worry about it, Agent Costilla," Hicks interrupted. "I've got just the man for it."

"Thanks, I really appreciate it, Sheriff."

"His name's Tom Jenkins. I'll send him right over."

49 | THE MOMENT OF CONCEPTION

"When I look at this picture, Doctor, I see a little foot right there. Am I right?"

Dr. Noreen Jackson leaned forward and extended the pointer in her hand to gently rap the large color picture that rested on its easel before the court.

"Yes. That *is* a foot, Mr. Mills," she said. "And just there you can see two hands. As you'll notice, there are fingers and toes as well. You can count all five of them in a fetus of this age."

"Eight weeks?"

"Eight weeks."

"The same age as Sarah Corbett's baby, maybe younger," Mills reminded the jury.

For the twentieth time that morning, Claire Davis circled a note to herself. She had to get one of her witnesses to discuss the problem of fetal ages. For convenience, OB-GYNs always marked the length of a pregnancy from the end of the woman's last period. But the age of the fetus itself, figured from the moment of conception, was usually two weeks less than that. Mills was getting a lot out of this two-week discrepancy. She wanted the jury to know that the fetus in the eighth week of pregnancy was actually only six weeks old.

Still, Claire reminded herself, it was pointless to get trapped arguing these day-by-day changes in the fetus, like medieval theologians discussing how many angels could dance on the head of a pin. She had to stay focused on the bigger picture: *Roe* protected abortions in the first two trimesters.

Riley Mills turned back to Dr. Jackson.

"What other organs would a fetus of this age have, Dr. Jackson?"

"A heart, for one thing. It is developed at this stage, and it is actually beating."

"A beating heart," Mills said sagely.

"And a brain," she added. "Fetuses at ten weeks have been shown to respond to stimuli. They can open their hands and even their mouths."

A tingle went up Claire's spine as Dr. Jackson spoke those words. The image of a fetus with an open mouth was at the center of *Silent Scream*. The haunting image of that purely reflexive action was dynamite; the fetus really did look like it was screaming, especially with the dramatic music the film shamelessly employed. Claire prepared herself to object if mention of the open mouth went any further.

But Mills wisely changed the subject.

"What about DNA?" he asked. "Does the fetus shown here have all the necessary instructions to become, say, a blue-eyed or brown-eyed child? A tall person or a short person?"

Dr. Jackson leaned forward, holding the pointer in both hands like a patient schoolteacher.

"From the moment of conception, the fertilized embryo has all the DNA it will ever have," she said, with awe in her voice. "That means that the way a child looks as an adult, his or her height, intelligence, susceptibility to disease, all those things you hear about that are genetic in origin, have already been determined. The potential is all there, Mr. Mills."

Dr. Jackson paused a moment, as if collecting her thoughts. Claire Davis wondered how many times she'd delivered this exact speech, word for word.

"If this embryo is allowed to grow," she continued, "it will develop into the child God meant it to be. Unlike any other in the world. Every fertilized embryo takes some of the mother's DNA, some of the father's, and therefore is unique, differentiated. You might say, each has its own soul."

"Its own soul," Riley Mills repeated.

On cross, Claire took up the issue of differentiation.

"Dr. Jackson, what about twins?"

"Twins?"

"Well, you said that each fertilized embryo has its own unique DNA. But identical twins share the same DNA."

"Well, that's true."

"Does that make them any less distinct as people? Does that mean that they share a soul?"

Dr. Jackson nodded her head as if appreciating a rich philosophical question.

"Well, they are not genetically distinct. And I have heard it said that twins share something between them that no other two people on earth do."

Claire sighed. Dr. Jackson had a way of turning all her pointed questions into mystical mush.

"Isn't it the case that every single cell in my body has all my DNA inside it?" Claire asked. "Just like a fertilized embryo, a drop of my blood has the instructions to make a unique human being."

"Not unique. It would be your twin, Miss Davis."

"Correct, my twin. But would you suggest that a drop of blood has the right to life, as it contains all the information to make an entire human being. As much potential as an embryo?"

"I'm afraid that I don't read much science fiction, Miss Davis."

Mills rose and interrupted Claire's response. "I'm not sure that I share defense counsel's taste for science fiction either, Your Honor."

"Let me rephrase, then, Your Honor," Claire said, taking a step away from the witness stand. She wasn't getting anything out of this witness anyway. Dr. Jackson was too experienced with cross-examinations. Claire could wait until her own witnesses were on the stand.

"You stated that a fetus, or even a newly fertilized embryo, contains the necessary DNA to become a genetically unique human being?"

"Yes, I did."

"Does a drop of blood contain that same DNA?"

"Yes, I suppose it does."

"A cell from my stomach lining?"

"Yes, I guess so."

"A bit of skin from the end of my fingertip?" Claire asked, pointing the pinky on her left hand directly at Dr. Jackson's nose.

"Yes."

"Is a skin cell from my pinkie a human being, Doctor?"

"No, of course not. But—"

"Thank you. Nothing further."

"Some proponents of abortion argue that a fetus is unable to think, can't rationalize or be self-conscious, and therefore doesn't deserve the same protection as a fully functioning adult."

Riley Mills nodded with concern. The prosecutor's witness was a philosophy professor from Fordham University. He must be a hell of a teacher, Claire thought. She found herself listening carefully to his measured voice, which was as compellingly soft as a whisper.

"What do you think about that, Dr. Helmut?"

"The important thing to realize is that many lives in the human community exist in various shades of gray, when it comes to self-determination, rational thought, and self-awareness. Very young children are often not rational, as I'm sure every parent knows. The senile sometimes lack self-awareness. People with advanced Alzheimer's disease lack a capacity to plan, to determine their life's course. A patient in a coma has no thought processes, has no self-awareness.

Even a person who has taken powerful drugs can be temporarily without rational thought. All these kinds of people, along with embryos and fetuses, do not meet the criteria that abortion proponents suggest is necessary to be full human beings. But they *are* human beings."

Helmut folded his hands, raised the volume of his voice by the slightest of degrees.

"All these kinds of people, by virtue of their conditions, cannot effectively challenge, choose, or determine the way they are to be treated. They cannot plan their lives. Some of them are temporarily unable to, some permanently. But can we simply say that therefore they have no rights? No protection under the law?

"On the contrary, people who cannot speak for themselves must have even *more* protection under the law. The infirm, the sick, and the unborn all must be protected with great vigilance. When you take an unborn child, you are talking about a lifetime's worth of potential. And you are talking about total dependence on others to exist. And finally, you are talking about absolute innocence. Who is more deserving of our care?"

Mills shook his head, as if unable to answer. Claire tried to think of a way to answer this man's quiet self-assurance.

"What we are talking about is power," Helmut continued. "The unborn are powerless. We must remember the dreadful consequences of allowing the humanity of a powerless class of people to be questioned by the dictates of another, more powerful class. One only has to recall when slaves were considered property, and therefore had no constitutional rights."

Claire looked anxiously toward the jury. One of the black jurors was nodding her head. My God, she couldn't believe anyone was buying this.

"So, Dr. Helmut," Riley Mills interjected, "what about someone who is undergoing surgery? For a few hours, they are under complete anesthesia, not capable of rational thought, volition. Why, they aren't even conscious. Like a fetus, that person is totally dependent on the care of others for his survival."

Dr. Helmut nodded furiously and joined in. "It would be absurd to suggest that this surgery patient is a *nonperson* for those few hours. No, the protection of the law must be extended to all humans, no matter whether they are capable of thought or not."

Claire realized that Helmut was the first of the prosecution's pro-life experts to avoid using the words "God" or "soul." Even the rationalists on the jury might be swayed by his calm words. She had to be effective on cross-examination.

"Dr. Helmut, what about someone with bone marrow cancer in the advanced stages? Someone who is unconscious and is about to die? Do they deserve the protection of the law?"

"Very much so," Helmut agreed with her.

"Well, then," Claire continued, "let us say that this person is your brother. You are his only sibling, the only person with the proper blood type to provide a transplant that he desperately needs. Like a fetus, he is totally dependent on others. On you and the doctors."

"Then it would be my moral responsibility to undergo the transplant," the professor proclaimed.

"Yes, I would agree with you; you should help your brother." Claire said this nodding, as if she had been swayed by the wise professor's words.

"Hypothetically, then, what if you said, 'The transplant is too dangerous'? Or what if your wife felt the operation was too dangerous, and didn't want you to make the sacrifice? And what if she let the air out of your tires so you couldn't get to the hospital in time?" Claire continued.

"Well, that would be wrong of her," he said. "To cause my brother's death. To disregard my choice in the matter."

"Wrong, yes," Claire said. "But would it be murder?"

"Objection!" Mills cried. "Counsel knows that question calls for a legal conclusion."

"Sustained."

Dr. Helmut seemed still to be thinking, however, for the first time at a loss for words. Claire let his silence stretch on.

"I'm not here to testify about the legal definition of murder," he finally admitted. "That's not my field of expertise."

"That's unfortunate," she said, "because that's what my client is accused of. Not moral cowardice. But murder in the first degree."

"Objection, Your Honor," Mills said. "Argumentative."

"Withdrawn," Claire said quietly, and strode back to her seat.

She needed no more questions. The puzzled, troubled expression on the distinguished professor's face was there for all to see.

The X-Acto knife cut through the thin pages with the sound of a snake moving over dry leaves. Peter O'Keefe had to concentrate to keep the soft rasping noise from hypnotizing him. Two bandages already graced his left forefinger, each the price of a moment's inattention. Two of the eviscerated Bibles sat to one side of the pile on the bed, their covers speckled with his blood.

O'Keefe pulled one of the bandages from the finger, inspected the wound, which was bright red against the pale skin around it. Somehow, the bleeding had helped calm him, like some self-punishing ritual of a medieval monk. The work of preparing the Bibles was tedious and exacting, but with an edge of danger that counting rosaries couldn't match.

O'Keefe finished coring the Bible in front of him, lifting the rectangle of cut pages out with a tug, the last few strands of paper tearing. He reached carefully for a small brick from the pile of C-4 pieces he had made, then hefted the explosive in one hand, the removed pages in the other. Close enough in weight. Tearing a six-inch piece of duct tape, O'Keefe secured the plastique into the Bible in a way that ensured that the little book wouldn't fall open.

To rest his fingers more than anything else, he counted the loaded Bibles again. Thirty-three finished, with just five more to go. He'd brought forty Bibles with him. Each held a half pound of C-4, perfect for his twenty pounds. But with the two Bibles ruined with blood, he would wind up with an extra pound of the explosive.

"What to do with you?" he said aloud, holding two of the small bricks against his cheek. They were as cool as clay, their pungent scent overwhelming the smell of coffee in the room.

Two half pounds, just what O'Keefe had used in his clinic bombing, before he had decided to make his war more personal. Perhaps God had guided his hand, to cut himself, and show with a trail of blood what should be done. These two bricks were just enough to focus the world's attention a bit more closely here on Lafayette, without tipping his hand.

"Of course," he said softly. "A small demonstration, before the lesson proper."

It was time to make his first play. Time to visit Dr. Ernest Magley.

51 | STAR WITNESS

Claire Davis carefully watched the jury as Sarah Corbett took the stand, searching for signs of pity, fascination, hostility. She couldn't judge their mood yet, so she let her eyes fall upon the witness herself. Claire had only glimpsed Sarah among the courtroom spectators, but now she took a long look. Sarah Corbett seemed older than she had those few months ago when they had met. She looked exhausted. The experience of becoming a national figure, a famous victim, and the center of a firestorm of controversy had evidently not been a restful one.

Claire wondered why Sarah had never told D.A. Mills that it was she, Claire Davis, who had arranged the rendezvous at the beach house. Claire was sure that if Sarah had told Mills, he would have made it his business to get her thrown off the case, if not charged as an accomplice. It was possible Mills had decided to wait for this moment to reveal it, a bit of courtroom dramatics to damage not only Daniel's defense, but also her career. But Claire thought that unlikely. She preferred to believe that part of Sarah Corbett was on the side of the defense, that in some small way the young woman wanted to make amends for all the trouble that had been caused in her name.

Claire intended to watch this testimony very carefully, trying to fathom how she might guide that part of Sarah into the open during her cross-examination.

Mills used a few questions to establish Sarah's identity, her age, how long she had lived in town. They were facts everyone knew, but the introduction of the star witness was one of the compelling rituals of any trial. Mills then asked her to describe her relationship with Daniel Wyatt.

"Daniel Wyatt has been my doctor for eleven years," she said. "Since I got back from college."

"When you were how old?"

"Twenty-two."

"How did he come to be your doctor?" Mills asked.

"He was my mother's doctor," she answered.

Claire didn't look around, but she heard the barest ruffle of sound in the courtroom. Riley Mills was going to play the age difference for everything he could get out of it.

"Is he still your mother's doctor, Sarah?"

"No. Both my parents are dead."

Claire took a deep breath. That Sarah was parentless was well known, the jury hadn't been sequestered long enough to be ignorant of the fact, but Mills wasn't missing any chances to paint his witness sympathetically. He must have every step of this day's testimony planned, every moment carefully choreographed.

The prosecutor spent a long time on Sarah's decade as a patient of Wyatt's, detailing her many illnesses, hitting again and again at how much she had trusted and respected him. To a member of the audience who didn't know where this was leading, it might seem that Sarah Corbett was here as a character witness for Daniel.

But eventually, of course, Mills's narrative reached the weekend at Baton Rouge.

"We met there by chance. He said he was in Baton Rouge for a meeting of Planned Parenthood."

The slightest of laughs rippled through the gallery, and Judge Thibodeaux raised his gavel in warning.

"And he suggested that you have dinner together?"

"Yes, he . . ." Sarah paused, a puzzled look on her face. "Or perhaps it was I who suggested dinner."

Riley Mills looked surprised for a moment, as if Sarah

had departed from the script, if only for a moment. But he quickly recovered.

"And what happened at this dinner?"

"He was very nice to me. He complimented my dress. We had wine."

Mills paused to let those three simple declarative sentences soak in.

"And what happened after dinner?"

"We went back to the hotel, where we were both staying. And he took me to my room."

Claire began to realize a hidden cost of not putting Daniel on the stand. This story would be told solely from Sarah's perspective, as stage-managed by Riley Mills. She noticed that Sarah had finally stopped making her statements sound like questions. However upset she was, this new Sarah sounded absolutely sure of everything she said.

"And that's where we made love for the first time. He made me feel so special."

The testimony lingered for a while on that weekend, the two nights they had spent together. Then Sarah grew tearful as she described the last night in Baton Rouge, when Daniel had tried to end the relationship.

"So, you thought that Daniel Wyatt was done with you?" Mills asked.

Sarah nodded mutely.

Mills guided her through her missed period two weeks later, and the tests that had confirmed her pregnancy.

"And this realization that you were pregnant with his child coincided with Dr. Wyatt's nomination to the position of surgeon general, did it not?"

"Yes. He was on TV that night, smiling and being congratulated."

"Did you call him then?"

"No. I kept it to myself for a few days. I didn't know what to do."

"Now, Sarah, I have to ask you one very important question," Mills said, his voice softening from his usual tone of courtroom bombast.

"Okay," she said, sounding small and vulnerable.

"In this whole time, did you have sexual relations with any other man?"

"No, I did not," she said.

"Are you sure?"

"Yes."

There it was, Claire thought, the one statement essential to Mills's case. If the jury disbelieved it, everything would change. But Sarah sounded pretty sure of herself. Claire decided to hit the subject of birth control hard in her cross. If Sarah Corbett wasn't sexually active, why was she on the pill?

The testimony wound through the meetings between the two after she had told Daniel about the pregnancy. The Cajun restaurant, the phone calls, the school play, she remembered them all very well. And she described each with an attention to detail that was almost touching, like those oft-revisited memories from a short, intense relationship.

Then Mills took Sarah through the missed appointment with Dr. Magley.

"Did you make the appointment?"

"Yes."

"Did you go to the appointment?"

"No."

"Why not?"

"I realized that I couldn't go through with it. I didn't want to lose this child, to lose this life inside me. I wanted to have this baby."

"Now, Sarah, please describe your weekend with Dr. Wyatt at the beach house."

Claire's muscles tensed. If Sarah was going to implicate her, this would be the moment.

"It was after the committee hearings in Washington. Daniel said that we needed to work things out. That I was very special to him, and that we needed to be alone."

Claire sighed softly with relief. Then a new thought came

into her head. Daniel hadn't spoken to Sarah at all about the weekend. Claire had handled everything, talking to her about it, giving her directions. This testimony meant that Sarah wasn't going to implicate Claire in the crime. It also meant something else.

Sarah Corbett had just committed perjury.

Her mind reeling from the realization, Claire tried to figure out how she might use this fact against the prosecution without destroying her own career.

As she tried to grasp the implications, Claire heard Mills continue the direct.

"What did you and Dr. Wyatt discuss the first night you arrived at the cabin?"

"He talked about a new drug, called RU-486."

"What was the purpose of this drug?"

"To give me an abortion. To end the life of my child."

"And did Dr. Wyatt have this drug with him?" Riley Mills asked.

"Yes. He showed me the box. He showed me the pills."

Mills paused. His voice took on a new measure of anguish.

"Now, Sarah. Do you remember Dr. Wyatt at any time telling you that this drug had dangerous side effects?"

"No. He didn't tell me that."

"Did he explain to you that a surgical abortion would be necessary if the drug didn't work?"

"No."

The testimony continued. Sarah explained that she had told Daniel she would consider taking the pills. Then she testified that she and Daniel had slept together again. For the second time, tears appeared on her face.

Mills then went through the night of the miscarriage.

"I was reading. I had felt dizzy all that afternoon, so I just sat in a chair to read. I suppose I fell asleep."

"When did you wake up?"

"About eleven o'clock. A little before."

"And what happened when you woke up?"

"I was covered in blood."

She had seen it in the evidence list, but Claire had convinced herself that Mills wouldn't produce it. But now he did.

"Is this the dress you were wearing that night, Sarah?"

The bloodstained sundress, its white cotton marred by the dark red of dried blood, provoked a hushed murmur throughout the courtroom. Even Thibodeaux seemed transfixed by it.

Sarah's hand reached out to touch the garment, brushing for a moment the stain that marked the passage of her child.

"Yes," she said.

The rest of her testimony took no more than half an hour. Riley Mills knew that he had directed a perfect performance and didn't want to end too long after that moment of high drama. Sarah wept again as she talked about her time in the hospital, when she realized her child was gone.

It was just lunchtime when the direct was finished, as if Mills had orchestrated the whole thing to get him on the twelve o'clock news right on time. He certainly looked happy with himself, and with good reason.

Claire could feel it in the courtroom. The momentum had swung Mills's way again.

Claire Davis began her cross-examination of Sarah Corbett after lunch.

Davis was careful not to go after Sarah directly, Mills noticed. That made tactical sense, of course. Part of the exquisite bind that the defense was in was a result of the jury's sympathy for Sarah Corbett. Any direct attack on her could anger them. Although there were important points she had to bring out, including impeachment, Davis couldn't risk upsetting the delicate balance of the jury's emotions. Any slip that would bring tears to Sarah's eyes would be disastrous.

But Davis couldn't leave her testimony standing. If the defense didn't strike a blow now, Daniel Wyatt would be convicted of murder.

Davis began by questioning Sarah on the dates of her pregnancy. When had her last period ended? When had she performed the home tests? Then the defense counselor went over the dates of her affair with Wyatt from beginning to the end. Sarah answered calmly, but that persistent hesitation in her voice, the sound of unsureness, had returned.

"October second?" she would say, about a date she should be sure of by now.

"Are you sure?" Davis would ask sternly.

Sarah seemed intimidated by the older woman. Like a schoolchild called on to speak in class, she sometimes seemed paralyzed, unable to bring a ready answer to her lips. Davis worked this insecurity, making Sarah seem unreliable.

Then she dropped her bombshell.

"Sarah, have you ever been in a court of law before?"

"Yes?"

"As a witness?"

"No."

"You were a defendant, is that correct?"

Sarah nodded, and admitted it. This was no surprise to anyone except the jury, of course. The media had long ago ground the story to dust. Sarah Corbett had been charged with a single count of perjury several years before, and had pleaded guilty. It was technical perjury; she'd backdated some forms that had to do with her parents' estate. Mills was surprised the case had even been prosecuted. Just his luck.

Claire Davis got all she could out of it. She went over the case again and again, using the words "lie" and "perjury" at every opportunity. Finally, Judge Thibodeaux asked her to move on.

Davis wrapped up soon after that. She sat down, probably thinking that she had pulled Wyatt's fat out of the fire with the perjury charge.

Mills leaned back and shook his head. Too little too late.

"Do you wish to question the witness in redirect, District Attorney Mills?"

Mills looked at Sarah sympathetically, letting all present know how reluctant he had been to subject her to Claire Davis's cold scrutiny.

"No, Your Honor. No more questions for this witness."

"Very well. May this witness be excused?"

"No objection," said Riley.

"Your Honor," Claire Davis spoke up. "I would like to have the witness remain available, as the defense may wish to call her as our own witness."

What? Riley thought. Corbett as a defense witness? It didn't make sense. Had Claire Davis gone crazy, wanting to put the prosecution's most devastating witness on the stand again? She must be planning something. Or perhaps it was just a ruse to rattle him.

Judge Thibodeaux looked as puzzled as Mills was.

"I . . . certainly, Counsel. You are to remain available in the event that the defense decides to call you, Miss Corbett. Next witness, Mr. Mills."

Riley Mills stood and took a deep breath. As always, he was reluctant to say the next words. Was there anything he had missed? Any fiber of evidence he had inadequately explained?

No. He'd done his best, and there was nothing Claire Davis could do to save her client.

"Your Honor, the prosecution rests."

Rita Moore always faced Tuesday mornings with a certain dread.

This was the day that Medicare payment schedules had to be filed so that they could be submitted by mail, arriving at the Medicare offices in Raleigh by Friday. Dr. Ernest Magley was very particular about getting them in ASAP. If they weren't there by Friday, the office might be reimbursed in five weeks instead of four. And if that were to happen, the sky would surely fall.

Imagine, Rita Moore thought, the federal government collecting all that interest for a whole extra week. Imagine having to hear about it from Dr. Magley for a month and a half.

She arrived at Magley's office, as she always did on Tuesday mornings, at exactly 8:00 A.M. Dr. Magley himself would be here soon, making sure that she was on the case. At this hour, the medical building was mostly empty, and she had to use her magnetic key card to open the outer door. The fluorescent lights that stretched down the long hallways flickered to life as she walked. It was just some sort of motion detector, but it made her feel that she was being watched.

When she arrived at Magley's door, Rita felt distinctly that something was wrong. She worried the magnetic key card in her hand, wondering what was preying on her nerves this morning.

Rita shrugged, and swiped the magnetic key card through its slot. Pushed the door open.

Then, as though a cold gust of wind had touched her, she shivered and looked upward.

A yawning black hole loomed above her. Several of the ceiling panels just outside the door to Magley's office were out of place.

Rita Moore looked through the open glass door into the office. She could see more panels disturbed inside. It was as if someone had climbed up into the space above the door, crawled over it, and then dropped down into Dr. Magley's office.

She stood there, paralyzed for a moment, the open door in her hand.

Should she run?

There was no sound. No sign of any person in the office. The phone on her reception desk was only a few yards away.

Rita pushed into the office and grabbed the phone through the hatch that separated her desk from the waiting room. She punched the numbers 911.

Dr. Ernest Magley arrived in the parking lot only a few minutes after Rita Moore. He parked his Jaguar in his marked spot and headed toward the main door of the medical building. His hand was on the handle when he realized that he had forgotten his magnetic key card.

"Shit," he said. He hated Tuesday mornings.

Glove compartment, his sleepy mind commanded. Yes, that's where the card key was. Dr. Magley turned back toward his car.

At that moment, 8:06 A.M., the explosion ripped through the walls of his office, two hundred feet away. The C-4 had been well placed, stuffed into holes cut into the cheap fiberboard walls all around the frosted glass that separated the two examination rooms. The glass wall disintegrated, spewing sharp, tiny shards throughout the office.

For the first half second, Dr. Magley didn't so much hear the explosion as feel it in the soles of his feet, as if somehow an angry subway train were passing underneath the parking lot. Then the muffled sound reached him.

He spun around, and saw through the glass doors and down the hallway a cloud of white fragments, plaster, glass, and crumbling ceiling panels.

Dr. Magley knew the blast had occurred in his office. The vague fear that had shadowed him since the beginning of the trial had now erupted into reality.

It took a moment for Magley to react at all. At first he was transfixed by the thought *I could have been in there. I could be dead now.* Finally, he reached into his pocket for his cell phone and dialed 911, and gave the address of the medical building.

For some reason, the dispatcher said that police were already on their way.

"An explosion, you said?" she kept asking. "Not a break-in?"

Dr. Magley said yes. An explosion.

It wasn't until he had dropped the phone back into his pocket that his mind fully cleared, and he said, simply, "Rita."

With the speed of a younger man, driven by a terrible and sudden anger, he ran toward his car for the key.

Millie's shift should have been over already.

She'd been at work since eleven the night before and had responded to three calls already. The first was a case of domestic violence. No one was bleeding, and she and her partner had let the police officers handle it. The second had been a run to take an eighty-year-old woman with breathing trouble into Lafayette General. By the third call, Millie was pretty tired. She'd been watching a lot of the trial on television during the days. Between that and holding Sarah Corbett's hand after Sarah got back from the courthouse, Millie hadn't had much time to sleep.

The third call was to assist one of the protesters, injured in a fall from a downtown office building. He and his pals had decided to graffiti a pro-life sentiment along the top of one of the old brick-front department stores across from the courthouse. His accomplices had hung him upside down by his heels while he spray-painted. That is, until they'd dropped him.

It was amazing that the young man wasn't dead or paralyzed. He'd landed on a convertible with its top up, and suffered no more than a broken collarbone. But the call had kept Millie late, filling in forms and waiting for two sheriff's deputies who had to come and arrest him for criminal mischief.

So there she was, standing in the ER waiting for the deputies, when the call about the medical building bombing came through. A minute later she was on the road, headed out the twenty miles to the outskirts of the county.

When she and her partner arrived, there was already a Louisiana state police car on the scene. Millie parked the truck at the main entrance and dashed through the door, which someone had thought to prop open. It was easy to follow the trail of debris, which the blast had blown down the halls of the building in all directions.

She found two police officers and a third man tending to a woman who lay stretched out on the floor.

The woman was in bad shape. Her face and arms were riddled with cuts and abrasions. When Millie pushed the officers aside, she saw shards of glass embedded in every wound. One of the woman's eyes was closed and swollen. She was breathing shallow and fast, as if one of the cuts on her throat were leaking air.

"Sir, you'll have to step aside," she ordered the third man in the room.

"I'm a doctor," he said. "This was my office."

Millie then recognized him from TV. Ernest Magley, the doctor who had testified about Sarah's missed abortion appointment.

Her eyes scanned the office to see what was available. It

was clearly a GP or an OB-GYN's office, without any emergency medical supplies.

"We've got an ambulance here," she told the doctor. "What do you need?"

At eight-twenty, running a little late and wondering why Millie wasn't home yet, Sheriff Mark Hicks left his house. He started his SUV, and the radio popped to life.

"Explosion reported at Stanford Medical Building. One serious injury. Lafayette General EMTs and Lafayette FD responding."

Hicks froze for a moment in stunned silence, listening as the dispatcher gave the location. The clinic outside of town, where Sarah Corbett had made an appointment to get an abortion. Hicks understood immediately. It was what he and Costilla had feared all along. A bombing. A clinic bombing.

The war had truly come to Lafayette.

He pulled into the growing morning traffic with his siren blaring.

As he drove, Hicks remembered what Agent Costilla had said about the man he'd been following for three years.

He's normally a shooter. Prefers it personal. But he has bombed a clinic. Did a good job of it, too.

Hicks found himself in traffic as he approached town. He pushed his SUV onto the shoulder of the road and let his horn blare.

Two bombs, not one, Costilla had said. *Timed thirty minutes apart. The first one was just to draw a crowd.*

"Damn," Hicks said.

Millie wasn't home yet.

Officer John Hardaway was blinded briefly when he stepped from the dark hallway of the medical building into the bright sunlight. The lights weren't working, probably because of the explosion. It was eight-thirty. The parking lot was starting to fill, and three dozen or so confused people had shown up for work already. He had stationed a young nurse's aide, the first to arrive, at the door to keep them from entering.

He shaded his eyes and ignored their questions. The truck from the Lafayette Fire Department should be arriving soon.

"What's going on, Officer? I run this building."

Hardaway glanced at the gray-haired old man. On his belt was a roll of keys as big as a fist.

"There's been an explosion. See if you can get the lights on in there," he ordered, waving the man into the building. The moment the old man was past him, Hardaway held out his palm to stop the others.

"The rest of you stay here. And *move away* from the door."

The crowd moved back a few feet from the door. The word "explosion" worked its magic, rippling through the crowd.

Hardaway looked out onto the highway. Still no fire truck.

With a threatening look at the crowd, he jogged over to his state police cruiser, where the radio was popping.

As he grew closer to the car, he heard snatches of the radio traffic.

". . . and the sheriff's department is warning that there may be a second bomb." Pop. "We don't know their source." Pop. "We have an FBI agent here—" Pop.

Officer Hardaway heard what sounded like a foghorn. There it was finally, the fire truck pulling off the highway. But *what* were they saying on the radio?

"Reports of a second bomb. Repeat: FBI and sheriff's office warn of a *second bomb* on the premises."

Officer Hardaway reached through the car window for the radio. But no sooner had his fist closed on the handset than he threw it down and turned to run back toward the medical building.

He'd heard enough. He had to get his partner and the EMTs out of there.

Hardaway had just reached the outside door when the second charge exploded.

Sheriff Hicks pulled into the parking lot with screeching tires, his fingers gripping the steering wheel so hard that they were dead white. He realized that he hadn't driven that hard in years. He'd made the trip in less than twenty minutes.

The SUV's wailing siren parted the panicked crowd at the building's entrance. His left tire bounced onto the curb with a jarring thud as he pulled in behind the Louisiana State Police cruiser parked at the door. As he saw the Lafayette General ambulance parked beside it, the color drained from Hicks's face.

He had heard about the second blast on his radio a few minutes before.

No! his mind screamed. He'd tried to warn them! He'd heard Costilla on the radio trying to do the same.

Maybe they'd evacuated before . . .

Sheriff Hicks pushed past two firefighters in the bright yellow spacesuits of full fire dress, dashed down the hall toward a concentration of noise and activity. A group of firefighters was huddled around a rag-doll form lying out on the floor. The downed body was dressed in bright blue Lafayette General coveralls. The smoke was thick in Hicks's lungs as he labored toward the group. There was glass everywhere, his cowboy boots slipping on the shards as he ran.

Reaching them, he pushed one aside to reveal the downed medical tech.

It was Millie.

Testimony had begun early that day. It was Claire's first day of witnesses, and she needed time to get through her experts on fetal development.

"Properly speaking? No. No heart is present in a fetus of that age."

"But we have heard testimony from other learned experts in the field," Claire Davis said. "And they have stated unequivocally that this fetus has a beating heart."

Riley Mills knew it was going to be a long day. Claire Davis was out to bore his jury, to confuse and bemuse them, to make them long for a quick and simple resolution. And Mills realized that his own version of that resolution, a guilty verdict on a charge of murder, was being sorely tested by this tedious and complex trial. But he couldn't complain about all this nit-picking, these semantic hairsplittings about fetal age and organ development. As Judge Thibodeaux had reminded Mills each and every time he tried to object over the last hour, the prosecution had opened the door to this symposium with its own witnesses.

"When we are talking about human beings, or any mammals, for that matter, the word 'heart' usually refers to a four-chambered organ that sustains the circulation of blood throughout the body. At this point, the cells that will eventually become the heart are present, but they are in the shape of a simple tube. That is, these cells are almost exactly like a fish's heart."

Mills rolled his eyes. Claire Davis's witnesses had compared the early fetus to a menagerie of animals: lizards, worms, fish. They seemed to believe that the human fetus traveled through the whole history of evolution on its way to becoming a person.

"This muscle may contract, but not in the consistent way a heart does. And, more importantly, the heart tube of the fetus is not supplying its own circulation——yet. The mother's circulatory system is still providing for the movement of blood throughout the fetus."

"So it's the mother's heart that's beating?" Davis asked.

"That's right," her expert agreed. The man didn't look like a doctor. At first glance, he might have been on the stand to represent the National Organization of Accountants. His delivery was deadpan, serious, and deadly dull.

"What about the brain?"

"The brain is considerably more complex than the heart," he said in his monotone. "And therefore emerges much later in development."

"But what about the testimony that we've heard from the prosecution's witnesses, that assures us that an eight-week-old fetus has a brain."

The witness shook his head emotionlessly.

"After the first month, there is a hollow cord of cells, called a neural tube, that runs from the head to the end of the fetus's tail."

"Tail?" Davis interrupted.

"Yes. Human fetuses have a tail for a while. Like a reptile."

Mills shared a tortured glance with Morrisey.

"This cord has a bump at the head end, smaller than a period on a printed page," the expert continued. "That is what some abortion opponents call the fetus's brain."

"What's in this bump, this 'brain,' at eight weeks?" Davis asked.

Mills noticed that a few of the jurors were leaning forward. Apparently, some of them thought that this argument had some merit. Mills wished that Dr. Helmut hadn't crumbled awkwardly during Davis's cross-examination. It had been his job to put aside questions of self-consciousness.

"At eight weeks, most of the cells in the head area haven't even become nerves yet. There are no special connections among them, such as neurons have. Even in the third and fourth months, long after the fetus you see here, this cord only carries reflexes. Twitches, blind responses, not thoughts."

"How does that compare to an adult human?" Claire Davis asked.

"The adult brain contains roughly a hundred billion neurons. Thought happens in the connections among these neurons, which number in the trillions."

"Trillions?" Davis asked. "That's a one with how many zeros after it?"

"Twelve," the man answered without hesitation.

"And how many neuron connections does a eight-week-old fetus have?"

"None."

"When does the fetus start to develop a brain like you or I have?"

"Between twenty and thirty weeks," her expert answered. "Brain waves can be detected at about thirty weeks. Before then, there are no thoughts, no hopes, no dreams, no intentions, no pain, no awareness at all."

"What would it be like to be a fetus at that stage?" Davis asked. "At eight weeks?"

"Nothing. Like nothing at all."

Mills's highly developed internal barometer of courtroom mood detected a shiver that ran through the spectators. Somehow, the slow, plodding testimony had added up to something, a moment of drama, of realization. With his even, measured words, the man had accomplished something for the defense. He had, at least for a few moments, quietly erased the victim of this crime.

And Mills couldn't even remember the man's name.

* * *

More defense witnesses marched to the stand. They discussed the first moments of conception. They quoted the Talmud and Exodus. They grappled with the question of what it was to be human.

Claire Davis had entered into evidence her own picture of an eight-week-old fetus, which she had often reminded the jury was only six weeks from conception. It was basically the same as the prosecution's, with one slight difference. It wasn't blown up like the one Mills had pointed to for the last week. It was exactly to scale. That meant that the fetus was only about an inch long, almost invisible, lost on the three-foot-by-four-foot poster board on which Davis's team had mounted the photograph.

Mills flinched every time one of the defense witnesses tapped on the photo with the courtroom's pointer. It looked so small and insignificant. He noticed that the jurors all squinted whenever the photograph was referred to, as if it were some distant and unimportant fact they were vaguely trying to remember.

Riley Mills's confidence had sunk a bit, as it always did when the defense started its case. Now that Claire Davis was calling the shots, he felt less secure. Anything could happen.

He would be glad when it was finally time to recess for lunch.

Claire Davis was happy to have her own witnesses on the stand. Until now, Mills had almost completely controlled the information presented in the courtroom. Claire had always felt this to be the greatest of the prosecution's advantages: the ability to put its case on first. She knew the D.A. could overwhelm a jury, and cause it to make up its mind before the defense had even started. But in her first morning of testimony, she felt she had already made headway, at least against the charge of murder.

Before court was recessed, a bailiff went up to the judge and handed him a note. Thibodeaux read the missive silently, a grave look coming over his face.

"Counsel," he announced, "in my chambers."

He turned to the bailiff and instructed him not to admit anyone into the courtroom, and to keep the jury in the box. Claire shared a confused look with Riley Mills. The prosecutor was as mystified as she.

Inside his chambers, Thibodeaux sat down heavily.

"There has been a bombing," he said.

"Where?" Claire asked, her mind leaping to WAG.

"An abortion clinic outside of town. A doctor and his assistant have been killed." Thibodeaux looked sadly out the window at the protesters. They looked agitated today. They must know, Claire thought. The whole world must know outside the courtroom, like the silent eye of the storm.

Then her mind grasped the description of the clinic. Magley's office was just outside of town.

"There were two bombs, actually," the judge continued. "A policeman and two emergency workers have been gravely injured as well."

Riley Mills was the first to shake himself from stunned silence.

"We've got to keep the jury from learning about this, Your Honor," he said. "The jury could hear something during a family visit. Even in monitored phone calls, the bailiff only listens to the juror's side of the conversation. They're bound to hear about it!"

"I thought you believed sequestration to be unnecessary, Riley," Thibodeaux said sarcastically.

Mills started to protest, but sputtered out of words.

"They'll find out," Claire said. "They'll know. We can't put them in jail."

Thibodeaux considered this, then nodded his head.

"Perhaps, but there will be no mention of this in my courtroom. We will start cross-examination of this last witness after lunch. Will you be ready, Mr. Mills?"

Mills nodded glumly.

Claire thought for a moment. Good heavens, no matter

how tightly the bailiffs controlled the jury, everyone else would know about the bombings within seconds of walking out the courthouse door. The rumor must already be quietly spreading among the courtroom spectators.

"Your Honor, you can't sequester witnesses," she said. "My experts are going to hear about this."

"She's right," Mills agreed. "Let's keep going."

Claire gasped. It would be crazy, driving the jury onward without food or rest.

"Your Honor, I request a recess until tomorrow," she said.

"But you just said—" Mills began.

"I want to give the witnesses time to recover from this news, Your Honor," Claire explained.

"I concur," Thibodeaux said. The judge himself looked too overwhelmed to continue. "You have your recess."

Claire entered the courtroom again, her mind ablaze as it tried to put this all together. Sarah had committed perjury. An abortion provider, possibly Ernest Magley, was dead. And every witness in the case, including Sarah Corbett, was about to hear about the bombing.

Claire shook her head. Nothing in her days as a lawyer, an organizer, a political animal had prepared her for this.

A trial was usually a carefully controlled dance, a ritual choreographed by judge, prosecutor, and defense following very specific rules. But this trial had a whirlwind surrounding it, a juggernaut that no one could have predicted. Events outside the courtroom were causing the wheels of justice to spin out of control.

But somewhere in this mess, a clear thought formed in Claire's mind.

Sarah would be shaken by this news. The woman would reconsider her earlier decision when she saw the horrors her accusations had led to; everything would appear to her in a terrible new light. Perhaps it would be enough to change the certainties of her testimony.

But Sarah had already testified. Of course, though, Claire realized, the defense could call Sarah Corbett again as their own witness, this time as hostile.

If nothing else, it was another chance.

54 | RESPONSIBILITY

Sarah Corbett drove alone to the hospital.

The feel of the steering wheel in her hands was oddly unfamiliar. Sarah realized that she hadn't driven herself anywhere lately. Usually, it was sheriff's deputies who drove her to the courthouse, or Assistant D.A. Kathleen Morrisey, or even Riley Mills himself. Without official plates on a car, it was impossible to find parking in downtown Lafayette, and impossible to get inside the courtroom without some sort of credentials.

Sarah realized that besides attending the trial, she rarely left her house anymore.

But here she was, unescorted and unrecognized, driving in her own car. She felt free, almost euphoric, as if she had stolen back in time to grab a few moments of her innocent life before this awful fall.

Then she remembered where she was going.

"Oh, Millie," she said to herself.

Dusk had fallen, but a few clouds were high enough to catch the light of the hidden sun, bright flecks in the sky above the dark highway. Outside of downtown this late, the traffic wasn't so bad. That was all you heard people talking about at this point in the trial. The citizens of Lafayette had grown weary of the weighty philosophical and legal issues, but the local talk radio still constantly lamented the crowded streets, as if this whole case were some grand conspiracy against commuters.

Of course, talk radio wouldn't be focused on traffic problems today, not after the clinic bombing this morning. Sarah hadn't listened to any news since Sheriff Hicks had called her. She hadn't dared. What if they were blaming her for all this?

What if Millie blamed her?

For the thousandth time since her miscarriage, Sarah Corbett talked herself through the sequence of events that had led to this moment. Somehow, the end result never made sense, never added up from the choices she had made. The exercise was like some awful, complicated tax form she kept filling out, the bottom line never coming out correctly, as if mathematical absolutes had been broken by the abuses of the last few months.

When had she, Sarah Corbett, ever asked to become a nationally known victim? A symbol of adultery? Of the end of moral decency? Of motherhood betrayed?

When had she ever asked for demonstrations on her behalf, or on behalf of her child? For news coverage, for celebrity, or for bombs?

The hospital parking lot was almost empty. Sarah braced herself before entering the vast building. The last time she had been inside its walls she'd lost her child forever.

It was strange to be anonymous. Certainly, a few passing members of the staff seemed to recognize her, but they were too busy to gawk. They didn't have signs or bullhorns, and no wall of police was necessary to protect her. She simply walked up to the elevator and entered the car. Mark Hicks had told her the room number when he'd called, his voice as broken as she had ever heard it. Sarah had never seen Sheriff Hicks cry, even when his wife had died on that terrible night eight years ago.

Deputy Mary Jackson was outside the room. How strange, Sarah thought. She had also had a guard during her days in Lafeyette General. Couldn't people stay at the hospital without protection anymore?

Again, the list went through her head. Look what her pregnancy had caused: Sheriff Hicks flushing reporters from the trees behind her house, Dr. Wyatt wearing a bulletproof vest, Millie under guard . . .

. . . and maimed. Mark Hicks had explained in halting words what the doctors had told him. She might walk again with crutches, but would never regain full movement in her legs. The second blast at the clinic had been packed inside a bag full of metal bolts, and one of the flying fragments had nearly severed Millie's spine.

The doctors said it was a miracle that she was still alive, that she was breathing unassisted.

A sad, shabby miracle by Sarah's reckoning. Where was the miracle that would have prevented all of this from happening?

Deputy Jackson smiled thinly and whispered, "I think she's awake."

Sarah went in.

"Hey, Sarah." Millie's voice was weak, but cheerful.

"Hey, Millie."

The room was covered in flowers. They occupied every spare surface, spilling onto the floor, crowding the top of the television. A small army of hospital pitchers had been deployed to hold them, the ugly brown and pink plastic containers shamed by the gaudy flora they contained. Of course, every member of the hospital's staff knew Millie. As did everyone in the sheriff's department, and probably a host of other people, too—friends, colleagues, old school chums . . .

Sarah felt insignificant, a small and contemptible presence in this splendidly decorated room.

"Oh, God," she exclaimed. "I forgot to bring flowers!"

"Don't be silly," Millie said. "I'm just so glad you're here."

Millie's voice was somehow distant, as if the room were on some mountain peak, the air dangerously thin. Her skin was pale, but the spark that always animated her features hadn't dimmed.

Sarah sat in the visitor's chair and reached out to hold Millie's hand. It felt healthy, warm and familiar. Sarah squeezed it, as gently as if the hand were a wounded bird.

"I'm so sorry about this, Millie. None of this would have—"

"Hush, silly. Don't make me go through that again. I just spent all day convincing Daddy there was nothing he could have done."

"By why would he—"

"He'd told the clinics in town to suspend any procedures, even had a deputy check on them every morning. But Stanford Medical was outside the county line. Out of his jurisdiction, even though Dr. Magley was called as a witness at the trial."

"Poor Mark," Sarah said, shaking her head. Sheriff Hicks's first name felt strange in her mouth. During her childhood, the presence of the sheriff next door had always filled her with awe, knowing that a power and an authority that exceeded even her own father's were just steps away.

"You take good care of him while I'm stuck in here, all right?"

"Yes, Millie. Anything."

The idea was crazy. Her, Sarah Corbett, taking care of Sheriff Hicks. But he had sounded so small on the phone, like a young and frightened boy trying to explain a medical problem by repeating the words of some kind, indulgent doctor.

"Where is he?"

"He just went down to the cafeteria for some coffee. Sarah, maybe you could make sure he goes home when you do. He needs to get some sleep, but he won't listen to me."

"All right."

Millie's eyes had grown glassy, as if even a few moments of conversation had exhausted her. Her eyelids drooped and her voice softened.

"And make sure he doesn't drink too much coffee. It upsets his stomach something awful."

Then, smiling, Millie had glided, as softly as a child, into a peaceful sleep.

* * *

Sheriff Hicks returned with three cups of coffee, as if he were determined to spend the entire night at Millie's side.

Sarah drank one, and she and Sheriff Hicks talked softly about the days when Millie's mother had been alive. Sarah sometimes forgot that Millie was a decade younger than she. Nowadays they felt like contemporaries, but back then "that Hicks girl"—as Sarah's daddy had always called her—had been a brat. Millie was prone to skip school, she dated older boys, and generally had the rebellious tendencies people expected of a preacher's daughter. Maybe sheriff's daughters were even worse, Sarah's daddy would often say. When Millie's mother died, all that had changed, and she and Sarah—whose own parents had died only a couple of years earlier—bonded powerfully, best friends forever. The difference in their ages seemed irrelevant.

"I wonder why I never told Millie," Sarah said to Sheriff Hicks as midnight approached. The halls of the hospital were silent now, all the other visitors departed. It felt as if the world had been emptied except for her, the sheriff, and the sleeping Millie.

"About Wyatt?" Hicks asked softly.

"Yes. About Daniel. I should have told her. But the whole affair just seemed to be so unreal, like if I told someone about it, it would all just disappear."

Hicks shook his head defeatedly. "Nothing just disappears, Sarah. You can pray all you want, but what's done is done."

She nodded, for a moment surprised that his words didn't bring a surge of guilt inside her. But she knew, was finally sure, that Mark Hicks didn't blame her for what had happened to Millie.

Besides, she was tired of guilt. Guilt had haunted her for so long, guilt about the affair, about her pregnancy, about what had happened to Daniel Wyatt and to Lafayette, Louisiana. Guilt for losing her child. No more. She hadn't caused all this, hadn't chosen any of it.

"Mark, I believe you're right. What's done is done. I think I'm past praying to change things. Past wanting revenge."

"What do you mean, Sarah?"

"I'm not sure. But I feel like for a long time now I've been letting other people choose for me. Letting them take all the responsibility. My father. Daniel Wyatt. And now Riley Mills."

"D.A. Mills is just doing his job," Hicks reminded her. "As best he can. Sometimes that means playing rough."

"Sometimes I think Daniel Wyatt was just doing as best he could, too."

"That man didn't give you a choice, Sarah. The law says you've got a choice about having a baby. You and you alone."

She nodded. "I know. Next time I'll make that choice myself."

The sheriff smiled at her, the expression breaking the sadness on his face. "I'm glad to hear that, Sarah Corbett. Now, I think I've got to take a little walk."

He rose, steadying himself with one hand on the back of his chair.

"Whoa. Just a little dizzy there," he said. "Got up too fast."

Sarah smiled and took his arm.

"Mark," she said, "I'm afraid I'm going to have to insist on something."

"What's that?"

"You're awfully tired. And I'm going to have to drive you home."

"But, I—"

"Shush. Millie's orders. Now go on to the bathroom, and then let's go home."

Agent Tabitha Samuels found herself shrugging as she walked down the crowded streets. Her weapon felt uncomfortable in its shoulder holster, larger than usual, as if the leather jacket that hid it had mysteriously shrunk a few sizes last night.

Normally, Samuels didn't mind carrying. She was used to it after three years with the Bureau. And despite her lack of enthusiasm for the gun porn her male colleagues shamelessly indulged in, she enjoyed the occasional hour at the shooting range. She just didn't brag about her scores, like she didn't brag about her car's engine or the size of her dick.

Leave that to the boys.

Today, however, the nine didn't feel quite right. Perhaps it was this new sports bra. Maybe it was the Louisiana weather, creepily warm even though it was late winter. Or possibly it was because she had the unpleasant feeling she was going to have to *use* the thing today.

Cost and the boys were out at the clinic that had been bombed, trying to collect evidence before the yokels pissed all over everything. So that left Samuels alone in town, checking the hotels one by one for any occupant using one of Steve Bartlett's aliases.

Legwork. A Yale degree in Fractal Calculations of Fundamental Chaos Theory, and she was doing fucking legwork.

Worse, she wasn't even sure if Bartlett was their man. Cost had a hard-on for him because he was ex–Soldiers of Christ and had probably sent that care package to Cost's (suppos-

edly secret) girlfriend. The guy was definitely a major ass-
hole, Samuels couldn't disagree with that, but Bartlett was a
total loser compared with the man they'd been tracking for
three years. This had been all too easy.

She walked unhappily into the Marriott and cut to the
front of the line at reception.

"FBI," she announced, thunking her badge case out on
the counter. Chaos carried her ID on a fat chain around her
neck, like all the pretty boys on nineties cop shows used to
do. The last word in guido jewelry.

"How can I help you?" the nice lady said, her already arctic smile freezing a bit more behind the layers of rouge and
lipstick.

Let's see. How can *you* help *me*? Lose the polyester uniform. Lose the big hair. Lose the smile.

"I'm looking for a someone who may be in this hotel,
ma'am," Agent Samuels said. "A very dangerous suspect."

The woman—Carrie, if she was wearing her own name
tag—answered with widened eyes.

"So could you please check a few names?" Samuels asked.
"I'll read. Just tell me if any of these people are checked in, all
right?"

Samuels read the list. One by one, Carrie tapped them in,
each keystroke from her long, lacquered nails setting
Samuels's teeth further on edge. Why did women do that?
she thought to herself. *Why* would you want to slow your
keyboarding down? For Samuels, it was as revolting as Chi-
nese women binding their feet.

"Nope. Not that one either," Carrie said when she'd
reached the end of the list.

Samuels breathed a sigh of relief. Another no-show. She'd
been on warehouse raids with federal marshals, and on a
DEA bust where shots had been fired, but her latest research
had showed that this Bartlett guy had been a Navy SEAL.
Tackling him without backup was not something Samuels
considered within her job description. She liked her chaos
on paper, thank you.

"Oh, but that's funny," Carrie said, her head leaning to one side in puppy-dog fashion.

Here it comes, Samuel's intuition warned. Of course, her intuition had been warning that all morning, and it had been wrong every time so far. Still, as Byron had once observed, even a stopped clock is right twice a day.

"You asked about an Arnold Bart?" Carrie said.

"Yeah . . ."

"Well, there's a fellow at the hotel whose name is Bart Arnold. Just the opposite! Now isn't that a coincidence?"

Agent Samuels looked deep into Carrie's bright smiling eyes and could only think to say, "Fuck."

"Cost!"

Costilla stepped lightly over the scattered metal fragments that covered the hallway floor. A sheriff's deputy was working on his hands and knees to mark each of them with a little circle of Magic Marker. They'd be reopening the building after noon today, and his team was trying to preserve as much of the blast evidence as possible.

"Chaos?" he answered. "What's up?"

"I found him. I think I have, anyway. There's a guy at the Marriott called Bart Arnold. Like Arnold Bart, but backward. The old name flip, the sort of lame cover Bartlett would use."

Costilla stopped short, steadied himself with a hand against the wall. This was it. His man, finally, after three years.

"Stay there, Chaos. Stanton and I are on our way. I'll call the locals and get them to your location. Wait for them in the lobby, but don't go in until we get there."

"No problem there, Costilla."

"All right, we should be there in twenty minutes. Try to keep the locals from being too obvious, all right?"

As he spoke, Costilla waved for Stanton's attention. Once the man was in tow, he started down the hall toward the exit. He had to restrain himself from running.

"By the way," he added. "Good work, Agent Samuels."

There was no answer.

"Chaos?"

"Shit," came her sharp reply. "I see him. He's in the lobby. That's definitely him. Fuck. He's gotta be three hundred pounds."

"Coming or going?" Costilla said, breaking into a run. He heard a sound of confusion from Stanton, then the man breaking into a run to keep up with him. "Talk to me, Chaos."

"Shut *up*. He's going. He's at the door."

Costilla reached the door, broke into the sunlight and heat. He struggled for his car keys with his free hand.

"Take him or trail him? Come on, Cost, I'm in motion. Do I follow or arrest his ass?"

Costilla stopped, car keys in his hand. Bartlett might be armed. Maria, he was almost certainly armed. The Soldiers of Christ were big on submachine guns. Four of them had murdered a radio host and his family in Tampa in 1994, using over seven hundred rounds to make the hit. You'd never take one without backup. And Agent Samuels was in a crowded hotel lobby, surrounded by innocent bystanders. The whole situation was stacked in Bartlett's favor.

But tailing a suspect alone was tough even for the most experienced field agent. And if Samuels followed him, Bartlett might spot her. He could disappear, go to ground, and never show up again, the opportunity presented by the Wyatt trial lost forever.

Costilla knew what he should do. Just have Chaos stand down. Let Bartlett go without a word. If he was registered at the hotel, he'd be back.

But Costilla couldn't give the order.

"Cost?" Her tense voice came back. "I am in motion. My cell phone is making me obvious. Take him or tail him?"

"Take him."

"**Y**our Honor," Claire Davis protested, "this is unconscionable. Discovery must be completed before trial."

"Counselor?" the judge asked, turning to Mills. The three were in sidebar, talking in hushed tones as the court waited.

"Your Honor," Mills answered, "I would have loved to have this evidence in hand earlier. I believe this trial would have been much quicker if I had. But this evidence was just uncovered. We didn't know about it until today."

Riley Mills spread his hands in a helpless gesture. Damn, Claire thought. He'd lucked out again. Just when the clinic bombing had threatened to turn the momentum back against him and his pro-life arguments, this had to happen. The jury was already in the box, waiting to hear her direct of the recalled Sarah Corbett, and now Mills pulls this out of his hat.

"Are you sure about that, Counselor?" the judge said. "You haven't been holding back on this tape?"

"Not at all. You yourself have commented on the huge amount of materials seized from WAG headquarters. This tape was on a backup tape that contained hundreds of conversations. We have been working with great diligence to get through everything," Mills explained. "Your Honor, this is a search for the truth. We can't keep this evidence from the jury."

"Your Honor," Claire butted in, "I appreciate the prosecution's great and lengthy efforts, but he made his case already on this matter. He has called many witnesses on the subject of the affair. A tape like this will greatly lengthen the trial and cause many witnesses to have to be recalled. The prosecution is sandbagging us."

"It was the defense that has made an issue of the affair," Mills interjected. "They have cast doubt upon the affair between Wyatt and Sarah Corbett, on whether she was pregnant, and on the paternity of the child. This tape speaks to each of those points. And if anyone would have known about this tape, the defense should have. Your client is on the tape, after all, Ms. Davis."

"All right," Judge Thibodeaux said. "I must weigh defense's right to discovery, which I take very seriously, against the importance of the evidence, then. The prosecution counsel is right, Ms. Davis. You have made the existence of the affair a central issue of this case. So let's listen, but in my chambers."

They retreated to the judge's office. Kathleen Morrisey stepped forward, placing a tape recorder on the desk.

As the tape played, Claire found herself flashing back to the night when this debacle had all started for her. She hadn't remembered what exactly was on the tape, but now as she listened, the words came back as clear as crystal.

Daniel? Sarah's voice. Sounding younger than it did now.

Are you okay? Wyatt's voice answered. It was undeniably his tone, his cadence.

Yes, I'm sorry. I'm sorry. It's just that I got scared. I don't know if I'm ready for tomorrow.

Claire looked at Judge Thibodeaux. He seemed transfixed by the soft confession of the tape. She knew the jury would be, too, if they heard it. It would blow apart her fragile structure of reasonable doubt like a hand grenade thrown at a house of cards.

Sarah, I thought we had agreed.

I know, but when you're not here I feel so . . . alone.

I'll be there tomorrow. I will.

But tonight has been just . . . ghastly. I keep thinking of the baby, our baby. It seems like this night will go on forever.

Our baby. Claire Davis remembered the words now. Two of the three pieces of her case would be destroyed. Yes, there was an affair. Yes, Sarah was pregnant with Wyatt's child. All that would remain was the question of how she had taken the drug.

Dr. Wyatt? I'm just lonely, I suppose.

Sarah. I could come over, if you need me. God, Daniel sounded desperate, Claire thought.

Oh, Daniel. Would you?

I'm leaving here soon. But I can only stay a little while.

Of course, Dr. Wyatt. I'll see you soon.

Morrisey stopped the tape. Mills looked at the judge with a shrug. His arguments didn't even need to be stated.

"Your Honor," Claire started, trying to find a way out of this, "give the defense time to draft a motion to exclude—"

"I'm afraid you would be wasting your time, Counselor. This evidence speaks to motive and opportunity," Thibodeaux said, shaking his head. "I will not exclude it."

Claire's mind flailed for something to say, but nothing coherent came into it.

"D.A. Mills, you may introduce this tape after the defense has rested," Judge Thibodeaux ruled.

The district attorney rose. Claire stood slowly, finally realizing the dimensions of this defeat. She now had to go out and begin her examination of Sarah Corbett, knowing that everything Sarah had claimed all along—about the affair, the pregnancy, the father—would soon be proven to the jury.

"We've kept the jury waiting all morning," the judge said, looking at his watch. "Perhaps we could break early for lunch. We'll begin testimony at one-thirty."

Claire nodded, knowing she'd been thrown a bone. Another two hours to prepare, to completely rebuild her murder case from the ground up.

She took a deep breath. There had to be some other direction to take this. But there was only one last argument she could make.

Two people, father and mother of an unborn child, go to

a lonely beach house to decide whether to continue their pregnancy. At the end of that weekend, a decision is made. She would have to press the jury with one question: is the father so completely irrelevant to the reproductive process that the father's decision on such a weekend could be murder, while the mother's decisions are constitutionally protected?

Claire took a deep breath. Although she had already touched upon this argument in her defense of Daniel Wyatt, Claire never thought that she would be left with it alone. But the course of events had led her here, to a stance she never would have imagined herself taking.

A father's right to an abortion.

"**C**ost, you cocksucker," Chaos muttered as she slipped the phone back into the pocket of her leather jacket.

She was on the street, watching the broad back of Steve Bartlett. Man, he was *huge*. The crowd parted before him. Agent Samuels felt exposed in the wake of empty space he created behind himself.

Something about him looked disproportionate. His legs were too thin for the bulky body. His green camo jacket spread like a tent over his torso. Steroids maybe. Skinny legs and a big chest. Always great for a man's disposition. Or maybe he was wearing a bulletproof vest. Fuck! That was it. The Soldiers of Christ had been total hardware heads. Machine guns, grenades—a couple of them had tried to buy nerve gas once from a con artist in Los Angeles. The man in front of her was definitely wearing pounds.

The weapon in her shoulder holster felt puny and toylike.

Chaos had a momentary fantasy. Use the vest to her advantage. Just walk up behind him and deliver four shots into his kidney area without warning. Like a prizefighter's punch, no chance of missing. That would take his cracker ass down. Then make the arrest. Sure, *if* he's got a weapon—which he's sure to have—then squaring her shots with an inquiry board would be a cinch.

Then she shook her head. What was she thinking? Shooting a citizen in the back without warning, on the assumption that he had a vest on? Man, carrying a gun did weird shit to your head.

Just do it by the book, she ordered herself.

Well, no. The book would probably demand two or more agents for a perp like Bartlett. The book would take it off this crowded street. The book would be kicking Costilla's ass right now.

Fuck the book.

Chaos pulled her weapon.

She flicked the safety and took a few quick steps forward, closing the distance between herself and Bartlett with sickening ease. A vertiginous feeling flooded her mind, like the rush of rappelling, when you push off from that firm base of rock and trust the thin rope, the clever metal clips, and black nylon straps to hold you. To save you from the unbelievably stupid thing you've just done. Just don't look down.

She'd timed her move right. Bartlett had just turned left, leaving Main Street with its milling pedestrian traffic. A long brick wall ran alongside and parallel with this smaller street. No stores or restaurants. Chaos took one last step forward, reached up—Bartlett had a solid foot of height on her—and tapped his left shoulder, then jumped to her right. It was that oldest of junior-high-school tricks, a second's disorientation before the sucker punch.

He bought it, turning around to his left. Now she was behind him, gun aimed down at his ass. The book said aim for the chest or the head. But Bartlett's chest was armored and head shots were missable if the man was fast. And the man had been a Navy SEAL. Chaos trusted a gun aimed at his groin to make him think twice.

"FBI!" she shouted. "Put your hands up!"

He was already turning around toward her, looking more confused than anything else. Who was this little bitch yelling at him? His hands were away from his body, but not in the air yet. Chaos kept her gun up where he could see it, but still angled down at his crotch.

"Put your fucking hands up, *now*!"

Bartlett was still frozen, but she could see calculation in his eyes. He figured he had a few seconds before she shot him for just standing still. He was weighing options. Chaos had kept herself well beyond arm's length. There were no hostages to grab, the few civilians on the street had cleared like magic. She saw a few bystanders frozen in her suddenly sharp peripheral vision. Everything was very slow and clear.

She saw it in his eyes. He gave up, just like that, like a good soldier.

His hands moved up slowly. They crossed behind his head, the jacket pulled tight by the gesture, its buttons straining until the top one popped. There it was, suddenly exposed, the black mesh of the vest. My God, she'd been right. And she'd beaten him. This giant walking arsenal. Chaos rules.

But the man was still moving, adjusting his position as slowly and carefully as a man defusing a bomb. His right elbow was still rising as the hand went further behind his head, as if reaching for something inside of it, something strapped to his back inside the collar. Fuck, she had time to think.

And then it was all in slow motion, because Steve Bartlett was making his move.

His motion was so fluid, so unexpected given that giant frame—Bartlett was as fit as a panther beneath the bulk of camo and Kevlar. His right hand swept up and over, going from its coiled position to straighten like a striking snake. A flash of metal caught her eye as she pushed off one foot, trying to dodge.

Chaos was firing before the pain hit. One shot at the groin and then, blinded by the lance of fire that erupted in her left arm, four more into his central body mass. She saw the shots push him back, like punches thrown by some invisible assailant. But the wall at his back stabilized Bartlett, and he pushed toward her.

She stumbled backward, into the road.

Chaos fired again, but now Bartlett's inertia was carrying him against the little slugs. She had to hit flesh. But she'd lost her steady footing, and her left shoulder was in blazing agony. She aimed downward again and shot for his knees, squeezing off the rest of the clip in a tight pattern.

Something connected, and Steve Bartlett went down onto one knee. A hand was reaching into his jacket as he fell face-down, his head only inches from her. She knelt, her knees on either side of his head, and put the empty gun against the back of his head.

"*Don't*, motherfucker!" she screamed. "I will splatter you."

She could see the tension in his arm. He probably had the gun he'd been reaching for in his hand. But it was trapped beneath the vest's weight and his own, and she pressed the hot metal of her weapon against the hollow where spine connects with skull. A pool of blood was spreading from his right thigh, another from his left knee.

"Do *not* move!"

He didn't move.

The high, angry screech came from her left. It was a car taking the corner too fast, with only seconds to stop for the pair lying bizarrely in the road. Chaos kept her eyes locked on Bartlett's head, screaming as if that would cancel the squeal of tires bearing down on her.

The car stopped with less than a foot to spare. Chaos could feel the hot air from its front grille on her cheek, as if some enormous predator were breathing down her neck, pondering whether it should bother eating such a diminutive meal.

But she couldn't look at it. Bartlett had a weapon in his hand; she had an empty gun.

"Don't move," she repeated hoarsely.

She tried to reach inside her jacket for another clip, but her left arm screamed with pain. Chaos saw it now, the knife handle thrusting obscenely from her shoulder. God, if she hadn't moved, the knife would be buried in her throat.

There was no way to reload without taking the gun from the back of Bartlett's head. And Chaos wasn't doing that.

So they waited there, Bartlett bleeding like a pig from the artery in his thigh that one of her bullets had sliced through,

Samuels kneeling over him with her useless weapon, holding him captive with nothing but the angry conviction in her voice as she ordered him again and again not to move.

They waited for an eternity that was in fact only three minutes, before the Lafayette PD showed with two cars, and then three more.

There was something unexpected in Claire Davis's manner as she began her questioning of Sarah Corbett.

Riley Mills leaned forward, trying to figure out what was making his courtroom instincts tingle. Davis was starting out slow, gently pulling answers about the affair from Sarah.

"So, Dr. Wyatt ended things with you on that Sunday night in Baton Rouge, correct?"

"Yes."

"And you thought it was over between you and him?"

"I did. I really did."

Davis nodded. She'd yet to disagree with anything Sarah Corbett had said. Mills wondered why Davis had bothered to recall the woman at all.

"So what changed that?"

"Well, the baby, I guess?" Sarah looked puzzled with her own answer.

"The fact that you were pregnant made you think again about your relationship with Dr. Wyatt. Made you think that in some way it was still going on?"

"Well, once I saw him again, just him and me together, it felt right."

"Even though he suggested that you have an abortion?"

"I'm not sure Daniel suggested it. I mean, at first I wanted to."

"At first you wanted to have an abortion." Davis paused to let that sink in, before saying, "But he agreed. He helped you get an appointment."

"Yes."

"So you asked Dr. Wyatt if you could abort your child, and he said okay, and tried to help you."

"Yes. That's what happened, Ms. Davis."

Mills began to realize what was happening here. Because of the taped conversation between Sarah and Wyatt, Davis's case had been yanked out from under her. Now she was floating in midair, trying to come up with something. She was improvising, trying to get Sarah Corbett, of all people, to help her come up with some new strategy. In a way, the new situation left her with more freedom than her reasonable-doubt strategy; Davis could drop the "alleged affair" nonsense and talk to Sarah directly and honestly.

Well, Claire Davis could improvise all she wanted to, but she and Daniel Wyatt weren't getting out of this one.

"Now," Davis continued, "why didn't you show up at Dr. Magley's office?"

The mention of the dead man's name sent a stir through the courtroom. At least a few of the jury must know by now, Mills thought. Even sequestered people heard things from relatives during visits or phone conversations. And sometimes they seemed to just know, like ants shoring up their hills before a rainstorm.

"I didn't . . . I don't know. Daniel had said he was coming by the night before. And he didn't make it. I mean, he drove all the way there, but he said he just couldn't come into my house."

"He stood you up?"

"I guess so. He broke his promise."

"So you stood him up?"

"Well, I was afraid he wouldn't be there. That I would have to face it alone."

Davis nodded sympathetically.

"Did you tell him this, later when you talked again?"

"Yes."

"You said you'd wanted to have an abortion, but you didn't want to face it alone."

"That's right."

Mills didn't like the ready agreement that Davis was getting out of Sarah. The younger woman was hanging on the defense lawyer's every word, being led by the nose. Mills hoped he could find something to object to soon in order to break the spell Davis had cast on his star witness.

"It was soon after that missed appointment that you went with Dr. Wyatt to the beach house, right?"

"Yes. It was Friday of that same week."

"Where you would be alone together?"

"Yes."

Yes. Yes. Yes. Didn't Sarah see where Davis was going with this? Mills looked at the jury. They were watching raptly. It must be surprising to them, to see Claire Davis suddenly so accepting of Sarah Corbett's story. Of *Riley Mills's* story, dammit. The defense lawyer's sudden switch from skeptic to supportive confidante might win them over as it had Sarah.

"So you'd wanted to have an abortion, but only with Dr. Wyatt at your side," Davis said. "And now you were headed out with him to a remote location."

Sarah nodded.

"And did you want to go there with him?"

"Very much so."

"And that Friday night, the first night you were out there alone together, he showed you the RU-486."

"That's right."

"Did that surprise you? That he had brought those drugs?"

"Well, a little."

A little, Mills fumed. Well, he would have to deal with this in his cross.

"Did it make you angry? Did you throw the pills at his face?"

Sarah looked thoughtful, as if she were visiting a fragile memory carefully, so as not to distort it.

"I thanked him."

A shocked sound went through the courtroom, but if Claire Davis was surprised, she didn't let herself show it.

"You thanked him for what?"

"I said, 'Thank you for giving me this gift.' "

Claire nodded. " 'Thank you, for giving me this gift,' " she repeated.

Mills could stand no more of this. He rose.

"Your Honor . . ." But nothing came.

"Mr. Mills," the judge ordered with quiet, angry intensity. "If you have no objection, please sit down and be silent."

Claire Davis turned to face Mills, as if he'd rudely interrupted a lovely tête-à-tête between her and Sarah Corbett to which he hadn't been invited. He sat, steaming. He knew that his face was turning red.

"Did Daniel say what he wanted?" Davis asked.

"Yes. He wanted me to take the pills. To abort our child."

"Did he say why?"

"He said it wasn't the right time. There was too much against us. His marriage, the people in Washington who were trying to get him. And he wanted to save his family. And he said that our child should have a full-time father, a family."

"He thought your child should have a family," Davis repeated. "Did you understand why he wanted these things? Did what he said make sense to you?"

"Oh, yes," Sarah answered. "He was so upset. He was just doing the best he could. I mean, I didn't want to mess everything up. I never wanted to become pregnant."

Another stir in the court. Claire Davis let it settle.

"That's why you'd been using birth control pills. Right?"

"Right."

"And then Dr. Wyatt offered you these abortion pills, correct?"

"Yes."

"And you thanked him."

"Yes, Ms. Davis."

"And you took the pills from him."

"Yes. He had me keep them."

"And where are they now?"

Sarah shook her head. "I don't know. I think I lost them."

Mills closed his eyes. *She thought she lost them.* That's what Sarah had thought before her miscarriage, but by now she should know better. The pills had disappeared for a simple reason: Daniel Wyatt had slipped them to her. Mills's team had searched the whole place for them, Corbett and Wyatt's cars, too, and hadn't found anything but an out-of-date flu prescription, some vitamins, and aspirin.

They'd found them in her blood, dammit.

"You lost them?" Davis asked in disbelief. "That night, Sarah, you went to bed with this question on your mind, right? Whether or not to take the pills?"

"Certainly."

"You were thinking about it hard?"

"Very hard, Ms. Davis."

"Did part of you want to take the RU-486?"

"Yes. Because I wanted my child to have a father, and Dr. Wyatt couldn't be that father. And things were so messed up."

"But another part of you didn't want to take the pills."

"That's true."

"Why not?"

"Because I thought that if I did I would . . . lose Daniel."

"You thought he might see you differently if you aborted your child?"

"Yes." Sarah was crying now. Her voice was steady, but glistening tears welled up in the corners of her eyes. Mills stirred, but Thibodeaux cast him a warning glance.

"Now, let me ask you something, Sarah. Something very important. Did you take the pills that Dr. Wyatt offered you? Did you take them and not tell him? Did you keep it a secret, maybe even from yourself?"

Sarah shook her head, but said, "I don't think so?"

Damn! Mills thought. I don't *think* so.

The words were like a blow to his stomach.

Claire Davis went on. She and Sarah talked about the miscarriage, about the sorrow. Davis did everything but hold Sarah Corbett's hand. Little else that was said that afternoon between the two women was exculpatory, it was just to show the defense attorney's human side to the jury. Davis knew she'd gotten all she could out of this witness.

The words rang in Mill's mind. *I don't think so.* The slightest of slips from Sarah Corbett, who was so used to making statements in a doubtful, uncertain tone of voice, to saying what people wanted to hear. Well, she'd done exactly what Claire Davis wanted.

Sarah Corbett had created reasonable doubt.

Riley Mills moved carefully during his cross-examination of Sarah, taking her back through the weekend at the beach house. He asked the questions slowly, like a man deactivating a bomb, Claire thought. Mills had looked tired this morning when he had arrived at the courtroom. He had a tough job today: the rehabilitation of his star witness. Finally, he reached the question upon which the case now turned.

"Sarah, do you remember willingly taking the RU-486?"

She paused just for a moment. "No."

"But, as evidence has shown, the drug showed up in your bloodstream. So someone must have given it to you."

"Your Honor!" Claire objected.

"Mr. Mills," the judge admonished, "you are pressing too much with that question."

Mills paused before attempting to rephrase. "What I suppose I mean, Sarah, is, don't you think you would remember if you had—"

"Your Honor," Claire interrupted, "if Mr. Mills wants to testify, then he should be sworn in."

"That's enough," Thibodeaux said, glowering at both of them. "Proceed with the proper question, Mr. Mills."

Mills sighed. "Sarah, hypothetically, if you were to take a pill designed to end your baby's life, is that something that you would remember?"

"Objection."

"Sustained. No more, Mr. Mills."

Riley Mills stepped back, his arms up in surrender but a

smile of satisfaction playing on his face. He had made his point.

Claire watched the jury. A host of expressions played across their faces: surprise, suspicion, uncertainty, but all had their questions. Claire realized that this was the moment she had long thought would happen.

Riley Mills, perceiving the world from his black-and-white perspective, in his absolute conviction that facts were facts, thought he had put doubt to rest by asking these last questions of Sarah. He really believed that the ambiguity of her earlier testimony was no more than a slip of the tongue, a sign of habitual insecurity.

But the jurors saw things differently, Claire Davis knew they did. They were beginning to see that Sarah Corbett and Daniel Wyatt had been caught up in this awful predicament together, and that both had tried to find a way out. Wyatt was no monster, he had been as confused and terrified as Sarah by the awesome consequences of pregnancy. In a way, he and Sarah had faced this decision as equals, as father and mother of an unwanted child.

So now it all came down to one question: who had put the drug in Sarah's mouth?

Claire knew what Mills didn't seem to understand, that the jury was no longer certain about the answer.

When it was over, Riley Mills sat down happily. Now that Sarah Corbett had returned to the script, there wasn't much left to do in this case. All the defense's attempts to create doubt about the affair and the paternity of the child would be destroyed by the tape. Mills watched Claire Davis with cool satisfaction. Everything had gone against her. Finding the tape this late had been a stroke of incredible luck. Davis had wasted her entire defense on issues that were now resolved.

The judge asked Claire if she wanted to examine Sarah again, and she declined. In fact, the defense rested its case. Did Davis really think that Sarah Corbett's slip on the stand had accomplished so much?

Riley Mills couldn't hide his surprise. Perhaps the woman had given up.

But that didn't sound like Claire Davis.

The playing of the tape turned out to be an anticlimax.

The judge announced to the jury that the prosecution was being allowed to reopen its case for new evidence. This caused a short stir, but Claire had steeled herself to appear calm. She hoped her frankness with Sarah had prepared the jury to hear a confirmation of the affair as a reality.

The court listened carefully as Mills explained the source of the tape, calling Sarah again to provide verification and context. She described the phone conversation with Daniel, when and why it had taken place. And the jurors listened intently to the tape, but it was not the revelation it would have been a few days before. Claire knew she had taken the wind from Mills's sails by tacitly admitting the affair in her cross of Sarah Corbett. Everyone in the courtroom accepted it as fact by now.

I'll be there tomorrow. I will, Sarah was saying.

Claire realized that this was the first time the court had heard Daniel's voice. He'd never been on the stand. In this strained, desperate conversation, he didn't come across as a calculating child killer. He and Sarah both sounded overwhelmed and vulnerable, like young, star-crossed lovers.

The tape might even create more sympathy for her client than hostility, Claire thought. She was relieved that she'd kept Daniel off the stand. If he had denied the affair himself, this revelation would have been devastating, and cause for charges of perjury.

But tonight has been just . . . ghastly, came Sarah's voice. *I keep thinking of the baby, our baby. It seems like this night will go on forever. Dr. Wyatt? I'm just lonely, I suppppose.*

Sarah. I could come over, if you need me.

Claire held Daniel's hand under the table. He flinched a little at the words "our baby," but she had warned him of the tape's contents. He hadn't known about the recording, of course. Daniel hadn't had time to think about it yet, but soon he would figure out how Claire had learned about his affair. He would realize that his lawyer, friend, and political ally had spied on him.

Her eyes fell to the table as the rest of the tape played. How thoroughly they had all betrayed each other, she thought.

After the tape was played the prosecution rested its case again in a bit of courtroom ceremony.

It was over. Only closing statements remained.

"**F**orgive me, Father, for I have sinned."

The priest was perched on the hotel-room bed, looking out the window rather than at the speaker of these words. Costilla faced in the other direction, on his knees as if in prayer. The priest had insisted that they be back-to-back, as if to create the anonymity of a confession booth.

"When was your last confession, my son?"

"It was . . . five years ago, Father."

The priest paused. "Five years? That's a long time to go without absolution, my son."

"Well, I'd done something that I didn't want my family priest to know about. I guess once I stopped, I got out of the habit."

"Confession is not a habit, my son. It is as necessary as prayer, as mass, as marriage, those other things that keep us in communication with God. What was your sin, five years ago?"

"My sister was in law school, in her first year. She wanted to become a federal officer, like me. She called me one night crying. She said she was pregnant."

"She wasn't married?" the priest asked softly.

"No. And she didn't want my parents to find out. My father wouldn't have let her go on in school. Even if she—"

"What was your sin, my son?"

"I helped her to get an abortion. I paid for it. I took her to the clinic, and I kept the secret from my parents."

"That is a grave sin, my son. Very grave. Not only did you

take life from an innocent, but you failed to honor your mother and father."

Agent Costilla sighed. He felt foolish, here on his knees in the priest's hotel room. But he couldn't function, hadn't been able to think straight since he'd heard what had happened to Agent Samuels. He'd stopped here on his way to the hospital, hoping that the childhood ritual of confession would somehow help him regain clarity and focus.

"But today, that's what I wanted to talk about."

"What happened today?"

Costilla closed his eyes. "I almost cost a young woman . . . another FBI agent . . . her life."

"What? How did this happen?"

"I sent her into a dangerous situation. Alone. I shouldn't have. It wasn't absolutely necessary. Now she's in the hospital."

"You are in a dangerous profession, my son. We sometimes choose paths that threaten our safety. Sometimes because our cause is righteous. Does this woman blame you for her injury?"

"Well, yes, actually. She even called me . . ."

"Tell me, my son."

"Well . . . She called me a cocksucker. I'm sorry, Father."

The priest chuckled a bit. Costilla felt more comfortable now.

"I can't judge your actions as a law enforcement officer, my son. Your superiors must do that. You yourself must. But tell me, why do you feel that you jeopardized this young woman's life?"

"She had found the man that I was sent here to capture. The man who bombed the clinic outside of town. I had to stop him."

"And did she succeed?"

"Yes," Costilla answered. "We have him now."

The priest sighed deeply.

"Then perhaps this was not a sin. Merely a hard decision, in times of war."

Costilla looked sidelong at the priest. The man looked gravely out the window.

"You accomplished what you were sent here to do. There was a price. Sometimes risks must be taken, my son," Father O'Keefe continued. "Sometimes the innocent are harmed even in a righteous cause. In every war, lives are lost, lives that shouldn't be lost."

Father O'Keefe didn't sound like the priests Costilla confessed to when he was growing up. Of course, he reminded himself, he was a member of an extremist Catholic organization. When Costilla and Hicks had interviewed them a few weeks ago, the two priests had talked this way, of wars and righteous causes. Perhaps he had come to the wrong place for absolution. Certainly the wrong place to talk about his sin five years ago . . .

Costilla remembered taking his sister Rebecca through the cordon of protesters. Usually, New York was a relatively easy place to get an abortion, without the legislative or political hurdles of the south or midwest. But in the mid-nineties, Operation Rescue had launched a campaign in the state, starting in Buffalo and moving down toward the city. Rebecca's problem had always been bad timing.

He had taken his sister into Manhattan, to the Planned Parenthood clinic, a plain building just north of Houston Street. The protest had been relatively small, fewer than fifteen people, but as Costilla and his sister passed the police barriers, a hand had reached out and grabbed Rebecca. There'd been only the briefest contact, a handful of hair pulled, a momentary yanking back of Rebecca's head that brought a sharp cry to her lips. But Costilla was already keyed up, nervous from guilt and shame, and he snapped. He pulled the young man who'd dared touch his sister over the police barrier and threw him to the ground, kicking him once in the stomach.

The sudden, unexpected violence silenced the crowd. They looked at Costilla in shock. He looked back and saw their fear. He could tell that they were used to outnumbering the people they taunted, prayed for, harassed. Crowds like this confronted women when they were at their most vulnerable. And now they had assaulted Costilla's family. He looked back at them defiantly.

"Come on," he said to the group. "You want it?" He yelled the fighting words of his old neighborhood into the mostly white faces.

Rebecca pulled him toward the door of the clinic.

The cop on barricade duty came up, his hand on his holster. Now under his protection, the protesters started pointing at Costilla and screaming for the officer to arrest him.

Agent Costilla flashed his FBI badge. The cop just shrugged and waved him inside, more perplexed than offended by his actions.

That brief loss of control ultimately shamed him; Costilla knew that he had failed a crucial test. He was a law enforcement official, not a thug. But the memory of that moment of anger as he faced the protesters stayed with him. In that second when they had laid their hands on his sister, he had irreversibly branded these people as cowards.

The anger was still inside him as he knelt here by the priest, who muttered words of absolution.

"Thank you, Father," he said.

Costilla stood. He didn't feel better. The ritual no longer worked. He knew he would have to find his own absolution. He looked at the stack of small Bibles on the priest's nightstand. For passing out to those who might heed the Word, he guessed. Bibles had once possessed a mystical power for Costilla. Now they were just books.

"You will start going to confession again, my son?"

"Yes," Costilla lied.

"*Gaudeamus igitur,*" the priest said.

Costilla nodded. The prayer sounded familiar, but he couldn't remember it. He had never been the best student in catechism class.

He walked out the door and headed for the hospital. Agent Samuels was being treated there. Costilla had to talk to her.

On the way, he called Agent Watson, stationed in Wyatt's house.

"You might as well pack it in, Watson. We've got our man."

"Should I tell the sheriff's department to stay put?"

"Sure. You never know."

"Think they can handle it?" Watson asked. "I hear we could have a verdict in a few days."

"That's not our problem anymore, Agent Watson." Costilla saw the massive hospital building just coming into sight before him. "From here on out, it's strictly crowd control."

61 | CLOSING STATEMENTS

Riley Mills began at the beginning. He took the jury through the facts again, making sure they didn't forget the basic structure of motive, opportunity, and intent.

Unlike the opening statement, the close wasn't required to be a clinical statement of the evidence, and Riley Mills allowed himself to indulge the full range of his oratorical gifts. He began to paint Daniel Wyatt not just as a killer, but as a deviant, a monster.

"He stepped outside the bounds of marriage, ladies and gentlemen, and lay with a woman other than his wife. He stepped outside the oath of his healing profession, the oath to do no harm, and brought bloody harm to Sarah Corbett. And finally, he stepped outside the most sacred of our society's laws, the commandment that 'Thou shalt not kill,' and reached into Sarah Corbett's womb to end her baby's life.

"The facts are not in dispute."

Mills spent the better part of an hour casting aspersions at Claire Davis's tactics.

"The defense has tried to distort this case by planting red herrings. They've blamed everyone besides the defendant. They've suggested that the medical experts were wrong, in error, lax in their work. They've claimed that the police forensics experts must have missed something, or may have confused month-old fingerprints with those left that weekend. But these experts are professionals, and to impugn their work is a simple tactic of desperation.

"And, yes, they've even blamed Sarah Corbett, one of the

two victims in this case. The defense wanted you to believe that she wasn't even pregnant with Daniel Wyatt's child, that she's some kind of hysterical woman accusing him falsely. They claimed that she may have had other lovers. But you heard that taped conversation between Sarah and Dr. Wyatt, and you know now what they both knew. There *was* a child, and it was their child.

"The defense has also suggested that Sarah Corbett may have taken those pills herself. But how can you believe that? Sarah has asked for nothing but justice since this case began, retribution for what the defendant stole from her. She wanted that baby, she has testified to that fact a dozen times. Don't let the defense confuse you for a moment on that score.

"And finally, look at how the defense has treated the other victim in this case, the unnamed child of Sarah Corbett. It has tried to erase this child from memory. First, they claimed that the child wasn't Wyatt's. But we know it *was* his. We've learned that from Daniel Wyatt's own words on tape.

"Secondly, the defense had tried to erase the *humanity* of the child. We heard from many witnesses for the defense that this was not a human being yet, just a clump of cells. But that baby had its own DNA, distinct from every other human the world has ever seen. It had its own heartbeat, a brain, hands and feet.

"Don't let the defense erase this child, ladies and gentlemen of the jury. Don't let them compound the crime that Daniel Wyatt committed. He ended this baby's life before it had a chance to start, before this child even had a chance to see the world. Don't let that tragedy end here, without justice being done, as if that baby had never existed at all."

Mills knew it was past lunchtime, but he kept going. He knew he would have one more chance to speak to the jury, to rebut the closing statement of defense counsel. But his own words kept him in motion, pounding the same points again and again. He wanted to keep his momentum, to make sure every last drop of anger was wrung from this jury.

Finally, Mills looked at the faces of the jury. He realized that they were exhausted. He had kept them too long, fraying their nerves after the long, difficult trial.

Perhaps he should have waited, to let his words sink in over the lunch recess. Now there would be a break, giving Claire Davis a chance to adjust her closing arguments to meet his attack. Mills wondered if his tongue had run away with him. But at least he would have another chance in his rebuttal, a privilege that the defense would not enjoy.

Mills closed with a polite thanks to all twelve members of the jury, then took his seat.

Claire Davis faced the jury. She knew that her closing statement would be short, so she wanted them to hear every word.

Riley Mills had probably stirred the pot a bit with his histrionics, but his artful attacks on Daniel Wyatt (and those on her defense) meant nothing if she could keep the jury's mind on one thing: Sarah Corbett wasn't sure.

Claire didn't start with Sarah's balk on the stand, however. She started where every good defense attorney starts.

"Thank you, members of the jury, for your patience and consideration during this lengthy trial," she began. "We all understand that jury duty is difficult, especially under sequestration. But I ask you not to think of yourselves as jurors anymore. You are now judges, with the same power that any judge has. You have the power to decide your own vote, individually, no matter what any other juror believes. And remember as you sit in judgment of Dr. Wyatt that the prosecution must prove each and every element beyond a reasonable doubt. I think you will see that they have failed to do so.

"Reasonable doubt. When this case began, the judge explained to you what that term means. Would a reasonable person have a doubt about the guilt of the accused? If so, the jury must acquit. Let's talk about the mountains of doubt in the prosecution's case.

"Many of you could look at this case and doubt that Daniel Wyatt terminated Sarah Corbett's pregnancy. There were no eyewitnesses. No one saw any drugs given to Sarah Corbett. No one has explained why traces of aspirin were found in the box that contained the RU-486. No doctor can say for sure what caused the miscarriage. We've heard expert testimony that twenty-five percent of all pregnancies end in a miscarriage, without any intervention whatsover.

"Twenty-five percent? That sounds like reasonable doubt."

Claire went through more of the medical evidence, the details of what had happened that night in the hospital, the complexity and accuracy of the tests used, but she didn't stay on the subject long. This case was no longer about forensics. It was about the vagaries of human beings, and of human memory and will.

"Others of you may doubt whether a crime was committed at all, certainly the crime of murder. 'Murder' is a very specific word, a word reserved for the killing of people. People, not ova or sperm or unique DNA groupings. We have heard that Sarah Corbett's fetus had no consciousness. It felt no pain and had no thoughts. Some of you may wish to believe that a fetus is a person, but how can you know? How can you be certain when humanity enters a fertilized egg? When it divides into two cells? Four cells? Eight? How can you be certain, beyond a reasonable doubt?

"Others may doubt whether this was a crime committed against Sarah Corbett. She sat here on this stand and told us she was uncertain."

Claire produced a sheaf of transcript.

"I said to her, 'Did you take them, and not tell him? Did you keep it a secret, maybe even from yourself?' "

"And Sarah Corbett replied, 'I don't think so.' "

" 'I don't *think* so.' "

Claire looked at each of the jurors in turn before repeating her mantra.

"Reasonable doubt.

"So, ask yourself this: What if Sarah Corbett did take the RU-486? What if in that beach house, she weighed the consequences of going through with this pregnancy? What if she thought about what it would require of her, and what it would cost the father of her child, and how it would shake the community? And what if she decided—perhaps with fragile conviction, with unsteady hand—that she wanted to take those pills?"

Claire closed with the jury, spreading her hands as if in confusion.

"And what if tomorrow, Sarah remembers that she did take those pills. Would we then reconvene this court, and charge *her* with murder? Same act, same consequences?

"Of course we wouldn't. The Supreme Court has decreed that we cannot. Sarah, as the mother, has the right to terminate her pregnancy. But Dr. Daniel Wyatt, the father of that child, sits here accused on flimsy evidence that he did that very thing. Can we condemn one and not the other? Can we be sure by which of the two parents this choice was made?

"Who here can reach into these two people's shattered lives and say—*without a doubt*—that Sarah Corbett and Daniel Wyatt didn't make this choice together?"

Claire stepped back, lowered her voice.

"I can't. The prosecutor can't. None of us can go back in time and see what really happened there. So, can any of you be certain, beyond a reasonable doubt?

"The events at that beach house, just like the moment at which life begins, are wrapped in unknowns. No one can be sure. The law cannot thrust blindly into this mystery and presume to do it justice. Some things are beyond its reach."

She waited a moment, then headed back toward her seat. Before she rested her case, Claire turned to the jury and said, "About some things, we must realize, there is *only* doubt."

The prosecution had the final word. In contrast to the defense, with their single shot at a closing statement, Riley Mills had a chance to rebut.

Mills believed that he had already won, but he decided to nail down the constitutional aspects of the case. Belt and suspenders.

"The defense has also argued that finding Daniel Wyatt guilty of murder will amount to an attack upon *Roe* versus *Wade*, and compromise a woman's right to choose an abortion for herself. But the Supreme Court was unambiguous. *Roe* guarantees a *woman's* right to choose, not a man's. No man can take away a woman's child without her permission. Not a doctor, not a judge, not a prosecutor, not even the father of that child."

Finally, Riley Mills stepped closer to the jury, lowering his voice to address each of the nine women on the panel in turn.

"Defense counsel seems to believe there is only doubt. Only doubt?

"How would you feel if this happened to you? What if a man—for his own gain, for his own career, for his own marriage and children—took it upon himself to kill your growing, healthy child inside you? A child you desperately wanted to keep? What if it were you?"

Mills ended with his eyes on Peggy Fontenot.

"What would you call it? You had a child, and suddenly you don't. You had a whole lifetime of loving, nuturing, and teaching this child before you, and suddenly you don't. This child lives inside you—you can feel it growing and changing you. And then you can't.

"What would you call the man who killed this child?

"I'd call him a murderer."

And with that, Riley Mills sat down.

As Claire left the courtroom and made her way toward the courthouse doors, she encountered a tall, good-looking man with gray hair.

Having to run the gauntlet of press and protesters every day, she had gotten used to pushing her way past any human obstacle, but something about this man stopped her. He had a presence, a weightiness, a solidity as he lightly grasped her forearm and said her name. His voice was low, his suit expensive and tailored. After a moment's look at him, Claire knew what had halted her.

Power. This man had power.

"Yes?"

"My name is Harry Thompson. I'm a partner at Emerson, Touche and Connelly."

The firm's name rolled off his lips as if it were one word. Thompson smiled a bit, as if he enjoyed saying the name. Of course, anyone associated with so prestigious a law firm would take pleasure in his connection. They were a legendary Washington lobbying group, whose partners numbered in its ranks former senators, House committee chairs, and cabinet members.

Claire had intended to give Daniel a pep talk before she met Eduardo. The jury would start deliberations tomorrow, and he would be on pins and needles. But she could give a moment to this man.

"Claire Davis," she answered, echoing Thompson's introduction reflexively.

"Of course, Ms. Davis," he said, his smile broadening. "We've been watching, just like the rest of the country."

"I'm flattered."

"No flattery. You're a damn good trial lawyer, Ms. Davis, especially given your limited experience. And you are very good on television."

"Thank you very much," she answered. "But at the moment, the cameras are waiting. And I have a client I need to see."

"We're concerned that now that this trial is over, your considerable talents will go to waste," he continued.

She narrowed her eyes. "I'm not sure what you—"

"We would like to offer you a position."

Claire swallowed. Emerson, Touche and Connelly was a kind of repository for many of the great old lions of Washington. It was where you went after you'd already made your mark in the world of public service and wanted to cash in on your connections. They lobbied the White House, the Pentagon, and both houses of Congress. Of course, she realized that they must have younger lawyers as well. At such a firm, she would have the ear of some of the most powerful men and women in Washington.

Claire felt a rush of guilt at her desire for the job. She would be a lobbyist. Not a policy maker, not an advocate of the disenfranchised. And more importantly, she would have achieved her position at the cost of Daniel Wyatt's career, the loss of the life he had known.

This man was offering her blood money.

"I'm sorry, but I have an advocacy group to run," she began

"We would be able to work out a very attractive package, I'm sure," Thompson said.

"It's not the money. It's just that your firm isn't what I had—"

"Please allow yourself to think it over, and give me a call," he interrupted, handing her a business card. Throughout the encounter, Thompson's smile had never left his face, the confidence that she would listen and obey never left his voice.

Power.

Claire made her way toward the shouting and pushing on the courthouse steps, where Riley Mills was already making a statement. She looked for a moment at the business card, its gold embossing flickering in the flashing bulbs of jostling photographers.

Lobbying. A form of advocacy to be sure, but not of her own beliefs, her own principles. The last major client that Emerson, Touche and Connelly had secured was a giant agricultural firm pushing for less stringent regulations for genetically engineered foods. She would become the servant of big money, a well-rewarded handmaiden of the rich and powerful. Claire shook her head. She had already given up too much on the road to this trial, had compromised her principles more than enough.

Everyone around her had suffered for her ambition. Suddenly the quest for power seemed a hollow and dirty pursuit.

She let the card slip from her fingers and headed toward the lofted cameras and pressing crowds on the courthouse steps.

That night Riley Mills broke out a bottle of thirty-year-aged Bowmore. As he poured the precious fluid into a glass, he realized that he'd been saving the bottle for almost fifteen years. Forty-five years total. That would make this whiskey older than Claire Davis.

He rolled the liquid in the glass, watching a bit unhappily as its legs formed. Now, there was a thought to ruin a good glass of whiskey. The feeling was definitely taking hold, an unfamiliar gnawing in the back of his mind. The confidence that he had felt after his closing statement had been slowly evaporating.

Claire Davis, somehow, had put the verdict in question.

Mills sighed. Sarah Corbett had proved unreliable. The

woman didn't have the fire that a good prosecution witness needed, a desire for justice, for revenge. As Morrisey had always warned him, Sarah still had a soft spot for Daniel Wyatt. But that wasn't all of it. Through careful management of his questions, Mills had managed to keep Sarah's unextinguished love for Wyatt out of sight. What he hadn't realized, until it was too late, was that Corbett also had a soft spot for Claire Davis. She regarded the older women with something akin to awe, and on the stand had seemed willing to follow her anywhere, as if under a spell.

Using this advantage, Davis had cast doubt into Sarah's mind, and thus into the jury's.

Still, the prosecutor thought, his closing argument had gone rather well, undoing much of the damage.

Mills took a drink, inhaling the heavy vapors of the whiskey as it burned his lips. The closing argument was the part of a jury trial at which Mills had always excelled. In a trial, closing statements were the purest moment of the storyteller's art, untainted by uncooperative witnesses and interrupted by far fewer objections. It had been Mills's opportunity to paint Wyatt as an arrogant misogynist and a child killer, and to override the jury's last doubts that murder was in fact the proper charge.

But Sarah Corbett's slip—her simple "I don't *think* so"—had tainted the factual part of the case with doubt, and that could cost the prosecution everything.

The phone rang.

Mills considered letting the call go, but he was happy to have his current thoughts interrupted.

"Mills."

"Prosecutor Mills, this is Senator Huffson's office. The senator would like to speak with you."

Mills sat up straight. "Certainly."

After a moment on hold, the voice of the old Cajun senator came on the line.

"District Attorney Mills?"

"Yes, Senator. What a pleasure to be speaking with you, sir."

"And with you, Riley. I just called to say that you've argued a hell of a case."

"Thank you, sir," Mills replied. "It was a case that needed arguing."

"You're very right, Riley. You've managed to get everyone's attention up here in Baton Rouge, I'll tell you that. Looks like you've got a sure conviction."

Mills wondered if the senator had seen the events of the last couple of days, when Sarah Corbett had managed to make his sure conviction a roll of the die.

"And I'll tell you, Riley, the party needs more leaders with conviction."

The old senator laughed at his own wordplay.

"Well, thank you, Senator. I'm just doing my part to give them boys in the White House a little trouble."

"You've done a good job of that, Riley. It'll be a while before they nominate another federal official before investigating his kids, brothers, and mother-in-law."

Mills wondered where this was going.

"Now, Riley, I just wanted to ask you what you're planning to do next."

"Next, Senator?"

"Well, as you know, the governor is a lame duck. We're going to need somebody to pass the baton to a year from now."

"Senator, I don't know what to—"

"Hell, you don't have to stay anything, just start raising money!"

The old man's cackle came sharply through the phone's speaker. Mills took a quick drink of the Bowmore; his mouth had suddenly gone dry.

"Thank you very much, sir. I appreciate your confidence in my abilities."

"Well, I guess we'll see what the jury has to say about

that. But I'm sure you got them under control, Riley. I'm sure you do."

"Thank you, sir. I'm positive we'll get a conviction."

"I hope so, Riley. That's what that fellow deserves."

Eventually, Senator Huffson said good night, leaving Mills alone with his whiskey. As he often did, the district attorney looked back over the case, trying to determine what he could have done better, where he could have pushed harder. Finally, he gave up and poured himself a second glass, and then a third.

The governor's office, he thought. Exactly as he had planned when this case had fallen into his lap so long ago. And after that? Well, old man Huffson couldn't live forever.

The only problem was the verdict. Huffson's tune would change pretty quickly if Wyatt was found not guilty. The jurors had to see through Sarah Corbett's lapse. Otherwise, Mills could lose everything. If only there was a way, Riley Mills groggily thought as the bottle grew empty, a way to make sure . . .

It was much later when a sleepless Daniel Wyatt was disturbed by a pounding on his door.

He heard a stampede of small feet running into the house, a high, sharp voice shouting.

"Daddy?"

My God, Wyatt thought. It was Dexter!

Wyatt burst from his bedroom, and was met by the sight of his family. The three kids swirled about their mother, then burst toward Wyatt.

"Daddy!"

Wyatt knelt, overwhelmed by the ability of these four faces to make him feel so happy. It seemed that this house, his home, had been a dead and solemn place these last months. And now, within the span of a few seconds, it had sprung back to life. The kids hugged him, then stood back to marvel at their father's face. Wyatt realized that the last months must have seemed much longer for his children, who were young enough for summers to seem like lifetimes.

Then, one by one, the three children charged off to explore the familiar house, running up the stairs. The sounds of them rediscovering their bedrooms trickled down from above.

Wyatt found himself face-to-face with his wife, for the first time since they had met through the glass partition at the county jail.

"Ellen."

"Daniel," she said, the name coming out like a sob.

They embraced. Ellen felt so small, Wyatt thought. It was as if some measure of her substance had been shorn away by the ordeal of her husband's trial.

Finally, they parted.

"We tried to call, Daniel. I just today decided to come. But you haven't answered your phone, and I suppose my message didn't reach Claire. Sorry to surprise you."

He shook his head at the apology. "I'm just so glad you're here."

Ellen looked out the window toward where the deputy's car was parked.

"Is it . . . safe here?"

"Yes," he said. "I mean, there've been a lot of reporters, that's all. That fellow's just here to give us some privacy."

Wyatt was glad that the FBI had found their man. It was good to have his family here, safe at home, rather than hiding in some hotel.

Ellen took him upstairs and began organizing, pressing her children into duty changing sheets and unpacking the clothes they'd brought back. It was late for the kids, but it took them an hour to wind down after the excitement of being home again.

Later, after the children had gone to bed, Wyatt was finally able to talk with his wife again.

"Daniel, you should know . . . we're leaving tomorrow

afternoon. The kids have to get back to school in Opelousas."

Wyatt's heart shrank a little at the news, but he nodded obediently.

"I understand. But the trial's almost over. They can go back to their old Lafayette schools next year."

"Daniel, I have something to tell you."

He looked into Ellen's eyes, and saw a hard certainty. He put up his hands against it.

"This is almost over, Ellen. Claire says we have a good chance of—"

"Daniel, it will never be the same for me again. Something's gone."

The words drove into him like cold bullets. He remembered when Sarah Corbett had first told him she was pregnant, just four months ago. Those simple words had started all this. Again, he felt that same helplessness, that sense that the world was changing under his feet. He struggled to somehow speak against it.

"But, Ellen, can't you see how good this is for the kids? They need to be with both of us. They need their father."

"If you're still here," she said.

"We don't even know the verdict yet, Ellen," he protested. "Can't you just wait until the jury comes back?"

"Daniel, I've decided to file for divorce."

Wyatt felt a tearing inside, as if every word were taking her farther away from him.

"No, Ellen. Don't say it . . ."

"I've tried to imagine us together again . . . for the kids. But I just don't know if I can. This whole thing has undermined something that we had. It's not all your fault, Daniel. It's me, too."

Wyatt brought his hands to his ears. He couldn't stand to hear Ellen blame herself. Not that, too, on top of everything else.

"Ellen, don't."

"Daniel, just don't blame yourself. Not for everything. I

may not have been as good a wife to you as I should have been. Maybe I wasn't sensitive enough to give you what you really needed. I'm so sorry, Daniel."

He opened his eyes, trying to hear what she was saying.

"But I know you're innocent, Daniel. I'm sure of it."

He looked gratefully into her eyes, overwhelmed that she still believed in his innocence. How did she have such strength?

"Just wait a little while, Ellen. Don't leave me, please. We've had fourteen years of marriage. Don't throw it all away."

Ellen shook her head, her eyes shut as tight as fists.

"I'll see if I can hold on, Daniel. We'll see."

Later, he lay awake listening to his wife breathe.

Tomorrow the jury would begin to deliberate. Twelve good people, a jury of his peers. They would decide whether Daniel Wyatt would spend years in jail or walk free, and there was no longer anything he or Claire or anyone could do to affect their verdict.

The die was cast. All he could do was wait for their decision.

But as he lay there, on what might be his last night under the same roof as his family, Daniel Wyatt couldn't bring himself to care what the verdict was. He had already pleaded his case to the person he loved the most.

And hers was the only verdict that mattered.

The feeling on the street had changed. The lawyers had wrapped up their cases. The energy of protest, of news gathering, of celebrity stalking now had no object on which to focus its intensity, nothing but the closed doors of the jury room, behind which the final decision would be made.

Father Peter O'Keefe walked toward the courthouse. He carried a satchel filled with small Bibles, bearing the heavy burden of the Lord's Word. He wasn't sure exactly where he was taking them, but O'Keefe knew that God's voice would guide him to the right spot. As the trial reached its conclusion, his growing need to act had been replaced by an almost holy calm, a certainty that his deeds were guided from the outside now. He suffered no more from indecision, confusion, or insecurity.

O'Keefe walked.

The demonstrators in the park across from the courthouse had grown in number this last week, new faces added by the trial's end and the increasingly warm weather in Lafayette. The rest of the country was suffering a March cold snap, but a bubble of gulf air had protected Louisiana from the inclement weather. Even the rains had held off through most of this winter.

It was as if God were drawing an audience.

Father O'Keefe's progress was impeded for a moment by a police action on the sidewalk in front of him. He watched as a group of demonstrators was corralled toward the door of a tall building next to the courthouse. A ring of police ushered them forward in a ragged line. O'Keefe saw that the protesters were bound with bright yellow plastic handcuffs. They must be pro-life, he thought, hearing the song they were singing.

"Every child sacred be . . ."

O'Keefe walked up to the group of police and their captives, and caught the attention of one of the officers herding the crowd into the building.

"May I ask where you're taking these people, sir?"

The cop looked at him for a moment with undisguised annoyance, then saw the clerical collar and turned to face the questioner.

"Into the old civic center here. The county jail's filled up, Father," he explained. "This is the best we can do for the moment. We've got beds in the gym."

"I see," O'Keefe answered, his eyes scanning the building. It towered over the low courthouse, and it was easy to see what the Lord intended.

"Is it possible for me to enter? You see, I'm giving out Bibles and counseling the demonstrators. Perhaps I could—"

"Talk to the man inside. Sergeant Rickles," the officer said, and turned back to the handcuffed, singing group. O'Keefe felt himself disappear from the man's awareness.

The priest hefted the Bibles in his bag. He waited patiently while the rowdy protesters were moved inside, then followed.

There was no Sergeant Rickles inside that he could see— at least, no one who seemed obviously in charge. The protesters who had been arrested were being processed, lined up before a row of folding tables, their names entered into ledgers by hand. It looked like some sort of preliminary voting procedure from a few decades ago.

O'Keefe found that his collar afforded him a kind of invisibility. He moved quietly among the shouting, jostling people, unchallenged and unseen. The lobby of the aging civic center had the same feeling as a hospital emergency room, a crush of needy and confused people guided among overcrowded stations by a few harried, uniformed authority figures, whose attention was fully occupied by the task of keeping things from succumbing to chaos.

No one paid any attention to Father O'Keefe. He felt as if an aura of anonymity surrounded him, cloaking him from suspicion. He realized as he found a staircase and headed upward that the ruse of the Bibles had been unnecessary. Amid all this madness, he could practically carry the C-4 openly.

But O'Keefe knew he had been guided to replace the Word of God with the deadly explosives. He no longer questioned the Will that moved him.

The staircase brought him past empty hallways. Apparently, the arrestees were all being held in the gym on the first floor. The classrooms and meeting areas of the civic center's upper floors were deserted. On the sixth floor, he stopped. His sense of direction told O'Keefe that the courthouse was to his left, behind the windowless walls of the classrooms on that side of the hall.

God be praised, he thought. He had indeed been guided to the right place. The two old buildings shared a supporting wall. The place where he stood now was probably only twenty feet above the courtroom in which Daniel Wyatt had been tried.

He stood silently for a few minutes, as if listening to the jurors argue through the plaster, brick, and iron that separated him from the courthouse.

Of course, he couldn't hear them, but he had no doubt that they would be able to hear God's Word when the time came.

He chose one of the darkened classrooms, picking the lock with tools from a hidden pocket in the satchel. Inside, he went to work, carefully unpacking the Bibles to gather the C-4 into several deadly masses connected by high-speed wire. A row of storage closets in the back of the classroom concealed the results of his efforts completely.

When he was finished, O'Keefe knew that the arrangement wasn't textbook-perfect demolition. He hadn't targeted any supporting columns, or packed the explosive to direct it toward the courthouse. But what his work lacked in grace the bomb made up for in sheer size and strength. He had little doubt the nineteen pounds of C-4 would destroy both buildings completely, tearing the supporting wall from between them, toppling the older, taller structure of the civic center onto the courthouse.

O'Keefe pulled a small radio receiver from the satchel. It was already tuned, fixed to a rarely used frequency. He didn't want the explosion to occur by happenstance. No, timing was everything.

Indeed, his message to the world might not need to be delivered. The vengeance of God could still be forestalled by a just verdict. O'Keefe understood now that his final act was merely the means to an end, a way to make it possible for the Lord to strike back at a world so empty of justice that it could not see murder for what it truly was.

God was merciful. But only if Daniel Wyatt were found guilty. Only then would God's wrath be stayed.

Deputy Tom Jenkins stood in his uniform and sweated.

Sometimes he wondered, as any good Christian did, what hell was really like. That was the anxious side of his faith, those intense and unforgettable fears forged in childhood: a world of torture, fire, the desperate, wailing cries of the damned. Well, Jenkins thought as he stood here in the direct sunlight and eighty-five-degree heat, now at least he had a fair idea of what the place was really like.

The stench was awful. That was the torture part. It smelled like more than just old garbage; like the overripe smell of a dead rat in a wall, amplified many times. It reminded Jenkins of a stolen Ford Taurus he had once checked out. It turned out that the car's owner, a Miss Tamika Rawlins, was inside its trunk, well stewed and swelled to twice her normal size, which had already been considerable before her untimely demise.

And it was hot here in the dump. Maybe not fiery-hell hot, but hot enough to cause his deputy's uniform to be soaked with sweat. The sun was unrelenting, and there was no shade unless he hid himself behind one of the mountains of garbage, but to do that meant traipsing farther into the dump. Besides, Jenkins was supposed to be here at the entrance when folks brought their garbage by, to make sure no one tried to dispose of any explosives residue.

As for the wailing cries of the damned, completing the analogy to hell, those were supplied by the ever-present gulls that wheeled dizzyingly overhead. Their mournful shrieks seemed to come from a great distance, like the souls of those condemned to perdition trying to make themselves heard across some ghostly divide. And, of course, two or three times a day one of them would drop some shit on Deputy Jenkins's hat.

Sheriff Mark Hicks could certainly act like a vengeful God, Jenkins had learned.

The sheriff hadn't much liked it that Jenkins had brought Riley Mills in on the Sarah Corbett case. And now here Jenkins stood, the only deputy in Lafayette County not earning beaucoup overtime doing crowd control. Certainly, he was the only deputy cleaning seagull shit off his hat every night.

Well, D.A. Mills had better make the deputy's reward worth this little stint in hell, Jenkins thought glumly. But so far, the D.A. had failed even to return Jenkins's calls.

A garbage truck was headed up the long access road.

Jenkins sighed, watching the garbagemen waving at him happily from the cab of the vehicle. He knew they were laughing at him, all of them.

So this is what Tom Jenkins had come to, the butt of garbagemen's jokes.

The truck pulled into the dirt turnaround, going into reverse and singing its beeping song, which sounded more like the damned gulls every day. The birds scattered as the machine crunched up to the newest garbage hill, but they didn't go far. The gulls probably thought of the trucks as some ancient, monstrous cousins, or perhaps as their benefactors, the Bringers of Garbage.

The vehicle made its usual sounds of straining metal. The bulk of black plastic bags mixed with occasional flashes of color rained down a new layer of garbage on the vast expanse of the dump.

Then it pulled away, its occupants waving again and, Jenkins was *sure*, laughing at him.

He stood there for a while, watching as the gulls descended carefully onto the new hill, gaining in confidence and number until their sharp beaks were pulling apart the plastic bags. Like demons coming down to rend the flesh of a new crop of the damned, freshly delivered to hell.

Jenkins stood still.

A wind came up, mercifully cooling the pool of sweat under his arms and on his back. He raised his hands like a captured perp. At least this breath of wind was coming from the road and not the deepest reaches of the dump.

Suddenly a host of white forms fluttered up from the garbage that had just arrived. The wind lifted the shapes— small pieces of paper, Jenkins could now see—into the air and began to scatter them across the dump. He took a careful step and pinned one onto the dirt with his cowboy boot as it flapped by. He looked at the small sheet of paper. Its edges were ragged.

He knelt, primly holding the fluttering paper by its edge, and read a line from the small text.

Be ye not only hearers of the word, but also doers.

"Well, I'll be," he muttered. "The Holy Bible."

It was the Word of God, delivered to Tom Jenkins here in his earthly hell. He looked at the newly arrived garbage. More of the pages were blowing out from a bag that a pair of gulls were attacking. More and more of them, like paper snow drifting across the fields of waste.

"That's funny," he said.

Tom Jenkins stood, no longer quite as miserable as he'd been, wondering who he should tell about this minor miracle.

"Just get me the knife," Chaos ordered.

"Come on, Samuels," Costilla complained. "It's evidence in the attempted murder of a federal officer. What am I supposed to do? Go into the Bureau's evidence room and steal it?"

"You're supposed to kiss my ass, Costilla!" Agent Samuels cried.

She looked very small in the hospital bed, her usually pale skin now bone white from the blood she had lost. Her left shoulder was bandaged, the arm in a sling. But she waved the captive arm wildly as she yelled at Costilla. Fortunately, the slim throwing knife had missed muscles, nerves, and important arteries.

But listening to Agent Samuels, you wouldn't know it.

"That's right. My ass. After sending me after that cracker motherfucker all alone, getting me almost cut in half. I want a fucking *souvenir.*"

"Hey, Chaos." Stanton spoke up. "Face it. You brought a gun to a knife fight, and you almost lost. That ain't Costilla's fault."

"Fuck you, Stanton," Chaos answered. "That mother was wearing pounds, and had about a foot and a half on me—"

"I'm just glad you're not dead, Chaos," Costilla interrupted.

"Yeah, me, too," she agreed sulkily.

"When the case is closed, I'll see what I can do. I know some guys in evidence," he added. From the moment Costilla had walked into the hospital room, Chaos had begun insisting that she wanted the knife that Bartlett had thrown at her.

"It was *in me,* man," she kept saying.

Costilla shook his head. Different people deal with stress in different ways, he decided. The first time he'd killed a suspect with a gun, Costilla had thought himself totally calm. The whole day, his superior kept telling him to take some time off, but he'd kept going, doing the paperwork, telling the story to anyone who'd listen. Finally, she'd ordered him to go home. The next day, he'd realized that his paperwork on the shooting was almost unreadable. His hands had been shaking so badly he had to do most of it again.

But somehow, in Chaos's burning desire to own the knife that had almost killed her, Costilla felt the beginnings of absolution. Her absurd demands assuaged his guilt far more than sullen silence or grudging forgiveness would have done. Chaos was just being Chaos.

Now that he'd seen Agent Samuels, and accepted the fact that she really was still alive, Costilla began to feel the stirrings of genuine relief. After three years, he'd caught his man. True, he hadn't been there for the capture, but the long hunt was over.

Finally over.

Just a floor away, Steven Bartlett was in his own bed, under heavy guard and still in serious—but not critical—condition. He'd lost a lot of blood, and one knee was probably ruined for good, but he would be fit to stand trial. Even if they never proved the abortion killings, they had him for attempted murder of a federal agent and possession of any number of weapons, both the Glock he'd had on him and the arsenal in his hotel room. With his priors, Bartlett was going to jail forever.

Unfortunately, however, the missing twenty pounds of C-4 hadn't been discovered. In the short interview the doctors had allowed Costilla with the prisoner, Bartlett had claimed he'd never had it. He said some other member of the group had stolen it before the feds had raided the Soldiers of Christ compound. Costilla didn't believe him. Bartlett must have stashed it somewhere. But it would turn up. A canine bomb unit was going through the Marriott right now, room by room.

Costilla said good-bye to Chaos, who favored him with a few more choice insults, and left her and Stanton to go over the encounter with Bartlett one more time.

"An empty gun!" Costilla heard as he walked down the hall. He smiled. Samuels had repeated those three words a hundred times during his short visit. " 'Don't you fucking move,' I say. And he *doesn't fucking move,* even though it's an empty gun!"

As Costilla walked down the hospital hallway, he saw the slumped form of Sheriff Hicks seated in a plastic chair outside one of the rooms. Costilla shook his head sadly. The man's daughter had been one of the EMTs responding to the abortion bombing. Only a few feet from the doctor and assistant who'd been killed, she'd taken the main force of the blast.

The older man looked up as Costilla approached.

"Sheriff."

"Agent Costilla."

"How's your daughter?"

The sheriff shrugged. "They're giving her a bath right now," he said defeatedly. Costilla realized from the way he said it that she wouldn't be taking any baths by herself for a while.

"I'm so sorry, Sheriff," he said. "You know we got the guy, right?"

"Yep," the man said, as if this fact didn't make it any better. "Wish you'd got him two days earlier, though."

Costilla just nodded. The guilt he'd felt all day settled down on him again. Tabitha Samuels was alive and healthy, but there was nothing he could do for Millie Hicks.

The sheriff shook his head, as if emerging from a dream.

"I'm sorry, Agent Costilla," he said. "It's good you got your man. I'm just tired."

"I understand, Sheriff Hicks." Costilla didn't know what else to say. "Thanks for all your help."

"Yeah. You're welcome. I guess I can pull Tom Jenkins off dump duty, now that you've got your man?"

"Sure."

"Darnedest thing," Hicks said, scratching his head. "Old Tom didn't report any signs of explosives. But he's been saying that he did see a sign."

"A sign?" Costilla asked. "A sign of what?"

"Just a sign," the sheriff said. "You know, a religious thing."

Costilla raised his eyebrows. He wondered what it could be. The Virgin Mary appearing amid some old coffee grounds?

"You see, someone threw away a bunch of little Bibles," Hicks continued. "But not the whole Bibles, just the pages— the *middles* of the pages, like they'd cut them out. So Tom's standing there in the dump, and all of a sudden the Word of God starts blowing all around him."

The phrase echoed in Costilla's mind. *The Word of God . . .*

"Now ain't that just the darnedest thing?" Sheriff Hicks asked.

Claire Davis waited in her house, sipping a glass of wine and feeling like some angry predator trapped in a cage that was growing smaller and smaller by the hour.

For the last three months, she had worked incessantly. First on the nomination, then on the Sarah Corbett situation, and finally on the murder trial. But now here she was without anything more to do, feeling useless and maddeningly restless, waiting for a bunch of strangers to reach a verdict.

Certainly, there was work to do for WAG. The trial had been damaging to the organization. A host of volunteers and about half of the paid staff had left. But Claire couldn't bring herself to attend to the details of administration while the jury was still out, and Daniel Wyatt's life and career were hanging in the balance. She kept playing the trial over and over in her head, searching for another point she could have made, a crucial change in the delivery or wording of some speech to the jury that would have made all the difference.

Where the hell was Costilla?

He said he would be here early tonight. Ever since the jar with the fetus had arrived, he'd been staying with her most nights. He made noises about her safety, but she knew he certainly didn't mind the sex. And right now, that's what she needed, a good exhausting bout in bed to take her mind off the jury's deliberations.

She heard his car pull up outside and heaved a sigh of relief.

"Agent Costilla," she said as she answered the door. Her head felt a little light. She must have drunk more than she'd thought.

"Hi, Claire."

Eduardo smiled and took off his coat. He looked like shit, in a handsome sort of way. Claire knew that he'd caught his man today, but had almost lost an agent in the process. But he didn't look triumphant. He looked almost puzzled, as if there were something vaguely wrong, some detail he couldn't get off his mind.

"Glass of wine, Agent?"

He nodded. "Just a little for communion, if you don't mind."

"Pardon me?" she asked as she reached for another glass in the cabinet.

"It's been a day for religious symbolism, for some reason."

Claire smiled to herself. "Oh, you're going all Catholic on me, are you? That sounds kinky."

She glanced up from pouring, but he hadn't found her joke funny. His limpid brown eyes were focused in the middle distance, as if gazing at some troubling apparition that refused to come into focus.

"I'm sorry, Eduardo. Tell me what you mean."

"Well, I confessed today."

"Confessed to what?"

"My sins," he said. "You know. I knelt before a priest and asked God's forgiveness."

Claire nodded unsurely. She realized that she was now holding both glasses of wine, and extended one to her lover.

He accepted it and took a grateful drink.

"It's been five years," he explained. "And I hadn't done it regularly since I was a kid. But I just couldn't believe that I'd almost got Chaos . . . Agent Samuels killed. I needed something. The funny thing was, I wasn't sure at first if I even remembered *how* to confess."

Claire sat next to Costilla on the couch and put one hand lightly on his shoulder. His mind was still far off, still worrying about something. It was a pleasure, actually, to let this dark, troubled man distract her from her own concerns.

"Isn't it kind of like riding a bicycle?" she asked. "I mean, they don't change the rules or anything. Right?"

"I suppose so. I mean, I knew the opening words. I remember the Ten Commandments, too. I bet you don't."

"Just the Ten Amendments for me, thank you," she said. A tipsy part of her mind began to list them inanely: Freedom of speech and religion, right to bear arms in an organized militia, no quartering of soldiers . . .

"But there was something that the priest said afterward," Eduardo continued. "A prayer that I didn't recognize. It's been bugging me all day. Something like *gaudeamus igitur*. It sounds so familiar . . ."

Claire laughed. "To me, too. It's an old college song, for one thing. The school song of my alma mater."

She leaned back and closed her eyes, trying to remember the words.

"*Gaudeamus igitur . . .*"

Claire stopped, suddenly embarrassed. The tension of waiting for a verdict must be driving me nuts, she thought. Claire Davis, singing the Vassar school song like some drunken sorority girl.

But Eduardo looked deadly serious.

"What does it mean?" he asked.

Claire frowned. "I did take two years of Latin. I thought it would help in law school. Anything for a leg up, you know? Let me think for a minute."

He was watching her closely, as if the world were riding on her answer.

"Hang on, Costilla," she muttered. "*Igitur* means 'therefore.' And *gaude/gaudere* is 'joyful.' No, it's a verb. 'Rejoice.' And *eamus* is the verb ending for the imperative, first person plural."

"What does it mean?" Costilla repeated very carefully.

She sighed. *Gaudeamus igitur.* It had been a long time since she'd conjugated any Latin verbs.

"I guess, maybe, 'therefore, let us rejoice'?"

Claire watched in astonishment as her lover's face underwent a transformation. The troubled frown was replaced by a look of surprise, then of horror.

He stood, the wineglass falling from his hand and crashing to the floor.

"God I must enter her!" he said. "*Gaudeamus igitur.*"

"What the hell . . ." Claire began.

Costilla put both hands to his face. "And I was right there, talking to him," he said.

Claire Davis sat up.

"He told me about Bartlett," Costilla said. "The priest. *He* was the one. Not Bartlett!"

"Eduardo?"

Costilla spun and headed for the door, crunching some shard of the glass beneath his heel.

"Eduardo!" Claire cried after him.

But then he was gone. She heard his car start up and peel away.

Her mind grappled with what had happened, adrenaline fighting alchohol. Something had gone terribly wrong. Claire ignored the broken glass, the spreading wine stain on her rug. She pulled a cigarette from her purse, filling her lungs with the stimulant to clear her mind. It came to her, as slowly as a drunken driver carefully navigating toward home.

He was the one, Eduardo had said. *Not Bartlett!*

Costilla had gotten the wrong man. Somehow the FBI had been fooled. The bomber, Wyatt's stalker, was still at large.

Then, a clear and singular thought filled her mind. They'd removed the FBI agents from Wyatt's house! There was only a single sheriff's deputy there now.

She stabbed out Daniel's number. His phone was off the hook, of course, as it had been for months.

Claire grabbed her keys. She ran to her own car, hoping she was sober enough to drive. To drive fast. Whatever was going on here, Claire Davis knew she had to get to Daniel's house as quickly as possible.

Eduardo Costilla raced toward the Hyatt, his cell phone in one hand. Stanton answered, but he was still at the hospital, miles from downtown. Costilla hung up without explanation and called Watson.

"Where are you?"

Watson named a restaurant downtown.

"Get back to the Hyatt, now. There's a Father Peter O'Keefe in Room 313. He's one of the Catholics for Life. Take him. Armed and dangerous."

"A priest?"

"Yes. Call me the moment you get him."

Costilla ended the call and accelerated. Dios mío! How could he have been so stupid? O'Keefe had just handed him Bartlett. Even Samuels had questioned the ease with which they'd found their man.

A fresh wave of guilt hit Costilla. He'd risked Tabitha's life for a red herring, a diversionary tactic. *Damn O'Keefe.*

Costilla's mind continued to piece the elements together as he drove. The Bibles stacked in the room. Of course, that's where the pages at the dump had come from. The old schoolboy trick of a hollowed-out book. The C-4 had been right there, a few feet from his elbow as he'd knelt and prayed for forgiveness.

Costilla feverishly tried to remember the conversation he'd had with the priest. There'd been his confession, of sins past and present. He'd talked about his sister, his guilt over Samuels, the capture of Steve Bartlett.

And the priest had talked about innocents hurt in wartime, the price of a moral cause. He'd also said something about *Your work here is over.*

Costilla pulled to the side of the road, shaking his head. O'Keefe must have realized that the FBI thought they had their man. He knew that they were standing down, and thought that Wyatt was no longer in danger.

Daniel Wyatt, who as of tonight had no one guarding him except a single sheriff's deputy.

Costilla pulled out his phone again, reached the Lafayette operator, and gave his badge number. He was put through to the police immediately.

"Send any available units to Daniel Wyatt's house," he ordered.

When he hung up, he sat and glowered at the lights of downtown Lafayette before him. Which way should he go? Toward the Hyatt and O'Keefe's room or to Wyatt's house? He couldn't think clearly. This whole day had been nothing but bad decisions, one botched call leading to another.

His phone rang.

"Costilla."

"Watson. O'Keefe's not here. But you wouldn't believe the stuff that is."

"The C-4?"

"Nope. Maybe traces, I'm not sure. But he's got an arsenal of guns. Also bomb-making materials: blasting caps, a transmitter, some high-speed wire."

"Any Bibles?" Costilla asked hopefully.

"Bibles?" Watson asked in puzzlement. There was a brief pause as he searched. "Yeah."

Costilla breathed a sigh of relief. O'Keefe hadn't planted the explosives. They'd reached the man in time to declaw him.

"One anyway," Watson added. "In the drawer by the bed. Good old Gideon. Why do you ask?"

"Shit!" said Costilla, and pulled back onto the road, spinning the car around in a wide arc.

"Stay there and lay low," he ordered. "If O'Keefe shows, take him. And don't touch that transmitter!"

Costilla completed the one-eighty and sped toward Daniel Wyatt's house, hoping he would be in time.

The FBI agents were gone, O'Keefe was certain of that.

The sheriff's deputy was still on duty, doubtless to ward off reporters and protesters. What O'Keefe didn't know was whether the warning devices the FBI had installed were still present and active. If Agent Costilla really believed that Steve Bartlett was his man, then perhaps the red-haired FBI agent had already come to disarm the alarm system.

O'Keefe was briefly saddened by the thought of Bartlett. He'd been a good man when they served together in the Soldiers of Christ, always ready to risk his life for the cause. So when God had guided O'Keefe to sacrifice his old friend, he knew it was what Bartlett would have wanted.

Daniel Wyatt was visible, pacing in the living room, no doubt pondering his fate with the jury. Now that he thought himself safe, Wyatt had left the blinds up. The lights were turned on in every room, probably more a sign of loneliness than fear. O'Keefe's thoughts returned to the alarm system. From what he had seen of its installation, it looked as if the transmitters were all short-range. The system was meant to be monitored by the FBI agent on-site. But the alarms might still be triggered to call the local police, or set off a loud wail that the deputy would hear and respond to.

Well, O'Keefe needed only a few minutes. And with the deputy out of commission, it would take time for any assistance to arrive. And he knew that God would guide him past any search efforts through the dark, empty night.

In the warm Louisiana evening, the windows of the deputy's car were open. O'Keefe stole toward the vehicle slowly, his approach covered by the short hedge that ran the length of the wide street's luxurious, oak-lined median. It was easy to be quieter than the rhythmic chorus of cicadas that filled the evening. The smells of fall—rotting leaves and rich earth—melded with the ether on the rag in O'Keefe's hand.

He leaped up to the window, grabbing the deputy with both hands, one forcing the rag over his protesting mouth and the other holding the head steady. The man cried out, but that only filled his lungs faster. In moments, he had gone limp in O'Keefe's hands.

Now there was one way to make sure that the alarms didn't go off. He took the deputy's hat and jacket and put them on.

O'Keefe walked to the front door.

It didn't matter if Wyatt got a look at him, after all. O'Keefe could go into hiding. The transmitter that would bring down the courthouse had a range of four miles.

He knocked on the door, his head down, hands in pockets a bit sheepishly, shuffling a little as if he had to urinate.

From the corner of his downcast eyes, O'Keefe saw Wyatt check through the window by the door. Wyatt opened it straightaway, as if glad for any interruption of his lonely night of waiting for a verdict.

O'Keefe pushed in, closing the door behind him.

Wyatt said, "You're not . . ."

"No."

Wyatt moved quickly for a man his age, running for the kitchen. The phone was there, perhaps some sort of alarm. O'Keefe took two long steps, hurled himself at Wyatt's legs. The older man fell hard in the hall between living room and kitchen.

Perfect. Here, they were invisible from the outside.

Wyatt gathered his breath, raising his hands as if expecting a blow. Then he took a deep breath, readying for a scream. O'Keefe punched him once in the stomach, driving up hard into the full lungs. Wyatt was silenced and reduced to harsh, gasping breaths.

O'Keefe released him and sat back. The physical contact was too intense. It made him want to end all this right now.

He felt terribly close to Wyatt, a man he had watched for so long, observed with the morbid fascination with which one studies the famous butchers of history. But Wyatt was here now, in the flesh, evil made real. It was almost peaceful, to be sitting in this hallway together, the quiet interrupted only by Wyatt's gasping and the sound of cicadas outside.

O'Keefe cleared his throat.

"Dr. Wyatt?"

The man was still speechless, clutching his stomach.

"I'm sorry for that. For hitting you."

Wyatt closed his eyes. He was trying to get his wind back. His breathing was rapid, but no longer racked his whole body.

"I see now that you aren't in control. You have been called here just like me."

O'Keefe didn't know where these words were coming from. He hadn't thought out what he would say to Wyatt when this encounter finally came to pass. He just knew he had to be in this house, knew that the message would come once he was face-to-face with Dr. Daniel Wyatt.

"You brought this great audience together. You gathered them in from the fields and towns, focused them on their televisions. Your singularly evil deed served God's purpose, as do all things."

O'Keefe could see them all now. The millions who would be watching in the next few days, waiting for a verdict, arguing and debating, then finally silent, in terrible suspense as they waited for word from the twelve.

"Before you, this holocaust of abortion was carried out in hidden clinics, in unmarked rooms of hospitals, in closed doctors' offices that were all invisible to the world. Not like the Nazis, who built great edifices as monuments to their crime. Rather, in a million tiny places, each one taking a life here or there each week, each one quiet and remote."

O'Keefe reached over and held Wyatt's shoulder. The man flinched. His breathing was normal again, and O'Keefe wondered if he would dare cry out. He leaned back and delivered another blow to the older man's stomach. It felt good to silence Wyatt again.

"But you built a monument to abortion, Dr. Wyatt," Peter O'Keefe continued. "Not a monument of steel and stone, but of newscasts and cameras and interviews, of websites and opinion polls. You made this trial, this monument to the crimes committed by doctors everywhere. You forced everyone to see."

O'Keefe held the gasping Wyatt closer, clutching him tightly as if forcing a recalcitrant child to pay attention.

"I won't see you again. But know that I will be there when the verdict comes. God's verdict will come as well. And His verdict isn't about you, Wyatt. It's a verdict on humanity itself. Can we see what we have wrought? Can we still see evil, even in a form as pure as you, child killer? If we can't, the sky must fall."

A sound came from the living room. Someone was knocking on the door. The deputy? O'Keefe wondered. No, he'd still be unconscious. The door creaked open. O'Keefe realized he hadn't locked it behind him.

"Daniel?" a worried voice. Then O'Keefe recognized it.

Claire Davis.

How fitting, that the other object of this great lesson would arrive at this moment.

Peter O'Keefe leaned close to Wyatt, grasping the man's throat tightly and whispering into his ear.

"So listen when your verdict comes, Dr. Wyatt. Pray that you are marked as guilty. That will be the only salvation for you, and every juror, lawyer, reporter in this trial. For if men find you innocent, God will know better, and He will strike you down so hard, all the world will know."

"Daniel?" came Davis's voice again.

O'Keefe released his captive and walked through the kitchen to the door, ignoring the blinking light of an alarm control panel as he pushed through it into the dark night.

* * *

Claire Davis heard something. Heavy footsteps here on the ground floor.

Fear almost paralyzed her. Why wasn't Daniel answering?

"Daniel?" she repeated, her voice dry.

"Claire," came a ragged shout.

It was Daniel's voice. He sounded wounded and breathless.

"Where are you?" she cried. She'd already dialed 911 outside, the cell phone in her hand, her finger poised over the send button. Now she pushed it, initiating the call.

As if in response, the painful, mind-numbing screech of an alarm filled the house. Claire dropped the phone and covered her ears.

"Daniel!" she screamed. Her paralysis broken, she ran forward.

There he was in the hallway, clutching his stomach. He looked like he'd been shot. She knelt and looked for blood.

"Are you all right?" she shouted over the piercing wail of the alarm.

He nodded, gasping for breath.

"What happened?"

"He was here," Wyatt croaked.

Claire looked around furiously. The house itself seemed to be screaming at her, the alarm driving into her ears like a pair of needles. She could see no one.

"Who?"

"The bomber," Wyatt gasped. "He's going to kill them all."

"What?" Claire shouted. Wyatt seemed crazed. She couldn't see any blood, but he was still clutching his stomach. As she had driven over here, her fear for Wyatt alerted by Costilla's strange behavior, she had tried to suppress her rising panic. But now in this hellish, screaming house, nothing made sense, as if the world had gone mad.

Where was the damn sheriff's deputy? The alarm had been ringing for thirty seconds. And what was Daniel saying?

"We have to change it."

"Hush, Daniel," she said, eyes searching for her cell phone.

"Have to change the plea. Or he'll kill them all," Daniel raved.

The alarm abruptly stopped. For a few moments, an echo of the sound rang in her head, a shadow-scream filling the sudden silence. Claire heard footsteps in the front room, in the kitchen, the pop of police radios.

Help was here.

"We have to change it," Wyatt repeated, shaking his head as if to drive the maddening noise from it.

"Daniel . . ."

"Have to change the plea . . . to guilty," he said.

O'Keefe hadn't shown.

Costilla had joined Watson in the priest's hotel·room after the situation at Daniel Wyatt's house had stabilized, and the two of them had been here all night. O'Keefe must have intended to return. He'd left identification, his clothes and luggage, and, most importantly, the transmitter that would set off the explosives, wherever they were.

But Peter O'Keefe hadn't returned. Something had tipped him off.

Perhaps some cop had let the priest's name slip over a police radio, or O'Keefe had spotted the agents that Costilla had put in the lobby as backup, or the bomb disposal team he'd brought in. It was hard to run a forensics investigation simultaneously with a stakeout, but Costilla hadn't had time to wait around. Hell, maybe O'Keefe had just gotten nervous that Daniel Wyatt would somehow ID him. Or maybe his God had told him to clear out.

Costilla hoped that it wasn't a setup. If O'Keefe had another transmitter, then they were wasting a lot of manpower. They had a plainclothes cop in every Radio Shack and computer store within a hundred miles. It wouldn't be easy to find another piece of hardware that would transmit the frequency that O'Keefe had left his transmitter set to, not on short notice.

If the jury would just hurry up . . . From what the priest had said to him, Daniel Wyatt seemed convinced that

O'Keefe was going to make his move when the verdict was announced.

As the two agents waited, the morning light crawling up the shaded window, Watson was suggesting how they might find the bomb.

"We could evacuate downtown, and just trigger the thing. We've got the frequency, after all."

"Smart, Watson," Costilla snapped. "We're talking about twenty pounds of C-4. That could take out a square block."

Watson was getting on his nerves. They'd been sitting here for hours, talking quietly in case O'Keefe finally returned and somehow slipped past the men downstairs. Costilla wished he could be down there, but O'Keefe knew his face too well.

Agent Watson shrugged. "If you're going to lose the buildings anyway, better they go up empty than occupied."

My God. Maybe the man had a point.

Costilla tried to imagine getting approval for such a move. Evacuating the entire downtown area to intentionally set off a terrorist's bomb. If they didn't have the right frequency, if O'Keefe had left the transmitter as a ruse, it would be a huge embarrassment for the Bureau. And it would be worse if the bomb actually detonated. Millions of dollars' worth of property deliberately damaged. Some detective work, to do the bomber's work of destruction for him.

At least Costilla had proof now that O'Keefe did in fact possess the Soldiers of Christ's missing C-4. The bomb team had found residue throughout the room. Some of the explosive was even found on O'Keefe's fingerprints, which matched the partials found at the bombed clinic back in 1996. The priest must have played with the stuff, making the little Bibles with his bare hands, a labor of perverted love.

The room still smelled of coffee, which O'Keefe had used to disguise the rich smell of the C-4. Costilla remembered it from that first morning when he had met the priest. He'd been so close. Twice.

The smell was making him hungry, and he was exhausted.

"All right, Watson. I'm going for coffee. Want some?"

Watson shook his head.

Costilla opened the door, taking a quick look down the hall in both directions. The room next door was the command post for the stakeout, occupied by the state police and Stanton. Costilla hoped they'd put a fresh pot on recently. He missed Samuels, who, like all computer geeks, took great pride in making decent coffee. Hot and strong, like her men, she always said.

Agent Stanton and the cops in the command post looked as tired as Costilla felt. They grunted at him, barely looking up from the images of the lobby and elevators that showed on their screens. Radio checks came in from the various observation points around the hotel. Costilla wondered if he'd pushed this stakeout too far. It had taken too long to get into place. O'Keefe must have returned and seen the signs as men got into position. Perhaps Costilla should have told no one about O'Keefe, just camped out alone in the priest's room, himself and a gun.

But he'd fucked up on the decision to have Chaos take Bartlett, so he'd done it by the book this time. And probably fucked up again.

The coffee tasted like shit.

Costilla looked at the row of little screens. Too much police work now was spent in surveillance, peering into cathode-ray tubes and listening over wires. He longed to get out on the street and look for his quarry with his own eyes, tired as they were.

The clock radio by the bed said a quarter to eleven. Was it really that late?

The room's television was on, set to CNN with the volume down. A graphic of a fetus entangled in a question mark flashed at the upper left of the screen—the graphic that represented the Wyatt trial. Costilla located the remote and brought the volume up.

". . . and Judge Thibodeaux has announced that the court will be convened at twelve o'clock—in just a little over one hour—for an announcement. We can only assume that the jury has come to a decision in both counts against Dr. Daniel Wyatt, the former surgeon general nominee accused of inducing an abortion to end the pregnancy of his alleged mistress, Sarah Corbett. Experts agree that the announcement is almost certainly not a hung jury, as the jury has been in deliberation for only one day. We don't know what the verdict is yet, but we are sure now that there will be no hung jury, a situation many legal scholars were expecting. Again, the jury has apparently reached a verdict in the case of . . ."

The men behind Costilla stirred.

The jury was coming back in an hour, and O'Keefe was still at large somewhere.

Costilla made a decision. Maybe I'm screwing up again, he thought. But at least I'll go down trying.

He finished off the coffee in a gulp and addressed the room.

"Stay here. I'm going to check out the courthouse again."

Stanton looked surprised. Dogs had scoured the entire building half a dozen times, including last night. Security in the hotel had been tight throughout the trial. But Costilla couldn't stand another minute of this useless stakeout.

Before anyone could question him, he walked out the door.

O'Keefe was out there somewhere, and time was running out.

Mark Hicks wished he'd gotten to sleep earlier last night.

News that the court was about to reconvene had spread among the ranks of protesters like wildfire, and things were heating up. The pro-choice demonstrators realized that any verdict would reflect badly on their cause; either Wyatt was guilty, which implied that abortion was murder, or he wasn't, which meant that a man had usurped a woman's right to choose and had not been punished. In either case, they were trying to get their mixed message across in the waning hours of the trial. The pro-life folks, on the other hand, thought that a quick verdict meant not guilty, and they were readying themselves to make a hell of a demonstration. They were chanting, screaming at the arriving legal teams, and staging sit-ins at downtown intersections.

This last bit of trouble had resulted in another round of arrests, and had forced Hicks to drag himself down to the old civic center. The county jail was long since full, and prisoners were being kept in three separate locations. Sheriff Hicks had received a complaint from the head of Operation Rescue that its members who were being detained had been mistreated.

The sheriff walked into the center, trying to find somebody in charge. He could see both local police and state troopers in the crowded lobby area. Who had jurisdiction? he wondered.

Hicks shook his head at the chaos all around the building. In almost twenty years, he'd never had a chain-of-command problem, and this trial had brought him nothing but. After the report of the intruder at the Wyatt house last night, even the FBI was back in the mix.

At least this addled state of affairs didn't leave him much time to think about Millie.

After fifteen minutes of being sent back and forth between state and local, Mark Hicks decided to call it a morning. According to the radio, this was all going to be over in another hour or so anyway. Maybe things would settle down a little after the verdict. Likely they'd probably get worse, Hicks thought glumly, but at least once it was over, things would eventually get back to normal.

In any case, he wasn't getting to the bottom of this Operation Rescue problem until after the verdict was announced. Hicks could feel the tension rising, building across the city like the electricity in the air before a bad thunderstorm.

Hicks left the civic center and headed for the courthouse. He was shorthanded there worse than usual today, as the FBI had requested a number of his men to help them find their suspected bomber before the verdict was announced. Maybe, Hicks thought, he wasn't too old to help with a little crowd control.

But as he neared his destination, Mark Hicks stopped and squinted. Before him was FBI Agent Costilla, standing in the middle of the courthouse steps, looking up at the sky.

"Hey there, Agent Costilla."

The sound of the old sheriff's voice wrenched Costilla from his thoughts.

"Sheriff Hicks."

"Find your man yet?"

Costilla shook his head. "He's disappeared. Just like he always does."

"That's too damn bad. I was hoping Deputy Scopes could get his hat back."

Costilla laughed. The sheriff's deputy had been mortified to have been found sleeping on his post, ether or no ether. "I wish that hat was all O'Keefe had. He's still got a lot of C-4 to play with. I don't know if it's true, but Daniel Wyatt says he's planning to make his move when the verdict comes in. I was going to check the courthouse one more time."

"I thought your boys were in there last night," Hicks said.

Maybe it was his exhaustion playing with him, but to Costilla, the sheriff sounded amused at his persistence.

"Yeah, I guess they were."

Costilla turned back to the sky. He had been looking at the large building that loomed over the courthouse.

"Sheriff, what's that building there?"

"That used to be the civic center. It's been closed about five years. They keep meaning to tear it down and build something else, but the zoning commission can't agree what. Some folks want a sports stadium. The site ain't big enough, though."

"So it's been wrapped up pretty tight, yeah?" Costilla asked. All the public buildings in the downtown area had been under close security throughout the trial.

"Was until three days ago, I guess."

Costilla looked at the older man questioningly.

"We're keeping prisoners there now. The county jail's been full up ever since—"

"Sheriff Hicks," the FBI agent interrupted. "Can you give me authorization to search inside?"

"Authorization?" Hicks chuckled. "It's a mess over there. Don't know who's in charge. I bet anyone could walk in there right now."

Costilla narrowed his eyes, again looked up at the structure. It rose up over the courthouse like a mountain. He wondered when the dogs had last swept it, if they ever had. If only they had time to call in the dogs now. But the verdict was going to be announced in less than an hour; there wasn't time.

"Sheriff Hicks," he said, "if you've got nothing better to do, come with me."

Hicks shrugged. "I reckon I don't."

* * *

"Daniel," Claire Davis said. "You can still back out."

Mills and Judge Thibodeaux were waiting in chambers, ready to discuss the deal. The judge had already accepted in principle the plea-bargaining arrangement that she and Riley Mills had spent all morning hammering out.

Dr. Daniel Wyatt was changing his plea.

"Claire, I have to. I caused all this, don't you see?"

"But you're innocent! You didn't give any drugs to Sarah."

Daniel smiled ruefully at her.

"That doesn't seem to matter. The press has already already convicted me. Regardless of the outcome, I'm ruined."

Despite his bitter words, Daniel didn't seem upset. He wore only a look of exhaustion, as if he were too tired to maintain any real emotion.

"I had some misconceptions about the law, I suppose," Wyatt continued. "We don't have presumption of innocence, we have assumption of guilt. We don't have a trial by one's peers. None of those jurors has a medical degree, and none has had to make the choices I've made. You've said I have a right not to incriminate myself, but we both know the jury thinks I'm hiding something because I haven't testified."

Claire nodded. She couldn't argue with Wyatt's words.

"Sometimes even innocent people have something to hide, Daniel."

"Thanks for still believing in my innocence," he said calmly. "I appreciate it. And you're right, I didn't slip her those drugs."

Daniel shook his head slowly.

"But, Claire, I broke an oath. I'm morally guilty. I'm a doctor, and I took advantage of my relationship with a patient. I broke my marriage vows, I betrayed your trust, and I gave Sarah medical treatment without adequate follow-up."

"Medication which you know damn well is safe," Claire exclaimed. "Her reaction was just a fluke!"

Wyatt just smiled sadly.

"I just want this to be over," he said. "No matter how many times you tell me I won't be found guilty, I can't get the fact out of my mind that I'm facing life in prison."

Claire looked at her client. Daniel seemed transformed since he had come to his decision the night before. He appeared, for the first time in months, to be at peace with himself. Finally, he had found a way to take responsibility for all that had happened. Claire wondered if the long ordeal of the trial, along with being assaulted by Peter O'Keefe last night, had somehow unhinged him.

But whatever was going on in his mind, he seemed happier now.

Claire realized that she desperately needed a cigarette. The calmer Daniel Wyatt got, the more agitated she became. It was too surreal, a client changing his plea while the jury was out, pissing away what could very well be a favorable verdict, and all based on the threats of a madman.

"Besides, this is the only way to stop him."

"Daniel, the FBI is combing the city for this Peter O'Keefe right now. They know his name, his face. They might catch him at any minute."

"Claire, I could see it in his eyes," Daniel said. "He will go through with this. Somehow he'll find a way to destroy more lives if I'm acquitted. I couldn't live with that. Not after everything else that's happened."

"Daniel, listen to yourself," Claire insisted. "I know you feel guilty for all this, for what's happened to all of us personally, and for the political consequences, too. But it's not up to you to sacrifice yourself. Let the FBI do their job."

"It was up to me to resist Sarah Corbett, and to tell the truth when I failed. It was up to me to tell the truth to my wife, to you, to the administration. I'm paying for that, no matter how this trial ends. But I can't ask others to pay for it also."

"Daniel . . ."

She couldn't think what to say. There had been too many

arguments over the last few months, trying to convince Sarah, Ellen, Daniel, the judge, jurors. Claire realized, quite suddenly, that she was all out of arguments.

"I have to do this," Daniel said. "Balancing everything, I can't take the risk."

The bailiff signaled that the judge was ready.

Claire nodded at Daniel, and walked alone toward the conference room.

Riley Mills looked uncomfortable. He must have known that in the end, the case had gotten away from him. Sarah Corbett had practically changed sides, handing the defense one last argument for reasonable doubt. The prosecutor was probably glad to save this one from being a defeat. Claire had heard rumors that Louisiana's senior senator was priming Mills for a run at the governor's mansion, the current occupant of which had served his allotted two terms. Politician Mills hardly wanted to have his case fall apart while the whole world was watching.

Mills had agreed to reduce the murder charge to involuntary manslaughter in exchange for a no-contest plea, and dropping the charge of furnishing medicine without a medical necessity.

Claire was determined that Daniel not admit that he'd administered the drugs to Sarah against her will, merely supplied her with them. Thus, he was only indirectly responsible for the death of her fetus. The involuntary manslaughter charge meant that he could eventually practice medicine again when he was released from prison. Representatives from the state medical board had explained it all to her that morning. He could reapply for his medical license when he was released.

He was, at heart, a healer. He could face any prison sentence that would eventually allow him to return to his life as a doctor.

Wyatt was already talking of going back to Guatemala.

"I'll be the anonymous medicine man down there," he'd said last night. "All us gringos look alike, you know."

Claire took her seat, and the judge began.

"Ms. Davis, I have in my hand a plea agreement between you and the prosecutor's office. I understand your client will plead no contest."

Claire nodded. She realized how much more confident Judge Thibodeaux was now than he'd been at the beginning of the case.

"Now, Claire," the judge continued. "I understand that your client had an encounter with an intruder last night?"

"Yes, he did."

"I want to make sure that regardless of what took place, his plea is free and voluntary. Is your client making this decision because he believes it is in his best interests to resolve this matter by way of plea agreement rather than to have the jury decide his guilt or innocence?"

Claire glanced at Mills, caught his eye. He looked away. Perhaps he had begun to feel as she did; she'd won the case for the defense, and Wyatt was throwing the victory away.

"Yes. My client wishes to act in his own best interests, Your Honor. He is not under duress."

"Well, during the plea negotiations, Ms. Davis, you made a plea for leniency that has been very persuasive. Although I can make no promises about what the sentence will be, my inclination—since this is an unusual circumstance—is for leniency."

"Thank you, Your Honor."

Mills sputtered to life. "Your Honor, the People strongly object and view this as a most serious crime!"

"Mr. Mills," Thibodeaux interrupted. "This is not a sentencing hearing. We will get a probation report, and both sides will be entitled to present additional evidence at the time of the sentencing hearing."

Thibodeaux seemed pleased with himself, Claire thought. He had won high marks for his handling of the case, and he had escaped the specter of a hung jury. And now he seemed to be promising leniency.

This deal was looking better all the time.

The judge closed the folder and leaned back contentedly.

"Well, if we are all in agreement, then, we shall take this announcement into open court, ladies and gentlemen. At twelve noon."

He stood, and those assembled followed suit.

"We have to inform the jury and thank them for their public service."

The upper floors of the civic center were eerily quiet after the chaos downstairs.

Costilla and Hicks walked down the long hallway, peering into the locked classrooms and meeting areas. Dusty bulletin boards were still layered with old announcements, of bake sales and cookouts and volleyball leagues. There was a ghostly feel to the place, a sense of abandonment, of ruin.

"How many floors?" Costilla asked.

Mark Hicks frowned. "Can't rightly remember. Five or six, I expect."

Costilla checked his watch. The verdict would be announced in forty minutes. Maybe they should call in backup. But every available man was covering local electronics stores, making sure that O'Keefe couldn't replace his lost transmitter.

"Maybe we should split up."

Hicks smiled indulgently. Costilla knew the older man didn't think much of this expedition, probably thought the FBI agent was spinning his wheels. Maybe the sheriff was right. Perhaps, Costilla thought, he was trying to compensate for having been taken in by O'Keefe. Well, it was better than sitting in a hotel room waiting for something to happen.

"All right," Hicks agreed. "I'll take the odd floors, you take even."

"Meet you on the top floor," Costilla said.

He watched the old sheriff walk slowly toward the stairs, then forced his tired brain to calculate. This was the second floor, and he'd also have to cover the fourth and sixth. That gave him a bit more than ten minutes per floor.

Costilla sighed and started walking.

Mark Hicks took the stairs slowly. He was getting too old for police work, dammit. Perhaps when Millie returned from the hospital, he should consider staying at home to care for her, at least until she could walk on her own. The next election for the sheriff's office was coming up the following November. Maybe it was finally time to sit one out.

He shook his head. He never thought he'd see the day when he didn't want to wear a badge. But this whole affair with Sarah Corbett had shaken his faith. So many good people had been ruined by it: Daniel Wyatt, Ernest Magley, and his Millie. And it had all stemmed from Mark Hicks's desire to enforce the Law. That's what had started it. Maybe some secrets were meant to be kept, or belonged hidden in those gray spaces into which the Law reached only at its peril.

Hicks found himself up on the third floor. He walked down the darkened hallway for a bit, checking the doors. Maybe that FBI agent was right, and a world-class terrorist had set up shop right here next to the courthouse.

But, then again, probably not.

For one thing, Costilla seemed a little unhinged today, with a wild look in his eye from the first moment Hicks had seen him. Maybe the FBI agent had been driven crazy by this case, just like the rest of the world.

Then Mark Hicks saw something that made him smile.

Sitting, dusty and abandoned in the hall, was an old wooden chair.

Hicks walked up to the chair and gave it a dust with one hand. Someone had left it here, forgotten it five years ago, abandoned for no particular reason. But now the chair had found its purpose.

Hicks sat down, making a little grunt of satisfaction as he did so. Soon enough, the verdict would come and go, and he could rejoin Costilla's search. For the moment, though, Mark Hicks was going to set a spell.

The sixth floor.

Costilla looked at his watch for the hundredth time since beginning his search. Only twenty minutes left before the court convened. The dark hallways stretched before him, slanting lines of sunlight bright with swirling dust. In his sleepless state, the abandoned building seemed to Costilla like something from a hackneyed dream. A row of doors, of possibilities.

Then he heard something.

Somewhere before him, a tinny voice was quietly buzzing. The words were indistinct, but the rise and fall of their uttering sounded like an announcer. Someone was watching television.

Costilla drew his gun and walked slowly forward, careful not to make a sound.

The noise of the broadcast seemed to be coming from everywhere at once. The empty halls echoed with it, or perhaps in his exhausted condition Costilla simply couldn't determine its direction. He paused for a moment at each door, gun raised, listening carefully.

Then he stopped short.

Just ahead of him, a thin line of light flickered from the gap beneath one of the doors. Costilla blinked and rubbed his tired eyes, but the flicker remained.

He edged forward, feeling adrenaline flow sluggishly into his veins. He reached out to test the knob. It turned slowly in his hand; the door was locked.

Costilla braced himself, flicking his nine-millimeter's safety catch off. Reflexively, he pulled an extra clip from his pocket and palmed it in his left hand. The doorknob mechanism looked formidable, the sturdy design of a few decades ago. Costilla pointed his gun at the wooden frame.

He took a deep breath, squinted his eyes to narrow slits,

and fired three quick shots. Ignoring the flying splinters that cut into his hands, he threw himself against the door and burst into the room.

Costilla swung his pistol toward the light. Peter O'Keefe stared back at him, a shocked expression on his face. The dark room was illuminated only by the tiny television. A few words from the little box reached Costilla's ears.

". . . rumors that some sort of deal is in the works . . ."

"Don't move!" Costilla shouted.

O'Keefe didn't shift a muscle. The FBI agent's eyes adjusted quickly to the almost lightless room. He saw the white collar of the priest's vestment flickering in the light cast by the TV, then he realized that O'Keefe also held a gun. But it wasn't pointed at Costilla. Nonsensically, O'Keefe aimed his weapon at a long open closet that stretched along the back wall of the room.

"Greetings, my son," O'Keefe said.

"Drop your weapon!" Costilla ordered.

The priest shook his head slowly.

"My son, the time is nigh, but not yet. It is too soon by a few moments."

"Drop . . . your . . . weapon," Costilla repeated. He moved to one side, getting behind the priest so that he could see into the closet. Had O'Keefe taken a hostage?

Then he saw what was inside the closet.

Stuck to the wall in a trail that stretched for several yards were little bricks of C-4, all connected by high-speed wire. It looked like all twenty pounds were there. Enough to level this building and the adjacent courthouse. O'Keefe's pistol was aimed at the largest of the bricks, which was studded with blasting caps. A twitch from his finger and everything would fall.

"My son, perhaps you should drop *your* weapon."

Costilla's exhausted brain tried to figure out a way out of this. Perhaps a volley of shots would stop the priest's heart before he pulled the trigger. But the angle was wrong. It was far more likely that one of Costilla's bullets would detonate a brick of the C-4. And once one of them went, they would all go.

What if he dropped his gun and rushed O'Keefe? Maybe the man wasn't ready yet, was unprepared to kill hundreds, including himself. O'Keefe had originally planned to detonate the explosives at long range, not make himself a martyr. Perhaps an unexpected attack would cause him to hesitate for a crucial moment.

But the priest had killed at least six times before. He wasn't some scared kid who'd taken a hostage at random, he was a confirmed murderer deludedly convinced of the righteousness of his cause. If anyone would sacrifice himself to commit this terrible crime, O'Keefe would.

Costilla realized there was only one way out, only one chance. The jury could come back with a verdict of guilty. Then, with justice served, O'Keefe might give this up and walk away.

The FBI agent lowered his gun, and knelt to set it on the floor.

Once he had done so, O'Keefe turned toward him. Costilla saw the man's weapon swing toward him in slow motion.

"I'm sorry, my son," the priest said.

And shot Costilla in the chest.

Sheriff Hicks sat upright in his chair, then stood.

The last of the sounds was still echoing through the empty halls of the civic center. It had been as sudden and sharp as a pair of two-by-fours banged together.

Or a gunshot.

There had been three quick sounds, then a fourth. At first, Hicks had thought it was something falling. Now he wasn't so sure.

Whatever it had been, it had definitely come from one of the floors above. Agent Costilla must be searching up there by now, frantic to meet his deadline of noon. Hicks looked at his watch; it was just eleven-thirty now. Maybe the man had hurt himself up there. The civic center had been closed partly because of structural problems, which is why Hicks had used only the ground floor for prisoners.

Mark Hicks sighed and trudged toward the stairway. Might as well find Costilla and see what had happened. It was time to move on, anyway. Once the verdict was announced, Hicks would be needed back at the courthouse steps.

Besides, he was mighty curious to know whether Wyatt was guilty or not.

The sound probably hadn't been anything, he reassured himself.

But as he climbed the stairs, he placed his hand on the butt of his revolver. It was always good to know it was there.

* * *

Riley Mills sat in his office watching the clock, his hands flexing nervously, a vague feeling of discomfort growing within him as the minutes moved toward noon. The clean result he'd wanted in this case—a jury verdict—was slipping away. He'd never know whether he had won or lost. A few of the jurors would give interviews, and claim they would have voted this way or that, but Mills never gave those statements much credence. A jury was an organism, a combination of personalities. Without the pressure cooker of a binding verdict, with a man's life at stake, you'd never get the same result.

The true verdict in this case was lost forever.

But Mills felt glad to be getting a guilty plea. He had accomplished what he'd set out to do. The state party was knocking on his door, the senior senator practically offering him the governorship—probably just to keep him from competing for the man's own Senate seat, which was also up for grabs next year. Maybe there was even a place for Riley Mills at the next Republican National Convention. The party needed reminding where it stood on abortion these days, and he was the man to do it. He wouldn't turn down a half-hour speech during prime time.

And to think that Sarah Corbett had almost blown it, with her last-minute "I don't think so." Riley Mills had half a mind to charge her with perjury.

But that wouldn't be good politics at all.

The problem was, when the plea bargain was announced in open court, it would create a media sensation. There would be some who'd say that Riley Mills had choked, hadn't trusted his own ability to get a conviction. In the heat of the moment, some might even say that Claire Davis had beaten him. Mills realized that the antipathy between Claire Davis and him was well known; the press probably expected to see a fight to the death. Perhaps it would be better if this ending weren't so dramatic, Mills thought.

Maybe a little spoiler was in order. News that had been leaked had time to spread a little more slowly, to percolate a bit, even to settle a little before it was confirmed. This way, at least, it wouldn't have the dramatic impact of an surprise announcement in open court.

Mills reached for his phone, glad to have something to do with his hands, to break the boredom of just waiting.

"KLIF News, Cynthia Feld," the answer came. The voice was choppy from a bad cell-phone connection, almost swallowed by the background noise of protest and traffic.

"Cynthia, this is Riley Mills."

The young reporter was struck dumb for a moment. Mills smiled and waited.

"Yes, D.A. Mills. How . . . interesting to hear from you."

"Well, I'm glad you think so, Cynthia. I wondered if we might have a short discussion about the announcement that will shortly be made before the open court."

"Certainly." Mills could hear her hungry anticipation.

"But this discussion would have to be off the record."

"Of course, Mr. Mills."

"Now, Cynthia, it sounds like you're on site. Ready to go live, as it were," Mills said. His office clock read eleven thirty-five. There wasn't much time left to trump the events in the courtroom.

"Yes, sir. I'm right here on the courthouse steps with my crew."

"Well, then I'm sure you'll want to hear what I have to tell you . . ."

When the conversation was over, Riley Mills turned on the small television in his office, switched it to KLIF. Talking heads counting down the minutes until noon. The usual shots of protesters and policemen, their ranks swelled by people awaiting the imminent announcement.

He wasn't forced to wait very long before KLIF interrupted its own coverage with breaking news, an anonymous tip about what lay ahead. Cynthia Feld appeared now, doing a stand-up from the outskirts of the courthouse crowd. Mills nodded to himself; he had done the right thing. This would cushion the blow of the plea-bargain announcement as rival news organizations reported this turn of events as rumor and speculation while they attempted to confirm it. He would leave them dangling when they called him, of course, saying nothing to confirm or deny.

"This is Cynthia Feld, KLIF News. We have just learned from a high-level source that the announcement soon to be made in the *Louisiana* versus *Wyatt* courtroom will be a plea bargain. The jury has not come to a decision, but the prosecutor's office and the defense have reached an agreement. Dr. Wyatt has agreed to plead no contest to involuntary manslaughter."

Cynthia Feld paused, gathering herself for the next barrage of hastily prepared remarks. Riley Mills had the momentary sensation that she was looking directly at him, straight through the television screen. Perhaps she knew she was being used for Mills's own purposes. But, of course, another scoop for Feld in the Wyatt case would help her own career immeasurably. Mills remembered now that it was she who had first made Wyatt a household name in Lafayette, after that business when the doctor saved a man's life in a restaurant a few years back.

Feld continued, but in a few moments her voice was drowned out by Mills's ringing phone. Already, the rest of the news pack was anxious to confirm.

Now he needed to play the media carefully, giving away the story bit by bit, like reeling in a big fish on a thin line. District Attorney Mills let the phone ring for a while before answering. Timing was everything.

"No contest?" repeated Father Peter O'Keefe. "And nothing about murder?"

Through a haze of pain, Agent Costilla watched the man's reaction. O'Keefe was deeply confused, upset by the rumors coming from the television set. He had been ready to become a martyr, or to walk away if the jury had found Wyatt guilty. But now the moral ambiguity of a plea bargain had intruded into his black-and-white world, his plan made irrelevant by this final twist of the trial.

Apparently, God hadn't warned him about this turn of events. How would he react?

Costilla sank back, struggling to breathe.

He felt as if some invisible elephant were sitting on his chest, easing more weight onto him every moment. With every breath, the pain grew worse, until traces of blue and red hovered in the corners of his eyes.

Costilla looked at his gun, only a few feet away. His fingers could clench and unclench, his arms move, but he couldn't seem to pull himself toward it. Now, with O'Keefe distraught about the events in the courtroom, Costilla had a chance. But he was too weak, the pain too great.

"What does this mean? Involuntary manslaughter? *Involuntary*?" O'Keefe shouted.

He looked at the gasping Costilla. "As if this crime were some mistake, a mere accident?"

O'Keefe knelt, clasping his hands in prayer. His face aglow with the flickers of the tiny television, the man looked as insane as he truly was, a cartoon version of a madman.

"No contest? Is this what you meant by *guilty*, Lord? I don't understand. He committed murder, not some petty crime."

The ravings grew distant. Something was happening in Costilla's chest, as if he were held in some medieval torture device. A slow but implacable screw seemed to be crushing his heart. His breathing grew shorter, a liquid and shuddering sound audible within his lungs.

Costilla's hand reached again for the gun, but he could no longer see. His pounding heart made a sound that filled up his ears.

"Yes, you're right, Lord," O'Keefe said, his words almost lost to Costilla through the din of his pain.

"This is not justice!" the man raved. "This is sacrilege. This must be avenged."

Costilla managed to open his eyes. O'Keefe was raising his pistol toward the closet again.

Then, a sound like thunder shook Costilla, and that was all he knew.

The scene in the room was burned into Mark Hicks's eyes by the flash of his revolver. Only as he blinked in those moments after firing did Hicks see what his single shot had illuminated. Agent Costilla on his back, eyes wide open, a gun inches from his grasping hand. O'Keefe raising a pistol to fire—not at a person, as Hicks had thought—but at a wall covered with explosives and wires.

Thank God I hit him square, Hicks thought.

His eyes adapted again to the darkness, and he walked hurriedly over to O'Keefe. The man was dead, his heart pierced by the bullet. The last expression on his face was a grimace of shock superimposed over grotesque rapture.

Hicks turned to the FBI agent.

Costilla had also taken a bullet in the chest. Low in the rib cage, probably through the left lung. Sheriff Hicks put a finger to the agent's neck, watched the blood-soaked chest for signs of breathing. Sighed.

He stood and headed for the door, considering what had to be done. The courthouse should be evacuated, in case this stuff was unstable. The whole civic center emptied of its prisoners. Now, *that* would be easier said than done.

The television was still blaring.

". . . if it turns out to be true, would be a strange conclusion to the case of Dr. Daniel Wyatt, once the surgeon general nominee and now a convicted felon. A conviction by plea bargaining. I'm sure both sides will be disappointed by this result . . ."

Hicks left the jabbering machine behind and headed for the stairs. His old bones were feeling their years, that was true. But there was no reason to rush. Both men were dead.

The case was over.

But then the words coming from the television gave him

pause. A plea bargain? That didn't sound like the Claire Davis that Sheriff Hicks knew. Hicks wondered if the events last night at Dr. Wyatt's house had had any effect on this decision. He'd heard from Costilla that the intruder had made terrible threats to Wyatt. Threats that might have something to do with this whole plea-bargain deal.

But now O'Keefe was dead.

Mark Hicks moved a little faster now, pushing his tired muscles into a slow trot. There was a phone downstairs.

Maybe, Hicks decided, he should give Claire Davis a call.

Claire Davis looked at the time on her cell phone again. Fifteen minutes. In fifteen minutes this case would all be over.

She had stopped trying to get Daniel to reconsider. If her client had achieved whatever closure he needed, who was she to demand a jury verdict? The risk was too great. And it would be a relief finally to end this whole matter, to let herself begin to heal. But still Claire felt inadequate when she considered the plea bargain. She always played to win, not to negotiate truces and half results.

These next fifteen minutes were going to be torture.

Daniel Wyatt reached out and touched her shoulder. She smiled back at him. Ironic that he, a man who was shortly to plead guilty to a charge of involuntary manslaughter, was comforting her.

Her phone rang. Claire pulled it out and checked the ID. She didn't recognize the number. Probably a reporter; they kept managing to get her private numbers. She dropped the phone back into her jacket pocket, and its ring was instantly muffled.

"Daniel, I'm not arguing with you anymore, but—"

"But I can change my mind at any time, right?"

She nodded. "The deal means nothing until you make your plea official in open court. You have every right to reconsider."

"Thank you for advising me of my rights, Counselor," he said, still smiling. Behind his smile there was such sadness, it broke her heart. Wyatt had suffered so much, had lost family and career, and would soon lose even his freedom. And he'd done so by following her advice.

Who was she to argue with him now?

The phone rang again, its high-pitched scream coming through the layers of cloth like the persistent whine of a trapped insect.

To escape looking into Wyatt's tortured face any longer, Claire pulled the phone out and pressed it to her ear.

"Davis," she answered.

"Miss Davis," a voice said. "This is Mark Hicks."

"Yes, Sheriff," Claire responded. "What it is?"

"I thought you'd want to know. We got him."

"What? Got who?" She forced her mind to focus.

"Me and . . . Agent Costilla. We got the bomber. The doctor killer."

Awareness hit Claire in an avalanche. Her heart leaped. Maybe this hadn't come to an end yet, after all.

"Thank you, Mark!" she said. "That's incredible."

"And I suppose I should tell you that Agent—"

"And thank Agent Costilla, too," she interrupted. "You two may have saved the day!"

She let the phone fall from her ear and turned to Daniel's expectant face. She took a few seconds to frame her first words; everything depended on the next few minutes.

"Daniel, the danger is over."

She saw understanding break over his face. "You mean . . ."

"They got O'Keefe. He can't hurt you anymore. He can't hurt anyone."

Wyatt nodded, sighing.

"Daniel, think about why we got into this agreement. You wanted to make a sacrifice; you wanted to make sure no one else got hurt. But now we're out of danger. All of us."

He held up one hand, as if to interrupt her.

She grabbed his wrist. "You don't have to go through with this."

"Claire," he said, his head still shaking. "Don't you under-stand? It's not just O'Keefe. It's everything that's happened. All the compromises I've made, all the mistakes. And finally, it's the fact that I'm . . . *guilty*."

"No, you're not," Claire cried.

"Yes, I am, Claire. I was her doctor, and I handed her those drugs. Knowing, *hoping* that she would terminate her fetus."

Claire's phone beeped in her hand, the connection lost. She looked at the time. Ten minutes to convince Daniel to change his mind.

There was only one way.

"Daniel, did you slip her those drugs?"

"No, Claire." He sighed. "But I *handed* her the RU-486."

"Listen, Daniel. O'Keefe is caught. If you go through with this plea bargain now, everyone will think that you slipped those drugs to Sarah."

The words silenced him for a moment, wiped the look of certainty from his face.

"Everyone will think that you took a woman's choice away."

"But, Claire . . ." he started. "You know that—"

"Everyone," she said flatly.

Wyatt's eyes darted back and forth in confusion. Claire saw that the one certainty he had clung to was evaporating. She had managed to make Daniel think that she doubted his innocence.

Daniel was reeling now, and she realized that she could press him one last time to do her will. "I've fought for you, Daniel, because I've been fighting for choice. Don't make me think I've been wrong about you. If you're really innocent, then let the jury decide."

He nodded. "Okay."

"We are going back before the court and taking the deal off the table," she commanded. She led him by the arm to-ward the courtroom doors. Wyatt shook his head but fol-lowed.

"Just let me do the talking, Daniel."

He nodded, just once, too tired to fight her anymore.

"We'll let the jury decide."

Her phone rang again in her hand. The caller ID read the same as before: the number from which Mark Hicks had called. She turned the phone off and propelled Wyatt forward.

Whatever further news Hicks had would have to wait.

69 | VERDICT

One week later, Judge Thibodeaux addressed the assembled court.

"I want to begin by saying how much I appreciate the service you have done for the State of Louisiana. Of all the duties of citizenship, being on a jury is one of the most sacred. You have given Daniel Wyatt one of the rights guaranteed him, and all of us, under the Constitution, trial before a jury of one's peers."

Riley Mills watched the jury's reaction. Of course, he would know in a few moments what they had decided, but his sharp eyes still sought those subtle clues that might reveal their thoughts.

"Madam Forewoman, have you all reached a verdict?"

"Yes, we have," responded Peggy Fontenot nervously.

Mills gathered his strength and pushed his doubts aside for a few more moments. Since the plea arrangement had fallen through, the papers were suggesting that he'd lost the case, that Sarah Corbett's balk on the stand had torpedoed the murder charge. But Mills still believed that this jury would see their way to a guilty verdict, murder one. He'd said so just this morning to Senator Huffson. He'd practically guaranteed it.

The old politico had simply sighed and said, "I hope so, Riley, I certainly hope so. We are all depending on you."

In an old piece of courtroom ritual, Peggy Fontenot extended a small piece of paper to the bailiff. There it was, Mills thought, a man's life in her shaking hand. And D.A. Riley Mills's political future as well, it seemed. The bailiff took the paper, handed it to the clerk, who handed it, still closed, to the judge.

Mills bit his lip. That plea-bargain business had made him look weak, had started people talking about how he'd overextended himself with the murder-one charge. If only he hadn't leaked the story to the media. Had that been Claire Davis's plan all along?

Mills looked over at Davis. She didn't look any happier than he felt. Her usual fire seemed to have gone out of her since Peter O'Keefe's death. Had talking her client out of the plea bargain made her afraid of this verdict? Or could the rumors about her and that dead FBI agent be true?

Thibodeaux opened the paper and read. Without any change of his countenance, he passed it back to the clerk.

Here it was. Despite his long experience, the number of times he'd faced this moment, Mills found himself unable to breathe.

The clerk cleared his throat and read, "We the jury, in the above-entitled action, find the defendant, Dr. Daniel Wyatt, not guilty of count one of the information, murder in the first degree."

Not guilty. Riley Mills seized the arms of his chair in an iron grip. Defeated. The governor's mansion, his speech at the Republican National Convention, it had all slipped away. Still, maybe something could be salvaged. He reached down into himself and tried to muster some anger; he would have to be outraged when he met the reporters on the steps. Perhaps this would be a clarion call to all Americans, for a murderer of a child to get a mere slap on the wrist . . .

There was a quiet rush to the door as reporters moved out to phone in the story. Only a few waited for news of the second count. The clerk waited patiently for order to return before he continued.

"We the jury, in the above-entitled action, find the defendant, Dr. Daniel Wyatt, guilty of count two of the information, furnishing medicine without a medical necessity."

Well, Mills thought, they had gone one for two. At least the good doctor would be losing his medical license. Perhaps even his freedom for a short time. Justice, and Riley Mills, hadn't failed completely.

"Is this your verdict, so say you all?" the judge completed the ritual.

Some of the jurors nodded, and Peggy Fontenot said "yes" so quietly it almost couldn't be heard. The trial was over.

The judge began his last few words, setting a date for sentencing, but Riley Mills hardly listened. He was still thinking of what might have been.

EPILOGUE | IRRECONCILABLE DIFFERENCES

The days were growing noticeably longer now.

It was almost April, and twilight was just beginning to fade into night. A last few fingers of red reached into Claire Davis's house, staining the rich wood of her rolltop desk and lighting the room like the glow of a distant fire. Through the crisscross network of bare branches outside her window, a single star was visible in the darkening sky.

Claire realized that she hadn't turned on a light. The law book before her was in utter blackness now; she'd been staring at but not reading it. She closed the thick tome, surrendering to her mood. Daniel's sentencing hearing was scheduled for three weeks from today, anyway. And Claire felt sure that Judge Thibodeaux had already made his true intentions clear weeks ago, back when the plea bargain had been arranged. If Thibodeaux had intended to show leniency for a charge of involuntary manslaughter, the lesser charge of furnishing medicine without a medical necessity was unlikely to land Daniel in jail for long, if at all.

The thought of a cigarette crossed her mind, or a glass of wine, but she shook her head. She had sworn off both smoking and drinking until she made her choice.

She sat in the darkness, listening to the soft noises her house made as the night grew cool. It sounded like a cranky old person, as if stirring in its sleep, troubled by some vague anxiety.

A car pulled into her driveway. Daniel's battered old Saab.

She watched him come up the walk, glad to see him, but a little sad that she would have to turn on the lights now.

"Good evening, Claire."

"Hello, Daniel."

It was strange to see Wyatt in her home. They were no longer constantly together now that the case was over, and Daniel's presence seemed familiar but out of place, like a visit from an erstwhile lover.

They sat in her living room, a single lamp shattering the darkness she had earlier let herself sink into.

"I talked to Ellen today," he said.

"How is she?" Claire asked softly. Somewhere on her desks were the divorce papers Ellen had filed. Irreconcilable differences.

Daniel seemed well enough now that his ordeal was over, ready to face whatever sentence the judge handed him. Claire had arranged a visit for him to a minimum security prison to allay his fears. But his estrangement from his family hurt him more than a stint in prison ever could.

"Well enough," he said. "The kids are beginning to understand, I think. It was one thing to lie to them during the trial; there was so much uncertainty then. But now that I'm going to prison—"

"Maybe," Claire corrected. It was possible the judge would hand down a suspended sentence.

"Well, they need to know, in any case."

"I'm sure Ellen will be strong enough, Daniel. She's a more resourceful woman than you might think."

He gave her a strange look.

"What is it, Daniel?"

"That's just it," he answered. "I was at the library today, the periodicals room. I've started to read about the trial, now that I can finally stand to. I've been trying to figure out why Sarah did what she did. Why she took the pills, then accused me."

Claire shook her head. "Daniel, don't even try. You're only torturing yourself."

He went on, ignoring her. "One thing that I kept reading again and again was that Sarah Corbett was my patient, my friend, and it said, my children's baby-sitter. I wondered where that had come from."

"Where what had come from?"

"Baby-sitter. It was something every newspaper repeated, part of the mantra: patient, friend, *baby-sitter*. But it didn't make sense. She offered once to baby-sit for us, but she never actually did."

"Daniel, that's what journalists do," Claire explained. "They get stuck on something that's good copy, and soon it doesn't matter whether it's factual or not. 'Baby-sitter' is vaguely salacious, I suppose. It makes her sound younger."

"I asked Ellen about it."

Claire sat upright. She didn't like where this was going. "Daniel. Don't torture yourself. It's all over now."

"And Ellen said that yes, Sarah had watched the kids for her just once, but she couldn't remember exactly when. I must tell you, I hadn't remembered that at all."

Daniel looked hard at his lawyer, as if expecting a reaction. Claire eased back into the depths of her chair and looked out the window, willing herself to relax. The sky was black now, a host of tiny stars surrounding that single jewel that had come out first.

It must be a planet, shining more steadily than any star, Claire thought.

"So I went through some of my records around that time. My day planner, old checks. I found a check made out to cash, just for a few dollars, signed by Ellen. The memo said 'baby-sitting.' When I turned it over, Sarah had endorsed it."

Claire sighed.

"The date was right. Ellen took the kids to her that Monday morning. And to use a check . . . She must have wanted me to find it."

Claire knew, of course, which Monday morning Wyatt meant. The day after the weekend at the beach house. The morning before Sarah's miscarriage.

"Daniel . . ." she said. But it was pointless trying to stop him. He had to say it now, had to hear himself speak the words out loud to someone. It was better that it be her than anyone else. She should have known that Daniel would eventually guess. Once she had confessed that the pills she'd sent with him to the beach house were placebos, his mind would worry the question until he finally understood.

"Ellen was there in the morning, about fourteen hours before Sarah's hemorrhaging began," he continued. "And seventy-two hours after you saw Sarah on Friday morning. The timing was perfect."

He stood, began pacing, gesticulating as he walked the confines of the small room.

"Of course, I'd always wondered about the aspirin," he said. "That crazy test result from the RU-486 box. Now I understand. You never sent me the RU-486. You *couldn't*, because you'd *already* given Sarah the mifepristone. You didn't want her to have two doses. And she was getting the second drug, the prostaglandin, on Monday, from Ellen. With aspirin, if she took the pills, it wouldn't matter. They were just placebos, the real drugs were already a certainty."

"Daniel, is that what you want to believe? Do you need to blame Ellen now?"

Wyatt stopped to look closely at her for a moment, as if she were some odd object passed on the beach, an unfamiliar creature deposited by the tides. Then he resumed his pacing.

"The whole time, the whole way through the trial, I was afraid you'd begin to doubt me, Claire. I thought that you would start to believe what Sarah said, that I had slipped her the pills, killed her child. But you never did, until the end, when you forced me to take a jury verdict."

Daniel sat and laughed bitterly.

"You stuck by me. You never doubted my innocence. And why should you have? You *knew* I was innocent."

He sighed.

"And Ellen believed me too. Even when she hated me, she *knew* I was innocent."

Claire hoped he was done. She wanted Daniel to leave so that she could return to the darkness, the night she enviously glimpsed through her window. Didn't Daniel know that she was in mourning?

"It should have worked," he continued. "She should have had a normal miscarriage, barely noticeable. Just like we always say about RU-486: it's indistinguishable from a natural event. And I would think that Sarah had done it, and maybe she would think that I'd done it, but she wouldn't say anything. Even if she asked me, I'd innocently deny it, and she would have believed me, Claire. She would have, thinking it was God's will. If only she hadn't had that coagulation disorder, then the prostaglandin wouldn't have made her bleed so heavily. Hell, if she'd just taken the fake pills, Ellen's and your actions would have been irrelevant. Neither Sarah nor I would ever have known."

"Maybe she did, Daniel."

He looked up at her. "What?"

"Maybe she did take them, the pills you showed her. The aspirin. Swallowed them out there, while you weren't looking, unsure of whether you would love her if you knew she'd killed her child."

He shook his head. "But she accused me . . ."

"Not before a small-town prosecutor got hold of her. Not before she went to the hospital, bleeding. She was afraid."

There was a long pause.

"Maybe," Daniel said, quieter now. "I have come to believe that anything is possible."

He stood.

"Anything."

For a moment, he seemed frozen; then he took a step toward Claire.

"The funny thing is, I can understand Ellen. Why she did it. She was defending her family, her good name, destroying something that threatened to destroy her. But you . . ."

He breathed hard, as if he were struggling to speak now.

"How could *you*?"

Claire curled up into her chair. The drafty house was still cold. She wondered what words would satisfy Daniel. She knew that nothing could ever really make him understand, so she said it simply.

"We're fighting a war, Daniel. Innocent people are hurt in wars."

"Damn, Claire. That sounds like something Peter O'Keefe said to me."

"Peter O'Keefe knew what he believed," she said quietly. "And if you believed as he did, that millions of murders were being committed every year, wouldn't you do something to stop it?"

Daniel sat back down. He was overwhelmed by her reaction. He'd wanted regrets, apologies.

"But he was wrong, Claire. A madman."

"Yes, O'Keefe was wrong. A clump of cells is not a human being. It's only potential, like sperm or ova. But a fetus inside a woman can change her life, utterly. That's why we must have a choice. A pregnancy nearly ruined your life, Daniel, so now you know. Unwanted pregnancies have shattered women's lives since the species began.

"That's why this is war," she finished.

"But you and Ellen . . ."

"We denied Sarah her choice."

"How could you do that?"

"Ellen was afraid of public humiliation and divorce, and she would do anything to save her family. I was afraid of your nomination failing, you being turned into a cautionary tale by the right wing, and all our work being squandered.

"And I decided to win. Or at least to try, whatever the cost.

"War, Daniel. A just war."

After Daniel Wyatt had left, Claire decided that she could allow herself a single glass of wine. Just one, drunk slowly, would be all right.

She returned the house to darkness, and attempted to picture Eduardo Costilla. She thought of his mouth, the rich color of his eyes, the angle of his jaw. But it was difficult; the image of him in her mind was fading.

Claire's hand moved across her belly. Perhaps memory would fade as this new life grew, a natural balance maintained between the past and the future. She could stop the process, of course, and maybe hold on to that picture of her lost lover. Like a photograph, fixed and unchanging. Or she could embrace this possible future, this potential life inside her, with all the chaos, sleepless nights, and unexpected wisdom it would bring into the world.

Her choice.

New York Times Bestselling Author
Lisa Scottoline

THE VENDETTA DEFENSE
0-06-103142-9/$7.99 US/$10.99 Can

MOMENT OF TRUTH
0-06-103059-7/$7.50 US/$9.99 Can

MISTAKEN IDENTITY
0-06-109611-3/$7.50 US/$9.99 Can

ROUGH JUSTICE
0-06-109610-5/$7.99 US/$10.99 Can

LEGAL TENDER
0-06-109412-9/$7.99 US/$10.99 Can

RUNNING FROM THE LAW
0-06-109411-0/$7.99 US/$10.99 Can

FINAL APPEAL
0-06-104294-3/$6.99 US/$9.99 Can

EVERYWHERE THAT MARY WENT
0-06-104293-5/$7.99 US/$10.99 Can

And Coming Soon in Hardcover

COURTING TROUBLE
0-06-018514-7/$25.95 US/$39.50 Can

Coming Soon in Hardcover from
New York Times Bestselling Author
LISA SCOTTOLINE

Courting Trouble

Anne Murphy, the redheaded rookie lawyer at Rosato &
Associates, opens the newspaper one morning to discover an
erroneous report that she has been murdered. She plays dead in
order to solve her own murder—and manages to look really
fashionable doing it. Then Anne finds herself locked in a lethal
struggle with the past, the police, and the killer. Not to mention
the boss—Bennie Rosato herself.

But when the going gets tough, the redheads get going . . .

PRAISE FOR LISA SCOTTOLINE

"Scottoline . . . sweeps her audience up in a luscious
whirl of unforgettable characters and crisp plotting."
Houston Chronicle

"Scottoline's satisfying mix of mischief, sex appeal,
action and legal analysis justifies her wide following."
Publishers Weekly

"Scottoline makes us remember why legal thrillers
became so popular and entertaining."
Ft. Lauderdale Sun-Sentinel

On-Sale Summer 2002